SALVATION
CONSPIRACY

BOOK TWO

CHAD JOSEY

COPYRIGHT

SALVATION CONSPIRACY
(Salvation Trilogy, Book 2)
Copyright © 2018 by Chad Josey

https://ChadJosey.com

Published by Hicks Creek Press

First Edition, 2018

ISBN-13: 978-0-9994959-2-6 (paperback

ISBN-10: 0-9994959-2-5 (paperback)

ISBN-13: 978-0-9994959-3-3 (e-book)

ISBN-10: 0-9994959-3-3 (e-book)

To my parents, Lonnie and Marsha, thank you for everything you sacrificed as young parents raising three children. Daddy, thank you for giving me your strong work ethic and sense of humor through your storytelling. Mama, thank you for your kindness and compassion for always being there.

PART ONE
ARRIVAL

1-FATHER

"**H**E'S MY FATHER!"

Joe's screams are futile to his wife, Mary. Shock consumes her as the rocket hurtles them into orbit above Earth. Her eyes shut tight protecting herself strapped into the flight seat.

His weightless arm reaches for her but falls short of contact. An image of Jacob Bishop, the Salvation Command Leader, reappears on the protective face-shield inside Joe's helmet.

"Joseph, I know to see me is difficult to understand. I'm aware of the feelings you must have. But, this is real. I'm real. I am your father, and I have so much to explain to you."

Joe shakes his head inside his helmet. At thirty-six-years-old, he had dreamt the fantasy of someday meeting his father. This dream had remained only fiction since Jacob had died in a car accident a few days before Joe's birth in 1979.

"I can tell you everything once you arrive at Salvation. But, for now, only you see my message. Not even the captain or the flight crew is aware I'm speaking to you."

Is this happening? Did I pass-out during take-off?

"I know you must be in shock… about Salvation… about the rocket you find Mary and yourself."

"In shock? You think!" Joe's yell at Jacob's recorded image is non-responsive.

The eight passengers inside the rocket's Living Module jostle in their seats. The engines stop.

Weightlessness provides a stomach-churning sensation for everyone. Mary faints; her two heartbeats record higher than average to the crew in the Flight Module. To the shock of the captain, Salvation Command allowed their rocket to takeoff from Earth given Mary's pregnancy while she remains unaware.

Humming fills the module. The flight crew engages the Photonic Receptor Shield extending from the rear of the rocket.

Lasers pulsate from The Eden Foundation's geo-centric satellite above Earth. The 1980s U.S. Government's Star Wars program had provided Eden a fantastic cover-story to develop their satellite.

The rocket's shield absorbs the laser, and its energy propels the ship forward exponentially with each pulse. This technology allows missions between Earth and Mars in three weeks versus six months.

No one feels the forward motion in zero gravity. The only evidence is Earth growing smaller behind them through the onboard windows.

Joe does not realize leaving Earth's orbit. His concentration never breaks from Jacob's image.

"Joseph, I can't even explain the torment I've felt having to leave you and your mother, Rachel. As you've learned from your recruitment by Gabriel D'Angelo, The Eden Foundation has long protected its secret from the Public. This ensures Salvation's survival."

Uneasiness consumes Joe hearing Jacob speak of his mother. Joe wants to punch, to run; but, remains trapped within his seat restraints.

"Joseph, I need for you to keep one more secret to help protect Salvation. We cannot have people here thinking you're joining us due to favoritism on my part. This is not the case at all. Your research findings are the true reasons we need you. It just happens to be that you are my son."

This can't be happening.

"Others, here, may not believe this... Hell, you'll probably never believe me. But, I need you not to tell anyone... that includes Mary."

You've never been a father to me in the first place. So, that won't be hard to do.

"I promise. When you arrive, I will explain everything to you. How I became involved with Salvation, and why I had to fake my death before you were born."

Joe closes his eyes blocking Jacob's image.

"And, Joseph... I'm so sorry... I've not been there for you in the past. But, we have our future together... and, I hope I can make this up to you."

The recording stops. Joe opens his eyes.

Not tell anyone, hell. I've kept Salvation a secret from Mary. And, I promised her no more secrets.

Within the helmets of the eight passengers, the Captain's voice echoes. "Well, everybody... that experience is over. From our readings up here, everyone seems to be doing okay."

Joe meets Mary's stare. Their focus locks onto each other.

"As we rehearsed yesterday, we'll disengage the seat restraints. Then, you can move about the module. The air and temperature inside have stabilized so you can remove your helmets."

Air-popping-bursts come from each seat as the restraints release. The passengers move in their places orienting to the zero-gravity environment. A drunk sensation consumes everyone.

Three passengers are quick to leave their seats. The California sisters, Heather and Joanie, stand to hug each other. The Austrian decathlete, Heinrich, stretches his muscular body.

Joe and Mary sit upright. As both reach to release their helmets, a live image of the Captain appears only to them.

"Hey, Guys. I hope everything is okay," the Captain said.

Since the Captain initiates a video call with them, the three can speak to each other.

"I have something I need to tell you and not the others, for now."

I know. I'm not supposed to tell anyone about Jacob being my father.

"That's why I'm communicating through the helmet. We'll talk more in person, later."

Joe grabs Mary's gloved hands shifting his focus to his wife.

"Mary, the delay in our takeoff was because we found an anomaly in your vital readings... " The Captain pauses. "There's just no easy way to say this... Mary, you are pregnant. Your heart monitor is picking up your heartbeat and one from your fetus... "

The pressure on Joe's hand increases. Mary focuses on Joe blurring her focus of the Captain's face on her shield.

"Everything appears normal. We don't expect any problems during our flight. We'll watch you closely and take necessary precautions. Once we arrive at Salvation in three weeks, you'll be in fantastic hands."

The Captain's voice falls silent in their helmets. Since their marriage in 2001, Joe and Mary had thought they were unable to get pregnant. Mary's diagnosed-health condition made pregnancy impossible... almost.

"How can this be happening?" Mary asked.

"Dear, I hope someone has explained sex to you before?" the Captain said attempting to lighten the mood.

"No, I mean— "

"Just kidding. At some point, before you arrived in Mauritius, Eden had received your health readings. This gives us our baseline to check everyone during the flight. From a timing standpoint, the Foundation must have acquired your data before your conception... "

"And, knowing this, you still let us takeoff, anyway?" Joe asked in a stern voice.

"Joe and Mary, that's why we had the delay. We had to check with Salvation Command as we take our orders from them. Salvation gave us the go-ahead after we verified we were receiving the correct readings."

"Do I need to worry about... " Mary pauses.

She had dreamt of being pregnant for many years but had no clue what to ask given their hurtling course to Mars.

"Antwan will be back there as soon as we complete the items on our flight checklist. As we said before we left, he's not only our navigator but serves as the flight doctor. And, he'll check you over completely."

Joe and Mary mumble into their microphones. The surreal announcement and traveling through Space overpower them.

"Well, let me be the first to offer my congratulations to you."

The Captain's image vanishes. Joe and Mary remove their helmets in unison. As they stand, they fall into each other's arms both crying. Emotion rushes over them.

They kiss through salty tears. Joe holds the sides of Mary's face with his gloved hands.

"Holy shit! We're pregnant," Joe said.

"I… I… can't even… I… " Mary's words escape her.

"That's why you've been nauseous the past couple of days."

"Oh, no. I drank alcohol… that can't be— "

"Sweetie, don't worry. I'm sure that wasn't enough to— "

"Oh my God, I'm pregnant!" Mary shouts.

The announcement silences the other six passengers.

"Well, congratulations," Heather said turning from her sister, Joanie. "I can't wait until I get pregnant."

Minutes pass. Attention leaves Joe and Mary, who find themselves alone in a corner of the Living Module.

"Joe, during takeoff, I saw you screaming and trying to tell me something?"

He opens his mouth and pauses his response. "Yeah, I was freaking out. It was nothing."

I can't tell her about Jacob… not at least until we get to Salvation… she has enough now to worry about… oh shit… I'm going to be a father.

EARTH DATE: MARCH 1, 2016
OUTSIDE MARS' ORBIT

THREE WEEKS PASS.

Mission Number 4,347 continues its approach to Mars. Six of the eight new, Salvation arrivals lie in slumber. Small amounts of halothane gas mix with oxygen inside the resting pods. The six are asleep. Joe and Mary float through the Living Module free of their helmets.

"What are you thinking about, Mary?"

Joe pulls close to Mary, who holds herself by an eight-inch-diameter window.

"I still can't believe what's happening. It doesn't seem real." Mary grabs Joe's hand. "Did you feel that?"

Joe places light pressure against Mary's stomach.

"Oh shit. I feel it."

"She's been kicking for hours."

"She?"

"Yeah, She. I just know it's going to be a girl."

Joe rubs her swelling stomach. "Has *she* been kicking a lot before?"

"I have no idea of time here. It was two sleeping cycles ago for the others." Mary said as she points to the other passengers.

"I know. It's weird. The sun shines all the time and who knows how long we've been traveling." Joe peeks outside the window. "Nothing ever changes since we left Earth."

Mary pushes away from the window gliding through the interior to Heinrich's chair. A muscular man, Heinrich appears as a chiseled statue wrapped in his gray-fabric flight suit.

"And, it's weird that they sleep so soundly. We are on our own most of the time," Mary said tapping on the glass of Heinrich's sleeping pod.

Joe joins Mary. "Yeah, I wonder what they are dreaming about when they sleep?"

He taps Lin Wu's pod beside Heinrich. Mr. Lin Wu from Shanghai is a fellow scientist, a nano-technology specialist.

"I kinda wish we could sleep like this to make the time pass," Mary said. She turns her attention to Heather and Joanie with their slim bodies on the other side of Heinrich.

"Well, at least the Captain was honest with us given your condition."

"Hell, my condition," Mary said as she rubs the glass of Heather's pod. "Do you think once I have the baby, my stomach will be flat like *hers*, again?"

Floating to Mary, Joe places his arms around her from behind reaching to her stomach. "You'll always be my beautiful wife." He spins her around facing him.

"I used to wish that we could sleep like them, too," Joe said. He changes the subject and bangs the pod belonging to Gary, the Boeing engineer. "But, it's for our good. Like Captain told us, the sleeping gas might have a side-effect of increasing our heartrates. We don't want to take any chances with our daughter."

Mary smiles. "See, you think it's a girl, too."

"I believe in you, and if you say so, then I can't wait to meet her."

Two, quick beeps interrupt them.

"Okay, You Two. Time to wake everyone," the Captain said from the Flight Module.

On command, Joe and Mary push-off from Heather's pod and float across the module to their seats.

"I'm getting tired of pretending to sleep like them," Mary said as she presses the controls as her seat reclines.

"At least we know about the gas. *They* don't. *They* think they're just sleeping normally."

Joe and Mary's seats recline flat.

"Normally? What's normal about any of this?" Mary said, her voice muffled.

Clear glass rises on the sides of their sleeping pods curling and forming a seal. After a few seconds, the passengers in each of their chambers slowly move their legs. Consciousness creeps within their lifeless bodies. Joe and Mary imitate their movements.

This is the twentieth time we've done this. Does this mean three weeks have passed? Joe turns his attention to Mary.

The glass enclosures reverse its course lowering as their chairs rise. After a few moments, the passengers stand and move inside the Living Module.

"Whoa, I had some crazy dreams," Mary said in an exaggerated tone. Joe senses her sarcastic frustration.

"How are you feeling?"

"Oh, Chantal, thanks for asking. The baby's kicking for sure."

"What... you're only about nine weeks along?" Lin Wu asks overhearing them.

"Yeah, there about's."

"Hmm." Chantal floats to Mary touching Mary's stomach.

"Hmm, what?" Mary focuses on Chantal, the nutrition scientist from Africa.

"Oh, I'm sure it's nothing. When I had my son, I didn't feel him kicking until after four months."

Joe joins the conversation trying to deflect Mary's concern. "So, you have a son?"

Chantal floats to the toilet area. "Had a son. He was killed in '86 in our civil war in Uganda."

"Oh... um, I'm sorry," Joe said.

"It's okay. If it wasn't for him, I wouldn't be going to Salvation, now," Chantal said as she zips closed the privacy screen.

Mary forces Joe's hand to her stomach. "You don't think anything's wrong, do you?"

Joe hesitates. "Sweetie, I'm sure everything is fine. You don't feel any pain. If she's kicking this early, this just means she's going to be a fighter."

Mary pushes up off the seat and kisses him. "Yeah... a strong fighter."

Two, quick beeps interrupt the passengers.

"Well, Everyone, I hope you all slept okay?" the Captain said. "I've got great news... we will arrive soon and begin our orbit of Mars."

The privacy screen unzips.

"Finally!" Chantal shouts.

"As we have reviewed, you need to prepare the Living Module. I'll come back to you shortly."

With the command, each passenger performs their assigned clean-up tasks. Small, loose items can become projectiles upon entry into the Martian atmosphere.

Lin Wu checks the food prep station. The area passes inspection.

Heinrich searches the top of the Living Module. He retrieves small articles lodged between a black hose and an electric conduit tray.

Heather and Joanie inspect the module walls. They make sure nothing has found their way stuck in any crevice.

Gary and Joe check for potential hazards wedged within the seats. The seats are safe.

Chantal clasps the toilet materials within their holders. She closes the privacy screen from the outside.

Mary watches everyone. She is not allowed to exert any effort more than she needs.

Satisfied, the passengers float to their seats and slip-on their gloves and helmets. Two, quick beeps chirp within the Living Module.

"Great job, Everyone. Now, we want to review what's going to happen," the Captain said from the helmets' speakers.

Joe turns to Mary, who already faces him.

"Lasers are already hitting our front Receptor Shield from our Martian satellite. This slows us down with each pulse. It's a strong jolt, but we aren't feeling it because of the zero-gravity."

Mary turns her head away from Joe glancing at the window.

"In a few moments, a vibration will return within your seats. This is from our engines preparing for ignition. When the vibration stops, our engines will fire, and this will press you into your seats. We'll go into an orbit around Mars. That's when you'll see out the windows your first images of the Martian surface."

Is this really happening? Joe thinks to himself.

"We'll orbit Mars three times as we prepare for the landing phase. That's when I'll get back to you to let you know what happens, next. So, with that, Everyone, get ready… and welcome to Mars."

Silence engulfs everyone's helmets as each secures their restraints. Joe reaches across the gap between them to Mary's outstretched, gloved hand.

Slow vibrations rattle beneath Joe. A strange feeling since it had been three weeks in weightlessness. Mary releases Joe's hand pressing both against her stomach.

The vibrations grow stronger. Teeth rattle. Then, motionlessness. Silence continues as the vacuum of Space makes it impossible for sound waves to travel.

Joe exhales. His breath presses hard out his lungs. The seat pulls him tight against itself. His eyes roll back into his head. The pressure against him returns.

Silence vanishes as the rocket enters the Martian gravity. Behind the ship, a stream of orange fire rushes from the engine exhaust. Plumes of white steam press from the sides of the ship slowing its rotation.

The Captain controls the ship. Spinning stops. The rocket levels into an orbit above Mars.

Two, quick beeps ring within the helmets.

"That wasn't so bad, was it? Okay, we're in orbit, now. We'll be here for a while. You can release your restraints and look outside. I'll return, later."

Excitement forces each passenger from their seats as they remove their helmets. An odd sensation returns. The weak gravity causes the passengers to exert more effort moving to the module's windows.

Awe overcomes them, as it does everyone who has ventured to Salvation. A rusty-red landscape zooms under them. Amazement follows.

"It looks like a movie," Mary said as Joe's cheek presses against hers. Her statement goes unanswered.

Time passes. Two, quick beeps echo inside the Living Module.

"Okay, Everyone, we're ready. Let me tell you what's next for our landing."

"Oh my God," Joe said turning to Mary, "this is it!" Excitement and apprehension envelop him.

"I need you to retake your positions and prepare for landing, and I'll explain what's next."

The eight passengers race through the air to their seats replacing their helmets.

"Great. Now, this will sound a lot scarier than what happened earlier. You will feel more vibrations as our heat shields lower around the ship."

Joe grabs Mary's outstretched hand.

"Once this stops, a few moments will pass. Then, you'll feel a jolt as our engines fire, again. The sound will get louder as we enter the Martian atmosphere."

Mary squeezes Joe's hand.

"We'll do controlled burns as we enter, and you may feel a heat sensation from your feet. But, we will be safe. We're just riding the wave down to the ground. As the sound gets louder, you will feel heavier as we reach the surface."

Mary releases her hand returning it to her side. Her maternal, protective instinct causes her to cover her stomach.

"As we get closer to the ground, we will invert our ship. The engines point to the surface. And, we'll fire them slowing us down allowing us to land at Salvation."

Mary rubs her stomach.

"There's nothing to worry about. We've done this many times. But, it's going to feel weird with the gravity sensations you'll experience after three weeks of nothing. So, hold on, and we'll be back when we land."

"Shit, she sounds like a plane pilot making it so simple," Joe said inside his helmet.

Alone, a suppressed feeling returns for Joe. He had not given a thought about the real possibility of Jacob being his father. The excitement of the pregnancy news and leaving Earth made this revelation secondary for him.

Oh my God, I will meet him soon... son-of-a-bitch.

Vibrations return underneath Joe. The rocket's heat shields enclose the ship. Blackness eclipses the red-reflected light from the Martian surface.

Silence. Joe holds his breath. Air rushes from his lungs as he jolts back into his seat with the engine's thrust.

Noise erupts. An unnerving rumble roars within the module. Everyone's lungs compress with their increasing weight. Rushing air sounding like colossal blow torches pierce everyone's helmets.

Joe jostles in his seat. His boots warm against the floor. Dizziness pushes his eyes in circles. He envisions the ship righting itself upward from the surface.

The roaring continues. Pulsating sensations release Joe from his chair, then pulls him hard against the seat. Flaming engines fight gravity slowing the rocket.

The red surface of Mars expands fast as the ship lowers to the ground. Long engine thrusts rip to the Martian surface. Joe bounces in his seat a final time. The roaring slows. Vibrations smooth.

Two, quick beeps regain his attention.

"Everyone… welcome to Mars… welcome home to Salvation."

Joe turns his head to Mary; her chest heaves quick. Tears stream across her face.

"Please stay fastened in your seats."

The familiar sensation of being upside-down returns. Joe does not press as heavy against his seat's restraints as he remembers on Earth. He now weighs sixty-two pounds versus two-hundred-ten given the gravitational differences.

"Technicians will enter in a few moments to help you from your seats and out of our ship. Our flight crew and I will be with you on the platform and will escort you inside Salvation."

White, silicone walls lift around the Landing Bay. The walls enclose the ship thirty meters above the ground.

A few seconds pass. An air-tight seal encases the ship. Oxygen pumps inside the building for the next fifteen minutes.

Air rushes inside the Living Module as the entry-door opens. Two women in similar flight suits crawl inside the module helping each passenger out of their seat and to the platform.

As the technicians unfasten Joe and Mary, he takes Mary's hand as they crawl to the door. They step onto the platform outside the ship.

Joe and Mary remove their helmets at the same time. Fresh oxygen fills their lungs.

"Mary... holy shit... we're here."

Mary says nothing. Joe lifts his face to the ceiling.

As Joe lowers his head returning to Mary, her face is pale white. Sweat dumps from her hair down her face. Her eyes roll backward. Mary's body matches the same motion corkscrewing into Joe's arms.

"Mary? Mary! Oh, God. Someone, please help! Mary!"

EARTH DATE: MARCH 2, 2016 (THE NEXT DAY)
SALVATION, MARS

MINUTES PASS. Time moves slow feeling like hours. Attendants rush Mary from the platform. Steps, four meters apart, are easy to maneuver given the lower gravity.

On Earth, Mary weighs one-hundred-forty pounds. On Mars, her weight is fifty-four. This reduction allows one attendant to hold Mary while the other guides her downstairs. Joe does not notice his ability to jump down four meters unharmed. His concern for his Mary is too strong.

A transport vehicle waits for them on the ground floor. Joe, Mary, and the attendants travel into the adjoining building where a team of medical technicians greets them.

Joe holds Mary's hand. She sits non-responsive in a bright, white room absent any windows. The technicians lower Mary onto a table connecting various electrical leads from machines on the opposite wall to her temples, chest, and stomach.

"What's going on? What's happening? Is Mary, okay... the baby?" His questions without their answers ache inside him.

Their arrival to Mars is the most important day in their lives. Joe is oblivious to the alien surroundings.

A small technician grabs Joe's hand holding Mary. "Joseph, please come with me. We will take fantastic care of her."

Joe refuses for a moment. He releases no longer resisting taking two steps away from her. Technicians enter and leave the room at a dizzying pace. Two beeps come from the machine in the corner of the room with one lead on Mary's chest and the other to her stomach.

The beeps are familiar to Joe; two heartbeats. One belongs to Mary, and the other to their baby.

Tears pour from his eyes. The water droplets hang in the air unnoticed by Joe.

Dear God, please let them be okay?

"Joseph," the technician who had grabbed his hand said, "her and the baby appear to be okay."

"But, she fainted, what— "

"Most likely, it was due to feeling the Martian gravity and from vertigo caused by the disorientation of the ship during landing."

The quick response provides comfort to Joe.

"She's in great hands. We will do everything to make sure she is okay."

Joe holds back his urge to push the technician aside to rush to his wife.

"The best thing to do right now is to step outside and give us a little room. We'll run several tests just to be safe." The technician pulls Joe's hand prodding him to the door.

Joe obeys. Stepping out, the door slides shut behind him. Joe scans the Launch Bay where his ship had landed an hour earlier. Various people inspect and connect a different assortment of hoses and cords from the bottom engines to the top of the Flight Module near the ceiling.

They wear the same clothing material as Joe except in a different color. Theirs are all-white while his is gray.

Gone are his fellow passengers and the three flight crew members. They had departed the ship exiting the bay on the opposite side from Joe. In the confusion of helping Mary, no one had greeted them when they arrived.

Amazement overcomes Joe.

Shit… I'm here… Mars… this is Salvation.

"Incredible, isn't it?" a voice said behind Joe. The voice has a familiar rich, bass tone.

"I... I... don't have the words," Joe said twisting around in the air to the source of the voice. "It... it's you?"

With his words, blackness slams across Joe's eyes. He slumbers to the ground as he faints.

"*You.* Take him to my quarters and make sure he's okay," the voice said commanding a passing medical technician.

"Yes, sir, Jacob," the technician said lifting Joe's now sixty-two-pound body from the ground with ease.

As the technician leaves, Jacob places his attention to the ship. After a moment, Jacob follows far behind the technician carrying Joe across the Launch Bay. Jacob stops in the middle of the floor.

"*You!* Make sure the payload is secure this time. We don't need a repeat of what happened with the last return flight to Earth."

Earth Date: March 3, 2016 (the next day)

A FAMILIAR FEELING washes across Joe. Light chases the darkness from the underside of his closed eyelids.

Is this another dream?

Joe positions his elbows up on the sofa. For a moment, the coziness of his office in the Stonehaven Laboratory near the university campus in Stony Brook returns.

I've got to stop working so late in the lab.

He twists his legs off the sofa. His feet fall heavy to the floor while his arms lift effortlessly on either side of his torso. Reality crashes beside him catapulting him off a couch.

An awkward motion of his lighter body accompanies his heavy footsteps. The office is twice the size of his in Stonehaven. White walls contrast against mahogany furniture.

Oh, shit. This isn't a dream.

"Mary! Mary!"

His calls go unanswered as he surveys the room. The wall has a black outline of a door frame. A glass panel sits recessed beside the door at waist-level.

Upon noticing this, a red light below the panel changes green. The frosted-glass door slides open. A man enters the room. The door slides shut.

"It's you!" Joe said standing still unsure as to lunge forward or step back.

The man walks the perimeter of the room away from Joe ensuring a distance remains between them.

"Yes, Joseph, I'm your father... Jacob," the man said.

Silence fills the space and years between them.

"I'm aware it's too much to understand... why I am here... why you are here?"

Joe takes one step forward. He pauses.

"Mary! Where is she? Is she okay?"

Jacob steps forward. Joe matches his step backward.

"Joseph, Mary is okay. We've been monitoring her and the baby, and both are doing well."

Joe lunges to Jacob. He walks like a toddler as Joe tries to familiarize his heavy feet and lighter weight. With adrenaline raging through his body, Joe does not realize how different the new gravity feels.

A brief smile comes to Jacob as Joe approaches. The smile disappears as Joe grabs Jacob by the shoulders pushing him against the wall.

"Who the hell are you, really? If anything happens to Mary, I swear to God, I will— "

"Will, what exactly?" Jacob said pushing Joe's hands from his shoulders.

Joe loses his balance and falls into a chair beside them. Jacob sits behind his desk.

"You're worried about Mary. I want you to know I will do everything in my control to protect her... to protect you, Son."

Joe regains his balance standing and lumbering to the opposite side of the room. "Son, don't you dare call me that... you... you... lost that right."

"Look around... look at me... Joseph, can't you see... I did what I had to do to build Salvation... "

Jacob studies Joe's reaction. Under his desk, in easy reach, an electric stun-gun awaits its use.

With each step, Joe gains familiarity with the strange sensation of walking. The metallic floor provides a bonding surface for the magnets in his boots. Martian gravity is thirty-eight percent of Earth's.

"How can I be certain it really is you? You died the day I was born by a drunk driver on your way to the hospital."

Jacob smiles and releases a short, muffled laugh. "And, you supposedly died in a plane crash in the Indian Ocean a few days ago?"

Silence returns. Joe loses his balance falling on the sofa.

"But, why? Why you? Why our family?"

"What I had to do to you, to your mother, Rachel... to my mama, Liz..." Jacob hesitates. "I learned about what would happen to Earth and of Project Salvation. And, the only way for me to join was for Eden to fake my death."

Agitation consumes Joe.

"I don't understand. Why not join Eden and stay alive to us... to Mama... to me?"

Jacob stands and paces behind his desk.

"I wish I could have. There was no other way. Joseph, why did you join Salvation?"

"Why did I join?" Joe stands. His gaze pierces Jacob. "I didn't have a choice. Gabriel approached me with the information. He said my work was vital to the future of humanity, and... and... " His retort stammers.

"Joseph, the same for me. I was recruited to join Eden with the promise of my family being taken care of as long as I took part."

"Your family would be taken care of... it was so hard for Mama? Then, the cancer... then, with Grandma... you bastard, some being taken care of."

Jacob leaves the sanctuary from behind the desk and approaches Joe.

"When I heard about Rachel, my heart broke. But, you were in good hands with Mama. I saw firsthand how strong Liz was after my dad, your Grandpa Eli, had died. Hell, I was only ten-years-old myself when that happened."

Silence returns. Jacob leans against the front of his desk.

"Eden recruited you as the leader, here?"

Jacob releases a short laugh.

"Not hardly. Someone like how Gabriel approached you approached me. He shared with me the origins of The Eden Foundation and Project Salvation."

"Why did they recruit you? I mean, weren't you and Mama freshmen in college?"

"Huh, that was my same response, too. But, Eden said they had identified special talents I had. And, hell, I was eighteen, then. I wasn't sure what my future held."

Jacob stands pacing before Joe.

"I fell in love with Rachel at the same time, and I... I... was just worried about our future. That's why Eden approached me."

"But, you were with Mama back then? Why leave us?"

"For security. After I learned what was going to happen in 2020, I realized I could become part of something. And, I thought maybe someday, I could return and bring my family to Salvation."

Joe jumps from the sofa. "So, my research didn't matter? I'm here because of you?"

"No! If that had been the case, I would have sent for you earlier. We make no exceptions in our program. Everything we have done is for the best interest of humanity. We play no favorites."

Joe matches Jacob by pacing while he listens. His balance adjusts to his new environment.

"It just so happens; your cancer research is the most promising Eden had come across. They knew if we were to survive in the long term on Mars, we would need the advances you have discovered."

"That shit is too hard to believe. I don't buy it."

"Joseph, this brings me to a problem we have, now. If you think you and Mary are here because you're my family, well, others will think the same."

Joe looks away from Jacob.

"As I said in my private message to you during your flight, no one can know we are related. I want no one to suspect favoritism."

"Then, how do you propose we handle our last names?"

A hearty laugh fills the room. Jacob pushes his backside off his desk.

"Joseph, you've only been here two hours. There's so much to learn. At Salvation, we have no last names. Everyone has a first name and an identification number."

Confusion engulfs Joe as he stops pacing.

"That information will come in due time, Joseph."

Silence returns. Jacob sits in a chair between his desk and the sofa.

"So… you are in command, the leader, here?"

"Yes. But, it was not always this way. Like I said, Eden recruited me because I had special talents. I always prided myself on being flexible and willing to take on any challenge. I guess you could say that I worked my way to the top, so to speak."

Joe reclines into the comfortable sofa. "I still don't understand this… how you became associated with Eden. Did they tell you about Salvation?"

"Eden was building the facilities we have here on the Moon. When they explained everything, my imagination was overwhelmed. My God… the possibilities of joining Project Salvation on Mars."

"That means you know the full history of Eden and Salvation?"

"So, to speak."

"I had so many questions for Gabriel… but, I never got the full truth."

"Joseph, what would you like to understand?"

Joe reflects on his past conversations with Gabriel. He had many opportunities from their first meeting in Colorado to their talks at Stonehaven. But, he never shared the full truth.

"Well, let's start from the beginning… Gabriel told me the planetoid was discovered in 1957… how about taking it from there?"

Jacob releases a deep breath.

"Okay, then. Soviet astronomers made the first observation in 1957. "

A green light glows on the glass panel by the black outline of the door. The frosted-glass slides open. The technician who had taken Joe from Mary's room enters.

Joe jumps from his reclined position. "Mary! Is she okay?"

The technician gives Jacob her attention. "Sir, you had asked me to let you know when she wakes."

"Thank you."

The technician leaves as Jacob and Joe stand.

"Joseph, let me take you to her. We have plenty of time. I will tell you everything you want to know about the origins of Salvation."

PART TWO
ORIGIN

2 - FORMATION

"MEN, WELCOME to the Advanced Research Projects Agency," Major General Betts said to the new scientists who had joined ARPA during the last month. The group of six is the second unit joining ARPA since its inception last month.

The men appear as clones. Each wears black pants with a white, short-sleeved, button-up shirt. Many pens and pencils rest inside the black, vinyl holders in their front shirt pockets.

The men have close-cropped, flat-top hair. A lone exception belongs to the eldest member, Simon Baptiste. His bald head shines through the thick cigarette smoke.

"Our mission is to maintain our technological superiority over our potential adversaries."

Major General Betts paces in front of the group. "Eisenhower has entrusted us with three initiatives: to get America into Space, protect the country from Soviet missile attacks, and to detect Soviet nuclear tests."

A murmur rumbles within the group. Betts continues with the introductions. After an hour, Betts leaves the group of six alone in the conference room as they acquaint themselves with each other around the table. The bald man speaks first.

"Good morning, my name is Simon Baptiste. I'm originally from Sarasota, Florida. I have Ph.D. in Astro-Physics from the University of Stony Brook in New York. I'm twenty-four-years-old, married to my high-school sweetheart, Janice. We're hoping to start a family someday."

Thick smoke rises above the table. Two bottles of whiskey empty as the next four men introduce themselves.

The last man to speak has a boyish face. Red splotches streak across his neck and cheeks as his turn is next. His chest expands with a deep sigh.

"Um, hello, Everyone. My name is Eli Bishop. I'm twenty-years-old. My wife, Elizabeth, and I, we just moved to Houston from Atlanta. No kids, yet, but we hope we will soon."

"So, only twenty, huh? What's your background?" Simon asked.

"Oh, sorry, I forgot. I have two Ph.D.'s, one in mechanical engineering and the other in psychology."

"But, you're so young?" one of the others said.

"I know. I get that all the time. I've been told I'm a prodigy, but I like to think I'm just a hard-worker," Eli said.

Simon straightens himself in his chair. He stares at Eli with his response puffing his lips while squinting his eyes. Simon stands and fills everyone's empty glasses with the last of the whiskey.

"Well, here's to us all. Looks to be the start of a great team," Simon said as he lifts his glass.

Clinking glasses echo through the empty conference room. Cigarette smoke swirls above the table with the sudden motion by the group.

APRIL 10, 1958
ARPA CAMPUS, ARLINGTON, VIRGINIA

TWO MONTHS HAD PASSED since the group of six had introduced themselves.

Their first, assigned project is the government's top-secret X-20 Dyna-Soar initiative. The X-20 space plane is a joint program between ARPA and the U.S. Air Force. Mission plans include aerial reconnaissance, satellite maintenance, bombing raids, and intercepting enemy satellites.

Bright fluorescent lights flicker above the dingy, white office containing the six men. With a sudden, unannounced bang, the office door opens slamming against the wall.

"Men, come, here. I've got some news I need to explain," Major General Betts said as he enters the office. Everyone huddles around Betts.

"I'm afraid that the news isn't good, Men." Betts scans everyone's eyes ensuring they are listening. "As we have feared, a new civilian organization is being developed to take over a good majority of our space programs. They're calling it NASA."

"What does that mean for our programs, Sir?" Simon asked.

Betts turns to him. "We are to transition our future programs to this NASA group, who will execute. We will continue with our work on the X-20. My concern is our future funding. But, Men, I'm here to fight for us."

The six men turn their heads side-to-side to their peers.

"That's all, Men. As I get further updates, I will inform you, accordingly," Betts said turning toward the door leaving the office.

Sighs and muttering fill the room. Gone with Betts is the team's motivation. Four of them call it an early day and leave.

"So, wanna get a drink?" Eli asked Simon since they are the only two remaining.

Simon pushes back from his desk. "Sure. Plus, I've got something I want to show you," Simon said.

The two friends leave the office. They walk across the ARPA campus in the cool, northern Virginia air. McGilley's Bar across the street is their familiar destination.

Simon and Eli open the door to the bar thankful to find it empty. An old man wearing a white apron around his waist stands behind the bar. A decade's stench of bourbon and cigar smoke pushes by the barkeep. He steps to them wiping the inside of two glasses with a white towel.

"The usual," Simon said holding up two fingers to the bartender.

"Some news, today, huh?" Eli said pulling himself onto the barstool beside Simon.

Two Budweiser beers in cold, pint glasses arrive. White suds roll down the frosty mugs. Simon pulls a red folder from his briefcase placing it on the bar between them.

"Eli, I want to get your opinion on something."

Curiosity creeps to Eli.

"Take a look at this. Tell me what you see?"

Eli opens the folder and scans through its contents while sipping his beer. His eyes scrunch together. Deep furrows radiate above his nose through his forehead.

"It's in Russian," Eli said pointing to the text.

"Focus on the object and the numbers. The text is the contact information of who sent me the information."

Eli studies the contents finishing his beer.

"Can we have another round?" Simon said pushing the two empty glasses down the bar.

"Is this a planet?"

"That's my conclusion, also," Simon said.

Eli lifts two pictures from the folder holding them side-by-side. "Looking at the stars in the background, it's the same sector of Space."

Simon pushes Eli's hands closer together.

"Hmm, it looks like the planet has moved… and from its appearance, it looks a little bigger," Eli said as he lowers the pictures away a few inches. "Is that right?"

Simon sips from his new beer. "That's what it looks like, doesn't it?"

"But, how can that be? Things that far out in space can't move that much. What… in the four months these pictures were taken apart from each other?"

"Exactly, Eli. I think what we are looking at is an object that is much closer to us than what we think. That would explain why we see such a variance in the position in these two pictures, four months apart."

Eli replaces the pictures into the closed folder. He drinks his new beer. "So?"

"So!" Simon slams his beer on the bar. "Did you not notice the equations on the next page?"

Eli opens the folder and removes the calculations. The handwriting looks different from what Eli had been familiar with as belonging to Simon. Several words are in Russian.

"Hmm… " Eli studies the equations. He finishes his second beer. "Is this real?" Eli releases a short laugh.

"Eli, this is very real. I've reproduced the calculations and even have seen *this planet* for myself."

"You've seen it?"

Simon finishes the last of his second beer.

"Yes, once I received this information, I re-did the calcs. And, I had to see if I could find it."

Eli sits unsure if the alcohol has created his buzz or if the excitement of a possible discovery is the culprit.

"It was hard to find it in the *Columba Noachi* Constellation, but I found it… it's there," Simon said. "That's where I went last week. I traveled out to Palomar."

"And they… they just let you use their telescope?" Eli asked.

Simon laughs. "It's amazing the access *this badge* will get you." Simon points to his identification clipped to his front, shirt pocket below his group of pens.

"So, what did you see?"

"Using the coordinates given, it took some time, but I found the object. It's only a faint smudge, but I assure you, I saw it," Simon said.

Eli again lifts the pictures studying them.

"Who sent you this information?" Eli asked.

"Do you know the name Doctor Sergi Mikannovich?" Simon asked.

"Huh," Eli said leaning to Simon, "is he a Soviet?"

"Ssh," Simon responds placing his index finger to his lips. "Just kidding. Yes, he is from the Soviet Union. I met him at a conference after college. He gave a presentation about near-Earth objects and the need to catalog them."

"The need to… why?" Eli asked.

"Well, if objects are out there, then it's possible for something to impact us."

"So, this Mick-o— "

"Doctor Mikannovich."

"Yeah, him. He sent you this? Why?"

Simon returns the pictures and calculations into the red folder.

"He's asking me for a second opinion."

"Second opinion about what?"

"What did you get from the calculations?" Simon asked.

"An approximation of its speed," Eli said.

Simon motions to the bartender signaling the need for the bill.

"The calculations show this thing is coming toward Earth."

Eli backs his torso away from Simon.

"It's going to impact Earth?"

"I don't know. I think it is too early to tell. Sergi sent me his contact information, but I've not been able to reach him."

Eli retrieves a black pen from his shirt pocket and scribbles numbers onto his wet, white napkin under his empty, beer glass.

A few minutes had passed. Eli finishes and turns his head to Simon after circling the number he had written.

"Okay, Guys, it'll be four dollars for the beer," the bartender said as he removes the empty glasses and napkins. "Huh, 2020? What's that?" the bartender asked.

"No, it's not what, but when?" Simon said handing a ten-dollar-bill to Joe, "Keep the change."

3 - PALOMAR

WEEKS HAD PASSED early in 1960.

Southern California is a modern-day Babylon for Eli compared to his Houston home and Virginia office. Beautiful women in bikinis and muscular men with surfboards are plentiful outside his beach-side Howard Johnson's room in Newport Beach.

Eli had finished installing a state-of-the-art telephonic answering system at the California Institute of Technology's Geological and Planetary Sciences Department. Caltech is the first university to receive this new technology for testing.

Warm, ocean breezes comfort Eli on his balcony. Fresh-squeezed orange juice refreshes his parched mouth after a late night at Caltech. His installation project there is complete.

A lime-green phone cord stretches from the hotel room through the opened, sliding-glass door. Ringing interrupts Eli's peaceful moment.

"Hello?"

"Hello, Eli. How did the work go?"

"It was easy, Simon. I finished the install and trained the astronomers on how to use the system."

"Who was included in the sessions?"

Eli gulps the remaining juice from his glass.

"All the Californian observatories and the tech team in the university."

"So, no problems."

"No, and I successfully completed the phone tap. We'll be able to hear all communications."

Passing seagulls fly by the balcony. Playful chirps emerge from the flock as they jostle for flight position scanning the ground below for morsels.

"Where are you?" Simon asked.

"At the hotel on the balcony. It's a beautiful day, here."

Silence.

"Simon, I noticed something while I was in their lab. Written on the chalkboard were observatory scanning coordinates for Palomar and Mount Wilson. And, our concerns are real."

"Why is that?"

"This week, Palomar will scan the *Columba Noachi* Constellation. And, Palomar is our greatest concern with the Hale."

More silence.

"Eli, you need to pay careful attention through next week."

"Well, in my training, I told them if they find anything in their scans, they're to call Caltech. And, I'll be able to intercept the call."

"We need a way to block observatories from scanning that part of Space."

"I'm working on a plan for that. I'll share it with you once I'm back there in a few weeks."

The call ends. Deep breaths of sea air refresh Eli before he leaves.

Clear-blue skies escort Eli's travels on California Highway 1-South. After ninety minutes, Eli turns off the highway in the town of Oceanside. A thirty-minute switchback drive up to Palomar Mountain lies ahead.

Caltech established Palomar Observatory in 1928. At two-hundred-inches, the Hale Telescope has been operational since 1949 directed by the world-renowned astronomer, Edwin Hubble.

Given its size, the research performed at Palomar is the first observatory Eli and Simon have targeted to monitor. The timing is perfect.

Caltech plans to study *Columba Noachi* this week. The same constellation where the Soviet astronomer, Dr. Sergi Mikannovich, discovered CIE.57.20 three years earlier.

Eli arrives at the observatory's parking lot. He is an expected visitor who has unrestricted access to the telescope building to finish installing the communication protocol with the Caltech offices. A perfect cover enabling Eli to connect a phone tap in the observatory's telephone system.

As Eli completes his work activities, he overhears a conversation of an arriving astronomer.

"What's our target, tonight?" the arriving astronomer said.

"The next area on the schedule is *Columba*. The constellation is coming into a good view, up from the Equator," the leaving astronomer said.

"*Columba?*" the arriving astronomer hesitated, "*that* is the most boring constellation to review. No bright stars. No meteor showers emanate from it."

"Jackson, we don't get to choose. Take it up with the boys at Caltech. They send the assignments down," the astronomer said as he collects his things to go home.

Eli studies the arriving astronomer. They pass each other as Eli exits the observatory building. He places his work items in the back seat of his parked car. He removes a brown, fabric bag from the front seat and walks behind the building to the telecommunications junction box.

A low hum reverberates from the top of the domed structure. Large-heavy, white shutter doors open along the building's sides. Eli looks upward in amazement at the maneuverability of the massive concrete.

His focus returns to the junction box. He inserts a blue-coated wire with an alligator-prong tip into the box's circuitry. He holds the end of a phone receiver to his ear.

Good... a dial-tone... it works.

Eli can listen-in on any phone calls to, or from, the observatory. In a well-hidden location, he is not visible to anyone if they arrive during the evening.

Two nights had passed. Eli has struggled to stay awake late each evening.

The time alone allows him to finalize his ideas on how to prevent the Hale Telescope and others from having the capacity to find the object in the constellation.

Eli sits alone in his thoughts. Chills from the night air keep him awake. The shrill of his tapped phone rings startling him. He lifts the speaker to his left ear.

Through the speaker, he hears the voice of the astronomer on duty.

"Hello, this is Jackson Wheeler at the Palomar Observatory."

Eli recognizes the dialed number. He knows Jackson is following his instruction calling Caltech. Eli listens. Jackson leaves a message providing the observed coordinates in the *Columba Noachi*.

"Shit," Eli said, his fear coming to reality.

"Anomaly identified. I'm going back to take another picture. I will contact your office in the morning," Jackson said.

Silence comes through the speaker. The rustle of wind blows through the California pines surrounding the observatory.

What do I do, now?

Eli has little time to plan his next move. The tapped phone line rings, again. Eli listens.

"Jackson! Jackson!" a woman's panic voice said.

"Tina, everything, okay?"

"Jackson, it's... it's time, my water just broke."

"Okay, we practiced this. Call your sister, and I'll meet you at the hospital."

"How long will you... " Tina said pausing. Two quick breaths blew through the speaker.

"The hospital is an hour away; I'm going, now. I love you."

"Love you t— " Tina said.

The line drops as Jackson hangs-up his phone in the office. Eli jerks the tapped line out of the junction box.

Shit, what do I do? It's too late to call Simon… I need to take care of this.

Eli's thoughts come fast only interrupted as the building's entrance door slams shut.

Out of view, Eli watches Jackson enter his pickup truck. Headlights illuminate Jackson's quick departure from the parking lot. Eli collects his items and runs to his parked car.

Eli throws his bag into the passenger seat as his chest heaves in-and-out. He starts his car and follows Jackson down the mountain. The overhead moonlight and brake lights before him guide his path downhill as Eli keeps his headlights off.

What am I going to do? Should I follow him?

The mountain switchbacks come fast.

I need to get to Caltech and erase the message… I still have five hours before anyone arrives there.

Jackson's truck is three minutes ahead of a closing-fast Eli. Halfway down the mountain, the road has a short straight-away.

As the road straightens before Eli, red-brake lights disappear ahead as Jackson follows the next switchback.

There he is. I'm getting closer.

Eli presses harder with his right foot. His car lunges faster stalking its prey. Around the next curve, the lion finds its target, Jackson. Eli reaches to his dashboard.

Sudden, close headlights appear blinding Jackson who adjusts his mirror. His momentary glance away from the road steals Jackson's attention. An unexpected veer left. Jackson's front wheel clips an outstretched section of a pine tree trunk.

Bits of rubber burn pushing through white smoke billowing from under Jackson's truck as it spins down a small, gravel gully. Eli slams his brakes stopping his car on the shoulder of the road.

Terror strikes Eli watching the truck flip. It slides on its side down from the road coming to a rest against large boulders forming a barrier to a cliff.

"Shit! Shit! Shit!" Eli bangs his steering wheel with each word. He takes two deep breaths to collect himself looking ahead and in his mirror.

Thank, God. No one is around.

Eli opens his car door. A low, whirring sound floats from the gully. Jackson's rear-passenger wheel rotates creating a funnel of white smoke spinning up from the truck.

Early morning fog lifts from the valley. The black sky lightens along the horizon.

Eli approaches the decimated truck. Glass and steel parts lie everywhere.

Oh shit, he's dead.

His thought ends as Eli hears the faint pleas of *help* from the wreckage. Eli makes his way down the gully. A small orange light flickers under the truck bed.

Eli opens the front passenger-side door. Blood drapes across Jackson's face.

Shit.

In one quick motion, Eli reaches into the truck wrapping his arms around Jackson. A rush of adrenaline surges through him as he pulls. Jackson's legs remain lodged under the crushed steering wheel.

Eli pulls again twisting Jackson. His legs free and Eli has him safe in his arms as he pulls Jackson from the crushed truck. The heat from the growing orange flame increases the sense of urgency.

Jackson lies on the ground away from his truck as Eli paces around Jackson's body. A rising heat sensation creeps up Eli's neck causing him to return his attention to the burning vehicle. Eli runs back to the truck's front seat grabbing a folder of thick, black photo prints from the upside-down ceiling.

"Help… " Jackson said through his blood-filled whisper.

Eli frisks Jackson taking a picture from Jackson's shirt pocket. Eli is unsure what he is taking, only that it is paper with possible notes about the discovery. No evidence of tonight's anomaly can remain.

Satisfied, Eli returns to his car and speeds away. The orange flames of the burning truck grow smaller in the distance until the next switchback ahead causes it to disappear.

"Shit! Shit! Shit!"

Eli catches a quick glimpse of himself in his rearview mirror.

I need to get to Caltech before anyone arrives and hears his message.

FEBRUARY 26, 1960 – 6:42 A.M. (6 DAYS LATER)

EARLY MORNING FOG lingers low against the frost-covered ground. A torrent of dust spins through the misty veil above the mountainside road. The purplish-orange hue of the pending sunrise teases over the horizon.

A sickening whir echoes from a roadside gully two miles from the Mount Palomar Observatory. White smoke billows through the fog. Shards of splintered glass fill the front seat of the Chevy pickup truck. Blood slips from Jackson's lips as numbness slithers below his neck.

"Help... " Jackson manages with a weak voice.

The spinning rear wheel vibrates throughout the cab keeping Jackson alert. His eyes open-and-close at a slowing rate. Blurriness fills his vision. With instinct, he lifts his left hand flipping open the sun visor. His bloody fingers snatch the picture of his wife slipping it into his shirt pocket.

In one quick moment, Jackson senses his body lift. A stranger's arms reach through his opened front door. The white fog and smoky haze eclipse his view of the crash as the stranger pulls him up to the roadside. Grunts and moans release from Jackson's lungs.

Heavy footsteps lumber around Jackson as cold, wet gravel poke the underside of his bloodied head. His body lies motionless as his brain does not allow either of his legs movement.

The moments feel like they last forever. In reality, a few minutes had passed.

Lumbering footsteps return around Jackson.

"Help... " Jackson said through his blood-filled whisper.

Strange hands frisk Jackson's helpless body. A blurry face enters his vision. His savior says nothing as he leaves.

Warmth falls across his face. Orange flames spurt through the fog. Gravel flies in the air as spinning wheels rush away from the scene. The flames grow higher as a rush of hot wind brushes across Jackson's body from the wreckage.

"Help… "

On the front, passenger seat, a manila folder bounces in the speeding car leaving the scene. Large, black-plastic photo plates vibrate out of their holder. Darkness rushes ahead of Eli's car as it speeds down the mountain without shining its headlights.

A few minutes later, lights appear ahead of the escaping car. Eli turns onto California Highway 76. His hands hold tight the top of the steering wheel with a picture of Jackson's wife staring back to him. The car slows not to draw any unwanted attention.

Red sun rays peek above the mountain ridge chasing the fog. A plume of billowing smoke rises from the hills inside the car's rearview mirror. Red and blue lights flash accompanying a wailing siren approach and pass his vehicle.

Eli adjusts his mirror as the firetruck disappears behind him. He places the picture in the folder with its photographs spreading across the seat. A grin reflects in the mirror as he wipes black smudges from his left cheek.

Smoke eclipses the sunlight. The sky holds patches of brilliant orange and purple. Sirens quieten fast behind him.

JUNE 13, 1960 (4 MONTHS LATER)

A WARM GLOW OF headlights round the front of the parking lot of the Palomar Observatory. Tires squeal as a pale-blue van parks.

Humming rattles from the side door. Jackson sits on a platform inside his wheelchair. He lowers himself to the pavement.

"Good evening, Jackson. It's been awhile," one of the leaving technicians said as he passes the van. "Do you need any help?"

The platform rises as Jackson closes the door. "No, thanks. I've got to do this myself."

"Sure. I understand." The technician continues to his car stopping halfway. "Oh, they finished installing the ramp and the lift to the telescope last night."

Jackson waives acknowledging the news. He wheels his chair up the ramp to the observatory's entrance. The familiar popping of the door opening awakes a four-month-old memory of his last night at Palomar.

His eyes adjust to the building's darkness as he wheels himself inside the observatory. The daytime astronomer approaches.

"So happy to have you back."

"It's great to be here. But, like I told the others when they visited me, just treat me the same as before the accident," Jackson said rolling by his colleague.

"Well, have a good one. I'll see you in the morning."

Jackson wheels into the side office. The coordinates for tonight's telescope-scan call for reviewing the *Aquarius* Constellation. He leaves them on the desk as he shuffles through a file cabinet.

He slams the drawer closed and spins around rolling through the office doorway. His chair squeaks as he heads across the observatory floor.

Jackson stops beside the steps and presses a green button on a metal pedestal. He rises ten feet to the telescope control panel.

He enters coordinates into the computer: Right Ascension 05 hours, 03 minutes, 53.8665 seconds and Declination minus 27.0772038.

The building's doors open as the warm, night air rushes inward. The platform hums and vibrates as the telescope spins and raises into position.

It should be here... I know it was here...

He inspects the *Columba Noachi* Constellation.

It was here... it's gotta be here.

Hours had passed. Frustration rages inside Jackson.

For three consecutive nights, he searches the same coordinates. After the accident, none of his colleagues has believed him or his story of the anomaly. His truck fire had destroyed his proof. He even doubts himself after finding nothing scanning the same location.

Hmm, I should have found it by now. Screw it; I'm going home.

The wheelchair platform lowers. Jackson collects his belongings from the office and exits the building.

As he fumbles with his keys, a car on the far side of the parking lot turns on its headlights as it races away from the observatory down the mountain.

Damn kids making out, again.

Jackson rolls onto the platform and raises himself inside the van closing the door behind him. He lifts his lifeless legs out of his chair and into the driver's seat.

Before starting his van, he lowers the sun-visor to see a picture of his wife holding their four-month-old daughter. He stops his ritual of kissing his index and middle fingers together and placing them on the picture.

"What the hell?"

Beside his photo is a new, but familiar picture. It had not been present when he had arrived earlier.

Jackson pulls the second photo closer. It is not new, but one he had thought lost in the fire. The picture is as he remembers except for a red, faint smudge along the top-right.

Jackson licks his finger and wipes the smudge flipping over the image. In black ink are words he had not seen or written.

"Stop looking, or she will have the same fate," Jackson said reading the text. "Stop looking for what? What same fate?"

He darts his head from side-to-side and checks his mirrors.

"Stop looking… "

Hairs on his arms and neck electrify. A chill shivers throughout the parts of his body with feeling. An uneasiness erupts from his gut.

His instincts tell him to run…

4 - Control

TWO YEARS HAD PASSED.

The group of six have journeyed from their Houston office to Washington. Today, the men have their first meeting with the President of the United States of America.

Simon's hotel room is the central meeting point for the group before their departure to the White House. Project plans in various levels of progress rise on a small table between four chairs at the window.

"Okay, Men, let's go over our discussion points one last time," Simon said standing before his seated colleagues at the table. Eli, as the youngest, rests on the edge of the twin bed.

"I will be the one speaking to the President unless he asks a specific question to any one of you. We want to show him we are a real organization with leadership."

Eli squirms at the foot of the mattress clearing his throat.

"We require more resources for Project Eden, so we need the government's help."

Unable to take the monologue instructions any longer, Eli stands.

"Yeah, but only to a certain extent, right?" Eli said sitting back on the bed as the seated men turn their attention to him.

"Eli, that's all in due time. Like we agreed, the President needs to buy into what we know before we can take the next steps in our plan," Simon said.

"I still want to go on record that I disagree with our plan. The only correct path should be to keep this information contained," Eli said.

"We know, we know. But, if we do this right, then everyone on Earth can go to Salvation. Better yet, we will be able to develop a way to save Earth itself."

"But, we're talking about almost sixty years from now. You've seen the world's population projections... it'll be impossible to save everyone." Eli reclines onto the bed staring at the ceiling.

"Eli, I know you disagree. But, fundamentally, you believe in our general plans," Simon said standing next to Eli's feet on the floor.

Eli stands fast from the bed. "Believe... well, hell, I'd say so with the lengths I've already gone to protect us so far."

Simon places his left hand on Eli's right shoulder.

"You did an excellent job handling the situation out at Palomar." Eli's muscles tighten under Simon's grip. "And, your idea to prevent other observatories from discovering the object was brilliant."

With two-hundred-three observatories in the world, the need to blind other astronomers from the secret had become apparent to the group of six. The group wants to prevent another "Palomar."

The group has formed a company specializing in upgrading telescopes with the latest, available technology. Their free service easily entices the observatories already strapped for funding.

As the company works, it hires technicians to install equipment within the telescope. This feature prevents the telescope from scanning the specific coordinates within *Columba Noachi.*

To the astronomer, they see a copy of the sky to the left of the constellation at the entered coordinates. This will make CIE.57.20 invisible.

The group had no problems convincing observatories to service their equipment. With this project, The Eden Foundation had officially come into existence.

Eli releases the tension in his back muscles as Simon releases him.

"But, for now, we at least have to give the President a storyline to believe to expose our organization to his resources," Simon said.

"How much information are you willing to share?" one man said seated with his back to the window.

Simon paces the room and reaches into his back pocket. A moment later, he searches into his black, leather wallet.

"Men, you see *this*," Simon said extending a small, color photo in his hand. "He is my newborn son, John." Simon pauses. "We will offer just enough information to make sure he and others will be safe in 2020."

Silence fills the room. Eli stands, again.

"John Baptiste, really? That's the name you and your wife came up with?" Eli said punching Simon's left arm playfully. "No, I agree... let's only give enough information to get what we need, but not everything, yet."

Simon puts away his photo. "We need to leave."

The six men stand placing on their black, suit jackets. Each pauses at the full-length mirror as they exit the room.

Eli holds the door for Simon, who is last to leave. The gesture is not a sign of respect or for the sake of manners. Subliminally, Eli is ready to take over the leadership of the fledgling Eden Foundation.

FEBRUARY 17, 1962 (10 MONTHS LATER)
PASADENA, TEXAS

SIMON GASPS AS HIS BARE FEET land on the cold, linoleum kitchen floor. Wonder Bread, bologna, and cheese position themselves across from him on the countertop in his dark kitchen. A sleepless night has forced him downstairs from his bedroom for a late-night snack.

With a huff, he re-opens the refrigerator retrieving a half-empty jar of Miracle-Whip. He completes his goal as he enjoys the simple taste, a reminder of his childhood.

Months of planning completed, the next step for Project Salvation is execution. The daunting task details ramble in Simon's thoughts.

Our two options are simple. We either figure out a plan to escape Earth or how to destroy it.

The soft bread melts with each bite.

Either solution will require so much funding and resources. I still think our efforts are well-suited to develop a way to deflect or destroy it.

The refrigerator door opens. Light rushes through the dark kitchen. Simon grabs and opens a carton of milk pulling it out as the light disappears into the room.

Eli really believes our best option is escaping Earth, but how?

The cold milk refreshes his throat with each sip.

We both agree the Moon is not far enough away... can we make it to Mars by then?

Simon staggers into his home office. Newspaper clippings from May 1961 of Alan Shepard's historic launch into Space lay scattered on his desk. Simon rests the remaining half-sandwich on the edge of a side table.

Hell, Shep is the first American in Space, and that was only eight months, ago.

Simon grunts.

And, Eli thinks we can make it to Mars.

Faint tapping against the office window awakes Simon from his daze. He peeks through the closed curtains. Eli is outside waving mouthing something to Simon. He realizes Eli is motioning him around to the back door of the kitchen.

Simon retrieves the rest of his sandwich, finishing it in two bites as he unlocks the back door. His lips smack together.

"Eli? It's three in the morning. What the hell are you doing, here?"

Eli turns his head looking over his shoulder as he enters Simon's home. His breath lingers in the unusually cool Houston night. Eli catches Simon's hand.

"Keep the lights off." Eli pushes by Simon into the room.

"Why?" Simon asked in a whisper tone as he closes the door.

Eli passes him again returning to the door. He peeks through the hanging blinds covering the window.

"I... I think someone is following me?"

"Following you?"

"Yes, ever since I left our office, I just had this feeling that— "

"Why were you in the office so late?"

Eli remains at the door. His gloved hands release the blinds. He turns to Simon.

"I finished the plans I have been developing for Project Salvation," Eli said as he leans against the kitchen table.

"You finished... which version?"

"Simon, you know which one. My vision."

"Mars?"

"Yes, Mars, it's the only alternative."

Simon slides a chair away from the table and sits.

"You know my thoughts on this. We have time to build a defense system to destroy it, or hell, at worse deflect it away from us."

Eli joins him at the table.

"Come on. We've both ran the simulations. The size and speed... there's no way we can— "

"But, can we build a city on Mars? We have only fifty-eight years. Even our best guess of when we can make it to the Moon is ten years from now," Simon said.

"And launching missiles at it... that will stop it? For God's sake, it's bigger than the Moon; there's just no way."

"Between the Soviets and us, our nuclear bombs are getting stronger."

Eli laughs.

"Shh!" Simon responds, "you'll wake *them* up."

"You think our countries will join together on this? Hell, neither country trusts the other," Eli said in a softer voice.

"That's why we have to go back to Kennedy. We need to share our new information about how big this thing is. We can share both our recommended plans. He seems to have faith in you since you wrote his Joint Sessions speech last year."

Eli stands from the table and paces the kitchen.

"Simon, you still don't understand, do you?"

"Understand?" Simon's eyes follow Eli.

"If our countries work together building larger weapons, eventually the reason will come out."

"And, you don't think that would be a good thing?"

Eli lifts the milk carton to his nose. Wrinkles appear between his eyes. Milk sloshes out of the container and onto the floor as Eli slams it onto the countertop.

"If there's one thing I know... people will do anything to protect themselves. If this secret ever gets out about this planetoid colliding with Earth in 2020, the closer it gets... there will be nothing by anarchy, everywhere."

"And, your solution is for Project Salvation to operate in secret?"

"Exactly, we've gotten great at making people do what we need them to do with our connections through ARPA and NASA."

Simon stands from the table.

"Yeah, but those things are done to convince government organizations to release projects," Simon said. "In fact, you're getting really good at getting us funding."

"You don't even know what else I've already done to keep this secret," Eli said.

"The situation in Palomar?"

Eli grunts his acknowledgment.

"See, that's a perfect example. You made a great point. We need to have controls at the observatories to make sure no one else discovers the object. At least until we can collect more information."

"Yeah, that was easy to manipulate those systems so no one will find it," Eli said with a smile which goes unnoticed to Simon in the darkness.

"I still think we can get even more of what we need by telling the government," Simon said.

"And, what happens then? I mean look at Sergi... we've not heard from him since he sent you the information. I'm telling you, the KGB is keeping it quiet on their side."

"That's their agency— "

Eli interrupts Simon. "And something as dire as this… you don't think our government would not try to silence us?"

Eli's question remains unanswered.

"Also, I've started my plans," Eli said.

"Your plan."

"Simon, you'll see. There's no way to destroy it… it's gonna happen, and that's why we need to leave Earth."

"And, what… by 2020, eight billion people will live on Mars," Simon said in a sarcastic tone knowing Mars at half the size of Earth could not sustain life for everyone.

"You finally are seeing it… it won't be for everyone. Only a select portion of the population, and that's why we must keep Salvation secret."

Simon grabs a paper towel from above the sink bending to clean-up the spilled milk on the floor.

"I disagree. People will come together. We will develop a solution to protect us all," Simon said, his voice out of breath as he cleans.

"I wish you would see it my way," Eli said.

Simon stands holding the wet towel. The whites of Eli's eyes pierce the darkness. He feels Eli's hands on his shoulders as Simon falls backward in a violent motion.

Darkness fills Simon's view. The heavy, quick motion pushes air from his lungs as the back of his head slams against the countertop in front of the refrigerator.

Eli kneels beside Simon turning his ear to Simon's nose. No breathing.

A growing pool of black liquid expands from under Simon's head. The darkness masks the flowing bright, red blood on the floor.

Eli pulls his right glove off his hand placing his index and middle fingers against the side of Simon's neck. No pulse.

He replaces his glove reaching up to the counter as he stands over Simon. Eli retrieves the near-empty milk carton pouring the remaining contents on the floor near where his bare feet splay on the floor. He returns the empty carton on the counter.

The scene is an apparent accident of slipping on the linoleum floor. The police will rule this as an accidental death.

Eli scurries to the back door. As his hand reaches for the doorknob, a faint cry from a baby grows quick and loud from upstairs.

"Awe, shit," Eli said in an exasperated whisper.

The back-kitchen door opens. Cold air rushes to Eli.

A woman's voice comes from upstairs. "Simon... Simon, can you take care of John... he's crying."

Eli looks back into the darkness of the kitchen releasing a sigh. He pulls the door silently behind him disappearing into the late night. With no witnesses, Eli leaves Simon Baptiste's house.

Before making the last turn down a side street, Eli stops. He looks behind him. The house is small in the distance. A downstairs light illuminates forcing Eli forward into the night.

Distant cries of "Simon! Simon!" quieten the further Eli moves away. His deed is done. Now, Eli is in command of The Eden Foundation... of his version of Project Salvation.

Eli is in control...

NOVEMBER 17, 1963 (NEARLY 2 YEARS LATER) LOCATION UNKNOWN

CIGARETTE SMOKE ENCASES the small conference room within the offices of The Eden Foundation. Uneaten doughnuts and cold coffee remain on the back table of the room.

Secret Service Agent Boyd and Eli have spent hours reviewing the plans for Project Salvation. Eli removes the last folder from the stack of papers handing it to Agent Boyd.

"*This* is the final plan," Eli said as Agent Boyd opens the red folder.

Wrinkles appear on Boyd's forehead. Eli finds amusement in the rapid pace Boyd's eyes scan the document.

"Is *this* even possible?"

"Mars, you mean?"

"Huh, yeah… Mars."

Eli stands. Smoke circles him as he moves.

"That's the vision. But, first, we have to get to the Moon."

"Hell, as much resources the government's putting into that, it should happen, soon," Boyd said.

Eli lumbers around the table. He pauses at the doughnuts before stopping behind Boyd's chair. He places his hands on Boyd's shoulders.

"That's why we have included you. We need your help to set up the security protocols for our foundation. You know the systems at the White House, and that's the same security we will need."

"But… but, I need to include the President in this discussion."

"We would prefer that you don't. This needs to remain on a need-to-know basis, only."

Agent Boyd stands to force Eli to release his grip.

"I'm sorry, but the President needs to know."

Eli pours a cup of coffee putting it to his lips.

"Shit."

Boyd smiles with Eli's reaction.

"I'll tell you, what… I have a special relationship with the President. Let me share this information with him. I'll convince him to work with you on this program."

Eli rejoins Boyd at the table.

"*Here,* give him *this folder* of information. It's the plans we've developed."

Agent Boyd skims through the folder.

"I don't understand… these look like CIA documents."

Before his recruitment to the Secret Service, Agent Boyd had spent five years working Covert Ops within the Central Intelligence Agency. After Project Tiger, a program of placing agents into North Vietnam and its failure, Boyd had sought an alternative way to serve his country.

"That's because they are… Eden has placed Assets within the Agency," Eli said.

"Assets?"

"Yes. We've been able to place our Assets into influential positions."

"To what, develop Project Salvation?"

"No. Well, not directly. We need to deflect attention away from Salvation, while at the same time set up ways to get funding."

"Funding?"

"Shit, Man. To be successful, we'll need trillions of dollars... and what a better way for the government to spend money than to create conflicts in the world."

Agent Boyd stares upward through the smoke. Stains from old water-leaks combined with the cigarette remnants have created a mosaic of brown and yellow stains in the drop-ceiling tiles.

"You're talking about Vietnam?"

Eli releases a low-rumble laugh.

"Korea, Vietnam... the Soviet Union... we Americans hate the Communists, don't we? Call it what you want, but we will develop ways to get our funding."

Boyd closes the folder on the table.

"But, surely the government will miss funds if you move them to Salvation, won't they?"

"Not if we also control the State Department, the Treasury, and Justice Department."

Eli meets Boyd's stare. "You have Assets there, too?"

"Let's just say we're working on that... hell, we've got almost sixty years."

Boyd pushes away from the table. Chair wheels creak underneath him.

"Sixty years... that's really the only reason I'm willing to help Eden." Boyd stands gazing out the window. "I'll be long gone by then, but I just had a daughter last month— "

"Rachel, right?"

Tears crest on Boyd's cheeks as he faces Eli.

"Yes... Rachel... I named her after her mom."

Eli stands and places his hand on Boyd's shoulder.

"I'm so sorry to hear about her death a month after giving birth."

Boyd steps to the back table and pats a napkin against his eyes.

"That's why I'm doing this," Boyd said, his voice muffles against his hand. "You've promised that Eden will protect her. Cancer took my wife, but I want your assurance that Eden will look after Rachel after my time is up."

Eli stands behind Agent Boyd with a grin.

"You have my word," Eli said extending his hand as Boyd turns around to Eli.

A firm handshake confirms the agreement.

"My little Jacob is only two. I would do anything to protect him," Eli said.

Boyd returns to the table. Sniffling precedes a deep explosion of wind through his nostrils.

"Okay, so you want me to take this information to the President."

"Sure, and tell him you have concerns about us. This will make him not suspect you're working with us."

"But, what if he wants to tell others in his Cabinet?"

"Then, call me at *this number*. It's my office phone. We'll re-evaluate our plans then... who knows, maybe it is a good idea to tell others?"

Eli provides the added comment to reassure Agent Boyd. Eli is well aware this will never be the case. The plans are too great for Eli to deviate from Project Salvation.

NOVEMBER 20, 1963
LOCATION UNKNOWN

THREE DAYS HAD PASSED.

Snow floats through the afternoon sky. Sketches and notes rest on a table by a window in a dark office. A black phone on Eli's desk rings startling him from his thoughts.

"Yes?"

"He wants to meet with you," Agent Boyd said through the phone.

"When?"

"Saturday... you promised me a place in Eden if I help you."

"So, he has seen our plans?"

"Yes," Agent Boyd replied.

A static-filled pause comes through the receiver.

"Good. Where will he be before our meeting?" Eli asked.

"Dallas."

"Okay, we will take it from here," Eli said replacing the phone in its cradle.

A grin as wide as the Cheshire Cat's overcomes Eli. He rises from his desk and steps out of his office. At the end of the hall, Eli opens another office door and enters. A man sits alone smoking a half-drawn cigar staring out his window.

"Our plan is in action," Eli said.

The orange glow from the tip of the cigar grows bright. White smoke puffs around the man.

"Good," the man said as the orange tip returns. "So, it's a go for Dallas, then."

"Yes, assemble your team… you know what you have to do," Eli said.

Eli exits the room closing the door behind him.

The thing about placing Assets in evil parts of the world, evil people follow. Eden has identified the perfect person to carry-out their grandest plan to date. A plan necessary to stun the world and to grow a conflict half-a-world away from the United States.

Two days later, the world will stop because of the events in Dallas… another step toward fulfilling Project Salvation.

5-After Apollo

SPEECHES FROM the three-man, Apollo 17 crew play on the large screen inside Mission Control. Replays show the crew of the aircraft carrier, USS Ticonderoga, plucking the Command Module, America, from the Pacific Ocean.

Men smile and cheer between their puffs of cigars in Houston. NASA's last mission to the Moon is a success.

Eli stands in the back corner of the Mission Control room. This is his seventh mission as Navigation Command Leader since the Apollo 11 Mission, man's first landing on the lunar surface.

While everyone celebrates the last lunar mission and prepares for their next endeavor with Skylab, The Eden Foundation will continue to the Moon. NASA has proven the capabilities funded by the Public.

Eden had started their secret recruitment of NASA engineers during the past two years. Eli knew those disgruntled with the government's decision to stop the lunar missions. His recruits are eager to start their new endeavor, albeit in secrecy in the southern Indian Ocean.

Timelines developed by Eden project their first return to the Moon will occur in 1976. What attracts the engineers the most are the outlandish promises of Eden to travel beyond the Moon… to Mars.

After each Apollo Mission, Eli collects flight data and plans. NASA has completed the work which he delivers to Eden's new Mission Control. An easy task to complete given his role in NASA Operations Command.

Once the video ends, the men head to the central conference room with lingering smiles. Eli remains to log the records into his files.

Hours had passed.

Sun has set early on this day before the start of Winter. Beads of sweat form across Eli's forehead as he walks across the parking lot. A remarkably warm, late-December evening in Houston.

Headlights flicker. Eli heads toward the signaling car.

A man exits. His knee-length black coat cloaks his identity. An orange glow illuminates from his face followed by a puff of smoke. The man extends his hand as Eli approaches taking the paper box of records.

"This is everything," Eli said. "You know the routine."

The man shakes his head in approval.

"Your flight to Buenos Aires is in the morning at seven," Eli said.

Another puff of smoke encapsulates them. The man opens the backdoor placing the box on the seat.

The car drives away. Red brake lights shine Eli's face. Tonight's full moon has risen. Eli tilts his head back looking sixty degrees above the horizon. The red light fades replaced by the dim moonlight.

Next, it's Eden's turn to go to the Moon.

Eli drives north from the Mission Control Center. Traffic is light this Texas evening. With every passing car, Eli darts his eyes into his rearview mirror. He slows when someone comes up behind him. His grip tightens on the wheel.

After thirty minutes, Eli returns to his Pasadena neighborhood; his headlights dim in the driveway. Lights from inside the small house glow as Eli approaches the front steps. The door opens as his wife, Elizabeth, greets him with a bear hug and a kiss.

"Oh, I watched the splash down on TV. I bet you and the boys are so thrilled," Liz said.

Eli did not respond squeezing Liz longer than usual.

"Daddy!" Jacob said, his scream separating his parents. "You're home."

"I have something for you," Eli said as his hands hold a small box.

"Ooh, for me?"

Jacob snatches the box, and in a flurry, pulls the ribbon holding the lid. "Cool."

Jacob holds a miniature replica of the America Lunar Module.

"That's, why Daddy is so happy… we had a very successful mission," Eli said.

Liz takes the empty box from Jacob as he runs through the living room. In his outstretched right hand, the model flies on an imaginary flight. Air purses through Jacob's lips; his imitation of rocket engines.

"I'm sure you have mixed emotions since this is the last mission," Liz said pulling Eli into the house and closing the door.

Eli smiles.

Liz places the box on a small, side table. Red, untied ribbon drapes across the gray box covering an emblem embossed on the closed lid.

Eli places his car keys on the table causing the ribbon to fall to the floor. The uncovered emblem reveals the logo for the Apollo Missions. Within a red circle, the letter-A sits on top an ellipse both outlined in white.

The logo steals Eli's attention as it stands out against the gray box.

Hmm… that's it… I need to create a symbol for Eden… this way, those working with us will know those who belong to the program quickly.

"Eli, I saved you some dinner. I hope you're still hungry?" Liz said from the kitchen.

Eli rubs his left hand across the Apollo emblem.

"Coming, Dear. It smells so good," Eli said his voice following the aroma of beef stew.

6-TROUBLED JACOB

THANKSGIVING, 1975 (3 YEARS LATER)
PASADENA, TEXAS

OFTEN, ELI IS ABSENT from the Bishop household. His wife, Liz, recognizes his sacrifice with his work on the new Space Shuttle program.

Excitement consumes the family with Eli's time-off for Thanksgiving. Jacob has looked forward to this week. At fourteen-years-old, having his father around means everything.

The savory aroma from the roasting turkey fills the small house. Liz has been awake since seven this morning to stuff the bird and prep the oven. Marching band music plays from the living room as Liz stands under the archway entrance to the kitchen.

"How's the Christmas parade, Jacob?" Liz asked as she holds a lime, green mixing bowl on her right hip.

Jacob lifts his head from a pillow on the sofa. "Oh, um... I'm not really watching it."

"You used to love watching this every year. How are the balloons? I know you like those."

"I guess all right."

Liz places the mixing bowl by the stovetop and returns to the sofa. She leans over Jacob putting the back of her hand against his forehead.

"Honey, you're hot. You, not feeling okay?"

Jacob winces rubbing his upper-stomach. "I'm sick. Bunch of kids at school have the flu."

"Honey, go back to bed and get some rest. I'll let you know when it's time to eat."

Jacob props his torso up supporting his weight on his elbows against the sofa.

"I can't, Mama. Daddy's home and I want to spend time with him."

"Well, you won't do anyone any good if you're sick. Eli's in the shower. Go take a nap, and I'll wake you in an hour."

Jacob is aware how pointless arguing with his mother would be as he leaves for his bedroom. As Jacob closes his door, the bathroom door opens.

"Liz, it smells wonderful in here," Eli said. His hair drips on his warm, white terrycloth robe.

"Thanks, Baby. It'll be ready by about two this afternoon."

Liz leaves the living room returning to the kitchen. Eli enters their bedroom resting on the bottom corner of the bed. Deep breaths fill his lungs.

Minutes pass. Eli changes into a pair of worn, blue-jeans with wide bellbottoms. His red-checkered, button-up shirt has a wide collar pressed against his collarbones. His wardrobe is strange attire given his daily uniform of a white shirt with black slacks.

Eli steps from the bedroom on the balls of his bare-feet in silence. He has an unimpeded view into the kitchen. Liz does not notice Eli as he admires his wife. A heavy sigh escapes his body.

Liz turns to place a dish into the sink.

"Oh, hi, Jacob, you scared me."

"Sorry, Sweetie. I was just watching you," Eli said with a sheepish grin.

He approaches her as she turns back to the countertop. Eli slips his arms around her from behind kissing her neck.

"Honey, I love you," Eli said whispering into her left ear.

The large mixing spoon clangs into the metal bowl as Liz turns to him. She places her hands behind his head. Her flour-stained fingers lock together against his neck.

"I'm so happy you're home. I've missed you," Liz said giving him a short kiss.

Liz pushes back from Eli; her hands stay on him. His chest heaves with a deep breath.

"What's wrong, Baby?"

Eli kisses her left cheek.

"Nothing's wrong. I'm just tired. But, I am happy to be home for Thanksgiving."

Liz stares up to Eli's dark-brown eyes.

"Well, I hope you aren't too tired. I need a favor."

"I thought you'd never ask," Eli said with a playful laugh pulling her tight against him.

"No, not that, Silly. That's for tonight… I need you to run down to the store for some ice."

Liz releases her grip.

"Ice? Can't Jacob go?"

"He's not feeling well. I'll wake him while you're gone. When you get back, dinner will be ready."

Eli steps away from Liz.

"Okay. But, I need to make a quick call with the project team to make sure they are on schedule, today."

Liz continues with her meal-prep; her hips shake mixing the bowl. Eli disappears into the living room turning his back to the kitchen. He turns the dial on the rotary phone calling a number.

"It's time… in thirty minutes… " Eli said with his hand held over his mouth and receiver.

Eli hangs-up the phone. His breathing short and fast as he places on his shoes. He grabs his wallet from the dresser beside the bed.

After a few minutes, he returns to the kitchen spinning Liz around to him.

"Whoa," Liz said with a heavy breath.

Eli tilts his head down to Liz pulling her closer. A passionate, long kiss presses between their lips. She swoons from side-to-side.

"Oh my, Eli, I can't wait for tonight." A sheepish smirk etches across her face.

"Liz, Honey… I love you, I always will," Eli said, his gaze longing to his wife. "I'll be back in a few."

Eli leaves. The corner grocery store is a short, three-block walk. Bells ring as Eli pulls-open the door.

"Hello," the clerk said from behind the cash register.

Eli nods to the clerk and wanders to the back of the store. White, moist air escapes from the icebox. The ice freezes against Eli's hands.

Bells ring from the front. Eli gulps. Two, fast gunshots blare through the store. Heavy footsteps approach. The ice bag slips from Eli's grip.

"Quick, go out back!" the gunman yells.

On command, Eli rushes across the back aisle of the store. As he opens the door, two men rush by Eli carrying a large, black duffle bag. The men position the bag on the floor by the ice box.

"Is that— "

Eli freezes seeing the contents of the bag. The two men unzip the bag and roll it on its side. The lifeless body of a man wearing bell-bottom blue-jeans and a red-checkered, button-up shirt with a large wide collar falls out onto the floor.

Eli stands over the body.

"He doesn't even look like me… we have the same build, and he's wearing my clothes, but— "

Two gunshots stop Eli cold. The bullets enter the man's face. Blood and brains explode across the floor to the freezer.

"Solved your fuckin' problem," the gunman said to Eli as the other men remove the duffle bag.

"Shit! Shit!" Eli yells.

"Quick, we need to leave! Go out the back door!" the gunman commands to Eli.

The door slams shut. A second passes. Eli runs back to the faceless body shoving his wallet into the pants pocket.

"Shit! Shit! Shit!"

The back door slams shut. Sirens grow louder.

SEPTEMBER 20, 1977 (2 YEARS LATER)
PASADENA, TEXAS

TROUBLE.

This follows Jacob the past two years after his father's death. Guilt and despair cause Jacob to travel down an uncontrollable spiral.

Jacob believes if he had been well that fateful Thanksgiving, his dad would be alive, today. Guilt pushes him into depression. Depression results in more trouble.

Days have passed in slow motion since. His mother is usually unsure of his whereabouts. High school is an afterthought as his grades will hold him back a year. At seventeen, Jacob is a lost youth.

After dinner, Liz watches television to lose her thoughts as she has every night since Eli's senseless death. Tonight is special for her. Last week's cliff-hanger episode of her favorite show, *Happy Days,* airs at eight. She has a friendly wager with the girls down at the hair parlor on whether Fonzie jumps the shark.

For thirty minutes, Liz loses herself in her program. Popcorn kernels rattle in the tin by her side. Her heart races as The Fonz approaches the ski ramp in front of a circular shark pin. At the exact moment his waterskies lift off the water, the front door opens startling Liz.

"Oh my, God, Jacob! What happened?"

Jacob staggers through the living room; the door remains open. Fresh blood drips across his lips from his nose. A trail of Jack Daniels lingers behind him.

"Jacob!"

Water rushes from the faucet as Liz holds paper towels in the stream gushing in the sink. Jacob rests at the small, kitchen table; he keeps his head against the wall.

"Are you okay? What happened?" Liz asked holding the wet towel against his upper lip.

Jacob grunts. Liz is uncertain if he is in pain or too drunk to respond.

"Poor, Baby."

Liz comforts him rubbing the space between his shoulders. His shirt is thick with sweat and specks of grass blades. He has been away the past two days.

Jacob grabs his mom's hands. His grip holds weak.

"Whatever it is, I can help you, Jacob. Just tell me."

His eyes close. Jacob opens his mouth. No words come.

Blue and red lights dance into the kitchen. Nausea churns in the pit of Liz's stomach. Nearly two years had passed since the first time these lights appeared. Rounds of knocking pound against the open, front door.

"Ma'am, this is the police. Can we come inside?"

"*Here*, hold *this* against your nose. I'll be right back," Liz said lifting Jacob's cold hand to his face.

She rounds the corner from the kitchen entering the living room.

"Good evening, Officer," Liz said approaching the door as she holds her bloody hands behind her hips.

The officer's eyes trace her body as he reaches for his gun holster.

"Ma'am, I'm gonna need you to show me your hands," the officer said stern without expression.

Liz gasps witnessing the officer's hand move to his gun. She moves her hands slowly in front of her. Watery blood from the paper towel drips from her left, index finger.

"Are you okay?" the officer asked releasing his hold on his gun.

Liz nods.

"We're looking for your son, Jacob. I was gonna ask if you'd seen 'em, but I bet that's his blood on your hands."

Liz gulps fighting back telling a lie to protect her son. This being the third visit by the police this year, she points to the kitchen.

"Yes, he's in there."

The officer enters the living room moving by Liz into the kitchen. He returns to the archway between the two rooms.

"Ma'am no one's here. Johnson, go 'round. He left through the door back yonder," the officer said motioning his partner remaining on the front porch.

"What's this about? What did Jacob do?"

The officer turns to Liz. "Ma'am, there was an argument in town. He fled the scene after gettin' into a fight."

"A fight?"

Officer Johnson yells from the back of the house. "Chuck, we got 'em."

"Excuse me, Ma'am. You can follow us to the station if you'd like," the officer said passing Liz leaving out the back door.

Fallen popcorn lays across the floor. Liz returns to the sink washing her hands after throwing away the bloody, wet towel. The blue and red lights fade from the house. Liz picks up the popcorn placing the kernels into her bowl.

Her recliner comforts Liz. The television images show smiling faces and laughter from inside *Arnold's*. She missed the big moment she had waited all week to watch.

The theme song from *Happy Days* plays queuing a wrenching cry from Liz. She throws the empty bowl from her lap across the room.

Her body's muscles relax removing their support as she slips from her chair to the floor. Liz pulls herself to her knees with her elbows resting on the sofa's edge. She clasps her fingers together to her lowered forehead.

"Dear God," Liz said pausing catching her breath. "Jacob is a good boy. Please watch over him and protect him. Please help him find his way. In Your name, I pray. Amen."

Liz stands wiping her face; her tear tracks dry and cold. The weight of worrying about Jacob falls across her shoulders like bricks.

She cleans her mess from the thrown bowl. Returning once again to wash her hands, she inhales a refreshing breath.

Liz walks through the living room turning off the lights and locking the doors. Her hand falls flat against the back of the front door in the darkness.

I'm sorry, Son. You'll have to sleep this one off, tonight.

She turns from the door and goes inside her bedroom closing the door behind her. The light under the door dims. Faint sniffles last into the evening.

SEPTEMBER 21, 1977 (THE NEXT DAY) PASADENA, TEXAS

DRIED BLOOD CRUSTS in Jacob's left eye. His throat is dry; his body in withdrawal as his system removes the alcohol coursing through him. His nose throbs as the right-side of his upper-lip grows numb.

Consciousness returns. Thin fabric under him supports his body. Jacob is alone inside the Pasadena jail cell resting on a cot in the corner.

His vision dims. The image of a man speaking to the officer remains blurry. Their voices are impossible to understand with the ringing inside his sobering brain.

The jail cell opens.

"Looks like it's your lucky day," an officer said approaching Jacob on the cot.

Footsteps pound inside Jacob's ears. A firm hand grabs him under his right armpit pulling him off the cot to his feet.

The officer leads Jacob from the cell through the corridor of the police station to the front exit. A man in a black suit wearing a black, flat-brimmed hat waits. A distinguishing feature visible even through Jacob's drunken-state is a small, red lapel pin against the breast of the man's jacket. The bright red pin with its white-outlined circle inside a triangle stands out clearly from across the room.

"Bishop, come with me," the man said.

Jacob's eyes open-and-close trying to regain his vision. The man's features remain fuzzy.

"Who... are... where are we going?" Jacob asked. His voice cracks as his throat clears.

"I'm here to help. You are free to leave as long as you come with me."

The man holds open the door to the police station. Night air rushes to Jacob refreshing him.

Jacob staggers down the steps following the man to a waiting black car. White exhaust rises like chimney smoke in the parking lot.

"Who are you?" Jacob asked the man, who holds the car's back door open.

"Please, get in."

Jacob presses the back side of his left hand across his numbing face. A mixture of snot and blood streak across his palm. He lowers his head entering the back seat. The man follows closing the door of the driver's seat.

"Who are you?" Jacob asked, again. His question stays unanswered.

One-mile from the police station, the car stops in a dark parking lot behind an abandoned factory. The man exits the car opening the passenger's side back door. The rush of air floods the car.

Another man enters the back seat wearing a full-length, black trench coat which seems too warm for this evening. A black scarf covers his face.

The car lunges forward leaving the parking lot. Jacob slides against his door leaning against the window. Relief soothes his throbbing head from the cold glass.

"Jacob," the man beside him said, "I'm sure you have a million questions."

The man removes his scarf. Jacob catches the man's profile from his peripheral eyesight. Passing streetlights flicker across the man's face. A stoplight captures the car. Red glows on the man.

Jacob turns his head fast to the man. He presses hard against the door as if he wants to escape the vision before him.

"What the— "

Worried wrinkles fill Jacob's forehead.

"Daddy?"

The man stretches his left hand across the empty seat. Jacob swats it aside.

"It's me... your father."

Jacob's mouth cannot open farther. Air escapes his body. Jacob cannot breathe.

"It's really me. I can explain."

"But... " Jacob rubs his eyes. "This can't be real."

"Son, I assure you. I am real," Eli said capturing Jacob's hand flat against the seat.

"No! You're not! We buried my father two years ago. He's dead... Let me out!"

"Keep driving," Eli said to the man in the front seat.

Pressure throbs in Jacob's temples. Alcohol has yet to purge itself from his bloodstream.

"Jacob, I know you don't understand what's happening. But, I didn't die. I left for a top-secret project for work."

"No! We buried you."

"That was not me. I'm here, and I'm real."

Jacob turns his vision staring out the window.

This isn't true. I'm still drunk and dreaming.

The car continues north on the highway. Suburbs disappear replaced by desolate north-Texas hill country.

Vibrations from the uneven road rattle the car. This relaxes Jacob. Alcohol is an excellent sleep-aid as he drools against the window.

Eli remains quiet. His stare never leaves his son.

Late night ticks into early morning. Orange sun rays peek above the rolling hills outside Oklahoma City.

Motion stops. Bright sunshine fills Jacob's awakening eyes. He is alone inside the car.

What the hell? Where am I?

With a sudden jolt, the back seat door opens. Jacob jumps to the middle of his seat.

"Come on, let's get breakfast," the driver said motioning to Jacob.

Jacob scans around the car.

I knew it was a dream.

He forces air from his chest as his muscles throughout his body relax.

Jacob exits the car. The warm, morning sun comforts him. He follows the driver inside the small, roadside diner.

The smell of eggs and bacon erupt through the diner's entrance. The aroma of coffee lures them inside.

Jacob follows the driver to a booth in the back corner of the empty diner. Sliding across to the window, the driver sits beside Jacob trapping him. Their backs are to the door.

"Where are we? Who are you?"

Jacob's questions remain unanswered.

"Good morning, Jacob."

The man claiming to be Jacob's father, Eli, enters the booth opposite Jacob and the driver. Jacob studies the man.

His father had brown hair; this man's is brown.

His father's hair was short; this man's falls below his shoulders.

His father was thin; this man is fat.

This man has his father's voice.

"I don't believe you? This is a sick joke."

"Jacob, let me assure you, I am your father... it's me, Eli. I faked my death to protect you and your mother."

Jacob's eyes dart side-to-side recalling the events of the past twenty-four hours.

I was sitting outside the bar... Someone came up to me saying I stepped on his girlfriend's foot inside... He punched me, and I beat the shit out of him... after that, it's so fuzzy.

Minutes pass as Jacob sits silently staring out the window. Eli speaks, but his voice does not register.

"Jacob!"

Hearing his name yelled snaps Jacob from his trance. It sends a shiver through his body. Jacob's lower lip quivers.

"Daddy?"

"Yes, Son, it's me. I'm sorry. We had to pretend that I was killed because of my secret project."

Jacob hides his head on the table; his arms wrap around him. Jacob's shoulders rise and lower.

"It's okay, Jacob. I know, I know."

Jacob lifts his head. His eyes become pink instantly.

"What the fuck do you know? I don't care about me, but Mama... Mama hasn't been the same."

Eli releases a deep sigh.

"Son, what I did was a shitty thing to do to you and Liz."

"You, think?"

"But, I did it because what I'm working on will save the world someday."

"Save the– "

"Here you go, Darlins. Two eggs over-easy with bacon," the waitress said.

Jacob had not ordered, but the food is exactly how he likes his breakfast.

"Scrambled eggs and sausage?"

Eli points to the driver.

"And, the pancakes they must be for you, Hon. Can I get y'all anything else?"

"No, thank you, we're good," Eli said smiling at the waitress.

Jacob pushes his plate away. The tempting smells lift to his nose.

"Son, I know you've been angry at me since that Thanksgiving. I'm sorry. But, I have been watching you and Liz to make sure you were doing okay."

Jacob pulls the plate closer caving to the temptation.

"And, I've been worried about you. I've heard about you being in jail three times. This fourth time, they would have sent you away even though you're only seventeen."

Jacob slams his fork onto the plate. Bits of egg land against the window.

"What the hell do you care. You weren't here. You've never been there. So, it didn't mean shit to me if you were killed or ran away."

The reality of Jacob's words silences the table. The crunching from the driver eating interrupts the awkwardness.

A minute passes.

"What kind of secret project forces you to fake your death?"

Eli leans forward with Jacob's question.

"That's why I'm coming to you, now. I have a job for you. This way, we can work together. And, I'll be there for you."

The food on Jacob's plate disappears.

"Mama said you were working on something called the Space Shuttle… is that why you left?"

Eli drinks his orange juice replacing the empty glass on the table.

"Not exactly. Yes, I was working on the Space Shuttle, but my real project goes way beyond that."

Eli was never home, so Jacob could never talk to him about Space, the Moon, or any of his projects. Curiosity creeps upon Jacob with his father's statement.

"Son, we've got a long way to drive. I will tell you the information on the road. But, before we leave, I need you to do me a favor."

Jacob's lips purse tight.

A favor for you, you bastard.

"Take *this* dime. There's a payphone outside. Call your mama. Tell her you're okay that the police released you. Don't tell her anything about me. I will stand beside you to make sure you don't."

"But— "

"No buts. On our drive, you'll understand why we need to keep this a secret. Just tell her you're okay. You need to get away from Houston and find yourself."

"Find myself?"

"Yeah, find yourself. That's what your generation is doing these days, anyway," Eli said with a laugh.

"I ain't no goddam hippie."

"I know, but that will be believable. Liz will hate this, but tell her you'll promise to call and check-in."

"Sorry, Sir, but we should get on the road," the driver said interrupting Eli's instructions.

The driver stands from the booth followed by Eli, then Jacob.

"Y'all have a nice day, ya hear," the waitress said as Eli and Jacob pass the driver who pays the bill at the counter.

Jacob opens the door. The mid-morning sun refreshes him. Eli spins around to Jacob grabbing his shoulders. The hug from Eli is uncomfortable for Jacob.

"It's okay. Now, I'm here for you, Son."

The driver exits the diner as Jacob turns to the payphone. Jacob slips the dime into the slot pressing the numbers for home. Three rings purr through the receiver.

"Hello, Mama, it's me, Jacob."

"Oh, Jacob!" Eli hears his wife's voice through the phone.

"Mama, I'm okay. The police released me… and… uh… "

Jacob looks at his father.

"I'm going on a road trip… I just need some time to myself… please don't worry… I'll call and check-in… I gotta go, now… I love you."

The metallic cord dangles from the receiver in the warm Oklahoma sun. Dust spits across the gravel parking lot from the payphone.

"Great. Liz will be okay as long as you check-in. But, you can never tell her or anyone about me."

Eli and Jacob approach the car as the driver holds open the back seat door. They get inside and continue north.

Jacob turns to his father. "So, tell me about this secret… "

7-YOUNG LOVE

MONTHS HAD PASSED since Eli had shared his plans with Jacob during their drive north from Houston; at least only those plans worth telling Jacob, for now. After seventeen hours in the car, their trip ended in the middle of the country, far away from everyone. Lynchfield Apartments in Sioux City, Iowa, is Jacob's new home.

Eli had forged information enrolling Jacob into the local high school. His new name is Eric.

Jacob, or Eric, is a model student his senior year. Realizing his father is alive has calmed him. He even has a job at the local ice cream factory.

With the information Eli had shared, Jacob knows his father has to leave town for weeks at a time. The relief comes when Eli calls Jacob every other night to check on his son.

Liz receives a phone call at least every other week from Jacob. Each time, he explains he is in a different part of the country. He lies to himself that she is not worried when they speak.

Jacob works in the maintenance department of the ice cream factory. Over time, a co-worker catches his attention. She is not like the other Iowan girls. Ruth has an edge to her.

Her work ethic attracts him at first. She does not shy away from the dirty jobs of cleaning the various, factory machinery.

Often, Jacob and Ruth meet after work for a six-pack of Budweiser in the back of Jacob's pickup truck. Both are eighteen-years-old, but Ruth often passes for being a few years younger than she is. After their few hours of debauchery, they go their separate ways home.

All seems perfect for Jacob. His father is alive. He is doing well in school. He has a job and a friend; they never call themselves boyfriend and girlfriend. It is the late 1970s after all.

More months pass. After the sixth-straight-missed call, Eli worries and travels to Iowa.

Eli unlocks the door of Jacob's apartment and enters. The stench of beer and musty clothes smacks his nose.

He storms through the rooms kicking a path through the hallway. Jacob's bedroom door is open were Eli finds his son passed out naked on his bed. He lies on top of Ruth, who is topless.

Given his son's smaller stature, Eli drapes Jacob across his right shoulder and carries him through the apartment to his car. He drops Jacob inside on the backseat returning a few moments later. Eli throws a pile of dirty clothes over Jacob who is still passed-out. His father drives the rental car away; away from Iowa, away from Ruth.

Hours pass. A sour smell of piss encroaches from the backseat forcing Eli to pullover. He stops at a gas station on the highway near Peoria, Illinois. The sudden stop startles Jacob from his drunken and drug-induced stupor.

"What the hell?"

"Dammit, Boy. Get out and clean yourself."

Jacob slides his hands down his chest.

"Why am I naked?"

"Why are you... just get out of the damn car. Go inside *there*, now."

Jacob grunts exiting the car. He stops half-way to the outside bathroom holding a shirt and pants over the front and back of his waist.

"Where are we? And, where's Ruth?"

Eli slams his car door and fast approaches Jacob pointing his finger between Jacob's eyes.

"Look, you will never see her ever again. That's Jackson Wheeler's daughter. She's off limits."

Jacob drops the shirt on the ground as he bends over to put on his pants.

"Oh, so now, you want to be my father, is that it?"

Eli's eyes pierce closed. Wrinkles furl across his forehead.

"Jacob, I am always your father," Eli said in a slow, loud tone. "You are jeopardizing our mission by getting too close to Wheeler."

Jacob buttons his pants and retrieves his shirt shaking off the dirt.

"Too close... our mission, ha!"

Eli leans closer to Jacob ready to pounce on his son.

"What? Our mission to steal secrets about rocket launches from NASA. And, what the hell does a science teacher in fuckin' Iowa have to do with any of this shit?"

Eli forces the wind from his lungs out through his mouth. Eli pauses. The wrinkles flatten; his eyes widen.

"Jacob, go inside. Clean yourself up and get back in the car. We're going on a trip... and, this time, I promise to tell you everything."

Eli's words appear honest. Jacob obeys the instruction. Five minutes afterward, he returns as Eli finishes pumping gas.

"Ready?" Eli asked as Jacob enters the passenger-side sitting in the front seat.

"Let's go. You better not give me any more of your bullshit stories."

Eli opens the driver's door. "No. It's about time I tell you the real story about everything," Eli said as he revs the engine.

Miles pass one small town after the other. Dramatic landscape changes rise between the lower Great Lakes region to the mountainous terrain of Pennsylvania. Several hours later, the lights of the Manhattan skyline emerge in the distance. The cityscape fades fast as they continue into Long Island.

Eighteen hours fly in an instant. A sense of relief overpowers Eli sharing the real details of The Eden Foundation, and his plans for Project Salvation.

Eli holds nothing back from Jacob. He explains the lengths he has gone through protecting the secret. He realizes his need to develop his son for his eventual takeover of Eden, someday.

Jacob listens to Eli as if he is hearing long-gone bedtime stories he had missed as a child. Each one is more fantastic than the earlier.

Stony Brook, New York, is their final destination. Eli parks at a hotel near the local university. The sun peeks between low-hanging clouds over the Long Island Sound.

"So, let me understand this, the organization you founded is based *here*… Long Island?"

Eli stretches tired from the drive.

"Yes."

"Why?"

Eli's eyes scan the side and rearview mirrors. A sense of paranoia grows.

"We needed to be close to a university for our various research projects. The development of the Stonehaven Laboratories is a perfect cover for us."

Jacob shakes his head matching his father's actions.

"We wanted a location in an unsuspecting place… I mean, look around. It feels like the middle of nowhere, but we're just an hour outside New York City."

Both sit in silence. Their eyelids grow heavy.

"Come on, let's get some rest. Later this morning, I'll share what my plans are for you here in Stony Brook."

Both doors open in unison. Without hesitation, Eli and Jacob stagger to their hotel room. The door closes behind them unaware of the approaching snowstorm.

JUNE 1978 (6 MONTHS LATER)
STONY BROOK, LONG ISLAND — NEW YORK

TWO SETS OF FOOTPRINTS meander through the sand between patches of seagrass. Small waves lap against the shore from the Long Island Sound, a tidal inlet of the Atlantic Ocean.

Orange hues illuminate the sky from the setting sun behind the shore over the island. Across the water, faint tinges of city lights from The Bronx brighten the darkening horizon.

A small, red blanket stretches on a desolate strand of waterfront. A shoe holds each corner against the sand providing security from the sea-breeze. The supports fail in their protection from the rolling two, young lovers. Embedded warmth in the sand from the early summer sun comforts the couple.

Six months since arriving at Stony Brook from Iowa, Jacob has not touched a single alcoholic drink. The information Eli had shared during their drive maintains his sobriety.

Eli's plans for Eden has provided Jacob safety given Jacob's future role with the Foundation. With Eli around most days, he helps offer stability for his son.

Jacob's newfound outlook with Eden forces a change in his appearance from his long-haired, hippy attire to a more clean-cut style. Short-cropped hair and a clean-shaven face; Jacob is unrecognizable to anyone he may have known in Iowa.

His new look pays off. Late one evening last month, Jacob finished his shift at the Irish Pub near the Stony Brook campus. His job as a server was an unassuming one as Eli has demanded.

One night, the pub had emptied, and Jacob approached a girl sitting alone in a back corner booth. She twirled a straw in an empty Coke glass with her fingers. Announcing the pub was closing seemed like a good excuse for Jacob to start a conversation.

With a smile between them, an instant spark ignited. Jacob walked the girl home to her dorm. Their conversation lingered for hours beyond his ten-minute escort.

Genuine excitement filled Jacob for the first time. During the day, she attended her freshman classes, and Jacob performed various tasks assigned by Eli. Both longed for the night as she would return to the pub for playful conversations over dinner with Jacob taking her home at closing time.

Last night, the late-evening talks turned more serious. She provided a lookout as Jacob entered the all-girls' dorm sneaking into her room.

Morning sunlight crept through the bottom window shade. Their naked bodies lie asleep under a white, linen blanket. Jacob was her first.

With today being Saturday, the beautiful morning sun called them to the beach, a thirty-minute stroll from campus. Jacob carried a basket of soda and sandwiches while she brought her favorite red blanket. A hundred-feet did not pass without a kiss between them. Love found a new couple.

Hours had passed. The water still cold after an unusually cool spring, they walked the beach dipping their feet into the lapping water before returning to the blanket.

The blue sky dims as streaks of orange stretch through the puffy, white clouds above the couple kissing on the sand. Gentle waves wash across their footprints disappearing along the shore.

Darkness surrounds the couple asleep on the blanket. An orange glow brightens in the front seat of a lone car parked beside the small, maintenance building behind the beach. White cigarette smoke puffs through the driver-side window. Eli is watching.

As the smoke clears, the view of the couple laying on the beach appears within Eli's binoculars. The cigarette smoke interrupts his sly grin.

He places the binoculars on the passenger seat flicking the last of his cigarette butt through the opened window. A faint hiss encroaches the car as the butt falls onto the wet sand.

Eli's plan worked. Jacob has met Rachel Boyd, the orphaned daughter of Special Agent Boyd, who Eli had promised he would protect.

After Agent Boyd's work with the Foundation in the 1960s, Boyd had become a liability to Eli. An accident on a construction site had left Rachel a ward of the State in the Houston foster care system.

A surprising scholarship offer had come to her from the university to study genetic biology. The surprise was not from her academics, but rather a school in New York which she had not applied.

Eli's plan was simple: a few unsuspecting fliers announcing Happy Hour Specials of Rachel's favorite foods placed around campus. The lure had worked bringing her to the Irish Pub.

Rachel was attracted to Jacob from the moment she saw him in the bar. It helped that Eli had given Jacob subtle hints on changing his hair and clothing styles to those Eli knew Rachel preferred.

But, after watching them together on the beach, something unplanned will occur. Something which Eli has not envisioned. In August, Jacob will approach Eli with the news Rachel is pregnant.

Eli had collected Rachel's medical records indicating she has a condition which should prevent her from getting pregnant. But, soon, Rachel will give birth to Eli's grandchild, Joseph.

While unexpected, the news will present Eli with a new plan. A grand strategy that Jacob will be all too eager to execute. This will mean Project Salvation is one step closer to reality.

8-Escape to Le Mars

CARS LINE THE ENTRANCE to the high school parking lot as parents and students arrive for the first day of class after the New Year in Le Mars, Iowa. A small town of eighty-two-hundred in the northwest corner of the state, Le Mars is thirty minutes by car to the northeast of Sioux City.

Those thirty minutes remain fresh in Jackson's memory even after eighteen years since he had arrived with his wife and newborn daughter, Ruth.

A blue van drives the straight-lined, neighborhood street coming to the one-story, brick school building. *What a Fool Believes* blares from the van's radio with its open windows on this unusually warm January morning. The same song echoes across the filling parking lot as everyone in town shares the pride of having one of their very own being a member of *The Doobie Brothers*.

The van stops in the only handicap-parking spot. Jackson sits with his closed eyes mouthing the lyrics coming from his radio, which tug at him with their words.

His wife had grown tired of living so far away from her California family. At least this is the story she has promised to tell everyone as the reason for their divorce. Both with their heavy dependence on alcohol, drove them apart.

For years, she had tried to understand Jackson's upheaval of their new family from California moving them nineteen-hundred miles to the middle of nowhere. Their trek along Route 66 through Arizona to Texas still comes vivid to Jackson, especially listening to the words of the song.

If it had not been for the hours of crying between his wife and daughter, Jackson would have continued to Illinois. This distraction caused Jackson to make a wrong turn on a new bypass in Oklahoma City taking their van north. After repeated screams asking him where they were moving, Jackson only replied with "away" numerous times.

Hours of pleading had endured. The highway had grown narrow as they passed Omaha, Nebraska.

Jackson grins in the driver's seat outside the high school. He remembers thinking even Omaha had seemed too big of a city to stop. They had advanced north stopping for gas in Sioux City.

Thirty minutes later, even the van had refused to move any further having released a grinding noise behind the panel wall below his feet. No one had passed by them in either direction for hours.

The road was straight flanked by wheat as high as the van's windows. A chorus of crickets serenaded them into the night. The van had died, and his passengers were deep in sleep. A green road sign reflected in his headlights: *Le Mars 2 Miles.*

Unsure where he was going, Jackson had driven his dying van outside a town with its ironic name. This was Jackson's sign to stop. He had decided in the morning he would wheel his chair into town hoping to flag down a passing car for help.

Jackson has never provided a reason for moving the family nor for stopping in Le Mars. There, Jackson believes he had found safety.

The song lyrics end. Jackson opens his eyes releasing a deep breath as he cranks-up his window leaving a small crack at the top. He slips to the right of his seat and pulls his chair from the back to him.

Once in his chair, he opens the side sliding door and presses a red button at the window. Hums and vibrations rattle the van as the platform supporting his wheelchair slides out the side lowering to the pavement. He presses the switch as the platform reverses up and into the van.

As Jackson wheels along the sidewalk to the brick school building, he replays the song in his mind. Words escape his lips. "A fool will believe anything, that's for sure."

Students move out of their way as Jackson rolls through the hallway. The last classroom on the right is his. Laughter and talking stop when Jackson enters. The freshmen do not expect to see the man in the wheelchair come in their class, especially being their teacher.

Jackson places his lunch and bag behind his desk and spins his chair to the class.

"Good morning, Students. My name is Mr. Wheeler, and it's the perfect name for someone like me isn't?"

Nervous laughter ripples across the classroom.

"It's okay. Let me get this out of the way. I was in a car accident a long time ago and can no longer walk. But, I am thankful to be alive, and I am thankful to be your teacher for this semester."

"Does it hurt?" comes a voice from the back.

"No… my legs don't hurt. I feel fine, except everything below my waist is numb."

"Wow, Man, that's not cool," the same voice in the back said.

Jackson grins. "Yeah, it sure isn't." He inches his chair forward.

"Okay, class, this semester I will teach you about our planet, how it was formed and about our neighbors in space."

"Like Martians," another voice said from the students. The class roars with laughter.

"Funny, Class. Like I haven't heard that one before living here," Jackson said.

A hand rises near the front of the class.

"Yes?"

"Um, Mr. Wheeler how long have you lived here? I don't remember seeing you in town before?"

Jackson backs away from the students. "Well, my wife and I moved here back in '61, a few years before you all were born."

"From where?" another student asked.

Jackson responds with his rehearsed reply, "From Florida."

A chorus of awe's come from the students. Jackson refuses to say California picking a state on the opposite side of the country.

"The reason you probably haven't seen me is that other than teaching, I don't get out much."

"But, how do you get groceries and things?" another student asked.

"Uh, my daughter, Ruth, helps. But, enough about me. Let's get started for today."

Jackson turns the lights off in the classroom and wheels to the center in front of the students. After a loud click, a bright, yellow light illuminates the room from the overhead projector.

"Okay, class, who can tell me what this is?" Jackson asked placing his finger on the slide. His fat, index finger creates a shadow on the screen.

Silence. No response.

"This is an illustration of the orbits of the planets in our solar system. Does anyone know what this planet is?" Jackson points to the third circle around the sun.

A voice erupts from the back of the room. "It's Earth."

"Yes, correct. This is Earth."

9-Con Man

THE SUN SETS BEHIND the flat Iowa horizon as Jackson arrives home. Untrimmed hedges surround a one-story, weathered-wood-framed house. Long strips of white paint peel from the siding. Gutter downspouts sit detached from the roof. This has been the Wheeler home in Le Mars for eighteen-years.

Gone are the happy smiles of his waiting wife and daughter upon his return home. The reality of his current life chases away those pleasant memories.

Jackson pushes his wheelchair up a dilapidated ramp. The rotting wood creaks as he opens the torn-screen front door.

Fist holes dot the plaster walls throughout the house. One would believe Jackson had created them given their two-feet height. But, his daughter, Ruth, was the culprit.

Jackson was not a loving father. His thoughts of Palomar has preoccupied him upon arrival. Ruth, his daughter, did not have a caring mother given her frequent love affair with Jack Daniels.

One thing Jackson did provide was protection. He had moved his family across the country to Le Mars. Fear had driven him East.

Jackson was overprotective not allowing Ruth to play outside their home during her childhood. In his mind, this was for her safety.

His chair manages through his house. Other than the creaking wood floors, no other sounds occur. Moldy bread and rotting bananas overwhelm him as he passes the kitchen with its overflowing dishes in the sink.

The house is dark with closed, dusty curtains. Through horizontal slats of the window shades, peeks of a lone streetlight illuminate his path. Keys jingle in his hand as he unlocks a door at the end of the hallway.

Jackson opens the door and reaches to turn on the overhead light. Fluorescent lights flicker until they entirely come alive. This room is off-limits to everyone including his wife and daughter when they had lived with him.

Pictures and scribbled notes provide the wallpaper around the room. Faces with red-marked circles and various black lines trace along multiple documents.

Newspaper clippings adorn the walls between the pictures and notes. Articles concerning missing scientists or unexplained laboratory fires are their common theme.

On the wall opposite the door, Jackson has drawn elaborate diagrams of various constellations. The most prominent is the *Columba Noachi* Constellation, the last one he had viewed at the Palomar Observatory.

For hours, Jackson would lock himself in this room when he had returned from his day of teaching. Not only had Jackson escaped whoever he believed was after him, but he had also retreated from his family, the very people he wanted to protect.

A familiar stare from Jackson occurs as he sits in his wheelchair in the middle of the cluttered room. *Columba Noachi* teases him with its secret. Within the constellation, Jackson had drawn a faint, small smudge.

As he has repeated for years, he breaks his gaze and rolls to the image. He lifts his hand reminiscing the time he had drawn his recollection of the mysterious object which he could not prove had existed.

Three, loud knocks interrupt his concentration. The banging comes from the front door.

With a huff, Jackson spins his chair to the room's door pulling it closed. Two more knocks muffle the jingling keys as he locks the door. Blue lights with a violent flicker sparkle the closed, window shades.

"I'm coming!"

Jackson slides his keys into his pocket and pushes his chair through the moldy kitchen smells returning to the front door.

"Who is it?"

"Mr. Wheeler, Mr. Jackson Wheeler, this is the Sioux City Police. Can you please open the door, Sir?"

"Awe, shit," Jackson said with disbelief. He peeks through the low, peep-hole he had installed. Two men in dark-blue uniforms, a blue so dark it looked black, stand outside his door. Blue flashing lights create a strobe effect.

Jackson opens the door leaving the torn-screen panel closed. The officers see him in his chair. One officer stands clear to Jackson through the part of the screen not ripped.

"Mr. Wheeler, my name is Sergeant Armstrong, and my partner is Lieutenant Collins."

"What brings you out this evening?"

"Mr. Wheeler, I am sorry. We have bad news to tell you, Sir."

Jackson backs his chair from the door a few inches bracing himself for what the officer is about to say.

"Is it about my wife, Tina? Is she okay?"

"No, Sir... I mean, yes, your wife is okay, I guess... " Sergeant Armstrong said.

Jackson fidgets in his chair.

"It's about your daughter, Mr. Wheeler."

"Oh."

"I'm afraid your daughter has been arrested— "

"Arrested? Arrested for what this time?"

"Sir, we were called out to an address at the Lynchfield Apartments in Sioux City."

"Shit, what did her boyfriend, Eric, do, now?"

Lieutenant Collins takes over from his partner. "Mr. Wheeler, we were responding to a domestic disturbance called-in by one of the neighbors."

"Hell, I'm not surprised. I've not seen him in a long time, but those two always seemed to fight about something... " Jackson wheels closer opening the screen door. "Do I need to come bail her out?"

"Mr. Wheeler, it's not that simple," the Sergeant said.

"Oh, no, it is. I've had to do this a few times for her... I know the procedure," Jackson said reaching for his van keys.

"No, Sir. I'm afraid she has been arrested for attempted murder," the Sergeant said

Silence falls between Jackson and the officers.

"Mr. Wheeler, we came here to get your statement to help us out."

Jackson lifts his head from staring at his dead legs. A single tear falls from his nose.

"Oh, God... I knew they were having problems... but... I never thought it could lead to something like this... "

Lieutenant Collins flips open his notepad. "Sir, you seem to have not been surprised about us being called out on a domestic dispute."

"Um... yeah... I mean, I have heard them fighting before. Then again, like I said, I've not seen him in a while."

"So, they fought a lot?"

"Usually about his drinking or coming home late. It never was anything serious like...attempted murder... what happened?"

"Sir, we can't go into those details, yet, until we finish our investigation. Did you ever see your daughter with any bruises or signs of any prior altercations?"

Jackson sits silently wiping the wet tear track from his face. A few seconds had passed.

"My daughter's always been a fighter standing up for herself."

"Did you see any signs of abuse or anything to cause you alarm?"

"Huh, a few weeks ago, she came home with a shiner on her right... no, it was her left eye. But, she told me she ran into equipment at the ice cream factory during maintenance."

"Maintenance?"

"Yeah, she works in the maintenance department. She can fix almost any broken equipment and doesn't mind getting her hands dirty."

"How long has she worked at the factory?"

"Since about '77, I think. It was right after high school."

Lieutenant Collins flips through his older notes. "Hmm, we don't have a record of her attending high school."

"Oh, no," Jackson said interrupting the officer, "we home-schooled her."

"Home-schooled? Would that have been Mrs. Wheeler, then since you teach at the Le Mars High School."

Jackson backed up in his chair. "Oh, God, this will kill her mom."

"Is Mrs. Jackson, here, Sir?"

"Uh, no. We're divorced. I don't even know where she is anymore?"

"You don't know where— " Sergeant Armstrong said.

"She left me. She's an alcoholic. I haven't heard from her in years."

Both officers scribble in their notes. A call from dispatch pierces through the doorway from the walkie-talkies affixed to their belts.

Sergeant Armstrong turns off his radio. "Sir, we can take you to our station in Sioux City if you'd like?"

Jackson grabs his keys and pushes by both officers.

"I'll follow you if that's okay."

The weathered ramp creaks with the accelerating wheelchair rolling over it. The officers follow behind walking to their patrol car. Their faces alternate between black from the night and blue from their lights. The police car leaves Jackson's driveway.

Rumbling comes from the van as white exhaust shoots from the rear tailpipe. As Jackson leaves, he stares at his reflection in the rearview mirror.

"Daddy's coming for you, Honey… my poor, Ruth."

MARCH 29, 1979 (LATER IN THE AFTERNOON) SIOUX CITY, IOWA

"MR. WHEELER, *THIS* WAY, *in here*, please," Sergeant Armstrong said directing Jackson into an interrogation room.

Gray walls absorb the dim, overhead lights of the room. Single, wooden chairs sit on opposite sides of the table. The sergeant pulls a chair away giving Jackson room to move his wheelchair.

As soon as Jackson positions his chair, the room's door opens. Lieutenant Collins ushers Jackson's daughter, Ruth, into the room sitting her opposite Jackson. The officer laces a chain from the table to her handcuffs and leaves.

Ruth slouches not making eye-contact with her father.

"Are you gonna tell me what happened?"

Ruth sits silent. Emotionless.

"They said you had a fight with Eric... is that true?"

A vacant stare lifts from Ruth to Jackson. Ruth continues to sit unresponsively.

"Did... did he hit, you?"

Ruth wears her factory's maintenance uniform. Red stains sprinkle across her white name tag, her face absent any apparent signs of a struggle. Jackson tries to make sense of why his daughter had attempted to kill her boyfriend.

At nineteen-years-old, she maintains a youthful appearance easily passing for sixteen. Ruth manipulates people with her looks while possessing the foulest mouth able to make a sailor wince.

"Honey, you have to tell me so I can help you," Jackson said pleading for her help.

A heavy sigh expels toward Jackson. The stench of Budweiser wafts across the table.

"Did he do something bad to you? Is that why... why, you... "

Ruth straightens in the chair and slams her hands on the table. The sound bounces off the walls.

"That motherfucker… " Ruth slams her hands again on the tabletop. "First, he gets me pregnant, and then that son-of-a-bitch tells me he's leaving me."

"What? You're pregnant— "

Jackson inches his chair from the table.

"He's leaving me for some bitch down in Texas," Ruth said yelling interrupting Jackson. "Supposedly, he's getting married and staying with her. That bastard got her pregnant, too."

Jackson holds his mouth open at her statement about being pregnant.

"So, I cut the fucker's dick off… that'll teach that cocksucker."

"Ruth!" Jackson said banging his fists against the table gaining her attention.

Her shoulders relax as her father always can calm her.

"We had a fight… and… I took a knife… and… " Ruth said; her breath comes short between words. "I was going to kill him… I guess… I don't remember too much after that."

With the admission, the door swings open as Lieutenant Collins enters.

"That's it, we've got what we needed," Collins said.

The officer removes the chain holding Ruth's handcuffs in restraint. He guides her to her feet. Her stare burns through her father.

"Honey, I'll find some way to get you out of here," Jackson said as Collins led Ruth from the room. "I promise."

MARCH 30, 1979 (THE NEXT DAY)
LE MARS, IOWA

THE SUN PEEKS THROUGH the closed blinds reflecting across Jackson's face. His breath reeks of stale Budweiser and of hours-old vomit. Morning arrives. Jackson pulls the yellow phone from the table beside him. His fat fingers, swollen from his evening gorge of beer, rotates the dial.

Jackson clears his throat. "Um... yeah, this is Mr. Wheeler... ack." Phlegm fills his lips. "Sorry 'bout that... I can't make it into class, today. I'm sick."

He does not wait for a response slamming the phone onto its base. The yellow cord sways across the table knocking over a half-empty, flat beer.

His eyes close. A rapid knock bangs against the door.

"Go away!"

Jackson keeps his eyes closed. The bangs repeat.

"I said go away!"

"Mr. Wheeler... Mr. Jackson Wheeler... I'd like to speak to you, Sir. I think I can help your daughter, Ruth, with the trouble she's in."

Jackson mumbles. The bangs repeat.

"Mr. Wheeler?"

"Jesus!"

Jackson opens his eyes and pulls himself from the rocking chair to his wheelchair.

"Wait a damn minute; I'm coming."

The door opens. A well-dressed man stands on his porch wearing a brown, corduroy suit with a matching vest. The giant collar of his brown polyester shirt compliments his tanned skin and close-cropped, sandy-blonde hair.

"Mr. Wheeler, my name is Eli Bishop. If I can come inside, we can talk about how I can help."

"You a lawyer?"

Eli laughs.

"Hardly."

"Then, how the hell are you gonna help me?"

Eli pulls open the screen door. Jackson sees the stranger holding a bright-red notebook under his left arm.

"Can I come inside? I've got an offer you'll want to hear."

Jackson pushes his chair back into the dark living room. He pulls a string on a table lamp as Eli follows inside the house looking behind him as he pulls the front door closed.

"Who did you say you were again?" Jackson asked reaching for an unopened beer from the bar separating the living room and kitchen.

"Sir, my name is Eli Bishop. I represent The Eden Foundation."

Jackson rubs his eyes. The morning sun cracks through his sobering brain. He does not recognize Eli. Their last encounter had occurred early, one-morning in 1960 on the mountainside roadway from the Palomar Observatory.

"The Eden, what?"

"Mr. Wheeler, I'm with The Eden Foundation. We are a philanthropic establishment, and we deal with cases like yours."

"Like mine? I don't follow."

"We have many connections. One of these is with the Sioux City Police Department."

Jackson lifts his gaze from his beer can to Eli.

"Is this why you're here? You've somehow learned about my daughter's situation. Are you a reporter?"

"No, Jackson. Our organization is becoming very powerful. And, our resources are vast." Eli peeks through the side of the living room's front window blind. "I came here because we can help get Ruth released by the police with all charges dropped."

Jackson pushes his wheelchair to the front door grasping the handle.

"I don't know who you are, but it's a clear-cut case. There's no way they're gonna release her... I think you should leave."

Eli pulls the opening door closed.

"I sense your doubts in our abilities, but trust me, we will make this happen."

Jackson backs from the door.

"How much?"

"How much, what?"

"How much will this cost me?"

Eli releases a low laugh.

"Nothing. But, we will ask for you both to join our group."

Jackson gulps the last drops of beer crushing the can and throws it into the kitchen. The metal scrapes across the linoleum floor.

"Sure, we'll join," Jackson said in a sarcastic tone. "We'll join your cult and pass-out flowers at the airport."

Eli slides a wooden chair to Jackson from the kitchen table and sits facing him.

"*Here*, in this folder is the proof you'll need to make you join Eden."

Jackson holds the folder scanning through its pages.

"The pictures will prove our capabilities of what we can achieve based on who we've worked with."

Pages reveal pictures of Eli shaking hands with President John F. Kennedy. Another shows Eli at a table with five men dressed alike sitting beside President Lyndon B. Johnson. Behind them is a wall map of Vietnam.

"Those pictures are only samples of the influential people we have partnered with during the past twenty years."

One picture stops his movement through the folder. A black-and-white photo of Mission Control. Being a former astronomer, the location in the image is unmistakable to Jackson.

"What was your role, *here*?"

Eli smiles. "I guess you can say, that's where it all started." He points to a thin man wearing a white shirt in the corner of the room. "*That's me.* I was on the Mission Control Team in Houston during the Apollo 11 Moon Landing."

Jackson rubs the picture. A momentary flash of jealousy floods his memory.

The months leading up to the moon landing had frustrated Jackson. By 1969, he had been in his eighth year of teaching science at the Le Mars High School.

As a child, he had dreamt of space travel. These daydreams had led to his passion for astronomy. A passion he has hidden given his new life.

"You… you were there?"

"Sure was. And, it was through my work at NASA where we developed The Eden Foundation."

This revelation calms Jackson. Envy works in his manipulation.

"A small group of us realized that with our journey to the Moon complete, we could take advantage of the situation."

"Take advantage of— "

"No, I don't mean anything bad. I mean… well, you know… everyone remembers where they were that night watching Neil step-out on the Moon… "

"Uh, huh."

"A group of us wanted to form an organization that fed off this excitement developing projects in the best interest of humanity."

"The best interest of humanity?"

"Yes. See that picture *there*?"

Eli flips to the next page in the folder resting in Jackson's lifeless lap.

"Yeah. You're shaking Doctor King's hand."

"Remember the outrage of his assassination?"

"Sure. It was terrible. I hadn't felt that sick since Jack was killed. Shit, not to mention a few months after King when Bobby was shot."

"Well… we were responsible… for bringing people together afterward. Eden developed outreach programs in various communities."

"But, I've never heard of The Eden Foundation? Especially considering these pictures of the famous people you've met, I would think I'd know about you."

Eli lifts the folder from Jackson.

"That's just it… our intent from the beginning was to stay silent, behind the scenes. The focus is, and never has been about us, but rather humanity. You can kinda say, we work in the shadows."

Wrinkles form on Jackson's forehead.

"I don't follow."

"Look, we made serious connections with very impressive people. We could convince them to pass changes… like the Civil Rights Act in '69 for example."

The wrinkles disappear. Jackson's eyes widen. Many years had passed since he had felt important.

"Nothing we've ever done has been for personal gain. We did these things to better society." Jackson relaxes his posture. "That's why no one knows about us. We don't publicize our works. The people we work with appreciate how we operate. They take the credit, and we surely don't mind."

Silence.

"So, getting my daughter released from the police should be a walk in the park. But, I don't understand why you're here talking to me?"

"It will be easy to get Ruth released," Eli said standing from his chair, "but, the only thing is, you both have to join Eden."

Jackson backs his chair from Eli.

"What... what exactly would we be doing for you?"

"Let's just say you both have specific qualities we need in our organization."

The wrinkles return to Jackson.

"What qualities?"

"We've been looking for someone like you who understands science and can adapt and keep secrets."

"Adapt... keep secrets?"

Eli returns to his chair.

"As you can imagine, with the high-profile people we work with, we have to know about the people we recruit to join our Foundation."

"Have to know about... "

"Yes, Jackson. We know you are originally from California. You used to work at the Palomar Observatory before your accident."

The news pushes Jackson's head backward. Only his divorced wife knows of his past profession.

"Um... well, yeah... I... was... " Jackson stutters unsure how to respond.

"It's okay. I'm sure your accident was heartbreaking for you and your wife, especially once Ruth came along?"

Jackson sits silent.

"So, you obviously can move and fit in within a community. I mean, does anyone here in Le Mars even know about your past?"

"No," Jackson replied through phlegm building in his throat. "I decided when we moved here not to tell anyone. I didn't want to answer questions, which would make me second-guess our decision to move."

Eli grins.

"But, what about Ruth? I love that girl, but why do you want her to join?"

"Let's just say she has proven her ability to take care of herself. And, we need someone like her in our organization."

"Well, hell, standing up for herself against her boyfriend, that's one way of saying it."

"She's obviously not afraid of anything, and we need her to scout new opportunities for us."

"Yeah, one thing's for sure. Ruth was born angry and brave."

Eli stands and moves to the front door.

"And, that's another reason we need you, Jackson. You must control Ruth in those situations."

"Control?"

The door opens. Sunlight rushes into the dark, smelly house.

"It's a crazy world out there. Our projects on the horizon, well... they will be unique."

"Unique?"

"I'll give you more information later about those projects. I'll set up a meeting with you all soon."

Eli enters the doorway. The sunlight illuminates the outline of his body.

"But, there'll be time for that information later. I guess with that... Jackson, do we have a deal?"

Jackson spins his chair around the living room. Beer cans crush under the wheels. He stops facing Eli stretching out his hand.

"Sure. Look around. My Ruth is in trouble. I have no choice, I guess."

Eli and Jackson shake hands; a firm grip between them.

"Jackson, I'm happy to hear. We'll be in contact soon. And, I won't be surprised if Ruth isn't home to you by this evening."

Eli leaves the front porch of Jackson's home. His black Buick drives away disappearing through the neighborhood.

Jackson rolls his chair down the ramp to the front yard. The sun feels warm and comforting against his face.

Huh, Mission Control… he will help Ruth out… The Eden Foundation… this sounds too good to be true… I need a beer.

Jackson pushes his chair back-up the ramp. The screen door slams behind him. A beer can cracks open piercing through the darkness from inside the dark house.

"Save humanity," Jackson said laughing between beer chugs. "That'll be something."

JANUARY, 1979 (3 MONTHS EARLIER)
PASADENA, TEXAS

WITH THE NEWS FROM last August of Rachel's pregnancy, everyone's plans have changed.

A self-proclaimed feminist, independence is a quality Rachel does not lack. This belief in herself is a survival trait she has developed since being placed in foster-care in Houston.

Her father's sudden death in 1964, when she was three-years-old, had left her alone. Her mother died a month after Rachel's birth.

Jacob and Rachel, both growing up without a father, had been one of their common bonds when they first met. One which Jacob would never confess the real secret about his father, Eli, being alive.

With a new life growing inside her, Rachel needs someone. She needs Jacob. Finishing university would have to wait.

Another attraction between them is the realization they both are from Houston. This became their inside joke living outside New York City to find each other.

Home, in Texas, called to them. Or, at least, Eli would make sure they heard this calling.

The pregnancy was the perfect cover for Eli to push Jacob's return home to Pasadena, home to his mother, Liz. Rachel agreed to leave Stony Brook with him.

Shock overcame Liz when she opened the door in early January. Jacob and his six-month-pregnant girlfriend stood unannounced in her doorway. Her lost son was home.

No matter how happy Liz was with the return of her son, the news of the pregnancy shook her core, church-going beliefs. Her only condition of them living together in her home meant Jacob and Rachel must get married. A small wedding would occur in two weeks.

All seemed right, again… at least for now.

Eli returned to fulfilling the work of The Eden Foundation. He completed designs for return missions to the Moon.

This meant Eli had disappeared, again. He visited his teams in the remote islands of the southern Indian Ocean where construction of launch facilities occurred.

During the final months of Rachel's pregnancy, she had grown close to Liz. She felt like the mother Rachel had never known. Liz reciprocated her feelings to Rachel as her daughter.

A familiar instinct revisited Jacob. Memories of a dead father returned upon his coming home. Unfathomable secrets remained locked inside his mind. His childhood home had grown smaller, tighter around him. Bouts of insomnia kept Jacob awake during the night.

Weeks had passed. Jacob needed a break. His father's wild tales, his very pregnant wife, his return home—Jacob could not breathe.

With an excuse developed in early March, Jacob fabricated a letter from the University of Stony Brook about Rachel's scholarship. The letter stated a requirement for the school to offer her financial aid. The University mandated her attendance in a meeting to discuss her plans. If she was unable to attend, the school was planning to re-direct her scholarship to another student.

On the afternoon of March 12, Jacob had left for the grocery store. From a payphone, Jacob called Rachel disguising his voice. He pretended to be an administrator from Stony Brook refusing to accept her pregnancy as an excuse of absence.

An hour later, Jacob returned home. Rachel greeted him crying at the door. Moving to Texas was to be temporary. They planned to stay only a year after delivering their child. But, the University threatened their plans or at least this was what Jacob wanted Rachel to believe.

Jacob knew what his next step would be in his plan. He told Rachel he would drive to Stony Brook and meet with the administrator. He assured her he would not return until he had straightened out the situation with the school.

As Jacob drove out of his childhood driveway, this would be the last time Rachel would see him.

MARCH 21, 1979 (3 MONTHS LATER)
SIOUX CITY, IOWA

MILES HAD DRIVEN by Jacob. Thoughts rushed over him… his dad was alive… The Eden Foundation… Project Salvation… returning to the Moon… future missions to Mars… the end of the world… the secrets his dad had confessed… the complete truth he shared.

Jacob's thoughts pushed him forward along the highway. When he had left Pasadena, Jacob had no plan for where he was driving. He needed to run away.

Two days later, Jacob arrived at his unintended destination. His subconscious has taken him north away from home.

A few days had passed since Jacob left when his father arrived back in Pasadena. Each time Eli returned to the Houston area, he disguised his appearance. After all, he was dead.

Eli met the person who he had positioned to watch the Bishops. But, Jacob had slipped unnoticed by the monitor from Houston. This upset Eli, who had not foreseen Jacob's departure from Rachel and Liz.

After a few days, Jacob called Rachel. He reassured her the conversation went well. The university will continue with her scholarship.

The monitor alerted Eli after hearing the phone call and informed him of Jacob's location after tracing the call. Jacob did not stay on the line long enough to pinpoint the complete origin of the call. But, Eli knew where

Jacob had gone given the monitor's report. The call had originated from Iowa.

Within the hour, Eli is on a plane for Sioux City. After landing, he rents a car and drives to his next destination. Fifteen minutes later, he arrives a few blocks away from the Lynchfield Apartments, Jacob's old place where Ruth lives.

No sooner as Eli walks across the parking lot late in the evening, Jacob steps outside the apartment carrying a trash bag to the dumpster. In the same instant, as the metal trash lid slams closed, Eli pushes Jacob forward against the dumpster.

"What the hell are you doing here?" Eli said in a threatening tone.

Jacob's face presses against the cold metal wall. His lips purse together against a sticky residue on the lid.

"I… I had to get out of there for a little… "

"Had to get out of there," Eli whispered as he releases his grip.

Jacob turns to Eli. "Yeah, it was getting to be too much."

"Okay… but, back *here?*"

The front window of his old apartment illuminates catching Eli's attention.

"Is that… is Ruth in there?"

Jacob does not return an answer or make eye-contact with his father.

Eli presses Jacob's shoulders back against the dumpster. The cold shivers his body.

"I… uh… I… "

"You, what?"

"I've still been seeing Ruth, but she's not home from work, yet."

Eli presses Jacob harder against the metal wall.

"What? You've been seeing her?"

"Uh… um… okay, only one time. When Rachel told me she was pregnant, I freaked out. How the hell am I going to raise a baby? What about Salvation? Holy shit, what about… everything else?"

As Jacob speaks, distant odors of beer spew from his mouth.

"What do you mean, *one time?*"

"Uh... I called Ruth after I learned Rachel was pregnant... I... uh, asked her if she wanted to meet. So, we met in Fort Wayne."

"Indiana?"

"Yeah. It was half-way between us. I knew I couldn't tell her about us being in Stony Brook."

Eli releases his grip. Jacob straightens his stance.

"What did you explain to her?"

"Um... nothing. She was mad at me for just leaving her."

"Did you tell her why you left?"

"No... we just met, and— "

"And, what?"

Jacob turns his eyes away from Eli.

"I slept with her."

Eli steps back. Wrinkles etch across his forehead in the darkness hidden in the shadows the dumpster cast across the parking lot. Eli runs his hand through his hair turning to the apartment and back to Jacob.

Eli charges to Jacob, again pressing him into the cold steel. He lifts Jacob off the ground.

"This is it... you will never contact her ever, again."

Eli releases his grip. Jacob's feet return to the ground as Eli flattens Jacob's ruffled shirt with his hands.

"Sorry, Son... I think it is time for me to share with you the rest of my plan. This is the reason you can never contact Ruth."

Jacob's eyes widen.

"You mean, I can finally join Eden?"

Eli smiles. "Yes, with all that's happening, it's time for the next step we discussed. But, I need to trust you... You can't be running off meeting Ruth or going back to Rachel, now."

Silence falls between them. Eli had planned to bring Jacob into Eden after Rachel gives birth, but the new circumstances require expediting.

"Okay, here's what we need to do... "

Eli explains a new plan while walking his son to his rental car. A plan involving how to handle the situation Jacob finds himself with Ruth. With his years of manipulating people, Eli has developed a talent for coming up with ideas fast.

"*Here*, take *this*," Eli said closing the trunk of his car.

Jacob holds open his hand.

"What is it?"

"Listen carefully, Jacob. When Ruth comes home after work, slip *this* into her drink."

"I'm not doing it unless you tell me what it is. I don't want to kill her or anything."

Eli huffs loud through his nose.

"It's LSD. Within an hour, she'll have a wild trip, and I'll handle it from there."

"Do I put all of it in her drink?"

"Yeah, it's just one hit, but it will do the trick."

"Then, what? What are you going to do to her?"

Agitation forces Eli's hands against Jacob's chest.

"Dammit, just take it inside. Do what I tell you. When she starts trippin' flash the living room lights to let me know."

Eli releases Jacob from his grip handing him the small plastic sleeve with a small pinch of white powder. He remains behind the dumpster watching Jacob return inside the apartment as the sky turns dark.

Ten minutes later, headlights brighten Eli's face. He ducks hiding into the shadows.

Ruth exits her car and enters the apartment. Eli waits. An hour later, the living room lights flicker.

Eli runs to the front door looking behind him. No one is around. Eli enters.

"Where is she?" Eli said whispering his question to Jacob.

"I… uh… did what you said. She came home. I brought her a beer after I placed the LSD in the bottle. Then, we started makin' out."

"Fine, but, where is she?"

"She pulled off me saying she felt dizzy. I helped her when she fell on the sofa. She laughed and asked me to help her get to the bathroom."

"So, that's where she is?"

"Yeah."

"Okay, good. *Here*," Eli said taking off his shirt, "give me your shirt and go into the closet. Don't come out… do you understand?"

"Yes."

Jacob removes his shirt handing it to Eli who places it on himself. Eli pushes Jacob into the small closet near the kitchen and turns out the living room lights. The only light comes from the kitchen.

Jacob peeks through the slats of the closet door. In the dim light, Eli appears like a taller version of Jacob, wearing his shirt.

Eli bangs against the bathroom door.

"Ruth, you okay in there. Come out," Eli said, his voice in a higher pitch to match Jacob's.

The light under the bathroom door disappears as the door creaks open. Ruth falls into Eli's arms laughing. She reaches behind Eli's head kissing him. Eli returns his kisses to her.

Jacob places his hand on the closet doorknob. He opens the door an inch and then pulls it closed.

Eli guides Ruth into the living room, her back facing the sofa. With a sudden push, Ruth falls backward buried into the cushions.

"Ruth, I wanted to come back here to tell you it's over between us," Eli said.

Ruth reaches her arms to the sides of Eli's waist pulling him closer. She moves her hand to his crotch unzipping his pants.

Eli steps back and zips up his pants.

"Oh, Baby, I don't know what it is, but I want you."

"Stop it! Ruth, it's over! We're through!"

Eli stalks the living room in front of her. Each time she tries to stand, he pushes her to the sofa.

Ruth's eyes sway back-and-forth.

"Eric, why are you upset with me. Come on, Baby, I want it," Ruth said as she unbuttons the top of her shirt.

Eli hearing Ruth call him Eric reassures him that Jacob has never shared his actual name with her.

"No, Ruth, we are through. I'm leaving!"

"Huh?"

Ruth sits quietly. Her eyes squint together. The smile she had worn vanishes.

"Are you leaving me?"

"Yes, I'm leaving, and I'm never coming back."

"But… why?" Ruth sits, her naked shoulders slump.

Eli marches around the room in front of her.

"I've been seeing someone else."

Ruth's head drifts side-to-side.

"Is that why you left me before?"

"Yes, and, we're getting married… she's pregnant, and that's why I'm leaving you."

Ruth's body stops moving. Her head lifts to Eli. In a fast motion, Ruth jumps from the sofa, her fists ball slapping against Eli's chest.

"Pregnant? Pregnant! You, motherfucker!"

Eli tries to catch Ruth's fists, but they fly fast against him.

Ruth stops her assault and turns away from Eli. Jacob continues watching from the closet.

She turns around facing the bar counter of the kitchen. Tears fall from her face.

"You can't leave me."

"Did you not hear me, I'm leaving. We're done."

"You can't leave me, you son-of-a-bitch… you got me pregnant, too."

Jacob stumbles against the back wall of the closet. The noise is audible to Eli but unnoticed to Ruth.

"What?" Eli said.

Ruth places her left hand on her stomach. Behind her back, in her right hand, she holds a butcher knife she has removed from the countertop.

"Yeah, I'm pregnant… " Ruth rubs her stomach, "we're gonna have a baby."

Eli stops moving in the center of the living room. Ruth approaches smiling. Her hand clenches tighter on the knife.

"So, see, you can't leave me."

"I'm sorry, Ruth, but I'm leaving. I'm in love with someone else."

Her knuckles turn white with the knife in her hand behind her back.

"Where does this bitch live?"

"Texas and I'm gonna be too far away to be with you. I don't want anything else to do with you."

Jacob watches as Ruth's shoulders heave up-and-down. As her back comes within his vantage point, Jacob sees the knife.

"Eric, don't leave me."

The arm holding the knife moves to her side, the knife is still hidden from Eli.

With one sudden motion, Ruth brings her right arm from her side lifting the knife above her shoulder.

"Motherfucker, I'll cut your dick off, Eric D'Angelo, if you leave—"

Ruth does not complete her words. Jacob rushes from the closet grabbing the knife and pushes her forward to the sofa at the same time. A dull thud bounces from the wall as Ruth hits her head.

Eli checks her pulse. She is breathing but unconscious.

Jacob presses his hand against the side of her face.

"Don't worry; she'll be okay. She'll have one hell of a headache when she wakes up. It's not like I've not done this before."

Jacob's eyes dart around the room.

"What the hell do we do, now?"

"*Here*, take *this*." Eli hands a black, fabric bag to Jacob.

"What the hell am I going to do with this shit?"

Eli retrieves the butcher knife from Ruth's frail grip holding it in his gloved hands.

"Just go out to your car. I'll take care of it."

"You're not going to hurt her, are you?"

"No! Leave, I'll be out in a few minutes."

Jacob rubs Ruth's stomach.

"Is she really pregnant?"

"I don't know if she was lying or not, but it doesn't matter. You're never seeing her, again."

Eli grabs Jacob and shoves him out the door.

Jacob stands frightened leaning against his car. Minutes had passed.

The scene in the apartment is complete. Jacob has placed Ruth, who remains passed-out, on the sofa lying on her side. A blood-soaked knife holds in her loose grip.

Eli has splattered blood across the floor to the front door. And, the last touch he provides is a faint trail of blood drops leading from the apartment to the adjacent wooded lot.

"Get your shit, and get in the damn car," Eli said pushing Jacob out of his horrific trance.

Eli throws the fabric bag into the dumpster. Small road kill had provided the blood source for Eli.

The car starts.

"What happens, next?"

"In a few hours, she'll wake up and think she most likely hurt you with all that blood."

"But, why do all that?"

Eli slams the brakes as the car had started to roll.

"Why the… " Eli laughed. "You don't get it, do you? She has to think you're gone. If she thinks she hurt you, then she will not be surprised that you never return."

The car starts to roll.

"You are never to see her, again. And, if she thinks she assaulted you, she won't come looking for you."

The car exits the parking lot.

"This is just how it has to be. When we recruit people to join us, there can be no suspicion about anyone. The best way to do this is… " Eli stops. Quick memories of him faking his death flood to him driving his son away from the scene.

"Let's just put it this way… no one will ever ask questions or suspect a dead person. And, that's how people join us."

Silence comes between them. The rushing roadside hums outside the windows.

"Shit, now, I get it. Like, when you— "

"Exactly," Eli said interrupting Jacob. "And, now the tough part. We need to execute our plans to kill you so you can join us at Eden."

Jacob smiles. Since Eli had shared the information during their drive to Stony Brook, Jacob had waited for the opportunity to join his father.

Eli stops Jacob's car in the parking lot of the nearby gas station.

"*Here*, follow me. My car is *right there*. I need to make a couple of calls," Eli said.

"To who?"

"The first is to the police... you know... I live nearby and heard a fight at the apartment, blah blah. That will take care of Ruth. The next is to execute our plan about you."

Eli steps toward a payphone.

"Wait, and I'll be right back."

Jacob obeys his father as Eli makes his calls. A few moments later, Eli re-joins Jacob who sits in the driver's seat of his car.

"Okay, it's all set," Eli said.

Eli recognizes something different about Jacob in the few minutes he had left.

"I know. It's Rachel and your baby," Eli said placing his right hand on Jacob's left knee. A tear formed across the top of Jacob's cheeks.

"But, what about Ruth's baby, too?"

"You can't believe what she was saying. She was so messed up from the drugs."

Jacob turns and looks through the window away from Eli.

"Listen, I know this is the hard part. Trust me, I know," Eli said between sniffles from Jacob.

"But, I promise you this. I will see to it that nothing bad happens to them. You've got an important mission. I need you to oversee the launch operations... this has to happen."

Jacob inhales a deep breath.

"Awe, screw it," Jacob said wiping his face with the back of his arm. "What's the plan? How do I fake my death?"

Eli smiles. "Son, it's perfect. You drove here, so what a better way than to have a car accident."

"But... how do I fake my— "

"Take *this*. It's an address just outside Shreveport. My associate will meet you there. I've got some things to take care of here with Mr. Wheeler."

"Ruth's father?"

"Yes, I need to tie up some loose ends with him. The next time you will see me will be in a few weeks on the island."

Eli presses his hand harder on Jacob's knee. A small sign, but an indication it is time to go.

The car door opens as Eli leaves Jacob returning to his car. Faint sirens grow louder approaching the apartment complex.

Jacob follows Eli from the parking lot. Eli turns left headed to Le Mars. Jacob turns right headed south… headed home to Texas… with a stop-over in Louisiana… headed to his fate.

10-A Monster Created

"GOOD MORNING, SIR," the hotel desk clerk said, "welcome to the Washington Hilton."

Eli reaches inside his front, coat pocket. He flashes a quick smile as he gives the clerk a forged driver's license.

The clerk scans the identification and flips through a stack of papers. Eli holds his head down avoiding eye-contact as people pass behind him in the expansive lobby. Several men in black suits stand at various locations throughout the entryway.

"Okay, Mr. Abagnale, here's your key. Your room number is 1204."

Eli takes the key.

"Your associate, Mr. Sawyer, checked in earlier."

"Oh, okay. Thanks." Eli slides the key into his jacket pocket with his wallet. He leans to the clerk. "What's with all the security, here?"

The clerk smiles and lowers her head. "I'm sorry, Mr. Abagnale. I can't say."

Eli peeks over his shoulder. "So, the elevator— "

"Yep, it's down the hallway and on the left. Please enjoy your stay at the Washington Hilton, Mr. Abagnale."

The elevator doors open on the twelfth floor. A red, velvet carpet leads through the straight hall. White doors line either side. Eli stops at Room 1204 and knocks.

A metal, door chain rattles coming unlatched from the other side, then opens.

"Dad, you're late."

Eli enters the room placing his black briefcase on the double-bed closest to the bathroom.

"How was traffic?"

"Okay, I guess. But, it got heavier the closer I got to the hotel," Eli said as he rests on the blue, floral-print bedspread.

The black leather of the briefcase is well-worn in his hands as the golden clasps pop-open.

"Good. Then, everything is normal."

"Jacob, I don't understand why you wanted to meet in Washington," Eli said as he rifles through several red folders.

"I know how much you like this city, and I thought it is the best place for us to meet," Jacob said as he opens the window curtains. Dim light enters the room from the gray, overcast D.C. sky.

"We need to catch up on our plans. We're two years away from our first landing on Mars, and we have so much to discuss," Eli said closing his briefcase. A stack of red folders falls across the bed.

"Yes, we're moving to the next phase for Salvation. My crews have been working the past year with lunar construction," Jacob said.

"Any problems with the workers?"

"None."

"If I've not told you, that was a brilliant idea recruiting construction workers from different prisons across the country."

"Dad, I learned from the master. Plus, who will miss those guys, anyway?"

Moon missions have pressed forward the last six years. The launch location has moved to a small string of islands in the southern Indian

Ocean. This remote setting is perfect; thousands of miles from the nearest population and shipping lanes.

Eli joins Jacob staring out the hotel window. "And, using those prisoners sentenced to death… I mean, they have nothing to lose."

Jacob's posture straightens, and his shoulders rise under Eli's firm hand.

"Not to mention it takes a special person willing to travel to the Moon to work there," Eli said.

A small, round table separates both men by the window as they sit reviewing their notes. One year had passed since each has seen the other.

After the Foundation had faked Jacob's death, Eli divulged every secret since the 1957 discovery of the planetoid. He shared how he has protected Salvation through cultivating his relationships within NASA, establishing false companies, lobbying political groups, and monitoring communication systems.

For Jacob, an eager understudy, time marches fast the first year under Eli's tutelage as CIE.57.20 draws closer to Earth. Only a few are aware of the planet's fate in 2020.

The majority who join Eden only receive bits of information, never the full story. Ignorance is Eli's best tool for manipulation.

When Eli started his recruitment activities, he realized the best motivator was a pride of Country. He became masterful in his ability to plant false information within the United States Central Intelligence Agency concerning the Soviets, and vice versa with the KGB about the Americans.

After all, everyone needs an enemy whether perceived or not. With enemies, countries will fund outrageous sums of money for programs to fight them. And, it is these funds The Eden Foundation siphons from unnoticed from the governmental agencies.

Hours had passed. Eli shares his designs for transporting the Salvation modules to Mars after the first Martian mission set for 1983. Given the lower lunar gravity, smaller Delta rockets will lift-off with their payloads piloted by two astronauts for their seven-month sojourn through Space.

Jacob studies Eli's notes.

"What's *this*?" Jacob asked pointing to schematic drawings of a satellite.

Eli smiles. "During the Apollo years, we discussed the possibility of launching rockets from a satellite."

Jacob pulls the schematics closer.

"Early on, when we learned about the discovery, I thought maybe we could send the satellite to the planetoid and launch nuclear missiles from it."

"Make any progress in researching that?" Jacob asked.

Eli slides the schematics from Jacob.

"Only in theory. But, what we are working on now is instead of missiles, maybe we can create a system of lasers to blow that son-of-a-bitch up."

"But, how do you plan to test this? I mean, it's one thing to block a tiny section of the sky so no one can see that bastard coming to Earth, but testing a satellite in Space is different."

Eli laughs. "Exactly, we have the perfect cover, don't we?"

"Huh, I'm not sure I follow?"

"All we need to do is convince the government to develop these tests to save America from a Soviet nuclear missile. I've even joked about having the government call this program *Star Wars*."

Jacob turns to Eli. "You already have this plan set up, don't you?"

Before Eli can respond, six rapid popping sounds pierce through the window glass from the street twelve floors below. Within moments, sirens wail. Both stand pressing their faces against the glass.

"What was that?" Eli asked.

They watch the myriad of ambulances and police vehicles rush around the hotel streets. People appear like ants scurrying through the intersection. Minutes pass.

Jacob releases a grunt passing Eli and turning on the television.

"Since when did you get hooked on soap operas? I'd recognize *One Life to Live* anywhere. It's Liz's favorite."

"Just wait a few minutes," Jacob said.

On cue, a black screen and the ABC logo in gold lettering replaces the sharp dialogue between Bo Buchanan and his father, Asa. A news anchor appears through the fading, black screen.

"Videotape of an incident that took place less than fifteen minutes ago at the Washington Hilton Hotel when shots were fired at President Reagan. Here, you see the President coming out, now. You just have to watch... I don't know if we can hear this or not?"

The same six popping sounds Eli and Jacob had heard earlier outside their hotel window repeat through the television screen.

"There it is... shots fired... we understand that one secret service agent, and maybe another Washington policeman was injured... the President had just come out of the entrance of the hotel... the President was immediately pushed into his car as the agents are trained to do in situations of this kind, and the car sped off..." the announcer said.

Jacob returns to the window. Eli turns to his son.

"Is this why you were insistent we meet here, today?" Eli said.

Jacob releases a short laugh. "You challenged me to prove my ability to develop a public diversion."

Eli charges Jacob. "What in the hell did you do?"

"Like I said, I've learned from the master."

Eli releases Jacob and leans on the edge of the bed.

"What I coordinated twenty years ago was necessary. Jack was going to go public about 2020," Eli said.

"Well, unlike Dallas, this President will live. We told John not to kill him," Jacob said.

"Not to kill him? Why shoot him in the first place?"

"C'mon, Dad, you know what will happen, now. This is the only thing that'll be in the news for weeks. We need the diversion. Just like you said earlier, we're moving to our next stage with Salvation, and we can use what happened here to our advantage."

Eli places his head in his hands. "I know we have to do this, but it is never an easy thing to do."

"Easy, hell, Dad, you've made it all look so easy. The President in Dallas, his brother, heck even King in Memphis."

"Yes, but— "

"No, buts. As you said, it's all necessary. You protected the secret. You put into motion so many things to fund Eden and now Project Salvation.

Hell, if it wasn't for your work, we wouldn't have continued to go to the Moon and now Mars."

Eli lifts his head from his hands.

"The only real travesty is no one's aware of the sacrifices you've made to save humanity after 2020," Jacob said.

"Of course, I know. But, it just never gets any easier."

"Sure, it does, wait to you see what's coming in a couple of months at the Vatican."

"The Vatican… uh, never mind… I agreed to turn these activities over to you while I focus on the Mars missions."

"Don't worry. I've got this covered."

Eli smiles at his protégé. "I must admit, I'm impressed with this. We're obviously not going anywhere for a while, so tell me the details about how you pulled this off."

Jacob spent the next few minutes explaining the coercion required and the chain of activities necessary for what had happened earlier.

"Foster… the actress? You mean to tell me he did this thinking it would impress her?" Eli said.

"Like you told me many times, make people believe what they want to believe, and that's when you can easily control them."

DECEMBER 11, 1993 (12 YEARS LATER)
GODDARD SPACE FLIGHT CENTER,
GREENBELT, MARYLAND

"SHUTTLE ENDEAVOUR. You are *Go* for redeployment of the Hubble Telescope."

"Roger, Flight Command. Go for redeployment," the Endeavour Commander said.

The fifty personnel inside the Flight Center collectively hold their breaths. Three years had passed since NASA launched the Hubble Telescope in 1990. Scientists soon realized the telescope's primary mirror contained a spherical aberration resulting in fuzzy images.

For thirty years, The Eden Foundation had controlled the global telescopes with the capability of identifying CIE.57.20. The Hubble Telescope presented a new challenge; it was the first placed into orbit above Earth.

In the late 1980s, Eli had used his influence with NASA to place an asset in the telescope's manufacturing facility. As production of the reflective mirror occurred, the asset had ground the outer edge of the mirror flat by a depth of 2.2 microns, one-fiftieth the thickness of a strand of human hair. A simple, but effective, flaw unnoticed during the final quality inspections.

Shuttle Endeavour Mission STS-61 carries the solution to the Hubble Telescope. The Corrective Optics Space Telescope Axial Replacement, or COSTAR, will counter the effects of the flawed mirror. COSTAR serves as a pair of eyeglasses correcting its vision of Space.

Flight Center engineers check readings from the Hubble Telescope as Endeavour places the telescope back into service. Video from inside the shuttle bay airs on television monitors in the room.

Each astronaut wears their royal-blue flight uniforms. Mission Specialist Granger stands out on the screen. A bright-red lapel pin affixed beside the flight insignia patch on her uniform shines like a beacon.

One person inside the Flight Center wears the same pin: Eli Bishop. Her pin catches Eli's attention, as he was not aware an Eden asset being onboard Endeavour.

Eli smiles as the readings from Hubble arrive showing normal operation. COSTAR appears to have solved the myopic telescope.

Images from the deepest reaches of Space will return to Earth with absolute clarity. Soon, NASA will discover the planetoid, CIE.57.20, and Eli's long-held secret finally can be revealed to the Public. This is Eli's intent.

Thirty-six years of operating The Eden Foundation and planning Project Salvation.

Thirty-six years of secrets kept and conspiracies executed.

Thirty-six years of planning successful missions to the Moon and Mars.

Eli has realized his overarching plan keeping the events of 2020 a secret has been fundamentally flawed.

Thirty-six years have made Eli exhausted. He believes it is time for the world to unite as he plans to confess his sins praying for absolution from the global public.

A significant anniversary has passed for Eli. The one, dark secret from his past which disturbs him the most. Still images of the president's brain exploding across the back of the open-air limousine constantly have replayed in Eli's dreams each night for thirty years.

"Sir, we have a problem," a Hubble engineer said seated at his computer monitor.

Eli and the Flight Center Commander peer over the engineer's shoulder.

"There is erratic data telemetry coming from Hubble," the engineer said.

Eli peers over the engineer scanning the screen.

"What does this mean?" the commander said.

"We'll troubleshoot this from here, but it looks like a new issue from the telescope. It may keep us from fully controlling what we can scan."

The engineer's words push Eli away from the monitor. Eli glances again to the television screens displaying videos of the astronauts. The red, Eden pin screams to Eli. Paranoia creeps to him as he looks around the room.

Eli slips out the back door of the Flight Center and walks downstairs at the end of the hall. The crisp, night air smacks Eli as he walks fast across the parking lot to his vehicle.

Headlights illuminate blinding Eli. The lights grow brighter as a car screeches to a stop blocking his advance to his vehicle.

"Get in," a familiar voice said through the blinding light.

Two sets of firm hands grab Eli's shoulders shoving him to the backseat. Once inside, the car speeds through the exit to a side street in the outskirts of Washington.

"What the hell, Eli? Didn't you think we wouldn't have a backup plan in place?" the driver said.

City lights dim. The car travels toward the hillsides of western Maryland.

"Our assets notified us that COSTAR was operational without any defects before launch, so we took countermeasures."

Eli sits pressed against the driver's side, backseat door. The windshield sends a shiver against his face as two large men take the remaining room.

"It's time we change plans for Salvation," Eli said mumbling against the glass. "I've had enough."

The car brakes stopping outside Gaithersburg.

"We've long suspected your thoughts were changing. We've been monitoring your activities," the driver said as he resumes moving forward.

"Where are we going?"

Eli's question goes unanswered.

"More than ten years... goddammit, over ten years... I've started a lot of shit in this world. We have the U.S. involved in Iraq, we're getting so much funding, and Salvation is almost fully operational... and you want to ruin everything we've worked for?"

"I... I... "

Eli was lost in his thoughts. Thirty-six years of guilt has created a burden too hard for him to no longer bare.

"There's absolutely no way we can share what we have done. You know this!" the driver screams slamming the steering wheel. "Don't be fucking crazy."

Eli stares at the driver's eyes through the rearview mirror.

"What? You want to tell everyone you're responsible for hundreds of thousands of deaths just to save ten-thousand even after billions of others will die?"

Eli looks away.

"It's too late; there's no way to expand Salvation beyond our capacity. And, you know there's no way to stop what's coming in 2020," the driver said.

Streetlights flicker across the driver's face... a familiar face.

"Jacob, what are you going to do to me?" Eli asked.

His son, Jacob, steals his attention from the road staring at his father through the mirror.

"You told me a long time ago that there is only one objective... to protect Salvation at all costs. I am not about to let you ruin everything I have worked for since you brought me into Eden."

Jacob drives into an abandoned warehouse area in Clarksburg. A building stands absent any lights next to a set of railroad tracks and a small parking lot. The car stops hidden in the darkness.

The firm sets of hands return on Eli's shoulders pulling him from the backseat. Jacob exits the car.

"Take him inside," Jacob said.

Large doors moan as the men push-open the rusted metal. Shards of dust float from the doorway with its years of closure. Ropes tighten across Eli's chest as the men strap him into a metal chair on the barren, concrete loading dock.

"Okay, leave us," Jacob said commanding the men.

Creaking metal reverberates through the empty warehouse as the men leave. Light from a battery-operated lantern dances across the roll-up, dock doors. Jacob paces the area.

"Just kill me. I've had enough. I can't take the secrets anymore," Eli said.

The dock door slams as Jacob punches his fist against the rusted metal.

"You know what has to be done," Jacob said. "Fuck!"

"It's okay." Eli's voice is low and soft.

"What the fuck, Eli? What happened? The things you've told me you've done to create all of this. If it weren't for you, Salvation would not exist... we would not have a plan to save humanity."

A slow, eerie laugh fills the empty, dark warehouse.

"What's so funny?" Jacob asked.

"Look at you," Eli stops laughing. "You used to be so lost and weak, and now... you're in full command of Eden."

Jacob charges Eli grabbing Eli's hands strapped to the chair arms.

"And, now, look at you." Jacob pierces Eli's gaze with his cold stare and bulging eyes. "You came back into my life, and you were the strongest man I've ever known."

Jacob pushes away from Eli and punches the door. His back remains facing Eli.

"Godammit, and now, you're fuckin' quittin'... you're wastin' everything you've worked for. I thought I had lost you once when I was a kid... "

Jacob bends to his feet. He stands holding a heavy, two-foot-long, steel pipe.

"I can't let you go through with this... "

Eli watches Jacob's shoulders tense as his fingers wrap tight around the pipe-end.

"Now, I really have lost you!"

As Jacob yells, he swings the pipe in a swift, violent motion to Eli's head. Wind echoes across the pipe-opening like a child blowing the top of an empty glass bottle. A sickening thud silences the whistling pipe.

The bloodied metal bounces on the dirty concrete floor. Clanging resonates in the empty building.

Darkness fills Eli's vision. Blood gushes across the side of his face from his temple down his left cheek. Sensation leaves Eli's body.

Jacob erupts with a primal scream. The groaning of the metal doors opening returns.

"Boss, you okay?" one man asked.

Jacob wipes his face. Blood splatter from Eli's head remains on the back of Jacob's hands.

"Take care of this," Jacob said pointing to his father's lifeless body. "You know what to do."

The sound of metal scraping across the concrete floor pierces the darkness as Jacob picks-up the bloodied pipe. He steps down from the dock to the front of the building.

"Call me when it's done," Jacob said before leaving.

Jacob enters the car. Glimpses of his face in the mirror show dots of his father's blood on his forehead. He balls both fists and slams them repeatedly against the steering wheel.

"Shit! Shit! Shit! Shit!"

Red lights emanate from the back of the car. Years of dirt spin-up behind the vehicle glowing in the red lights. Jacob leaves, now entirely in control of Eden… in control of Salvation.

11-Cry for Help

November 24, 1996 (3 years later)
Greystone Psychiatric Hospital, New Jersey

"COME, THIS WAY," the Admissions attendant said.

Two officers push a lifeless body in a wheelchair into the front lobby of the Greystone Psychiatric Hospital of New Jersey.

"So, what happened?" the attendant asked.

"We received a call of a possible homicide at the Newark Airport Hotel. When we arrived, we found a suicide note beside the body. Her vitals were weak, but paramedics were able to revive her," one officer said.

"We ran her information and cannot identify any next of kin. So, our policy is to admit her here until she recovers," the other officer said pushing the wheelchair.

The attendant leads the officers to a room at the end of a ground-floor hallway. Gray strips peel from the walls as if even the paint wants to escape the hospital.

"Place her in the bed and we'll take it from here."

The wheelchair stops as the officers lift the woman onto the bed.

"What about her clothes?"

"An orderly will be here in a moment. Follow me. I need to get some information."

The attendant takes the officers back to Reception. One officer pushes the empty wheelchair.

"Okay, what's her name?" the attendant asked.

An officer retrieves his small notepad from his back pocket, flipping it open.

"We got the information from the front desk of the hotel. Her name is Ruth D'Angelo. She didn't have any identification on her when we found her. The hotel said she paid in cash. We ran the name in our database, but nothing came back."

The attendant enters the patient's information in her computer. Long, red-painted fingernails click the keyboard. An annoying, rhythmic melody comes from behind the counter.

"And, you said there was a note?"

The other officer lifts a small, plastic bag with a piece of paper inside as if he holds a prized-catch.

"Yeah, here it is."

He opens the bag and places the note on the linoleum counter between them and the attendant. The attendant's eyebrows raise as she reads.

"Hmm, there's not much here. It says she has had enough and couldn't go on… so, sad." Clicking resumes from behind the counter. "And, the call came from the hotel?"

"Yes, but, the hotel couldn't identify who called. I'm sure the manager there doesn't want any bad publicity."

"And, what time?"

The officer reads from his notes. "We got the dispatch call at 14:00 and arrived at 14:14. Once we determined she was still alive, we called for an ambulance which arrived at 14:42."

"Okay, so now it's… " the attendant stops and checks the round, white wall-clock, "16:10. Did she ever regain consciousness?"

"No," both officers said in unison.

"Charlie 31, come in," a woman's voice said over the officers' radio attached to their right shoulders.

"Go for Charlie 31," an officer said into the black microphone.

"We have a… " the voice trails as the officer approaches the sliding glass door of the lobby and leaves.

"Ma'am, we have to go. Here's my card if you need more information," the other officer said.

"Thank you. We've got what we need for now."

The clicking continues behind the counter as the officer leaves pushing the empty wheelchair to the police cruiser.

After returning the chair inside the trunk, the officer joins his partner in the front seat. The driver lowers his rearview mirror. A man sits in the back seat; his head remains turned to the sliding doors of the psychiatric hospital.

"Sir, she's okay. They'll take great care of her, now."

The man returns his gaze catching the officer's eyes in the mirror.

"Thank you, let's go."

Raindrops pelt the top of the car as it moves forward through the parking lot. The man turns one last time viewing the front of the hospital. A tear falls from the tip of his nose.

The man rubs a small photo. A much younger version of himself stares back under his thumb. He forms a smile as he caresses the image of an infant girl in his lap as he sat in a wheelchair.

"Baby Girl, they'll take care of you," Jackson Wheeler said in a whisper.

NOVEMBER 27, 1996 (3 DAYS LATER)
GREYSTONE PSYCHIATRIC HOSPITAL, NEW JERSEY

"AND, *THIS* IS THE TELEVISION AREA," the nurse said.

Ruth shuffles her feet behind the nurse; her hair disheveled. The thin, white robe pulls up tight around her neck providing comfort.

"This is the common area. I will leave you in here. If you need anything, just ask anyone you see wearing pink scrubs."

The nurse left Ruth alone. Her hands shake inside her robe's pockets.

Half the room is empty. Several plastic chairs in various hues of blue sit alone. Others hold patients. A few talk to themselves while some rock violently. The stench of body odor and soiled clothes wafts through the room.

Ruth slides a chair across the floor to the window. A light snowfall mesmerizes her heavily medicated mind as she stares.

A slow, rocking motion comforts Ruth. Sixteen years of drug abuse masked the longing for the father of her baby. Jacob, or Eric D'Angelo as Ruth had known him to be, had left before her son's birth. A son, Gabriel, who she had never known leaving him at a church near Des Moines, Iowa.

Her father, Jackson Wheeler, had arranged for someone to take her baby. He knew she was unable to raise a child. The help came from The Eden Foundation as they had plans for Ruth and Jackson.

Jackson's primary responsibility with Eden was monitoring the Bishop household in Texas. He often required Ruth's help with tasks Eden assigned. She never knew of Eli Bishop or the Foundation, as her direction came from her father.

Ruth obeyed without question. She developed loyalty to him given his ability to free her from prison. The tasks from Jackson preoccupied her mind from her absent boyfriend and abandoned son.

She stares at the falling snow. Memories over the years come hazy through her drugged mind. Tears stream across her face; tears of sadness and frustration.

A gentle hand falls across her left shoulder. This sensation snaps Ruth from her trance. She turns looking into the eyes of an elderly man. His eyes seem familiar, but only in passing as the man staggers by her leaving the room.

Hours had passed. Ruth sits motionless. The ground covers in a fresh blanket of white.

A plastic chair shuffles across the floor shaking her attention. The sound stops beside her as the elderly man returns. He joins her staring. Silence is their companion.

Ruth twists her head to the man. Her eyes shift as far right as possible.

The man fidgets his fingers together rocking side-to-side in slow motion. A jagged scar runs the length of his left cheek to the top of his head and across to his right eye. Unlike the other patients, over his white gown, the man wears a gray jacket. A frayed, black Yankees cap covers his head. Ruth scans his arm; on his wrist is a name-tag: *Robert*.

A scream comes from the left side of the room stealing her attention. Ruth turns back, but Robert is no longer there.

They never spoke, but his gentle touch on her shoulder and their fondness of scenic beauty comforted Ruth. She twists her torso around scanning the room. She is alone.

As she returns her stare to the window, Ruth spots a small slip of paper remaining in the chair where Robert had sat. She reaches across to the seat and pulls the paper to her lap.

Wrinkles emerge across her forehead as her eyes scrunch together. Scribbled numbers and letters arranged five columns across, and five rows down, stare back to her .

THANKSGIVING, 1996 (THE NEXT DAY) GREYSTONE PSYCHIATRIC HOSPITAL, NEW JERSEY

TWO DAYS OF THE YEAR, the hospital provides its patients and staff with hot-cooked, savory food: Thanksgiving and Christmas Day. Scents of turkey and fresh-baked bread fill the five-story building. Most patients stay impaired from their drug therapies, but the familiar smells awaken most from their stupor.

Ruth finds her way to the cafeteria. In the back corner, she sees Robert sitting alone staring at his uneaten food. The nurse who had provided her with a tour of the hospital stands next to the buffet table.

"Ex... excuse me," Ruth said.

"Um, yes... Ruth, isn't it?"

"Yeah." Ruth turns and points to Robert. "What's the deal with *that* man?"

The nurse straightens her posture and leans to her right. "Oh, Robert, he's a sweet man."

"Is he okay?"

"Oh, he's harmless. He's normally catatonic."

"How long has he been here?"

The nurse pulls Ruth closer. "It's so sad. A few years ago, before Christmas, we found him outside. He was face-down in the snow. Thankfully, that jacket and cap kept him warm."

Ruth turns to Robert and then back to the nurse.

"His head was wrapped in so many bloodied bandages. Poor thing was unresponsive for months."

"What's wrong with him?"

"The doctors say it's brain damage from a blow to his head— "

An argument at the buffet table interrupts the nurse.

Ruth fills her plate with turkey and mashed potatoes. She approaches Robert.

"Mind, if I sit?"

Robert does not respond. She sits enjoying her meal unable to remember the last warm food she had eaten.

"I figured out your little puzzle."

Ruth slides the paper with its numbers and letters across the table.

Robert's eyes widen; his head remains lowered.

"It was simple."

Ruth explains how she deciphered his encoded matrix. She had many faults, but one talent she inherited from her father, Jackson, is her ability with numbers. Ruth easily sees patterns in the figures, which also had aided Jackson with his astronomy.

"But, I don't understand how to use it once it's solved?"

Robert lifts his head. A full smile emerges. His white teeth shine through his unshaven face.

"E... E... "

Ruth leans her head to Robert as he tries to speak.

"E... Elizabeth... it... it's you."

"Oh, I'm sorry, but my name is… " Ruth observes how Robert's demeanor has changed. His eyes have brightened, and his shoulders have straightened. She takes his hand. "Yes, I'm Elizabeth."

Robert lowers his head and slips a pencil from his jacket pocket. He scribbles a set of numbers under the puzzle Ruth had solved.

"Here."

Robert stands and leaves Ruth with the note.

She pulls the paper to her. Without instruction, Ruth knows the numbers correspond to the new matrix she had created. The first number provides the column and the second the row to obtain the corresponding letter.

A few minutes had passed as she matches the numbers to the letters.

"I miss you," Ruth said whispering her result.

Weeks had passed.

The only words Robert would say to Ruth were *my Elizabeth*. He passes her written strings of numbers; which Ruth deciphers against the matrix. Most of the short sentences make little sense to her.

Jacob loves Evel.

Miss home.

John I sorry Dallas.

Salvation Eden real.

We all die.

Liz so pretty.

On Christmas morning, Robert gives Ruth a ball of paper as he leaves their usual meeting place by the window returning to his room. She feels something hard inside and unwraps the gift.

Her face radiates as she lifts a stainless steel watch from the paper. Her fingers massage the timepiece not believing it is real. Ruth flips it over and sees the words inscribed: *Eli + Liz = Forever*

"Who's Eli?" Ruth said returning her stare out the window.

The next day, Ruth sits by the window in the television room. She waits for Robert. Her time with him takes her mind away from her past troubles. But, today, she has questions about Robert's gift.

Ruth feels a light grip on her shoulders. She turns around. Her smile disappears.

"Honey, how are you doing?" her father, Jackson, asked.

She does not respond and returns her attention to the window.

Jackson wheels his chair beside her sliding away the empty, plastic chair she had placed for Robert.

"The doctor says you have responded well to your medication."

Ruth maintains her focus straight ahead.

"I've come to take you home."

As Ruth turns her head to Jackson, Robert enters the room. The man in the wheelchair seems familiar to him. His damaged brain will not allow him to remember the man, but Robert knows not to be seen. He turns and shuffles away.

After thirty minutes, Robert returns to the television room. Ruth is gone.

He taps the shoulder of the nurse, who he had seen before with Ruth. He points to the two, empty chairs by the window without saying a word.

The nurse follows his pointing.

"Oh, Ruth?" the nurse said lightly touching Robert's shoulder, "I'm sorry, but her father has checked her out."

Robert releases a grunt and shuffles to the empty chair by the window.

Liz... come back...

He lowers his head and rocks side-to-side.

12-ON THE RUN

DARKNESS HAUNTS THE empty hospital room. Another lost night of sleep. Eli remains frozen in his bed staring up toward the black ceiling.

Jagged memories rush to him as he is unable to piece them into chronological order. His jumbled mind stays confused.

Liz, I miss you... Believe in my plan, Simon... Join us... the Earth will end... Salvation... Salvation...

An eerie red light creeps into the room through a growing crack in the doorway.

"Who's... " Eli grunts pushing his uneaten dinner tray from his bedside. The plasticware bangs against the underside of the plate with its cold macaroni-and-cheese.

The redness grows filling the room with a blinding light.

"Who is it?" Eli said forcing the words from his mouth.

A silhouette emerges through the light.

"Who are you?" Eli's question comes slow.

Eli sits up in his bed throwing his legs to the side away from the door. The red light grows dim. Footsteps approach behind him forcing him to stand and slink in the farthest corner of the room; his teeth chatter.

"Eli, how are you?" a familiar voice said through the darkness.

The corner feels rough against Eli's backside as he slides crouching on the floor.

"I've been worried about, you?"

"Who are— "

"Eli, you don't remember me?"

Eli places his hands over his ears and presses his head hard as if he were trying to smash tight a snowball.

"It's okay, I'm here for you, Daddy."

The pressure against the sides of his head releases as Eli stands.

"Jay… Jacob?"

Eli stands stroking his head along the path of his scar.

"Yes, it's me. I've come to take you home."

"Home… Tex… home… " The words come incomplete.

"Yes, home to Houston. I'm taking you back to Liz."

Eli rubs his wrist where his watch used to be.

"Liz?"

"Yes, Liz, we're going home to live together again as a family."

"Family!" Eli screams.

"Shh, Eli, they will hear you."

The skin around his wrist feels raw.

"They?" Eli said.

"Yes, they. They are watching you."

Eli closes his eyes tight. Red and white dots flicker behind his closed eyes. Dizziness rushes through his head causing him to open his eyes wide. Eli charges to the voice bolting across the room.

"Let me go, Eli."

The cold glass from the full-length mirror shocks Eli's palms as he presses against the source of the voice.

"No," Eli said.

"Shh, they are watching."

"No!" Eli screams.

"Shh, be quiet. They are watching."

Eli balls his right fist pulling it behind his head. Air buzzes by Eli's right ear as his fist pounds toward the voice.

The voice falls silent. Shards of glass break against Eli's fist and to the floor. He screams in frustration and pain.

He opens his eyes staring into a kaleidoscope of his reflection. The red light from the emergency exit flashes into the room through the small window above the door.

Eli is alone.

Tears flood as Eli wipes his face; his pale skin smears with blood blending with the flashing red light. Within the kaleidoscope image of himself, Eli smiles. His white teeth shine brightly through the blood and the darkness.

Eli flashes his eyes open-and-closed multiple times. He presses his face closer to the broken mirror admiring his teeth.

A grunt escapes his lungs as he moves his right hand to the shattered glass remaining affixed in the plastic mirror frame. Eli forces his fingers against the sharp, barbed glass. Blood oozes from his fingertips as he squeezes his hand tight against a triangular shard pulling it away from the wall.

Blood gushes from his knuckles and fingertips as he holds his face close against the remaining pieces of the hanging mirror. Eli opens his mouth as wide as possible and positions the tip of the glass at the base of his front teeth at his gums.

With a sudden jolt to the front of his head, Eli balls his left fist and jams it quick into the back of the glass in his right hand. Eli's reflection disappears in the glass covered by spurting blood from his mouth.

Eli drops the glass to the floor. His eyes roll inside his head as he staggers back against the foot of his bed. Uncontrollable hemorrhaging pumps from his face. Eli falls to his knees slipping on the bloody floor.

Both hands flat against the sticky floor, Eli pats his hands up-and-down. A sharp pain jolts against his left palm; he closes his hands returning to the bed.

He pulls the lamp string. Four, bloody teeth drip on the white sheet from his hand. He reaches for the largest tooth bringing it close to his eyes.

Eli purses his lips together and spits on the tooth between his fingers. He rubs it clean of blood.

With his left hand, he uses his index-fingernail and pries at the inside of his broken tooth. A few seconds of scraping, Eli removes his hand away; the tooth falls on the bed bouncing to the floor.

Eli turns to the lamp and holds his index-finger into the light. A small computer chip rests on the pad of his fingertip. He places the chip on the table with the lamp.

In the dim light, Eli retrieves the plastic knife from his dinner tray. With the rounded-end, he slams the hard plastic against the table shattering the chip into pieces.

Eli stands. Clotting across his gums slows the dripping blood. He reaches into his closet and places on his gray jacket and Yankees cap. With the knife still in his hand, he steps to the window and wrenches it open.

Cold, snowy air refreshes him. The sensation shivers his body from his exposed, bleeding mouth.

The window provides his escape as Eli bolts through the buildings' shadows into the darkness of night.

JANUARY 15, 1997 (2 WEEKS LATER) NEWARK, NEW JERSEY

"RUTH, DINNER IS READY," Jackson said calling to his daughter.

The smell of Salisbury steak leads Ruth to the kitchen. They sit in silence while eating.

Three weeks had passed since Jackson discharged Ruth from Greystone and returned to their apartment in Newark. Ruth had always been a quiet person. But, he cannot recall a single utterance since she had been home.

For years, medication had been effective for Ruth helping with her sense of uncontrollable rage. A strong side effect was a depressive state, which calmed her.

Years of switching between rage and depression, Ruth had had enough and overdosed. Jackson found her unresponsive and contacted The Eden Foundation who sent two officers to their apartment where they admitted her in Greystone.

Steam rises from the black, plastic TV dinner trays. A shimmer from the overhead light catches Jackson's attention.

"Oh, that's a pretty watch," Jackson said trying to make small-talk with Ruth. "It looks a little big."

Jackson sees Ruth smile as she glances at her wrist.

"Was it a gift?"

Ruth finishes eating and looks at her dad.

"This nice man at the hospital gave it to me." Ruth removes and admires her gift.

"Can I see it?"

Ruth extends her hand across the table. Jackson takes the watch.

"Someone gave this to you? It's very— "

Jackson pauses as he flips it over.

"Eli and Liz, forever," Jackson said.

Jackson holds it close to his squinting right eye and lowers it to the table.

"Eli? Was this his name?"

Ruth takes the watch from Jackson. "Um, no. It was Robert. He seemed nice, but didn't really speak much."

"What, what did he look like?"

"I don't know. Just an old man. He had gray hair, but the most memorable thing was this bad scar on his face."

"So, he said nothing?"

Ruth stands from the table taking the empty plastic dishes to the trash.

"No. We played this game with a code. I think he was trying to tell me something, but the nurse said he was heavily medicated."

Jackson backs his wheelchair from the table as Ruth cleans the kitchen.

"What did he say?"

Water runs in the sink.

"Hmm, I don't remember. Just random words, really."

"Yeah, like, what?"

Jackson is relieved Ruth is talking as he tries to carry on the conversation. The water stops. Ruth freezes; her eyes lift to the right trying to recall.

"Something about a *Jacob*, and *home*... he mentioned *Liz*, that's what he called me. I think he thought I was her?"

Jackson rolls his chair closer to his daughter.

"Anything else you remember?"

Ruth hesitates, her eyes closed.

"He must have been a churchman or something."

"Why do you say that?"

"Well, the only other words I remember him saying were *salvation* and *Eden*."

Jackson drops the glass he held. The shattering jolts Ruth as she jumps spinning around to him.

"That's okay; I'll get that," Ruth said.

She kneels to clean up the glass pieces. Jackson grabs her wrist.

"There's something I need to tell you... " Ruth returns a worried expression. "... it's something I should have told you a long time ago."

Jackson and Ruth return to the table. For the next several minutes, Jackson confesses everything to Ruth. A sense of relief leaves him as he had carried his burden for so long. A burden which drove his wife away and had caused so many problems with Ruth.

"So, you think this group that hired me and you to work for them... that they are the ones responsible for running you off the road that night?"

"I don't have any proof. Things never added up for me. How they found us in Iowa? The things that Eli asked me to do."

"And, you think this Eli is the same man I met in the hospital?"

"Yes."

"But, how, why's that?"

"The names on the watch... Eli and Liz. Liz was his wife. That's the reason we used to live near Houston. My job with Eden was to monitor Liz and her family."

"So, if that's true, why was he in a hospital in New Jersey, and his name was Robert?"

Jackson does not return a quick answer to Ruth's questions. He backs his chair from the table.

"I'm not sure. I've not heard from him in years. Different people with Eden have been contacting me with their instructions."

"I don't know. Robert just didn't seem capable of being this Eli person. Someone must have given him this. I mean, he could barely move or say anything."

Minutes had passed.

"What makes you think this Eden group created those events you told me?" Ruth asked.

"Remember back in 1993?"

"Yeah, in Waco... How can I, not? That's when you had me drive those women to that place."

"And, what happened?"

"Oh, you mean the next day when the FBI raided that compound?"

"Exactly, Eli told me to have you drive them there. It just seems too convenient that the following day is when all hell broke loose."

"What? You think they had something to do with that? With that fire?"

Jackson huffs in frustration.

"Not at that time, I didn't. But, if we connect all the dots of the things Eden has asked us to do, it becomes clear. It seems like something bad happens after we completed our jobs."

"Yeah, like what else?"

"What about New York in 1981?"

"You mean when I got out of prison, and the cleaning job you got me in Manhattan?"

"And, what happened, then?"

"Hmm... I don't remember."

"There was that blackout in New York City. I mean, Eli told me about a job he had for you."

"Yeah, that was the best job ever. That building was so nice."

"While you were there, that blackout lasted for four or five hours. All those banks and brokerages… the timing just always seemed weird to me."

"Oh, I see what you mean. Like when we had moved to Florida, and then the next day the Challenger exploded? I remember that 'cause we could see the smoke from our backyard."

Ruth stands and fills two glasses of water.

"But, what about Oklahoma City?" Ruth asked returning to the table.

"What about it?"

"Well, it was my idea to move there a few years ago. And, I got that job— "

"The job cleaning at the courthouse?" Jackson said interrupting her.

"Yes."

Jackson sips his water. "Actually, it was me that caused us to move there and helped you get the job. Eli asked that we move there, but he wanted you to work across the street from that building."

"But, it was my idea."

"Eli gave me magazines about Oklahoma and the area and told me to leave them around our house."

"I remember seeing those. That's how I got the idea for us… oh, I see, now."

"Yeah, and it was Eli himself, or he had someone call you about that job."

Ruth gulps her water and returns her empty glass to the sink.

"So, what are you saying? We move somewhere, and something bad happens? Well, don't you think, so? I mean, you started that job, and then the following week the explosion."

Jackson wheels his chair into his bedroom and returns a few minutes later to the kitchen. In his lap, he has his wallet and keys to his van.

"Come on."

"Where are we going?"

"We're going back to the hospital and talk to this man. We need to find out how he got this watch. I need to see if this is Eli. Maybe he's ready to tell his secrets of what the hell has been happening all these years."

Ruth follows Jackson out the door. The apartment sits in darkness.

An hour later, Jackson and Ruth arrive at Greystone. The familiar face of the nurse who had spent time with Ruth greets them in the lobby.

"Oh, back so soon?" the nurse asked.

"No. I mean, uh, that man, Robert, I used to sit with him in the television room, can we see him?" Ruth asked.

The nurse looks behind her and returns her attention to Ruth.

"You said, the man… in the… hold on." The nurse walks around the counter and flips through a ring-binder affixed on her desk. "Hmm… "

The nurse types on a keyboard. "What did you say his name was, again?"

"Robert, his name was Robert. You remember, he was the man who always wore a jacket and a hat… he didn't talk, and we always sat by the window in the television room," Ruth said.

Tapping comes from behind the counter. "No, I'm sorry. There is no Robert… do you have a last name?"

"I don't know his last name."

"Maybe he's checked out?"

"You know, his name is Robert… you were the one telling me about him?"

"I'm sorry, Honey, but we have so many patients here— "

"What about an Eli… Eli Bishop?" Jackson asked.

The tapping returns. "Nope, sorry. No Eli either."

"But, but… I don't understand. His name is Robert. He wore a jacket and a Yankees hat."

"Oh no, that can't be. We don't allow any patient to wear anything but hospital issued gowns."

"Not true. His name is Robert." Ruth's voice becomes loud and aggressive.

The nurse places her hand over a button under the counter. One press will alert orderlies to the lobby.

Jackson grabs Ruth's wrist. "Come on, Ruth. We'll go home."

The nurse removes her hand from the button. Ruth turns from the counter and walks with Jackson as he rolls with her through the exit door.

As the glass door slides behind them, Jackson's grip grows firm on Ruth's wrist.

"Get in the van. We need to leave here, now."

Jackson positions himself behind the steering wheel. Ruth places his wheelchair in the back of the van.

"So, what now?" Ruth asked joining Jackson in the front seat.

"I'm not sure, but it may have been a mistake coming here. We need to find Eli… Robert, whatever his name is. I just hope we've not alerted the people he worked for by coming here."

Outside Denver, Colorado, a phone rings in an office complex under construction by The Eden Foundation.

"Hello?"

"Yes, you told me to call if anyone came looking for Eli," the nurse from Greystone said through the phone.

"Yes."

"They were back asking to see him."

"What did you tell them?"

"Nothing…just like you told me to say, that we had no records of him."

"Okay. Good job. Call me if they return."

The phone line clicks silent.

Inside the Colorado office, the man who received the call stands.

"What do we do, now, Boss?" one of two men asked sitting at a table.

"I want you to find *him*. Do whatever it takes."

"Yes, Mr. Jacob, we understand," the other man said as they stand to leave the office.

As the door closes, Jacob throws his right hand toward the office wall. "Dammit!"

Pieces of a small, computer chip bounce off the wall and roll back on the floor to Jacob.

"I should have killed you."

JUNE 11, 1997 (6 MONTHS LATER)
PASADENA, TEXAS

ELI'S BLACK, LEATHER SHOES melt in the Texas, summer heat even at sunrise. His soles have worn thin the last five months from his sixteen-hundred-mile walk from New Jersey.

After his escape from the psychiatric hospital, Eli ran unsure where he was going. The voices in his head have jumbled his memories. But, Texas pulls him south.

His fear of Jacob and The Eden Foundation kept his profile low during his journey. As the northern snow gave way to southern warmth, his internal voices had quietened.

One voice breaks through his internal noise. Encouragement comes from his wife, Liz, who Eli remembers always having kind words to say to everyone she had met.

Eli has traveled along a straight, two-lane highway for hours. A few miles from the Pasadena, Texas city limits, Eli stops walking. A massive roadside billboard captures his progress.

"Chatham E... states," Eli said. His words stutter softly through his parched, chapped lips.

Eli presses forward on the road. A long-hidden instinct guides his path. Thirty more minutes of walking, Eli arrives home: the neighborhood of Chatham Estates.

Shoulder-high shrubs outline property borders. Eli walks behind the shrubbery remaining hidden as he comes to 207 Chatham Lane... home.

Sunlight fills his old backyard as morning pushes to noon. A row of bushes under a back window gives Eli a resting place. He closes his eyes as his internal voices return.

Jacob's voice comes to Eli as he sleeps leaning against the house.

"And, now, look at you. You came back into my life, and you were the strongest man I've ever known... now, you're quitting... you're wasting everything you've worked for. I thought I had lost you once when I was a kid... I can't let you go through with this... "

Silence joins the darkness of Eli's dream. A faint, woman's voice pushes through the darkness. The voice is from his wife.

"Martha, I'm sorry you and James had a fight last night. Is there anything I can do, Hun?"

Sunlight enters Eli's eyes. The bushes create a green kaleidoscope within his vision. Liz's voice in his head soothes him.

"Are you coming to Joseph's graduation tonight at the high school?"

Eli slinks under the bushes against the ground. Her voice is loud.

"Oh, that's okay, Darlin', I understand."

Eli turns his head to the house. He notices the open window above him. Liz is inside the kitchen.

"I'll take plenty of pictures."

His skin turns pale unsure if the voice is real. He crawls through the thicket of bushes and into the opened door of the backyard shed. Eli lies on the wooden floor.

The small building has a strange sense of familiarity. He collects his breath. Long-faded memories bounce in his absent mind. Eli had used the building as his personal workspace when he and Liz moved to their new house in 1958.

He rummages through the shed crawling under the workbench to the back corner. He wedges his index finger between two floorboards lifting one revealing a rusted, square box unopened in thirty years.

Nail heads press into his back as Eli leans against the wall under the bench. Water forms within Eli's bottom eyelids. A rusted groan releases as Eli opens the metal box. A chill shivers his mouth as air rushes over his front gums as he smiles pulling out a wad of at least ten-thousand dollars. But, what makes Eli smile the most is an old Polaroid camera hidden under the money.

Memories of a Christmas morning decades ago come to Eli. Rustling wind created by the sweltering sun interrupts his memories. He closes the box and returns it to its hiding spot replacing the floorboard. As Eli leaves the shed, he stuffs his pants with the cash.

He holds the camera to his eye looking through the viewfinder. A sight startles Eli forcing him back inside the shed. For a moment, he thinks maybe Jacob has discovered his hiding place. Eli sees Liz step outside and yells to her grandson, Joseph, who turns to her.

Eli rubs his eyes. He had only seen Joseph one other time at a distance when Joseph was ten-years-old. A rainy afternoon, Eli had stood behind a large oak tree in the cemetery of Middle Creek Baptist Church witnessing the burial of his daughter-in-law, Rachel.

"Joseph… my grandson… high school… " The words stutter from Eli.

Seconds pass after Joseph enters the home. Eli sneaks from the shed carrying his camera underneath his gray jacket. Beads of sweat drop from his Yankees hat as he walks from Chatham Street meandering through the neighborhood to Bethlehem Senior High School.

A few hours had passed into the sweltering afternoon. Eli stands among the tall, slender east-Texas pine trees lining the perimeter of the school parking lot. He fixes his gaze on a green Oldsmobile pulling into a parking space.

Eli steps through the trees; dry pine needles crunch with each move. He steps onto the blacktop. His feet sizzle.

His dehydrated body aches as he makes his way through the parking lot. Eli continues stalking the car as he walks. He stops less than a hundred feet away as Liz steps from the car.

People pass by Eli as he stands motionless in the middle of the parking lot. They give him double-takes given his jacket attire in the terrible heat.

"They are calling for storms, tonight," a lady said to her husband as they pass.

Eli moves closer to Liz careful not to be seen. He follows as Liz approaches Joseph in his graduation gown. She stops to take Joseph's picture as he yells "Graduation!"

Liz leaves the graduate and makes her way to the football stadium. Eli shuffles well behind her almost getting too close when Joseph runs to her as she stops.

Eli hears Liz say, "It was all I could do. I did it all for Rachel, and I am so very proud of you."

A slight smile on Eli's face disappears as the voices return to his confused brain. Paranoia spins him around in the parking lot.

A deep breath fills Eli's lungs as he calms himself. He looks but has lost his sight of Liz and the graduate. He presses on to the stadium.

"Would you like a program?" a young girl said wearing a white dress standing at the stadium entrance.

Eli pushes her hand away and releases a faint grunt passing her. Once through, Eli finds Liz again. He watches as she goes into the football stands at the fifty-yard line stopping beside a seated, balding man.

The muscles in Eli's shoulders tense and his face flushes red watching the man stand to hug Liz. Eli releases another grunt as his body relaxes.

Minutes had passed as Eli remains stationary on the walkway. Music plays signifying the start of the ceremony.

Oppressive humidity swamps the stadium. Flashes from cameras throughout the stands match the flashes of lightning along the horizon.

The graduates file onto the running track around the football field. Eli smiles, but he is unsure why.

"It is now time to present the graduating class of 1997 with their diplomas," the high school principal said, her voice booming across the stadium.

Eli unzips his jacket and reaches inside its pocket pulling out his old Polaroid camera. He zips up his coat and steps down the side of the stands onto the field.

He stands to the left of the seated graduates near the side of the elevated stage where the graduates walk down after receiving their diplomas. During the ceremony, cameras flash around him. The lights conjure his internal voices on their return.

"I'm watching you... I see you..."

Eli stands resolute. His camera is firm in his hands by his waist.

"Joseph Jacob Bishop," the principal said.

Eli's shoulders swell, and his chest expands. His attention goes to the graduate he had seen with Liz earlier in the parking lot.

Eli flashes a broad smile. Gone are his teeth; his gums visible under the camera he holds to his eye. He stands close to the steps, ten feet from Joseph as he walks down from the stage. Eli snaps a picture.

"Hey, Jacob! Is that your name?"

A shivers shutters through Eli's body upon hearing his son's name yelled by the students greeting Joseph at the bottom of the steps.

"I'm watching you... I see you..."

Someone bumps into Eli scaring the voice inside his head to silence.

Eli turns and runs across the football field in the shadows cast by the stage. His feet lumber underneath him as his knees ache with each pounding step.

The tall pines offer sanctuary to Eli. He bends at his knees with both hands flat against the pine bark. His chest heaves violently as the camera swings side-to-side in front of him.

Eli stands patting his jacket and pants.

"My picture... where... is it?"

Eli steps from the trees determined to find the Polaroid picture.

"I'm watching you... I see you..."

Jacob's voice inside Eli's head pushes Eli back as he disappears into the forest.

13-LOOSE ENDS

NOVEMBER 1997 (5 MONTHS LATER)
PUEBLA, MEXICO

JACKSON SENSED A long, familiar uneasiness after leaving the psychiatric hospital in New Jersey. The same sensation he had felt during his first week back at the Palomar Observatory after his accident thirty-seven-years earlier.

Driving the van with Ruth in the passenger seat, memories had returned to Jackson. Quick flashes of headlights in a parking lot and finding a lost photo with a handwritten note, forced a repeated action. He ran.

Months had passed. Jackson and Ruth have established themselves in Puebla, Mexico. They live in a small villa in a valley at the base of Popocatépetl. Located near an active volcano, the house is cheap and more importantly secluded. Jackson is confident they are safe.

To restock their supplies, they travel an hour twice per month to the nearest grocery store. Tonight after arriving home, Ruth discovers a large envelope shoved under the entry.

"What's that?" Jackson asked noticing the door slightly ajar.

"Don't know. There's a note saying it's for you," Ruth said as she handed the envelope to her father.

Jackson opens and reads the contents.

"Ruth, it looks like we're going back to Washington."

"Washington? Is that from Eden? How did they find us?"

Jackson places the envelope on his lap as he wheels his chair through the house.

"I shouldn't be surprised that they discovered us?"

Nervous energy fills the pit of Jackson's stomach. He realizes if Eden wanted to harm him or Ruth, the item under the door would have been more than an envelope.

"Do we really have to go?"

Ruth has found peace living in the valley relaxing for her thoughts. Her moods have evened.

"If they found us, then we will need to leave," Jackson said.

"What does it say we are to do?"

Jackson scans the papers.

"I've got to read through this. I'm not sure of the details, but it's something called Project Lewinsky."

"When do we leave?"

"Tomorrow."

The next morning, Jackson and Ruth leave before sunrise arriving sixteen hours later at the U.S. Border in Laredo, Texas. Two lanes of vehicle traffic move forward. After a fifteen-minute wait, the border agents allow them to pass.

"Pull over, I need to use the bathroom," Ruth said as they pass a gas station.

Jackson complies parking the van. Ruth gets out while Jackson fills the van with gas. She returns a few minutes later.

"Dad, I will meet you in Washington in a couple weeks."

The gas pump stops before the van's tank is full.

"What? You can't leave me."

"You will be fine. I'll take a bus there… I just need to clear my thoughts more before going back."

Jackson stares at Ruth a few seconds. He resumes filling the gas tank.

"Fine. You know what hotel we're staying. Do you need money?" Jackson said knowing it was pointless to argue with her.

"No, I've got enough. I'll be fine and will see you, soon."

Ruth turns and leaves. Jackson watches as she turns the corner of the gas station out of his sight.

Two days later, on the day before Thanksgiving, Ruth knocks on the apartment door of a friend she had made during her time with her father in Pasadena, Texas. Her last time visiting was four years, ago.

The door opens. A tall man stands in the doorway. He is twice Ruth's size with tattoos snaking up his arms and chest under a white undershirt. He is the same age as Ruth, thirty-six.

"Ruth, is that you?"

"Yeah, hey, Luther, I'm sorry I haven't called you in so long."

"Come *here*. You look as beautiful as ever," Luther said as he reaches through the door to hug her.

"Can I come in?"

"Sure, come in… pardon the mess; I've been watching my cousin's baby."

Ruth laughs. "I was going to ask you what woman in her right mind would let you fuck her when I saw all the baby toys."

"Oh, Ruth, I've missed you," Luther said through his belching laughter.

"How have you been?"

"Good. I've been able to get some handyman jobs here and there. You know… payin' the bills and shit. What about you?"

Ruth spends the next hours telling Luther everything which has happened to her since her last arrest as a teenager. She needed to release the burden inside her building the previous twenty years.

She had met Luther at a bar one night while her father monitored the Bishop's house in Pasadena. Theirs was a passionate relationship induced by beer and cigarettes, and never one about sharing their past.

Luther was a child of the foster care system, who found himself in and out of trouble over the years. He had a violent streak but was always a pussycat around Ruth.

"So, this Eli, they said he wasn't a patient in that hospital?"

"Yeah, ain't that some shit?"

"And, your dad thinks finding him may be the key to whatever he thinks is going on?"

"I think so. That's what he said. You remember when we met, I told you someone asked my dad to watch a family here in Pasadena?"

"Yeah, I guess so."

"Well, it was Eli's wife he was watching."

"Holy shit and this is the man you met in New Jersey?"

"I know, right? That's too weird if you ask me."

Luther slides closer to Ruth on the sofa.

"So, why did you stop by?" Luther said as he rubs her shoulders.

Ruth releases a sigh.

"I'm not sure. I'm thinking about meeting this Liz person, tomorrow."

"So, you came, here?"

"I need a place to sleep. I've hitched rides here from Laredo."

"No problem. My bed is always open for you," Luther said sliding his hand to her chest.

Ruth smacks his hand.

"Not that. I'm sleeping on the couch."

"Sorry."

"That's okay... maybe, tomorrow," Ruth said as she smiles. "I also wanted to talk to you about joining Jackson and me?"

"Huh?"

"Yeah, the company he works for pays him well. He's getting older, and I need someone to be around to— "

"Kick somebody's ass."

"Something like that," Ruth said touching his thigh. "I can protect us, but it will help me out knowing you're there too to help."

The sound of crying from the other room interrupts them.

"Can I?"

"Please... she never shuts up once she starts crying."

A few minutes later Ruth returns to the living room. The baby is asleep in her arms.

"Oh, you're a natural."

"Luther, I need to ask another favor… can I borrow her for a few hours tomorrow?"

"Borrow?"

"Yeah, I want to take her with me when I see Liz. I can use her as a way to start a conversation with her."

"Sure, whatever you want."

"I also need to borrow your car."

"On one condition."

"What's that?"

"Tomorrow night, it's me and you."

"No problem. I was going to fuck you, anyway."

SEPTEMBER 11, 2001 — 8:15 A.M. (4 YEARS LATER) WORLD TRADE CENTER, NEW YORK CITY

A COOL, CRISP MORNING greets Luther as he pushes Jackson in his wheelchair with Ruth following them. Lower Manhattan bustles with people and noise. Small puddles from an overnight storm look like landmines along the pavement. The sky is bright blue absent a single cloud. Scents of bagels blend with the aroma of the many coffee shops around every corner.

"Which way, now?" Luther asked.

"You can't miss it. The World Trade Center is just ahead," Jackson replied.

People rush entering the lobby of the South Tower pushing Luther toward the bank of elevators. Their identification badges grant them access through the security turnstiles.

"Which floor?" Ruth asked.

"Seven," Jackson replied.

The elevator jolts upward stopping after a few seconds. A small chime dings throughout the full car. Like Moses, Luther pushes Jackson out of the elevator as the crowd parts.

"We're to go down the hall and wait by the windows in the waiting area," Jackson said instructing Luther which way to turn.

Lemon-colored, leather chairs sit around a coffee table. Various magazines and newspapers hide the mahogany wood grain. Luther positions Jackson by the window allowing him to enjoy the view of the North Tower. Two, young men stop in the waiting area in the middle of a heated conversation.

"Pay up; you owe me fifty dollars."

"Hell no, the Broncos got lucky last night."

"Luck, hell? The Giants suck, you guys should have never moved out of the Meadowlands."

"What do you mean, we suck? We are Super Bowl Champions."

"Yeah, but that was last year. Now, pay up."

The conversation fades drowned by the ever-increasing population of workers entering the floor.

"Did they tell you what the meeting was about?" Ruth asked.

"No. I only know Eden used to have an office here, but they moved out last week."

Ruth flips through a newspaper. Several articles reference today's New York City mayoral elections.

"In fact, a long time ago, Eli told me the Foundation had bugged several offices here. Supposedly, Eden was able to be successful in the stock market because all the financial companies headquartered here," Jackson said in a hushed tone.

Ruth replaces the newspaper on the table.

"What do you mean, they moved out? If that's true, then why are we here?"

Jackson stares out the window admiring the beautiful day. He pulls a note from his front pocket.

"We were asked to meet a representative with Eden here at 8:45 this morning… awe, shit."

"What's wrong?"

"We're in the wrong damn building. My memory is getting bad."

Luther looks at the note Jackson holds.

"Your handwriting is shit, too, Old Man," Luther said with a laugh, "plus, that looks like a seventy to me, not Floor Seven."

Jackson studies his note, again. "Hell, you're right." He looks at his watch. "Shit, we're gonna be late. It's already 8:45, now."

Ruth and Luther stand. At the same moment, as Luther places his hands around the handles of the wheelchair, the floor and windows rumble like an earthquake. Bright orange illuminates the windows.

"What the hell— "

"Oh, shit! I thought I saw a plane," Jackson said interrupting Ruth. "Go! Get to the elevator, now! We gotta get out of here, now!"

Jackson's face is bright white. Luther spins the chair from the window to the hallway.

"Hurry! Run!" Jackson's commands come fast as people pass them going to the windows.

Jackson presses the *down* button at the elevator in a continuous fashion like a telegraph operator. He moves his right hand behind him and returns his wallet to his lap.

"Luther give me your wallet… Ruth, put our wallets in your bag, and leave your bag, *here*."

The elevator doors open. It is empty. A small, down-arrow light teases them with a pleasant ding.

"But, my money… my license," Ruth said.

"Take *these* and leave them, *here*. We need to go, now!"

Jackson grabs Ruth's hand as she throws her bag holding their wallets behind a potted plant beside the elevator.

"Okay, let's go."

Luther pushes the chair inside the elevator and presses the button for the lobby.

"What's going on?" Ruth asked.

Jackson places his finger over his lips. "Shh."

His eyes lift to a security camera affixed in the top corner of the elevator car.

The doors open. A wall clock catches Jackson's attention. Its hands move to nine o'clock.

"*There…* go *that way*, get out of this building." Jackson points to the side lobby door.

Luther follows his directions. They run to the exit; the chair's left wheel squeals. Most people in the lobby are conducting regular conversations, oblivious to the terror happening next door. To them, everything seems normal… for the moment.

The glass door closes behind them as they exit onto Liberty Street. Shouts and gasps capture people standing still looking up, as they pass.

"Go that way… to Battery Park. We'll catch a ferry— "

A roar from the sky interrupts Jackson. All three tilt their heads backward at the exact moment a jetliner crashes into the South Tower.

"Run!" Jackson yelled.

His command snaps Ruth and Luther from their trance as they run pushing Jackson. People around them remain frozen in terror with their heads lifted skyward. Paper with bits of concrete and glass rain down around them.

"Go! Go!"

Luther dashes forward as Jackson holds tight onto his chair. Ruth sprints in front of them leading the way.

"*There,* the ferry is leaving," Jackson said as an attendant remains motionless allowing them to get on without a ticket.

Winded, Luther spins Jackson around facing the direction they came. They watch the horror of both towers of the World Trade Center. Black, billowing smoke rises to the heavens. Paper floats like snow in front of orange flames soaring through the gaping holes near the top of the buildings.

"Oh my God… we were supposed to be up, *there,*" Ruth said.

Jackson relaxes his closed fist. The small note with its smudged instruction for the 8:45 a.m. meeting on the seventieth floor stare back to him. He lifts his head staring at the North Building. As he watches in horror, he rips the note into small sections.

The cold water of the Hudson River splashes across Jackson's outstretched hand. The ferry escapes fast heading to Jersey City. Paper falls like confetti from his hand into the river churned by the roaring engines in the water.

Ruth turns to Eli. They hold an unspoken acknowledgment between them. They know someone meant for them to be at the top of the North Tower. Fate has intervened.

Months later, someone would discover among the Ground Zero debris their identification. To the world, to The Eden Foundation; all three had perished.

Jackson, Ruth, and Luther watch the news from a secluded cabin in the Appalachian Mountains of East Tennessee. Their new base until they decide their next course of action.

14-Finding Eli

LIZ HAD FIRST MET RUTH at the Pasadena Homeless Shelter on Thanksgiving Day in 1997. Volunteering on this holiday had brought Liz peace given the sadness she felt during the holidays.

In the past, men had visited the shelter for Thanksgiving. But, in 1997, Liz saw a lone woman with a baby join the men.

Ruth had faked her inability to speak English with her recent learning of Spanish during her and Jackson's seclusion in Mexico. With the stories she had learned from Eli in the psychiatric hospital a year earlier, Ruth had to face Liz.

From her meeting in the shelter, Ruth realized Liz was a special person. She showed kindness that day helping Ruth with the baby which she had borrowed from Luther.

Ruth's other motive for meeting Liz was to decide if Liz knew Eli's whereabouts. As Ruth observed her interact with the people, she realized she could not confront her with the news about him.

An idea came to Ruth while finishing her plate of fried chicken and baked beans. Eli had shared with her the communication matrix in the hospital. Eli said he used this to hide specific conversations with Liz. Ruth used this matrix to communicate with Liz pretending to be Eli.

Ruth finished her food and flipped over her white, paper plate. She pulled an ink pen from her jacket pocket and created a matrix in the center of the plate. Below the matrix, she wrote a string of numbers. Once solved, the matrix would reveal a straightforward sentence, which Liz would believe came from Eli.

I am alive.

Ruth spied through the windows of the shelter later in the afternoon as Liz found the plate. She followed Liz home and continued watching her the next few days. Ruth hoped her note would cause Liz to search for Eli. But, Liz never deviated from her routine.

Ruth left with Luther the following week as she had promised her father joining him in Washington. Luther had agreed to go encouraged by Ruth.

Over the years between task assignments from The Eden Foundation, Ruth sent Liz pictures with encoded messages about various world events. She hoped Liz would think Eli was alive and try to look for him. Ruth could then follow her to Eli where they would kidnap him and force the truth.

Alas, Liz never looked. Liz kept the pictures with their encoded messages hidden within a scrapbook, uncertain why she had been receiving them.

Six years after their first encounter at the shelter, Ruth sent a final encoded message to Liz. This message was different than the others containing detailed instructions for Liz to meet Eli at the Houston Airport Ramada Inn.

To Ruth's surprise, Liz obeyed this time following the instructions to the hotel on Christmas Day as she watched Liz enter the hotel room. With Ruth dressed in a cleaning uniform, she was non-threatening to Liz who allowed her entry to the room.

After the initial shock of explaining what was happening, Ruth shared with Liz the information about Eli being alive. Liz believed Ruth to be lying. Not until Ruth gave her Eli's watch, would Liz change her mind about the unfathomable possibility of her husband being alive after twenty-eight years.

Ruth left the hotel room giving Liz instructions to take a parked car to a specified address. Once there, Ruth promised to share everything with Liz about Eli.

When she left Liz, Ruth joined her father, Jackson, in the hotel room, one floor above where Liz remained. They waited peering out the window to see if Liz would obey Ruth's instructions.

Alone in the hotel room, Liz's heart races under her hooded sweatshirt. Curiosity eats at her, as she spies through the thick, fabric curtains. The hum of the heating unit blows warm air against her thighs.

I can't wait an hour... I don't see anyone out there... I'm going, now.

She clinches the keys to the lone Toyota in the parking lot Ruth had given her before she left. The ridges of the silver key imprints against her smooth left palm. With one last peek through the curtain, Liz takes her plastic bag off the bed with her clothes she had brought with her from the airport and presses her eye against the peephole of the door.

Looks quiet. No one is out there.

She gulps pulling open the door. The outside light floods the dark hotel room. Cool air flushes through her hair as she enters the hallway and hurries to the stairwell at the end of the corridor.

The stairs are dark. A red, neon exit sign flickers guiding her way downstairs. At the bottom, the second-floor door, where she had exited, slams shut frightening her.

At the same time, Liz pushes on the exit door as cold, night air smacks against her unmade face. The sudden chill pushes her faster across the parking lot to the waiting car as Ruth had instructed.

Liz flips out the key from her sweaty palm and unlocks the door getting inside the cold front seat. Her plastic bag tips over in the front passenger seat. A glance in the rearview mirror presents an unusually disheveled Liz.

Oh, Dear, I look absolutely terrible.

Unsure of her destination and whom she may meet, Liz searches her fallen bag for her lipstick applying a fresh layer of a pink hue across her lips.

There, that's a little better.

With a final flip through her hair with her hands, she starts the car and reviews the directions Ruth had provided.

What am I doing? I should call Martha or Joseph.

As fear once again approaches, something pinches against her right thigh inside her sweatpants pocket. A simultaneous smile and tear appear on her face as she opens her right hand revealing Eli's watch Ruth had given her.

No… I will face whatever this is…

Liz leaves her parking space turning out onto the street fronting the hotel. Headlights of a black pickup truck illuminate her former parking place as the truck follows far behind her.

Huh, this address isn't that far away.

The small Toyota continues down the highway leaving the airport complex. Heavy traffic from earlier on this Christmas Day has lightened as most of the holiday air travel has ended. The black truck stays well behind Liz unnoticed.

Liz obeys the handwritten directions driving for ten minutes as she enters a business center complex.

I thought this area seemed familiar. There's Mr. Spivey's Law Office, there.

She parks her car in front of the building with only two front doors. Liz had entered the right door last month when she visited her lawyer to update her will.

I wonder if Bobby knows anything about this? Surely, this can't be a coincidence to go to the office beside his?

Liz runs across the parking lot to the left door as instructed and knocks. Her sixty-four-year-old body shakes smothering her caution.

The door opens.

"Who are you?" a deep voice said from the other side of the closed door.

"Uh, my name is Liz… Elizabeth Bishop… Ruth sent me."

A small chain clangs. An eerie yellow light escapes from the opening door. A large man stands in silhouette within the doorframe.

"Please, Liz, come on in. Ruth will be here in a moment."

An old pickup truck passes by the parking lot, slowing down as it turns on a side street behind the building. The vehicle stops; the driver has a perfect vantage point to the front of the building from the side, hidden in shadows from the street lights.

"Would you like some coffee?" the large man asked.

"No… no, thank you." Liz's voice shakes.

The empty office is absent any furnishings. One table stands in the corner with a Mr. Coffee machine and yellowed-cups.

A stench of stale coffee mixes with old sawdust from the renovation underway in the office. A cutting table propped against two, empty fifty-five-gallon barrels are the only other items inside.

"Liz, I'm sorry. Please let me introduce myself. My name is Luther. I'm a friend of Ruth's."

"Nice to meet you… uh… so, do you know, Eli?"

Courage propels the question from Liz. Thoughts rush to her of her long-dead husband, who had supposedly died in a robbery in 1979.

"Uh, well… Ruth will explain when she gets here."

"Do you know when this may be?"

"I'm supposed to take care of you until she arrives. Should be a few minutes."

Sizing up Luther, Liz said, "Sure, then, I'll take a coffee, that sounds great, actually."

Luther returns from the corner station.

"Here ya go."

"Do you know Bobby, I mean Robert Spivey? His office is next door."

Before Luther can respond, the front door opens as Ruth enters. Rather than walking straight into the room, she holds open the door.

Familiar squeaking approaches Ruth's outstretched arm. A man in a wheelchair enters through the doorframe. The man makes eye contact with Liz.

"Hey! It's you. You were on the elevator with me at the hotel?"

The man smiles.

"Yes, very observant, aren't we?"

Liz's shoulders tense. Both fists clench beside her. Eli's timepiece presses deeper into her palm.

"What's goin' on? Who are you? Why are you following me? What do you want?"

The man in the wheelchair rolls to Liz. Ruth peeks outside one last time and closes the door.

"Well, Liz, my name isn't important, now. What is important is Eli."

Liz steps against the far wall. Her eyes dart around the room.

"Eli? I don't understand... he's dead."

The man wheels closer to Liz.

"There, there. I'm sure Ruth told you about being with him at the hospital several years ago."

Liz clenches the watch in her hand.

"Uh... like I told her, I can't believe it. I mean I buried my husband."

"And, the watch you're holding... that was also in the casket with him?" The man smiles looking up at Liz.

The wall lost its support as her knees buckle. Her back slides to the floor. Tears and emotion pour from her.

The man's wrinkled hand pats the top of Liz's head.

"I know... I know... it's a lot to take in, but Liz, I can assure you he is alive. We need your help to find him?"

Ruth approaches Liz curled on the floor kneeling beside her.

"Sweetie, it's okay. Go ahead and cry it out. It's okay."

Liz feels comfort from Ruth and the man. Their words help stop her crying. She slips Eli's watch onto her wrist.

Through sniffling, Liz asked, "I don't understand... why are you looking for him? How am I supposed... I mean, to me, he's dead... been dead?"

Ruth helps Liz to her feet.

"Here, come sit *on this*. We'll have some coffee, and I'll explain," Ruth said as she points to the barrels. "They're empty, but they make perfect seats until we get some chairs in here."

Luther brings Liz her coffee, which she sips from the warm, yellow Styrofoam cup.

Huh… it's just the way I like it… how did he know?

The man in the wheelchair spins to Liz.

"So, let's begin, again. When you received these pictures and codes in the mail, what did you think?"

"Uh," Liz said sipping the coffee, "well, I don't really know. When I found the first code at the shelter many years ago, I thought someone was pulling one on me. I thought someone else must have known about Eli's codes and sent that to me… I don't know, to somehow remind me of him?"

"We had learned about his code and thought this might be a good way to approach you," the man said.

"But, why not just come to me with this instead of leaving it on a paper plate during a dinner?"

"As I'm sure Ruth explained, we had to be careful. We're not sure if we're being followed and wanted to approach you this way to see if you understood the code."

"I still don't understand… following… watching, who would do this? Why?"

The man rolls closer to Liz.

"It's so complicated. But, think about it. We are telling you that your husband, who you've thought has been dead for over twenty years is really alive… why would he fake his death? What would drive him to do that?"

"How would I know? I'm having a hard time with this?"

"But, you saw him. You said you did at your grandson's high school graduation," Ruth said.

Liz wiggles on top of the barrel.

"I don't know… I thought it was him. It was an emotional night, and my mind was playing tricks on me, I guess."

"And, the watch on your wrist… how did we get that, then?" the man asked.

"Uh… " before Liz could respond, a sense of worry rushes over her. She takes a deep breath. "I don't know… maybe y'all dug it up or something?"

"I can assure you, Sweetie, Eli gave this to me in the hospital," Ruth said.

"Now, this hospital, where did you say that was again?"

"It's a psychiatric hospital in New Jersey," Ruth said.

"New Jersey?"

"Yeah."

"That's crazy. Eli's never been there."

"Just as crazy as us asking about him, now?" the man asked.

Liz pushes herself off the barrel which falls to the floor.

"Here, I'll get that," Luther said pushing by everyone lifting the empty barrel upright.

A few moments had passed. Silence surrounds everyone.

"What's going on, here?" Liz asked, again out of frustration.

"Like we said, we're looking for Eli," the man said.

"But, why?"

The man moves to the middle of the floor.

"Finding Eli will give us a chance to prove everything to the world."

Liz turns to the man walking to him and placing her hands on either side his armrests.

"What do you mean… prove what?"

Her stare pierces through the man. He holds his head back.

"Eli can prove the end of the world is coming," the man said.

The man rolls backward as Liz pushes against his chair. She stands erect.

"What the hell… the end of the world? That's it; I'm out of here."

Liz approaches the door. Luther moves to block her path. Liz freezes.

"Eli has known about this since his work with NASA," the man said behind Liz.

"Move! Get out of my way!" Liz yelled at Luther.

Ruth grabs Liz's shoulder. Liz pushes Ruth's arm away.

"Get off me; Y'all are all crazy. Let me the hell out of here!"

"Liz!" the man in the wheelchair yells. She calms from her manic state. "Liz, we believe Eli faked his death to protect this information from everyone."

Her body relaxes; her shoulders release their tension. She turns to the man.

"But, why?"

The man wheels closer to Liz taking her hand.

"He's part of an organization that knows information about the end of the world."

"The what?" Liz tenses the muscles in her legs eyeing the front door.

"Do you recall the pictures with the codes we sent you?"

"Uh, yeah... you mean those of 9/11 and different wars over time?"

"Yes, we believe the organization responsible for faking his death was also behind those events."

"But, why? What could my Eli have anything to do with all that?"

Liz paces the floor.

"Did Eli say anything to you about something called The Eden Foundation?"

Liz paces in silence.

"Uh, you mean like from the Bible?"

"Not exactly... what about *this* symbol?" Ruth holds a picture of a red circle inside a red triangle all outlined in white. "Does this mean anything to you?"

Liz takes the photo from Ruth. She stops in the middle of the room.

"Huh, I've seen this before... " Liz paces again. " ...I'm not sure... "

"That symbol is used by a group called The Eden Foundation as a way for its members to identify each other," the man said.

"Identify each other?"

"Eden has members across the world in various positions of power or control. It's worn as a pin or a patch on clothing."

"Ha, that's it! I have seen this before. It looks like a pin my grandson used to have?" Liz moves the picture closer to her face. "It's been a long time, but I think it looked like this."

"Your grandson, Joseph. Where did he get it?" Ruth asked.

"I remember he used to wear it for good luck in college. He got it from Rachel, his mom, but... " Liz studies the picture more. "But, I remember her telling me my Jacob gave it to her and it had the university's name on it."

"And, Jacob, he's your son, right?" the man asked.

"Yes, my son."

Ruth, Luther, and the man look at each other. The answer comes before the question, but the man wants to test her reaction.

"Oh shit, what the hell was *that*?" Ruth said as she rushes to the door, "outside... I thought I heard something."

Luther steps to the only window beside the front door and peeks through the curtain.

"See anything?" Ruth asked.

He leans from the window and lifts the waistband of his shirt. Luther holds a black Glock 26.

"I'll check it out," Luther said.

The sight of the gun pushes Liz to the back corner of the room as Ruth follows behind Luther out the door. A few moments later, they return.

"It was nothing. We didn't see anyone," Ruth said.

As the front door closes, the excitement leaves the room. Liz's question breaks the silence.

"The end of the world... what did you mean by this?"

Luther and Ruth stand guard on either side of the window's curtain. The man inches his chair to Liz.

"So, Eli never told you anything about it during his time with NASA, what he was working on?"

Liz leans against the empty barrel.

"Eli worked on the Apollo Program and was on the navigation team in Mission Control," she said.

"That was his official role, but did he ever talk to you about his work?" the man asked.

The watch she had given Eli many Christmases ago presses against her skin as she leans on her wrist. Quick memories of her dead husband rush to Liz.

DECEMBER 25, 2003 – 8:15 P.M.
WAREHOUSE DISTRICT, SE HOUSTON, TEXAS

ONE HOUR EARLIER...

Headlights from a blue Toyota illuminates the parking lot as Liz drives from the Houston Airport Ramada Inn. At the far end of the lot in the shadows, Eli follows Liz in his black pickup truck without its lights. He remains far enough behind to view Liz as he turns on his lights joining the rest of the airport traffic.

Three vehicles behind as Liz stops at the light, Eli wrenches his hands on the truck's steering wheel. The distance remains between them as Liz turns left moving through the vast number of warehouses used by air freight companies.

The traffic thins as Liz turns right onto Highway 3-North heading toward downtown Houston. Yellow flashing emanates from the rear-right turn signal, as she pulls into an empty parking lot of a small, brick building. Liz parks in the spot closest to the two, front doors in the center of the building.

Lights from the following truck disappear as it passes the lot. Eli slows his forward momentum careful not to touch the brake pedal to draw unwanted attention. The truck passes the building and coasts into a parking lot within sight.

A smile creeps across his toothless face as Liz steps from the Toyota and enters the left door which closes behind her. Eli holds his hand on the door handle to leave his vehicle.

Blinding lights flash his face as a candy-apple, red Corvette pulls into the parking lot followed by a pale-blue van. Eli releases the handle pulling down his black, Yankee's cap over his face. He peeks from under the brim spying a woman exit the Corvette going to the van helping its driver exit in a wheelchair.

Eli pulls his hat back into position. The man in the wheelchair is familiar to him as his heart pounds under his gray jacket.

Why after Liz? Eli thinks.

After escaping from Greystone Psychiatric Hospital, Eli had led a nomadic life. His jagged memories fade in-and-out. The injury sustained from Jacob lingers. Complete sentences and memories remain incomplete.

Eli's lucid memories come to him as haunted, dream-like sequences. However, he was sure of two things: Eden cannot track his location given his self-inflicted dental procedure, and Jacob will surely kill him next time.

Conflicting sensations overcame Eli over the following years. Feelings of guilt have antagonized his knowledge he was only doing what he thought was right to save humanity. But, memories of his plans for Salvation and the reason for its development never reappeared in his mind.

After running away from Joseph's high school graduation, Eli had spent four years hidden near Santa Fe, New Mexico, biding time as a ranch helper. One day, no one had shown up outside the barn where he would meet the workers each morning.

A pickup truck had roared passed the barn with torrents of dust spinning behind the Dodge Ram. Gravel flew through the air as the truck skidded to a stop. The ranch owner yelled at Eli to get inside where he drove Eli to his house on top the hill.

Once inside, the owner joined the other ranch hands and his family in the living room of the one-hundred-year-old white, farmhouse. Everyone huddled around a television in the room. Several people cried as scenes of the North and South Towers of the World Trade Center fell.

The billowing smoke above New York City seemed to push Eli from the house. Eli ran down the hill; he continued running east, back to Pasadena, Texas. A familiar feeling ached over him; the crashing buildings replayed in his mind. He knew Eden had to be involved.

Eli had vowed to protect Liz from that moment. Upon arriving in Pasadena, a roadside motel near the interstate provided him a room for fifteen dollars a night.

The motel was close. Eli would walk behind Liz's house and watch over her from his hidden vantage point in the bushes.

With age, the constant walking took its toll on his sixty-five-year-old body. A rusted-out, pickup truck had a *for sale* sign in its back window at the motel parking lot. The driver only wanted two-hundred dollars.

After having followed Liz from her house, shock came to Eli as he followed her to the parking lot of the Houston International Airport. He was unsure how he could follow her once she boarded a plane.

Eli was leaving the airport arrival area. In his rearview mirror, he saw Liz walking out of the terminal to the bus area. She had a very different appearance, almost unrecognizable to him.

Gone was her flowery blouse and skirt. Liz wore gray sweatpants and a black hooded sweatshirt. Eli followed the Ramada Inn shuttle bus with Liz inside to the hotel as he parked in the far corner away from the hotel's entrance. A few hours later, he witnessed Liz walk across the parking lot in front of him. He followed the Toyota as they left the hotel.

Now, sitting in a dark parking lot across from the building after following Liz, Eli sees Jackson in his wheelchair enter the same left-side door. A woman follows him closing the door.

Eli has not seen Jackson since his time with Eden. His memories still not fully recovered, he cannot recall Jackson's role with the Foundation which was to monitor Liz. Eli closes his eyes shaking his head trying to clear his mind.

His eyes open fast-and-wide. Eli remembers he had run Jackson off the road at the Palomar Observatory, but he could not recall, why?

A sudden sense of concern comes to Eli. *Is this his revenge?*

The cloud-covered sky chases the moonlight. Most of the streetlights are out in the parking lot. Darkness is the perfect cover for Eli as he leaves his truck and sneaks behind the building. Only windows with closed blinds are in the front of the building. Blank, brick walls make up the sides and rear.

His breath pushes out in the cool air from his lips and nose as he walks the complete perimeter of the building. Having watched everyone enter the left door, Eli props a crowbar, which he had taken as protection from his truck, into the slat between the frame and door. With a quick motion, the right door opens.

At the same time as Eli had closed and locked the door behind him, he hears the other front door open. Eli's heart pounds. He holds his breath. The beating pulsates from his chest to his ears. He holds his left-hand flat against the back of the door while pulling the crowbar over his head with his right.

The whispers Eli hears in the other room vanish as the front door opens-and-closes, again. Eli lowers the crowbar and releases his grip on the front door. His breathing returns to normal.

Voices come murmured from the closed door between the two offices. Eli presses his ear against the door. The voices grow louder but remain unclear.

Eli jars his head back as Liz's voice shouts. The raised voices come loud to Eli.

"I don't know what you're talkin' about?" Liz said.

"I think you are lying." Eli heard the woman following Jackson say.

Eli stands unsure what to do. In his hand is only the crowbar. He knows Liz is inside with the woman and Jackson. Eli plots his rescue.

He lifts the metal bar to the door hinge. As it contacts the metal, he hears the woman scream from the other side.

"Oh God, I think she is having a heart attack."

Eli hears an unfamiliar man's, deep voice.

"Quick, hold her head."

"Is she breathing? Does she have a pulse?" Jackson asked.

A few seconds had passed.

"Shit! What now, Boss?" the man's voice said.

"Goddammit, goddammit," the woman said repeating her words.

"Leave her. We need to get out of here. Her lawyer is next door, so that can explain why she is here," Jackson said.

"But, Boss— "

"Luther, go! You and Ruth leave. We can't be seen carrying a body. It's over," Jackson said.

Eli holds the crowbar against the door.

A trick? Liz okay?

As Eli stands contemplating what to do, the front door opens-and-closes in the other room from Eli. Two cars speed from the parking lot. Silence returns to the building.

With a sudden push, Eli presses the crowbar through the space between the latch and doorframe. A sliver of light from the parking lot slips under the window blinds across Liz's face.

She holds her bottom jaw gaped apart. Both eyes are frozen open in horror.

"Elizabeth! Elizabeth!" Eli screams. "Elizabeth! Oh, no… Elizabeth!"

He presses his right ear against her chest. Calmness overcomes him for a moment as he has stood over many a dead body in the past. Terror returns as her lifeless body lays limp against the barrels.

A moment of clarity returns to Eli. He slips his arms under his wife's lifeless body and carries her from the building to his truck. Heavy breathing fogs the front windshield as Eli starts his vehicle and returns to the airport satellite, parking lot.

Eli is thankful a space is available beside Liz's car. He parks and catches his breath. Eli slides down in his seat and watches across the area for any sign of people. Certain he is alone, Eli exits his truck and unlocks Liz's car with the keys he finds in her pocket.

He lifts her body from his truck and positions her behind the steering wheel of her car. He presses his lips against the top of her cold forehead. Tears stream from his eyes falling to her face.

He feels a lump on her wrist causing him to look at her arms. A familiar stainless steel watch looks back to him. Eli slips the watch from her wrist and places it on his.

"I will love you forever, Elizabeth. I'm so, so sorry," Eli said in the most lucid sentence he has managed in six years.

Eli returns to his truck and leaves the parking lot. An orange-hue breaks through the clouds as the moonlight shines over Houston.

15 - REVENGE

ELI LEFT LIZ'S BODY in her car at the airport. His pickup truck drives a reasonable pace from the complex returning to Chatham Estates. He turns onto Chatham Lane; his headlights darken as he parks at the dead-end of the street.

He leaves his truck walking four blocks to the rear of Liz's house propping open the door. His instincts force him inside without turning on any lights.

Absent twenty-eight-years, familiar smells lead Eli through the darkness of the house. He remembers his way through the kitchen walking to the living room. The corduroy arm of *his old* chair greets him.

He sits leaning his head back. Gasps of air fill the room between deep sobs. His memory remains jagged, but he knows what he has done. Guilt consumes him feeling responsible for Liz's death, tonight.

His elbow slams against a book on the small table next to the chair. Eli reaches into his shirt pocket. The flicker of a short flame from a cigarette lighter highlights the book.

With his right hand, Eli flips open the cover while holding the lighter in his left. Light dances across the plastic-protected pages revealing photos of Liz and him. A quick puff leaves his lips causing the flame to extinguish.

He flicks the lighter turning more pages. Pictures of Jacob emerge causing him to flip multiple pages at a time. Close to the end of the book, Eli pauses. Something familiar stares at him, a string of numbers.

Eli rubs his fingers across Liz's handwriting below the numbers. The plastic page crinkles with the contact. Liz had written the words, *I am alive*, at the bottom of the page.

He turns the last pages. More strings of numbers appear below pictures of world events. Liz had solved coded messages explaining the images.

Was Liz involved with Eden?

A rumbling noise from the front yard forces Eli to slam the book closed. He peeks through the narrow, door window. A red Corvette pulls into the driveway.

Eli runs to the kitchen and exits the back door as the front door opens. He hides in the bushes below the kitchen window. A perfect hiding place giving Eli the ability to listen inside through the thin window panes.

"Luther, get those microphones you placed in here," Ruth said.

Last year, Luther had visited Liz's house disguised as a cable repairman. Liz had allowed him access where he installed listening devices in the home.

A crash of books comes from the living room.

"Dammit, Luther, don't ransack the place. We don't want it to seem like someone murdered her."

"What else are we looking for?"

"Anything that can connect us to her. Dad's working on our next plan to locate him."

"Hey, check *this* out... aren't *these* the pictures you sent to her?"

Luther hands Ruth the scrapbook Eli had been reviewing. She inspects the book.

"Jesus, she kept it... and all of 'em... look for another book because I sent her several of these."

"Shit!" Luther yells kicking his shin on the corduroy chair.

Eli ducks unsure if someone had discovered his hiding place in the outside bushes.

A few minutes had passed. Luther paws over the bookshelf, while Ruth studies the sheet with the words, *I am alive* written on it. She rubs the missing center-section of the paper torn with frayed edges.

"Found it."

"Here, let me see… yep, they're all here… good. Is there any place else you think of? We need to find this section of the paper with the numbers and letters I wrote. It looks like she tore it out of here for some reason."

"Well— "

"Well, what? It's important… we need to locate the missing piece."

"Come over *here*."

Luther leads Ruth to an antique, roll-top desk.

"Sure, it's probably in there," Ruth said.

He lifts open the covering. An elegant wood-grain surface appears in the soft glimmer of Luther's flashlight. Ruth examines the different slots searching for the paper.

"So, when I was here last year… I put a microphone… *here*."

Luther stretches under the tabletop removing a small wire.

"Feel under *there*," Luther said pulling Ruth's hand to the bottom of the desk four inches from the floor.

"Rub it… don't feel anything do you?"

"No… should I?"

A loud bang slams on the tabletop as Luther pounds his fist against the surface. A muffled pop comes from where Ruth had her hand.

"After I installed the wire, I was crawling out and hit my head under *here*."

Luther points to the area under the desktop where one's legs fit when seated.

"I heard that pop, and I thought I had broken something."

Ruth bends down on her knees, her head sideways against the floor as she shines a light under the desk.

"Holy shit… it's a hidden drawer."

Ruth slips her hand inside and pulls out a small section of white paper. In the light, she turns it overseeing a rectangular set of letters and numbers.

"Damn, Luther... that's it... this is it."

Ruth rubs the paper she had written on six-years earlier. She stands holding the paper, then paces in the darkness of the bedroom.

"Luther, I've got an idea... she hid this *there* for a reason... she either didn't want someone to find it or hid it knowing that this is the place only someone who knew where this drawer is would look for something?"

"I don't follow... what's your idea."

"Jeez, give me a moment."

Ruth continues pacing in the darkness. Eli lifts his head to listen better.

"Okay, there's only one person alive left in Liz's family."

"Her grandson?"

"Yeah, Joseph."

"So?"

"If anyone, he's the only person who could know about this hidden drawer?"

Luther bends down examining the desk.

"Guess, that's possible."

"What if we send those scrapbooks to him with a note saying the truth is hidden in the desk... then, Joseph will know where to find the matrix and associate it with the photos in the book?"

"But, how does this help us find Eli?"

Eli pokes his head from the bushes looking through the window after hearing his name.

"We don't know if Joseph knows where he is? But, if we make him discover this matrix, he'll ask questions... maybe he knows something or where he is and will reach out to find him... we can follow Joseph to him."

Luther stands as he moans stretching his back.

"Okay, but how do you just send Joseph a box of pictures and a note out of the blue from his dead grandma?"

Ruth turns to Luther.

"You're right... that may make her death look suspicious... we can't have that... "

"How does this sound? Liz is dead—"

"But, we didn't kill her," Luther said interrupting Ruth.

"Yes, but someone will find her... what was that building we were in you found?"

"Jackson told me to find a secluded place, and I did... it only had a law office next door."

Ruth paces more.

"That's it... we need to go back there and move her body so someone will find her," Ruth said as she pulled Luther's hand toward the front door.

Eli listens but cannot hear any more talking from inside the house. Lights creep around the edges of the walls following the rumble of the Corvette.

Eli lowers his body to the ground. His back leans against the vinyl siding.

"Joseph... "

Eli stands running from the backyard. Four blocks away the faint purr of the truck starts and passes the house. A long drive is ahead of Eli.

JANUARY 15, 2004 (3 WEEKS LATER)
STONY BROOK, LONG ISLAND — NEW YORK

STONY BROOK IN JANUARY can be brutal in January. A nighttime chill follows an unusually warm afternoon. Large, fat snowflakes fill the early evening air across the Stony Brook campus.

Crunching below his feet follows Eli through the snow as he lingers in the shadows of a two-story apartment building. He had arrived in Stony Brook two weeks ago trying to locate his grandson, Joseph.

Eli's protective instinct was to find him to ensure his safety. He had driven the eighteen-hundred-mile trip to Stony Brook... a drive Eli knew well. Upon arrival, he searched for Joseph but could not find him for two weeks causing him extreme concern.

Joe was not in Stony Brook. He was with Mary in Texas attending his grandmother's funeral. Airport paramedics had ruled her death a heart attack upon arrival to her parked car.

While in Pasadena, Joe and Mary visited the law offices of Robert Spivey for the reading of Liz's will, unaware last week she had died next door. They left disappointed with his childhood home being given to Liz's church. The only items Joe would receive were old pictures and an antique desk which had belonged to his grandfather, Eli.

Luther had played a convincing role as Spivey as did Ruth as his secretary. Jackson's instruction to them was to do what was necessary to find Eli. To them, what was required meant killing both the attorney and his secretary to meet with Joseph and Mary.

Laughter emerges through the falling snow from the sidewalk startling Eli. He jumps behind a bush growing white with the passing seconds. His sixty-five-year-old knees crack as he squats out of sight.

"Joe, it's so beautiful, tonight," the woman said.

Eli watches as she sticks out her tongue trying to catch one of the many snowflakes. Joe stretches his hands out from his waist, his palms face-up to the sky.

"Yeah, it's crazy, Mary. A few days ago, we were in eighty-degree weather back home in Texas," Joe said.

Two flakes land on her tongue as she pulls herself closer to Joe. Through the growing snowfall, Eli watches as Joe and Mary approach the building where he is hiding.

"We better not get sick because of it..." Mary pauses as she hugs Joe's arm tight. She looks up into his eyes. "That's the first time you've said the word *home* when talking about Texas in a long time."

Eli ensures they do not see him. His black jacket merges with the dark shadows and the white specks collecting on the wool fabric.

He remains frozen crouched in the bushes. A large book presses into his ribcage protected by his overcoat. The sharp pain eases as Eli looks under his jacket and pushes the corner from his side.

I will not allow you to get pulled into this by Eden.

With Eli's thoughts, he rubs the book under his coat.

The sky grows whiter as the canopy of falling snow causes the front-stoop lights above the door to shine. Light illuminates above Eli's head as he remains hidden. The plastic-coated pages reflect the overhead luminescence.

Flickering catches his attention away from the young couple as he fingers through the book. Eli recognizes Liz's handwriting.

He caresses his fingers above the letters and numbers she had written with a black Sharpie pen. Underneath the writing, several pictures are familiar to Eli.

The photos are not of people at least anyone he knew. They are of the World Trade Center, children stricken with famine, and battle scenes from the Middle East. The horrific images stay unnoticed as Eli smiles reminiscing over his wife's handwriting. The cold air shocks his toothless gums.

"Mary," Joe said returning Eli's attention to the young couple, "this whole funeral thing got me thinking. We should try to have a baby."

Eli shoves the book deep under his jacket. The pain is numb in his side as he stalks the couple.

Snow-muffled footsteps grow closer. Eli shrinks even smaller beside the steps to their apartment.

The door opens; clunking sounds escape from the entry. Four feet stomp against the wall knocking the sticky snow off their shoes.

"Mary? Did you lock the door when you left?"

Eli hears the faint question from the other side of the closed door. Before the couple had returned, Eli entered their apartment searching for the scrapbook. He was determined not to have his grandson involved with Eden.

Foot impressions in the snow lead from behind the bush down the sidewalk into the veil of the white night. Eli walks away from the apartment building.

A unique phenomenon occurs as snow covers the ground; silence. It not only blankets everything in white but provides a perfect sound-dampening effect. Through the quiet, an engine hums as a van slowly drives toward the apartment.

This sound captures Eli stopping his progress. He darts between another row of bushes as a familiar vehicle passes his hideout.

Through the fogged windows, Eli witnesses Jackson behind the wheel with the same woman Eli had seen with him in Texas in the front passenger seat.

Heat burns through Eli's chest. He clenches his fists tight. Eli remains hidden holding back his urge to charge the van. Jackson continues the vehicle's slow progression through the snow-covered street turning right at the stoplight.

Eli bolts from his position running through a courtyard behind Joe & Mary's apartment. Jackson drives down another alley away from the courtyard. The snow glows red making the van a natural object to follow given its slow pace through the night.

A quarter-of-a-mile away, the van pulls into a driveway of blue row-home. Eli pants; his breath hangs in the snowy air. Eli stops short of the home.

The passenger door opens followed by the side-wall. Jackson lowers himself in his wheelchair to the ground. A strange man to Eli exits the house. Eli watched as the man goes to Jackson pushing his chair into the building as the woman follows.

A few minutes had passed. Silence reigns in the neighborhood. A light interrupts the darkness shining in the backyard.

Eli steps through the snow toward the house. The bottom of the windows is at his eye-level as he balances his toes on the ground. He peeks inside. Through the darkness, Eli makes out the faint outline of a naked woman straddling the man.

Eli continues to opposite side of the house attracted by a light. He peeks inside the window. Jackson sits in the kitchen reading a newspaper. Eli clenches his fists.

The snow crunches as Eli lowers his feet to the ground. He turns around and shuffles through the thickening ground cover returning to the courtyard and his parked truck.

Snow falls heavier; a perfect canopy hiding Eli's vehicle.

Hours had passed. A bright, white light chases the darkness from the windshield. The morning sun rises warming the snowy landscape. Eli rolls his window down and punches his fist through the snow.

Cold shivers through his bare left hand as he clears a small path on the front window. Jackson's row-home is in view.

Another hour had passed. Eli has fallen asleep. Jackson's van starting awakens him.

Jackson and the man drive from the house followed by the woman in a red Corvette. The car's 450hp engine manages its way through the plowed streets near campus.

Eli waits. Silence returns. He exits his truck. The sun has chased away the previous evening's clouds. It is a beautiful day.

JANUARY 16, 2004 (THE NEXT DAY)
STONY BROOK, LONG ISLAND — NEW YORK

NIGHT FALLS. The day's sun and warming temperatures have melted most of the fallen snow from the previous night. The area around campus bustles with students emerging from their short-term hibernation.

Through the student-filled streets, a blue van and red Corvette return. Luther and Ruth help Jackson inside the home. The three sit in the front living room.

"So, Boss, we've followed them for a few days, now... not a damn thing," Luther said between gulps of his cold Mountain Dew.

"How long are we staying, here? It's so fuckin' cold," Ruth said glaring at her father.

"Until we get a sense if Joseph can lead us to his grandfather," Jackson said.

"I still find it strange that someone moved Liz's body before we even got back there," Luther said finishing his soda.

"I've told you both; the Foundation was surely watching her. Hell, that was my job for the longest time," Jackson said.

"Do you think they are watching us, now?" Luther said.

Jackson pauses. "I don't know. We've kept such a low-profile for the last three years... that's why we have to make this quick to see what Joseph knows."

Luther stands pacing the living room.

"Let's just grab him and bring him here to talk."

"Sit down, Dumbass," Ruth said.

"God, I hope it doesn't take too long. We'll watch him a few more days to see if he acts differently after finding the hidden matrix," Jackson said as he wheels his chair to the kitchen.

"Ruth, this was your idea to send the scrapbook with the pictures to Joseph. So, now we just wait to see what happens."

"I hope we didn't make too big of a deal out of hiding the picture and matrix in that desk," Luther said injecting his way into the conversation.

"No, I agree with Ruth. Joseph probably doesn't know his grandfather is alive. If we make it seem like his grandmother was hiding a secret and communicated it to him in her will, then maybe after he finds those things in the desk, he will try to find Eli," Jackson said.

"Well, I delivered the box with the picture albums and scrapbooks yesterday, so I guess we just have to wait," Luther said. "Plus, we killed that lawyer and his secretary to create this plan, so we need to let this play out."

Their conversation frustrates Jackson. His plans for uncovering Eden's true intentions are falling apart.

For years, one question has infuriated Jackson. He needs Eli for the answer. *Did the Eden Foundation know about Columba Noachi?*

"Okay, that's enough for now. We'll figure out our plans for monitoring Joseph, tomorrow. I'm going to take a shower if you two will fix dinner."

"Sure thing, Boss," Luther said as he stood pulling Ruth's hand lifting her from the sofa.

Jackson rolls his chair into the bathroom at the end of the hall. Ruth and Luther enter the kitchen yelling at each other.

"What the hell?" Luther said.

"Just shut up and heat the leftover beef stroganoff."

"That shit was nasty."

"Sorry, make yourself a goddam sandwich then, I don't give a shit."

Jackson spins his chair around in the cramped bathroom. He places his right hand on the doorknob.

"Do you smell that?" Jackson hears Ruth ask as he stops short of closing the bathroom door.

"Yeah, it smells like gas," Luther replied after a few seconds.

Jackson hears quick chirps coming from the microwave.

"Don't press start!" Ruth screams.

Her command prompts a flight instinct from Jackson. In an instant motion, Jackson slams the bathroom door shut pushing his chair backward. He throws himself into the white, porcelain-enameled cast iron bathtub.

Searing heat and a roaring flame of orange fire rush behind Jackson's falling body in the tub. The moment his body falls hard against the bottom, an avalanche of caustic air ejects the tub through the back wall of the house.

Mud and snow splash through the air as the tub tumbles across the backyard. Jackson remains flat against the bottom given the centrifugal force of the rolling tub.

Billowing, black smoke presses from the home like escaping kettle steam. The tub slows its rotation as Jackson slams hard against the cold gravel in the yard.

His eyes focus on the burning building. Warm blood oozes from his nostrils down the side of his left cheek pooling under his head. Jackson had long lost any sensation in his legs from the Palomar accident forty-four-years earlier. He is unsure of the extent of his current injuries.

Even though that accident had happened long ago, the memories flood over him. The sensation of being on the ground watching a billowing fire is too familiar. His entire body goes numb.

At this moment, Jackson knows Ruth and Luther are dead. Jackson's breathing grows difficult; his eyes open-and-close at a slowing pace. The last image Jackson maintains his focus on is a small picture on the ground facing him which has fallen from his shirt pocket.

A blood-soaked smile appears on Jackson as the image becomes clear; his young wife, Tina, holding their infant daughter, Ruth. Darkness fills Jackson's eyes. A deep sigh escapes his lips.

Black smoke and orange flames rush high into the sky from the back of the row-home. Headlights of the parked pickup truck illuminate on the opposite side of the courtyard.

Red brake lights disappear as the truck lunges forward. Eli's grip on the steering wheel releases as he drives away from the raging fire disappearing into campus. The flames grow dim in his rearview mirror.

Eli has his revenge.

16-R.I.P.

SWEAT DUMPS FROM Eli's face hunched over a desktop computer. A cold spell this week has forced, the Kave Internet Café on Roosevelt Street in Brooklyn, to not use their air conditioner. Today's unexpected return to eighty-degree temperatures makes it uncomfortable.

Eli slips off his gray jacket. Yellow stains run the length of his backside from his armpits. The salty beads of sweat streak through the jagged scar on his face from under his faded, black Yankees cap.

The heat does not concern Eli. He focuses his attention on the computer screen with a lukewarm cup of coffee beside his keyboard. His presence is a common site to the patrons. At seventy-six-years-old, they know Eli as the old man in the corner.

Kave has been his refuge over the past years. With his computer experience during his early NASA days, Eli is a master of hiding his location online. His tool of choice is a virtual private network application, which hides his IP address. But, he is aware any internet expert can easily decipher his actual location if they know how to follow the cookie trail.

Eli masks his IP address through the VPN stringing together thirty-two proxy servers connecting to his final location. This spiderweb of virtual connections makes it almost impossible to trace his location from anyone trying to locate him.

He was one of the first internet hackers with the ways he had accessed global observatories in the past. Eli needed to know if any observatory had scanned the *Columba Noachi* Constellation, and if so, did they discover CIE.57.20?

Today, Eli has one target with his hack; his grandson Joseph's computer. While Eli can never make his presence known to him, virtually Eli can watch his online activities.

Last month, Eli had accessed Joseph's email from The Eden Foundation. The email was their invitation for Joseph to deliver a presentation about his scientific research. A shiver had shot through Eli's body upon seeing the sender.

This realization troubles Eli, who is unsure of his son Jacob's intentions. For years, Eli had no indications Eden had been monitoring Joseph.

But, there it was, an email and a link to a webpage. As the page opened, Eli recalls the hairs on his arms standing electrified. A familiar logo had spun on the screen; one he had created for the Foundation fifty years, ago.

The future of mankind is your responsibility.

Eli had read the words to himself as they scrolled across the screen.

"Can I bring you another coffee?" a petite waitress asked Eli.

The question startles Eli, who blocks the screen with his hat. An equally startled face returns her stare to him as she steps against the wall.

With his removed head covering, Eli is bald with patches of hair in various spots around his scalp. The jagged scar on his cheek snakes its way up to his right temple across the top of his forehead where his hairline should be.

Eli's missing teeth are visible as he snarls his displeasure at the waitress who rushes to the front of the small café. He replaces his hat and continues reading Joseph's email.

Years had passed since Eli's encounter with the end of a metal pipe by Jacob. Time is a wonderful healer for memory and speech. But, sudden motions or loud noises jar Eli back to primal grunts.

"Who is *that?*" the new waitress said to the young owner standing by the air conditioner controls.

The owner turns to the direction the waitress points. "Oh, George... he's been coming by for years, almost every day."

"He looks... scary," the waitress said turning her attention back to the owner.

"Oh, he's harmless. He always sits at the same terminal and keeps to himself. I usually bring him just a small black coffee."

"Old school."

"Yeah, for sure. I feel sad for him. He's always wearing the same clothes and that hat," the owner said.

"I bet. You're a Mets fan."

"Yep. I don't hold that against him, though. He's a paying customer and tips well and never bothers anyone."

The conversation with the owner helps, but for the days following, she still refuses eye contact with Eli when he visits Kave.

Since discovering the invitation, Eli had struggled with what he should do. Does he intervene and stop his grandson from joining? Or, should he do nothing? Maybe Joseph will be safe in five years when the Earth ends?

Eli knows whatever his decision, Joseph will never know the full extinct to which Eden has gone to protect Salvation... the full extent of things Eli had been responsible for performing.

One thing is clear to Eli. He knows if he tries to contact Joseph, it may jeopardize his location. Eli knows the Foundation must be monitoring his grandson... that's what he would do.

As a child, Eli's unique talent was his ability to remember any list of numbers or words he reviewed. He later self-diagnosed himself as having Eidetic or photographic memory. As he grew older, Eli could glance at something for only a second and recall it at any time in the future.

This ability has eluded him for twenty-years since the blow against his head. Now, the images return drowning the manic voices in his head.

One vivid memory is crystal-clear. He recalls the night Liz had died and his standing in her living room flipping through her scrapbook, which he later had stolen from Joseph.

The string of numbers which Liz had solved yielded the words; *I am alive.* Since the method of the encoded matrix was Eli's creation, he reverse-engineered the result to create the original matrix.

Before Eli had run away from Liz's home that night, he remembers overhearing the woman and the man who had been with Jackson talking. She had told him her plan of hiding the matrix in the desk to manipulate Joseph to find it and possibly search for Eli.

Eli sits behind the computer remembering the conversation.

I wonder if Joseph found the matrix… if so, I can reach out to him and warn him about Salvation.

Eli logs into xmail.com and creates an account. He copies pictures online of JFK, Princess Diana, Oklahoma City, 9/11, and various viruses; and composes his email.

Using the original matrix from the scrapbook which Eli has determined, he types a string of numbers at the bottom below the pictures: *5.1 3.5 2.5 5.2 3.5 1.4 2.4 3.1 1.2*

He sends his email to Joseph configuring it to transmit at 12:56 a.m. to further disguise his location. Joseph will receive an email from Eli only identified as *friend@xmail.com.*

Eli hopes his grandson can connect the photos to the code he sent. Once deciphered, it will read as *SALVATION.*

Aware the Foundation may be monitoring Joe's internet activity, Eli avoids any keywords associated together with Eden, Mars, the end of the world. Eli feels safe sending the single word, Salvation as his encoded message.

With a quick chug of his cold coffee, Eli logs off his computer terminal and leaves Kave. He disappears among the pedestrian crowd in the new, trendy Brooklyn neighborhood.

His familiar friend, paranoia, returns to him as he passes people.

Was I too careless sending that?

Did I put Joseph in danger?

Is Jacob able to locate me?

As Eli wonders through the crowd, he is unaware Jacob is no longer on Earth but had left years ago assuming command at Salvation. Jacob's replacement at Eden, Gabriel D'Angelo, has taken over operations of the Foundation.

This email and its pictures will send an alert to the Foundation. A new threat has appeared to Salvation.

OCTOBER 4, 2015 (3 WEEKS LATER) STONY BROOK, LONG ISLAND – NEW YORK

SINCE SENDING HIS EMAIL to Joseph, Eli no longer visits the internet café. It is too risky. He has returned to Stony Brook to watch over his grandson.

Eli is quick to acknowledge his need to change his appearance. He must blend into the surroundings on campus as best he can given his age and injury.

He enters his hotel room across from the campus parking deck carrying a shopping bag. Inside, Eli has new clothes, toiletries, and foundation makeup.

The white lights of the bathroom flicker as Eli flips up the wall power switch. He removes his hat holding it on the countertop beside the sink. With a heavy sigh, he releases the hat into the darkness of an empty, black trash bag. The hat, a Christmas present from Liz many years ago, is gone.

Eli stands silent for minutes in the bathroom. The mirror reflects his weathered age of seventy-six years.

He rubs the patches of hair over his scalp. Shaving cream squirts in his hand. With one quick motion, his scalp becomes white. The cream is cold on his head.

With each stroke of the disposable razor, water races down his face finding the jagged scar an easy escape path. Eli lowers his head into the sink splashing hot water on his shaven head standing after a few seconds.

Water drops from his face drenching the gray hairs curled on his shoulders and chest. Steam rises from his cold scalp. He dries himself with the hanging, white hotel towel.

From the shopping bag, Eli holds a tube of makeup primer. He presses the tube's end; tan-colored makeup emerges from the opening.

His fingers are sticky as he applies the primer across the scar which leads from his right temple down across his cheek. The scar is a painful reminder of his son, Jacob, and his taking control of The Eden Foundation from him.

He follows the primer application with two tubes of color-correcting, makeup fluid; green to cancel the redness of the scar and yellow to cancel the purple tones held within the injury. Eli daps the liquid with a small sponge blending each color.

The green and yellow fluids mix appearing as a light bruise across his face. Eli uses a brush to apply concealer to his skin followed by talc powder to set the total application. This is not the first time Eli has applied makeup to conceal his identity.

After fifteen minutes of application, Eli lowers his face close to the mirror. The jagged scar, which had been his visible reminder for twenty years, has disappeared.

He realizes with his age, he can easily assume the role as a tenured professor allowing him entry into classrooms and laboratories. He needs to get closer to Joseph.

Days had passed. Eli walks unnoticed by Joseph in the hallways of the various campus buildings and within the Stonehaven Laboratories. With each passing, Eli looks for any visible signs of distress in his grandson.

The university campus is serene in early October. Golden, fat maple leaves float from the sky; the trees prepare for the onslaught of another Long Island winter.

One day, Eli observes an erratic behavior from Joseph. He follows him in-and-out of multiple businesses along Main Street, even exiting through the back of a theater.

Joseph's actions are evident to Eli of not wanting to be followed. Eli recognizes the paranoia; he had performed the same moves before many times.

A golden canopy of trees hides a flowing creek through campus. Eli shadows Joseph from a distance as they stop walking. Sixty-feet is too far to hear his grandson.

Eli reaches behind him to a small bag strapped across his back. He holds an iPhone and places a Bluetooth earbud over his left ear. His phone vibrates as he opens an app.

He lifts the phone to his face simulating a video call. Rather than video, the opened app allows for minimal sounds to amplify in his ear. Eli listens as Joseph talks to himself in the distance.

Joseph paces back-and-forth. Eli senses his grandson's nervousness as he appears to be waiting for someone. After ten minutes, Eli sees a large, black man approach Joseph. Eli knows from his weeks of following Joseph, this man is his best friend, Charlie.

"Boo!" Eli hears Charlie say sneaking behind Joseph who jumps spinning in the air.

"Damnit, Charlie! Scared the shit out of me."

"Sorry, Man. Couldn't resist. You've been fun to watch walking and talking to yourself."

"Oh… uh… yeah."

"That's okay. I do it now all the time… here's your beer."

Eli watches as the two friends share their beer while he overhears their conversation from a safe distance. Joe confesses he had concerns someone could be following them.

The two walk away from the trail to a large collection of boulders juxtaposed against the creekside and the grass bank. Eli positions himself on the other side of the path, closer to them.

Golden leaves enrapture everyone offering an appearance of being trapped inside a yellow snow globe. A colorful scene of contradiction to the darkness of his grandson's confessions to Charlie about Colorado, of the coming obliteration of Earth in five years, and of Salvation on Mars.

Eli stands dumbfounded. Old instincts creep over him. He had performed the most horrendous actions in his past protecting the secret of Salvation. And, here, his grandson is divulging the secrets in public. The conversation Eli overhears creates an uneasiness inside him. Dread consumes Eli.

"You know how crazy you sound?" Charlie asked Joseph. "No way in hell is that going to happen… "

"The organization has done terrible things to protect its plans," Joe said.

"Sounds like all this conspiracy theory shit about 9/11 being perpetrated by the government or some evil corporation or something."

A snorting laugh comes from Eli hearing Charlie. His comment brings Eli a sudden, clear thought.

There's nothing theoretical about anything Joseph is saying.

"Next, you're going to tell me you know who the second shooter was who killed JFK?"

Eli drops his phone catching it before it crashes against the gravel pathway. Crunching beer cans recapture Eli's attention as he sees both friends leaving the area splitting their path between them.

Joseph heads down along the creek, while Charlie walks up the hill to the student quad. By instinct, Eli follows Charlie.

Students loiter about the grassy area between buildings. It is a beautiful sunny day. Eli remains in the shadows of the tree-line watching Charlie cross the yard to the bicycle rack.

Eli knows where Charlie lives on the other side of campus. Rather than follow on foot behind Charlie, Eli returns into the woods and crosses over the creek taking a short-cut across campus.

After a few minutes of pulling himself through the thick underbrush on the other side of the creek, Eli emerges from the trees walking down the sidewalk of Charlie's neighborhood.

He stands opposite Charlie's house across the street. Eli stops as he sees Charlie's wife in the front yard pruning weeds from a small flower garden. Young, twin daughters play on the front porch.

Eli feels compelled to watch Charlie. He needs to determine what Charlie's next actions are once he returns home after being told the secrets from Joseph.

Charlie emerges from a small park near his house riding his bike on the sidewalk. Eli scans the distance to Charlie and prepares to listen via his phone app once Charlie arrives home.

A horrific scream erupts from the porch as Eli lifts his head from the phone focusing on Charlie. He witnesses a black, pickup truck plow through Charlie on his bicycle. The truck had ridden up onto the sidewalk as Charlie's body rolls under the tires. Before Eli could react and snap a picture with his phone, the truck speeds away from the scene.

Eli's knees buckle. His stomach spins. Pain throbs from his masked scar.

He knows the Foundation will protect its secret. After all, this is what he would have done twenty-years, ago.

With a deep breath, Eli picks himself up from the ground and disappears back into the woods. The screams grow silent behind him in the distance as paranoia returns.

December 24, 2015
Stony Brook, Long Island — New York

TWO MONTHS HAD PASSED.

The golden leaves have rotted to brown and black. Bare tree limbs stretch to the sky like deathly fingers to the heavens. Cold and thick clouds of winter have established themselves over Long Island.

Eli had continued his observations of Joseph; careful not to get too close knowing the Foundation has many eyes.

No longer a pariah, people never give Eli a second glance with his new appearance. Clear memories have returned with Eli's current mission — to protect his grandson, Joseph, from The Eden Foundation.

The crowd is thick of people on Main Street of downtown Stony Brook this mid-afternoon. Eli follows Joseph zig-zagging through the maze of mostly men and their procrastinated Christmas shopping.

Eli waits across the street of the front door to Stony Brook Floral & Gifts. After ten minutes, Joseph appears pushing through the scrum entering the store. Eli crosses to the opposite side of the street remaining at a distance.

Warm pastry smells tempt Eli. Brief memories of his early days with his wife, Liz, come back to him. A quick horn chirp of a passing car steals Eli's attention back to Joseph as he approaches Eli crossing the middle of the street. Eli lifts the collar of his jacket over his throat and face. His right elbow grazes his grandson as Joseph passes entering a jewelry shop.

Eli watches through the window as a tall, gray-haired woman assists Joseph from behind the counter. Diamond rings sparkle under the glass as the woman leads Joseph to other displays of pearl necklaces. Joseph stops mid-way with the woman who continues to the end of the counter.

The woman rejoins Joseph as he points to a blue, heart-shaped pendant behind her. Eli smiles witnessing Joseph's posture change holding the necklace.

Fifteen minutes later, Joseph leaves carrying a small bag with the store's logo on the front. Eli follows. Christmas music continues louder, then softer, as various shop doors open-and-close as they walk.

The spire of the Catholic Cathedral of Stony Brook increases in size as they approach with Eli twenty-feet behind his grandson. After a brief pause, Joseph walks up the cathedral steps and enters.

Eli waits a few minutes and pulls open the cathedral door. Air and snowflakes push him inside as the door closes behind him.

Few people wander inside the vast church. Dim candlelight flickers throughout the decorated, stonewall sanctuary. The smell of incense fills the air. Wooden pews lead to the front alter with a ten-foot-wide aisle between the seats. Joseph sits alone in the front pew; his gaze transfixes to a statue of Jesus on a crucifix above the altar.

Eli pauses. A frail, elderly woman shuffles by Eli as she meanders down to a prayer table next to the altar. Eli watches Joseph stare at the woman.

A moment of inspiration overpowers Eli drawing him to the back corner of the sanctuary to a hanging black shirt on a coat rack.

Eli slips off his jacket and buttons the black shirt over his clothes, affixing a white square under the neck collar. The back of a wooden chair holds a white, linen robe. Eli places the robe over his black shirt.

The old woman smiles at Eli as she passes. With a quick gesture, Eli lifts his right hand making the sign of the cross over his chest. He walks between the pews grabbing a Bible from a seat and holds it tight to his body.

Eli stops behind Joseph.

"Good afternoon, my son. Merry Christmas."

Joseph jumps in his seat turning around to the voice.

"Oh, I'm sorry. I didn't mean to scare you," Eli said with a quick laugh. "My name is Father Alvaro... Merry Christmas."

Eli pauses his introduction. Years of living in Texas, Spanish comes naturally to him, causing the name to escape his mouth without thinking. Since Eli's mission is to look after Joseph, subconsciously, Eli chooses a name meaning protection.

"Oh... Merry Christmas to you, too, Father," Joseph said.

Eli smiles and steps up to the altar. After making the sign of the cross, Eli walks to a nearby table lighting a candle assuming the role as a priest.

"Excuse me... Father. Do you have a moment?"

Joseph's question causes Eli to open his eyes scanning the sanctuary.

"My son, I'm about to step into the confessional, if you'd like to join me?" Eli said leading Joseph to the side of the church.

"That's okay. I'm not Catholic."

"Son, God has no teams in Heaven. You can tell me what's on your mind in *there*."

Joseph follows Father Alvaro into a confessional. The doors close as they enter.

Eli inhales two deep breaths to clear his thoughts. His heart pounds through the borrowed priest clothes speaking for the first time to his grandson.

A moment later, Eli slides open a small door on the wall revealing a crisscrossed, wooden screen between them.

"So, how can I help you, my son?"

"Aren't you supposed to say, *how long has it been since your last confessional?* Like they do in the movies?" Joseph asked.

Eli releases a soft laugh realizing this would have been the same comment he would have made to a priest.

"Yes, you're right, but you've already told me you weren't Catholic… something's on your mind isn't it, my Son?"

Joseph pauses. "Well… I've been keeping a secret from my wife, but I am telling her about it soon. And, Father, it's been killing me not telling her."

Eli knows what secret Joseph keeps. They are the same ones which have haunted Eli for decades.

"Are you keeping something from her that will upset her or hurt her once she finds out?" Eli asked.

"I don't think she will believe me, but after that, I think she will be angry at me for not telling her sooner."

"Do you think the reason you have not told her before is you're trying to protect her from something?" Eli responds with his reasoning he had developed keeping the secrets from Liz.

"Yes, and I was told not to say anything to her about it," Joseph said.

"Sometimes, we protect those we love by doing things that most times we would never do."

In a quick flash, the guilt of his sins Eli had committed the past sixty years overcome him. Warmth fills his body. He feels lighter in his chair. The confessions from Eli through his questions to Joseph push his impersonation of the priest further.

"In God's eyes, if you have committed a sin, and this is what you are not telling her, then you are sinning against God based on the marriage vows you took."

"Oh no, I've never lied to her about any of the questions she has ever asked me. I just never explained or told her any additional information about what I'm keeping from her. And, I feel so guilty not telling her."

Joseph's words feel like the same words Eli would say.

"If she loves you, once she gets beyond the shock of what you're planning to tell her, she will understand your reasons," Eli said delivering his justification he had realized decades in the past.

A single tear falls down Eli's face. Silence fills the confessional chamber. "Thank you, Father."

Eli catches the words about to escape his mouth. Instead of calling him *Joseph*, he said, "You're welcome, my son." Eli asked, "Is there anything else?" Eli did not want his brief time with his grandson to end.

"Well… um… yes. I grew up down South and attended a Southern Baptist church. It's been so long now… how does the Catholic Church view the end-of-the-world?"

Joseph's question catches Eli off-guard. "Oh, my… that's a deep question for this time of year. I can tell something is troubling you if you're asking me this."

Eli is aware the guilt Joseph experiences. This same guilt has manifested itself to Eli at different times since he had learned a planetoid would incinerate the Earth in 2020. A man of science, he had often sought Biblical passages as a source of comfort for the fate which he knows will befall humanity.

Various Bible verses rush to Eli, who hesitates with his delivery. A phantom pain erupts from his right temple with twenty-year-old memories of the metal pipe crashing into his head from Joseph's father. Troubled, Eli selects a verse to alert Joseph.

"In the Book of Matthew, God warns us to *beware of false prophets, who come to you in sheep's clothing but inwardly are ravening wolves.* This time of year is when you hear proclamations from so many claiming the end-of-the-world is coming."

"Yes, but Father, if we knew for certain when the world would end, shouldn't everyone on Earth know about this?"

Eli pauses. The first person who said the same thing to him about telling people was his partner, Simon Baptiste. The second person was President Kennedy. Eli had dealt with these original responses in different ways, but with the same outcome.

Joseph now is saying the same thing to him albeit as Father Alvaro. Eli knows the secret has to stay safe to ensure the survival of humanity, and for the survival of his grandson.

Eli collects his thoughts and delivers to Joseph a verse from First Thessalonians. The verse discusses the believers rising to heaven to be with the Lord in the end. Eli had always thought this verse alludes to the Salvation Station on Mars. But, Eli had long lost the sense that he was the Lord.

"But, what about the survival of humanity, how can we trust they will be saved?"

Without hesitation, Eli responds, "My son, the only way to *Salvation* is through Christ, our God in heaven."

"Salvation?"

Hearing Joseph say the word, *Salvation*, Eli realizes he had to stop his conversation. He does not want to give away his identity or what he knows.

Silence comes from Joseph's side of the confessional.

"My son, I can tell you still have a lot of questions. I would love to see you come back and attend a service, and we can talk more."

Eli wants the conversation to end.

"Oh, okay, Father… thanks for listening."

"My pleasure. Merry Christmas and peace be unto you, my son," Eli said.

Eli closes the small door between them and places his palm flat against the wood divider. He releases a heavy sigh as Joseph's door opens-and-closes, as his grandson exits.

Eli stands to leave the confessional cracking open the door. Four people stand in line as the door opens on the opposite side where Joseph had sat.

He realizes people must have seen him enter with Joseph. The role of Father Alvaro has to continue longer as Eli opens the small door on the wall to the next parishioner.

Thirty minutes have passed. Eli has heard the confessions of two women, one teenager, and an elderly man.

After the fourth confession, Eli re-opens the door. With a heavy sigh, he closes the door again as the back of a large man in a black suit opens the confessional door.

Eli reaches and opens the small door on the wall. Concern encroaches Eli as he expects the real priest of the church to open his door at any moment. But, Eli remains safe inside hidden.

The crisscrossed-wooden screen blurs the images of the people who sat across from Eli. As he spoke to the parishioners, Eli imagines their appearances. He likes the indemnity the screen provides.

"Forgive me, Father, for I have sinned," a man's deep voice said through the screen.

Eli peers through the screen trying to establish the facial image of the man.

"How long has it been since your last confession, My... Son?"

Eli pauses his words. Against the man's black suit, Eli makes out an unmistakable figure through the screen... a familiar image... an image Eli had created fifty-years-ago. The white outline of a circle inside a red triangle sears itself into the back of Eli's eyes.

With a sudden flash, Eli's vision blurs. His head jolts violently against the back wall. Spurts of red blood ooze down from the center of Eli's forehead into both eyes.

A single bullet had entered Eli's head originating from the side of the confessional with the man. Light, gray smoke lifts from the end of a suppressor attached to a Glock 17 barrel.

Before the man had entered the confessional, he had slid a black screen around the doors as a typical signal to the parishioners of a closed confessional. This screen makes for a perfect cover. After cleaning the blood from the back wall, the man exits and pulls Eli's dead body out of the confessional.

The man places Eli's body in a wheelchair he had found earlier in the church. A plastic bag covers Eli's head preventing further blood dripping to the floor, as the man places a black robe over Eli.

The confessional area is clean; no sign of murder is left. Squealing wheels from the chair echo under the vast sanctuary ceiling as the man pushes Eli from the church to an outside side alley. Seeing no one on the dark street, the man lifts Eli from the chair to the bed of a black, pickup truck.

Red brake lights illuminate the dark street. Snowflakes appear like drops of blood floating behind the truck.

From the truck cab, the man lifts a cellphone to his ear.

"Sir, our little problem… I have taken care of it," the man said.

The voice through the phone replies, "Excellent, Thomas. You know what to do with the body."

Christmas music from Main Street fades as the truck races away from Stony Brook. Under a burlap canopy, a blood-filled plastic bag covers Eli's head.

Potholes bounce the truck bed. With each jolt, a blood-soaked Bible vibrates from Eli's dead hands to the open-air. The truck speeds at fifty-miles-per-hour without slowing for a speed bump. The violent thrust of the truck bed lifts the Bible over the tailgate.

Eli's blood splatters from the Bible as it rolls across the road stopping on the yellow centerline. Snow falls on the opened pages soaking to red as the warm blood melts the flakes.

Gushing wind turns the pages of the opened Bible. The first page of the *Book of Revelation* stares up to the black, night sky. The white page turns an eerie red from underneath through the wet, blood-filled book.

Silence fills the air. Eli's life is no more. He is finally at peace.

PART THREE
Salvation

17-CONSTRUCTION

TO THE PUBLIC, APOLLO 17 is the last manned mission to the Moon in 1972. Three years afterward, The Eden Foundation has renewed lunar missions in secret. Gone were the experimental endeavors led by NASA; Eden has a precise purpose... to save humankind.

Eden's first missions establish construction facilities for the eventual Salvation Complex on Mars. Each lunar operation tests various orbital and landing systems to prepare for the first mission to Mars in less than a decade.

The Foundation's engineers copy the Apollo technology for launching, orbiting, and landing. Recruiting engineers is straightforward; finding recruits as lunar laborers presents a challenge. Workers need construction and survival skills besides being crazy enough to travel to the Moon.

A demand to maintain secrecy develops a strict order-and-control system within Eden. Participants only have one option: to follow the

Foundation's commands. The optimal recruit is one capable of following orders and who has a disconnect from society; having no family or friends — a loner.

Eli Bishop has no difficulty locating these recruits. Being the 1970s, many Vietnam War Veterans return home to a country who show them little respect. Consumed with a myriad of emotional issues advanced by the horrific actions they had seen; this particular population serves Eli's purpose.

Some veterans Eli approach had added special military skills. Many have flight experience with different aircraft allowing them to work as pilots for launch and orbital vehicles.

Once recruited, the chosen person starts rigorous training programs at Eden's Mission Command facilities in the far reaches of the southern Indian Ocean. A few hundred miles from the shores of Antarctica and thousands of miles from the nearest population or oceanic shipping lanes, Eden has an ideal, hidden location.

Eli approaches these men on the pretext of carrying out Top Secret projects for the U.S. Government. Having served their country, Eli finds their manipulation easy to obtain their service to Eden. Prestige and honor drive the men; never learning the true secrets the Foundation hold.

With Eden's first lunar missions in 1975, two transport vehicles leave Earth: one containing material for the genesis of establishing the lunar base, and the other occupied with workers.

The early missions are merciless. Crews live inside the same modules used for the Apollo Missions. With each new visit, more of the construction base and living quarters form on the lunar surface.

Within five years, twenty workers live on the Moon building structures, which Eden will deliver to Salvation on Mars by the mid-1980s. Six months occur between the first lunar missions; within a few years, they will occur monthly.

By 1982, Eli has turned over the authority of Lunar construction to his son, Jacob. This transition allows Eli to concentrate his recruitment for the scientists and engineers developing technologies for the Foundation's next development phase… on Mars.

The daunting task of recruiting construction personnel with the eagerness to leave Earth decreases. Jacob approaches Eli with a solution; an untapped, regular supply of laborers for not solely the Moon but Mars.

Jacob recognizes the penitentiary system presents an impressive resource pool, notably once the Foundation promotes the War on Drugs initiative for the U.S. Government to conduct. A motley gang of welders, plumbers, and tradesmen join Salvation assured of Eden's power to secure pardons for their crimes. But, Eden has no intentions with following through with this promise.

The selection process yields an arrangement where Jacob approaches the worst of the worst criminals who have nothing to lose. Society has already identified these men as disposable, why not Eden?

Each serves their purpose. When this purpose ends, Eden promises them safe passage on their return to Earth. However, no one ever leaves the lunar surface unbeknownst to the remaining workers.

As the Salvation modules complete their construction, the engineers develop their designs to transfer the materials to Mars. With the lower lunar gravity, the ability to launch from the Moon with a heavy payload of materials bound for Mars requires smaller rockets compared to the Saturn V technology used between the Earth and the Moon.

This research leads Eden to the current technology of reusable rockets with the new added benefit of producing enormous cost savings. Another breakthrough coincides with the Foundation's concept of a photonic propulsion system from the advances produced in laser development.

One parallel project Eden had developed was the prospect of generating a powerful laser to impact the incoming planetoid hoping to deflect the incoming monster. However, a laser of this strength is only workable in science-fiction films and not in reality. But, the research develops photonic propulsion creating the opportunity of traveling to Mars from Earth in three weeks instead of six months.

Eden has several programs running in parallel to be complete in time for ten-thousand colonists at Salvation by September 11, 2020.

The Earth-date of November 13, 1983, produces the most unheralded event in human record: the landing of the first manned mission to Mars.

The world should have heralded this event more than Neil Armstrong's first, giant step for mankind. But, only twenty people observe on their video monitors the first, red footprints left on the Martian surface.

After this proving-ground mission, two flights to Mars occur later in the year with people and equipment to set up the assembly process for the Salvation Complex. The first trip has an unexpected discovery.

Hundreds of barren lava tubes formed millions of years ago by volcanic events make excellent material storage sites. Over time, the early Martian construction workers transform these tunnels into living quarters larger than their planned living conditions.

Salvation takes shape on the red, alien surface. Underground lava tubes support the lunar-built walls assembled above ground. Once done, the workers erect polyurethane-framed outer structures which extend over the exterior of the composite-material walls.

Earth has the advantage of supporting life better than Mars. Gaseous layers of ninety-five percent carbon dioxide form the thin, Martian atmosphere. Earth, by contrast, has a dense atmosphere composed of nitrogen and oxygen with a barometric pressure a hundred times greater than Mars. Another protective element comes because of the Earth's iron core developing a strong magnetosphere which deflects solar radiation.

With its thin atmosphere and lack of a magnetosphere, radiation bombards the Martian surface. Any individual living on Mars requires security from this radioactivity, or the Foundation cannot sustain human existence at Salvation beyond a generation.

Eden's scientists test a variety of elements for this protection. Using technology from the nuclear power industry, the scientists determine a protective barrier of water will suffice even in the form of ice.

A cold planet farther from the Sun than Earth, Mars once was a planet of flowing rivers and lakes. Through millions of years of planetary evolution, surface ice in the polar regions and sub-surface ice captured trillions of gallons of water. Eden's third mission confirms this theory.

The construction workers complete the polyurethane frames and insert small pipes extending twenty meters into the ground. Heated elements within the pipes warm the ice below the surface. As the ice thaws, water percolates to the surface filling the plastic molds and refreezing on contact.

With the thin atmospheric pressure and the solar distance, Mars cannot retain its heat energy. Temperatures can soar above freezing during the day and plunge to minus eighty-degrees Fahrenheit at night even during the warmest of summer, Martian months.

The exterior, ice shell does not thaw even with the limited time conditions above freezing. With the eighteen-inch-thick ice shell, radiation does not pass through to the interior.

The 1980s turn into the '90s. Salvation continues its growth.

Solar arrays extend beyond the perimeter of the complex providing power. Underground ice fields provide potable and drinking water through filtration systems. Hydroponic plants grow providing greenery and oxygen.

A large domed, glass structure in Salvation's center houses a hydroponic greenhouse. The vast structure creates a Central Park Hub producing fresh oxygen which combines with the mechanical oxygenation systems. A glass encased elevator shaft lifts to the top of the dome emptying to an atmospheric viewing room.

Ice-covered facilities radiate out like the spokes of a wagon wheel from the Central Park area extending across the red landscape. Causeways join the spoke corridors at various connection points as walkable shortcuts throughout the complex.

Salvation will sustain the facilities to support ten-thousand people. A small city develops on Mars.

In the late 1990s, as 3D-printing technology develops, the ability to build faster and more elaborate structures becomes possible. Salvation no longer has first to build the modules on the Moon, then transport them to Mars for assembly. Now, Eden can travel direct to Mars.

By 2005, Salvation develops into a self-sustaining city for its one-hundred permanent staff who further prepare for receiving thousands of others and supplies. The operational phase of Salvation begins.

The foundation's Command Center transfers from the southern Indian Ocean to Salvation. With this transition, Jacob Bishop became a permanent resident in 2011. Jacob has less than ten years to complete all activities and prepare for receiving the final inhabitants.

After 2020, there will be no more arriving personnel, no more arriving supplies... Salvation and its ten-thousand pioneers will have to sustain humanity... alone.

18-MARY

THE TECHNICIAN LEADS Jacob and his son, Joseph, through a white corridor from Jacob's office. Fresh oxygen fills Joe's lungs. His footsteps labor like a newborn as the magnetized floor produces a sense of gravity similar on Earth.

Lost in the expansive complex, Joe is oblivious of his whereabouts. An advantage as the Salvation Leader, Jacob has his private wing connecting to the Command Center.

They approach a glass door which remains closed at the end of the passage. The technician presses her palm flat against the waist-high, red-illuminated board. Green chases away the red light as the door glides open to the right with a faint swoosh sound.

"This way," the technician said. She reaches out her arm into a simple room.

"Mary!" Joe sees his wife awake in a bed covered in white sheets; her eyes open.

An older man with gray hair approaches the bed as Joe kisses Mary and wipes the hair from her forehead. Jacob stands beside the man.

"Joseph, Mary is okay," the gray-haired man said.

"The baby— "

Mary grabbed Joe's hand. "She's okay. I just got light-headed and passed out."

"Joseph, I'm Doctor Johanisson. Mary and the baby are okay. She's three month's pregnant, and that alone is exhausting her body. After orbiting Mars and the rapid gravitational changes, this caused her to faint."

Joe squeezes Mary's grip.

"We have run an extensive body of tests, and everything is okay. Her blood-sugar levels are a little low, so we are administering fluids. We'll keep her in bed for the next couple days just to make certain. This will allow us to watch her closely."

"Mary, I was so worried."

She draws him to her. Joe's ear presses to Mary's mouth.

"I can't believe we are here," Mary whispers.

With hormones flooding her body, tears erupt from her gushing across Joe's cheeks as his face is flat against hers. He wraps his arms around her shoulders rocking back-and-forth in comfort.

"It's okay, Sweetie… shh… it's okay."

"Everyone, let's give them a little time," Jacob said motioning the doctor and technician from the room.

As the three left, Mary steals a brief glimpse.

"Is that man, Jacob, from the video?"

Her words come slow through her sobs as she catches her breath.

"Uh… Yes, that is Jacob… he's… he's… my…. He's the leader here. He helped comfort me while the doctors were watching after you." Years of keeping secrets feel once again too familiar for Joe.

Mary pushes against Joe as he remains on her bedside. She wipes her face with her bedsheet.

"Wow, that was nice of the leader to meet with you, as I'm sure he has to be busy here."

Joe caresses her left cheek. Her skin is cold and damp.

"Yeah, it was. He seems okay."

"How long was I out?"

"I'm not sure. I have no idea of time, here. It's been maybe a few hours since we landed."

"Ha, since we landed," Mary said repeating Joe. "I know we are not on Earth anymore, but it feels like a dream."

Joe smiles to comfort her while hiding his nervousness.

"Are you sure, Gabriel didn't slip us more of his water, again. I'm mean, are we really on Mars?"

"I've only been down the hall where Jacob lives and through the landing hangar."

Mary's eyes widen.

"After we landed, glass walls lifted over our ship. I saw mountains for a brief moment. That's when you fainted."

"Was it red?"

"Was what red? Oh… duh… yes, the land was red." Joe wipes Mary's hair from her eyes. "You remember that field trip to El Paso we took in high school?"

"You mean, where we had our first beer?"

"Yeah, there. It kinda looked like that, at least in the distance."

"So, what did you talk about with Jacob? Did he give you a tour?"

The medical room is small. Mary's hospital bed sits in the center of the floor. An intravenous drip station pumps a clear solution in her left arm. Two rhythmic beats come from the heart machine in the corner. One beats slow, the other fast. Both are normal.

A mirror behind the bed reflects the room making it seem larger. On the other side of the glass, Jacob stands alone… watching.

EARTH DATE: MARCH 6, 2016

THREE DAYS HAD PASSED. Strength fails to return to Mary.

In this time, Joe only leaves Mary's bedside to go next door to the bathroom. Worry consumes him.

"Joseph, do you have a moment?" Dr. Johanisson catches his attention as Joe leaves the restroom.

"Sure, everything okay with Mary?"

"I'm glad I ran into you out here. I needed to talk to you before telling Mary as we will need your help?"

Joe's face brightens white; his eyes swell.

"I don't like the sound of that? Oh God, is it the baby?"

"Joseph, come with me to my office so we can talk."

Dr. Johanisson leads Joe through the corridor. Halfway from the end, they stop before a closed, glass door. The doctor places his right palm against the entry glass as the door slides open.

"Come, in. Please take a seat."

Dr. Johanisson's office is bright. White, luminous walls surround the room. A glass desk and black leather chairs are the only furniture present.

The doctor stands behind his desk holding his palm flat against the wall. Numerous charts and data-sets scroll below her name.

"Joseph, we had hoped that her vitals would recover."

Joe gives Johanisson his complete attention.

"Doctor, I don't understand. You have been telling us it was her pregnancy and the change of gravity causing her issues with vertigo… what do you mean, her vitals."

Dr. Johanisson places his fingers on a line graph enlarging the scrolling numbers.

"*This* is showing both Mary's pulse and the baby's."

Joe approaches the wall.

"Your baby's heart is extraordinarily strong. But, I'm a little concerned about Mary. Hers seems to be a little slow for our comfort."

The doctor scrolls through files he keeps on a tablet.

"From her medical records, we don't have any notes of any pre-existing heart conditions. Do you recall any doctor mentioning this in the past about her?"

Joe scratches his head. He had accompanied Mary to most of her past appointments.

"No. The only condition we ever knew about is her polycystic ovarian syndrome. I can't think of anyone saying anything about a heart problem. Hell, that's the reason we never thought we could get pregnant in the first place."

"Joseph, I don't want to scare you. Everything is checking out okay for her and the baby. But, I would like to keep her in bed longer. We can watch her closely and this way she won't exert too much energy as we need her body to continue developing the baby."

Wrinkles encroach Joe's forehead. He rakes his hand through his hair.

"But... how long? Should I worry?"

Johanisson places his tablet on the desk. He returns to the wall and swipes the translucent surface. Mary's information disappears.

"No, don't worry. This is more of a precaution. As far as time goes, it may be just a few days."

"How many births have happened so far here at Salvation?"

Johanisson walks to Joe and places his firm left hand on Joe's shoulder.

"Don't worry. We've had dozens of births in the past years. The first one was during Earth-year 2010."

"And, everything has been okay with those?"

"As okay as births go... Don't worry, we are experienced with prenatal care, and both will be great. But, we need to be on the safe side, here, with Mary."

Joe's shoulders relax under the doctor's hand.

"I wanted to tell you so you can prepare yourself when we give her the news."

"Thank you for that, Doctor. Just please keep me updated. I don't want to worry in front of her as I don't plan to ever leave her alone through this."

Johanisson leads Joe to the door as they both return to Mary's room. Joe inhales a heavy sigh as he enters.

EARTH DATE: MARCH 7, 2016 (THE NEXT DAY)

A BELL CHIMES INSIDE Mary's room as a video display illuminates above the access panel.

"Look, Joe, at the door," she said.

Joe picks up his head from the side of her bed. He twists his body around with minimal effort and settles on the floor.

"It's Jacob," Joe said.

Joe raises his right palm against the panel. The glass entry swooshes open.

"Hope I'm not disturbing anything?" Jacob asks entering the room.

He passes Joe to Mary's bedside and takes her left hand in his.

"Mary, it's so nice to meet you. My name is— "

"Jacob. I know. Joe told me."

Jacob glances to Joe remaining by the door then returns his attention to Mary.

"Yes, that's right. What else has your husband mentioned about me?"

Joe walks to the other side in direct eyesight with Jacob.

"Oh, he had nothing but great things to say, like how you personally welcomed him in your office when we first landed when I had my fainting spell."

"Yes, we were so concerned about you. And, the best thing to do was to preoccupy your husband so our physicians could examine you."

Joe shifts his balance from side-to-side.

"I'm sorry that Doctor Johanisson had to tell you yesterday about his need to keep you in here for a while longer."

"It's okay. I actually don't mind. I mean at least this way the doctor is very close in case the baby or I need him."

Mary rubs her swelling stomach as Joe joins her on the bed.

"So, Joseph, how are you dealing with this?" Jacob asks.

Joe takes Mary's right hand.

"I'm just doing my best to comfort her while she's stuck in here."

Mary squeezes Joe's grip.

"And, he's doing an excellent job, but I'd be lying if I didn't say I'm so curious to explore the facility," Mary said.

"There's plenty of time for that, but our primary objective is your and your baby's health."

"I know, but my God, we're on Mars. I can't believe it."

"Mary, I've been here, now, roughly five years, and I'm even in awe too sometimes."

Joe rubs Mary's right arm.

"So, what's this I understand? You've not left this room, yet?"

"I'm not leaving Mary's side until we can leave to our area together," Joe said grinning at Mary.

Jacob releases Mary's right hand stepping back from the bed.

"I understand. Hopefully, it's just a matter of a few days, and then we'll get you both situated in your assigned room. And, Joseph, we'll introduce you to your lab staff."

Joe stands from the bed sensing Jacob's intention to leave.

"Jacob, to be honest, I know you've brought us here for my lab work, but it'll have to wait until she's out of here."

"Oh, no problem. Take whatever time you need. I'm confident you being with her will only help."

Joe steals a quick glimpse to Mary.

"Well, I need to go. I'll check in later to see how you're doing. If you need anything from me, just tell Doctor Johanisson."

"Thank you, Jacob, for dropping by to check on me. That means a lot."

"I'm responsible for everybody here. I'm delighted to stop by."

Jacob steps to the door putting his palm flat against the entry panel. The door opens as Jacob leaves.

"He seems awfully nice," Mary said.

Joe releases a huff stepping to the door. He holds his hand flat above the access panel swiping his hand down against the wall. The room lights dim as Joe returns to Mary's bed.

"Let's try to get some sleep. You need your rest after that visit."

Mary slides over in her bed as Joe sits beside her. He removes his shoes, which fall heavy to the magnetic floor. His feet float as he rotates his body shifting on his side cuddling her.

"I love you, Joseph."

EARTH DATE: AUGUST 9, 2016

FIVE MONTHS HAVE PASSED since Joe and Mary arrived at Salvation. The excitement of Mars has long been missing for Joe. His concern for Mary exerting too much effort exhausts him as she remains bed-ridden in her medical room.

Joe refuses to visit their assigned living quarters until they can leave together. Since their second week, a technician had placed a separate bed in Mary's room.

Mary is eight months pregnant. The baby is strong with tests showing a regular heart-rate and fetal development.

"Dammit, my back hurts, Joe."

With Mars' lighter gravity, moving for Mary should be easy. But, with her time in bed, her muscles have weakened. To compensate for her pregnant belly, she rocks back-and-forth gaining momentum to raise her body from the mattress.

Joe steps from his bed and massages her lower back as she rolls to her side.

"Does this help?"

"That's great. You always have the magic touch."

"Yeah, if I recall correctly, it's my touch that got us into this situation."

Mary laughs.

"Can't believe we've been stuck in this room the whole time we've been here on Mars."

"I hate you've had to be in this bed this long, but it's been for the best."

Joe struggles to console her knowing the doctor's concern caused her bed-ridden situation.

They entertain themselves by fantasizing raising their daughter on Mars. Both agree on things to share with her concerning Earth and their family. With separate reasons, each concedes to be always honest with her as she becomes older. Years of secrets between them force this understanding.

Doctor Johanisson and numerous medical technicians have been their regular visitors. Jacob makes it a point to stop by every few days to say hello. With each visit by his father, Joe struggles with the secret he now keeps from Mary.

"You know, Joe. I was thinking while you were asleep how ridiculous this whole situation is."

Joe stops rubbing her back.

"What's funny about this?"

"If you think about it, you are Joseph, and I'm Mary. We've traveled far to arrive to a new place, and I'm pregnant. Remember how your grandma always made us perform the parts of Mary and Joseph in the church Christmas plays?"

"Uh, yeah."

"Don't you think this is ironic?"

Seconds pass with no reply.

"Oh, I get it... Mary and Joseph... so, this room is our stable?"

"Yeah, and Salvation is Bethlehem," Mary said.

Joe releases a hearty laugh rubbing Mary's belly.

"So, you're giving birth to Jesus?"

Mary matched Joe's snicker.

"See, I told you. That's hilarious."

"You've got a weird sense of humor."

"Well, I'm preggo and have to amuse myself someway, especially being stuck in here."

A chime rings inside Mary's room. A familiar group of people appears at the door.

"Oh, shit, Joe! Look! It's Heinrich, Joanie, and Heather from our ship."

Joe rises from the bed.

"Well, there you go Mother Mary. Here's your visit from three wise people," Joe said as he laughed sarcastically opening the door.

"Joe, how's Mary?" Heinrich asked as the two sisters pass them going to Mary.

"She's hanging in there, and the baby is okay."

Joe led Heinrich into the room joining Joanie and Heather at the bed.

"I was talking with Heather the other day, and we were thinking about you. So, we asked if we could stop by. Hope that's okay?" Joanie asks.

"Oh, it sure is. We've not had many visitors other than doctors. So, it's great to see you. How have you been? What's it been like being here?"

"Fantastic. Joanie and I are working in the Children's Wing. Everyone has been very nice. And, my God, this place is like beautiful. Have you seen the garden area?" Heather asked.

"Oh, Darlin', I've not been able to escape this room since we landed."

"Wow," both sisters said in unison.

"Heinrich, what about you? What's your job, here?" Joe asked.

"I am in maintenance and deliver materials to different locations in the facility."

"Hey, we brought you gifts," Heather said.

"Please don't say it's frankincense," Joe said in a sarcastic tone causing Mary to smirk.

"Frankenstein? Joe, I forgot how funny you are," Joanie said.

"*Here*," Heather said as she stretches out her hand, "We thought you could use this lotion oil they have here. It really makes your skin so soft."

"Oh, that's so nice, thank you."

"And, I brought this," Joanie said holding a small, white box with open holes on top. "*Here*, smell it."

Mary picks up the box and places her nose above the holes.

"That smells nice," Mary said.

"Yeah, they have these boxes put out in the common areas to help make things fresh. I thought maybe you would like it."

"So, you brought frankincense, and Heather brought myrrh," Joe said.

"Myrrh? I brought oil," Heather said.

"Never mind." Joe turns to Heinrich. "So, I suppose that means you brought us gold?"

Mary releases a raucous laugh.

"Gold?" Heinrich said to Joe, "I didn't know we were bringing gifts?" Heinrich whispered to Joanie who stands beside him.

A chime sounds, again. The doctor's image is visible at the access panel. Joe opens the door.

"Hi, Doctor Johanisson."

"Hey, Joseph. Oh, I didn't know you had guests?"

"Doc, these people came to Salvation with us," Mary said motioning Johanisson into the room.

"Hello," Johanisson said, "this explains it."

"Explains what?" Joe said as the door closes.

"I received an alert in my office, Mary, that your heart-rate suddenly increased... must be from your guests— "

A deafening shriek from Mary interrupts Johanisson.

"Mary!" Joe screams as he rushes to Mary. A second scream erupts from her.

"Everyone, please leave," the doctor said ushering the visitors from the room.

As the door opens, two technicians run by the leaving guests accompanying the doctor beside Mary.

"Mary!"

Joe jostles his way between the medical team to seize Mary's hand. She crushes his grip as she surrenders a savage roar.

Doctor Johanisson grabs Joe's hands pulling them from the bed. Joe gives a cold stare at the doctor.

"Joseph, she's going into labor."

The doctor takes the hand of one technician.

"Please, get Joseph out of here."

"Hell, no! I'm staying."

"Joe!" Mary screams.

"Sweetie, I'm right here."

"Joe!"

"Joseph, you need to leave. We need room in here. Please!"

"Sorry, but I'm not leaving. I'll stand behind the bed out of the way."

"Joe!"

"I'm, here, Mary."

Joe forces his body by the doctor and technician. He positions himself behind Mary's head between the bed and mirrored-wall rubbing her shoulders. They are soaking wet from her instant sweat.

"It hurts!"

A shrill from the depths of Mary's body chases away her words. Doctor Johanisson props Mary's legs into stirrups the technicians affix to the sides of the bed.

"Okay, Mary, your baby is deciding she wants to visit us a little early," Johanisson said.

The translucent walls come to life. Various graphs of her and the baby's statistics flash across the surface. Mary's heart-rate has tripled its previous speed approaching one-hundred-forty-beats-per-minute.

"Joe, grab Mary's hands and help her with my instructions."

"Mary, when I tell you, I want you to push until I tell you to stop."

Mary screams.

"Okay, push!"

Numbness stings Joe's fingers as Mary squeezes hard against his hands. She releases a guttural groan as she pushes.

"Push, push, push, Mary… that's good. Okay, stop."

Mary grunts. At the same time, intense pain thrusts from her pelvis through her opened legs upward through her chest through her arms.

"Joe! I love you."

He kisses her wet forehead.

"I love you, too. I'm right, here, Sweetie."

Tears stream from the sides of her head dripping into her ears.

Mary opens her mouth, her lips move. No sound comes.

Joe lowers his ear over her face.

Mary whispers, "Promise me. You will protect our daughter."

Joe turns his ear away from her and kisses her.

"I promise."

Mary screams. Air rushes from her lungs. Joe watches Mary's eyes roll upward inside her eyelids.

"Mary! Mary!"

A sick, familiar feeling overcomes Joe. An instant memory flashes to his childhood and his mother at church as Mary's body falls limp in his hands.

"Joe! You stay here! We need to take her to the operating room for a cesarean."

A technician pushes the bed as the another opens the door. Joe follows in a daze.

Doctor Johanisson grabs Joe's shoulder.

"Joe! You can't go. Stay here. She's passed out, and the baby's coming."

Joe relents and freezes in the middle of the empty room. The door closes. Joe is alone.

EARTH DATE: AUGUST 13, 2016 (4 DAYS LATER)

JOE SITS SILENT in the blackness. A faint light glimmers in the room packed with monitoring equipment. Disheveled hair accompanies his unshaven cheeks and neck.

Beside him is a narrow table with locked wheels. A clear glass box with two, oval openings on each long side rests on top the table.

Sniffles echo in the room as tears fall across his face with his forehead resting on the box's top edge. He stretches each hand through the holes in the glass facing him.

His fingertips graze the exposed skin of his daughter's backside. The premature infant's lungs swell and shrink under Joe's fingers.

Wire-leads run from various positions on the baby through the glass to the nearby monitors. The newborn is responding well.

"Hey— "

Joe's breathing becomes labored as he breaks down. His shoulders shake with each gasp of air. A few minutes pass.

"Your Mommy and me... we love you, so much."

Joe strokes his daughter's tiny shoulders.

"We both promise to always love and protect you."

Sniffles return to him with his bending head.

"We thought we could never have a baby... we're so thankful... you are our little miracle... "

With each hand gesture, Joe feels his daughter's body react.

The room's door opens as Doctor Johanisson enters.

"Joseph, how is she doing?"

Joe strokes the thin hair of his daughter's head.

"Her breathing is regular, and I know she can hear me when I speak."

Johanisson bends to the glass staring at the monitors beside them.

"Everything is checking out perfect. Her oxygen levels are normal... So, I think in a couple days we can remove her from the incubator."

Joe sits silent.

"Have you slept any?"

Joe continues rubbing his daughter's shoulders in silence.

"You really need to try to sleep. I can give you something to help. You won't be doing her any good if you don't get some rest."

Joe's fingers stop moving.

"It's been three days, now."

"Lie down on the bed. You're right beside her. Take this. You'll get a good night's sleep."

Joe releases his touch from his daughter and removes his hands from the incubator complying with Johanisson. With a glass of water, he takes two tablets and lies on his bed.

"Don't worry. We'll continue monitoring her. She's in great hands. Now, get some sleep."

Joe complies in silence as Johanisson leaves. Darkness chases away the light.

A lone tear from each eye rolls to his ears. Joe slips his right hand below his throat. Mary's blue-diamond pendant is heavy against his chest as he caresses the stones.

His breathing slows.

"I love you, Mary... good night, my little Emmanuelle."

On the other side of the mirror, Jacob watches Joe with his daughter. The door behind Jacob opens.

"Great work given the circumstances," Jacob said to Doctor Johanisson as he comes in the room with the door closing behind them.

"Do you think he suspects anything?" Johanisson asked.

"No. With his concern about Mary and the baby's health, he never suspected the reasoning for a slowed heart rate. Fantastic idea with that as a reason to keep her in bed."

Johanisson joins Jacob by the one-way mirror.

"I feel bad for them," the doctor said.

Jacob grabs Johanisson's shoulder getting his attention.

"Don't. As you recognize, we only have a precise capacity within Salvation. It was either Mary or the baby," Jacob said.

"Sir, you made the right call. Our conception and birthrate plans have been lower than expected."

Jacob turns back to the mirror.

"We have to figure out an approach to help the mothers keep their muscle-strength during pregnancy," Jacob said.

"Given Mary's muscle atrophy, an actual childbirth may have killed her, anyway."

"Well, not a chance we needed to take… it's done, now."

"I'll monitor the baby closely— "

"Let me know at once if she develops any complications."

Johanisson leaves the room. Jacob stands alone by the window placing his right hand flat against the glass.

"My choice was easy between them. Emmanuelle, you will love me as your grandfather."

19-Depression

JOE HAS NOT VENTURED from the Medical Wing in the six months since he had arrived to Salvation. Tears no longer come to him. His newborn daughter, Emmanuelle, steals his attention with her struggle of early life born one month premature.

With the aid of medication, sleep comes and goes to him through the night. Dreams and memories of his deceased wife, Mary, torment his visions when he is not giving Emmanuelle attention.

Joe sits with his left arm inside the incubator. Emmanuelle holds the tip of his index finger with her tiny left hand as she sleeps on her stomach.

A bell chimes inside his room as a video display illuminates at the door. Doctor Johanisson enters.

"Good morning, Joseph. How's she doing, today?"

Joe wipes his eyes trying to wake himself.

"Emma is doing great. She's able to hold my finger."

Johanisson steps to the incubator and examines the monitors. He reaches to the clamps holding the incubator's top sealed.

"Joseph... " Johanisson unlatches the top of the glass, "I've got great news... "

The doctor reaches inside the opened enclosure and unsnaps the monitor leads to Emma's chest. He removes his hands from the incubator holding Emma. "It's now time to take your daughter home."

Home is unfamiliar to Joe. Concern creeps to him having never been to his living quarters.

"But, she's still two weeks premature... " Joe takes Emma from the doctor holding her tight against his chest. "Are you sure she's okay?"

"Emma is very strong. She has fully developed, and everything checks out completely normal."

A bell chimes, again. The video display shows Jacob standing outside in the hallway. Johanisson opens the door.

Jacob enters seeing Emma in Joe's arms. A smile broadens on Jacob's face.

"Johanisson gave me the good news about Emma this morning, Joseph. I'm so happy for you," Jacob said.

Joe pats his right hand lightly against Emma's back as he stands shifting side-to-side.

"We've arranged everything you'll need to care for Emma in your place."

Joe stands silent slowly rocking Emma.

"Once you get there if you need anything, you let me know personally. We'll give you some time to get settled and then we'll talk about setting you up in your lab," Jacob said.

In the opened doorway, a familiar face appears. Heather, one of the sisters who had traveled to Salvation with Mary and him, enters the room.

"Hi, Joseph. Awe, is this her?" Heather steps beside him placing her hand next to his on Emma's back. "She's like adorable and all."

"Show, Joseph and his daughter to his room," Jacob said to Heather.

Joe follows Heather in silence to not wake Emma. Preoccupied with his precious baby in his arms, Joe is unaware of what Heather is saying or the path she takes him to his room.

"Okay, we're here. This is your room. Just place your hand flat against the access panel."

Joe complies. The glass panel is cold against his palm. Letters scroll across the panel: *Joseph 17WD21.*

"What's that mean?" Joe asked.

"Oh… uh… they didn't tell you? That's okay. I bet you've been busy with your baby. It's your identification."

Joe scrunches his forehead. His eyes narrow.

"Obviously, Joseph, well, that's your name. Seventeen is the Martian year you arrived. WD21 means you are *here* in the West Wing of the complex in Section D, and Room Number 21. It's pretty simple."

"Whatever," Joe said mumbling his response.

"All right, let's go inside."

Heather enters with Joe holding Emma following her as the glass door closes behind them.

"Lights on," Heather said as the room's lights brightened. "Everything is voice-activated. You can like set it up to react only to your voice when you want to for your security."

"Lights off," Joe said as the room dims.

"See, you got it. Lights on."

For the next few minutes, Heather shows the features in his living quarters and shows him around the different rooms.

"The toilet and faucets like work the same as you are used to in the Medical Wing. The only difference here is like uh every living area has a limit to the amount of water you can use in a twenty-four-hour period. Yours is twenty liters per day. Sounds like a lot, but it goes fast."

Joe follows Heather into the bathroom still holding Emma.

"Above each faucet in the bathroom or kitchen are like three, little lights. Green means, you have the full twenty liters available. Yellow means like you have ten liters left. Then, when you have two liters left, the red light will like blink and everything. If you run out, the red light stays on. But, don't worry, you'll get used to it."

"What about food? So far, it's been brought to us."

"You have several options."

Heather leads him into the kitchen.

"We don't have like stoves or ovens, thank goodness. Me and Joanie can't cook anyway, so we're thankful we have just microwaves. Most food requires water to uh... awe, Man, what's the word?"

"Rehydrate?"

"Yeah, rehydrate the food. So, it's like important to save enough water for cooking and all."

Joe listens. New information feeds his brain. A welcomed distraction.

"Use the room's tablet to order your food for the next few days, and it's like delivered to your room's delivery box outside in the hallway. It's pretty awesome."

Heather demonstrates a food order on the tablet.

"Okay, just place your hand on the tablet's glass."

Joe obeys.

"This uses your handprint to authorize the purchase on your account." Heather watches him follow her instructions. "Wow, you're set up nicely. You basically can order anything you want."

"What do you mean, I'm setup?"

"Well, you see, like me for instance... I am like what's called a *Restricted.*"

"A *Restricted?*"

"Wow, no one told you, huh? Figures. Most of the people here have like restricted access to certain areas within the complex. That also means we have other restrictions on the types of food we can have, and sometimes our water amount may be reduced for a few days if there are production issues and crap."

"Really? Does that happen a lot?"

"Huh, we've been here five—"

"Six."

"That's right. Six months and Joanie and me have been on water restrictions twice. It's only ten liters instead of a twenty, but it hasn't lasted too long. Only a few days."

"That doesn't seem fair."

"Well, you're a *Privileged*, well that's what we call you all, anyway. Maybe you can work to correct that someday," Heather said with a playful laugh.

"You mentioned several options?"

"Oh yeah, we have like restaurants here. But, don't get your hopes up."

"Restaurants?"

"Sure. They try to make it feel as close to Earth as possible. You can access them all, but I'm restricted to the main cafeteria. I'm sure someone will be by to show you."

"What about baby formula? They brought this into the room. How do I take care of that?"

Heather smiles.

"May, I?" Heather extends her arms to him.

Joe hesitates but relents passing Emma to her.

"Oh, she is adorable. Her name is Emma?"

"Actually, Emmanuelle, but we liked Emma for short."

"Hey, there sleepy head. Is it a family name?"

Joe holds back his tears.

"Mary and I loved that name ever since we were little kids and heard it at church."

"A beautiful name for such a beautiful little girl." She sniffs Emma's head. "Oh, I just love that baby smell. It's like been so long since I've held one."

A moment of normalcy comes to Joe.

"Well, I should go. Someone will stop by later today to show you around," Heather said as she gives back Emma to Joe.

"Thank you for showing me around my place."

"No problem. Hope to like see you around."

Heather leaves. Silence returns to Joe. A memory from onboard the rocket with Mary comes to him. The moment Mary first had mentioned the name Emmanuelle comes clear. Joe smiles as he looks at Emma.

"Well, it's a good thing you are a little girl because we never settled on a boy's name."

Joe copies Heather's action and bends placing his nose against the top of her little head. Wisps of faint-auburn hair tickle his nose.

"She is right. You do smell nice."

As soon as the words escape from Joe, he lifts his head fast.

"But, oh my God, that does not smell nice."

Joe scans the room worried as he enters his bedroom. Beside his bed is a small crib for Emma. Inside, to his relief, he finds cleaning supplies to change her

Her little eyes open staring at her father as she lays flat on the changing table. A slight smile emerges across her face catching his attention forcing a returned smile.

"I… I can do this."

EARTH DATE: AUGUST 27, 2016 (3 DAYS LATER)

IN A BED FOR TWO, Joe lays flat on his back diagonal across the mattress. Unshaven and disheveled, for the past three days, he has only moved his position to care for Emma or to relieve himself. His nemesis of insomnia has accompanied him to Salvation from Earth.

The bedroom's lights dim and brighten in slow, repeated turns. Joe stares to the white ceiling whispering his commands as his virtual assistant obeys.

"Dim lights… turn lights on… dim lights… "

Soft breathing escapes from Emma's crib beside Joe's bed. He rolls to his side. Through the crib's vertical slats, his daughter sleeps on her stomach; her face turned to him.

"Turn lights on… " he said whispering his command.

Joe's eyes do not blink. A vacant stare focuses on Emma.

"Isn't she beautiful?"

The words come to him in Mary's voice inside his head. Her voice remains vivid in his memories. Joe returns to the discussion. Words do not leave his mouth; only his thoughts.

She looks like you.

Maybe so, but, Joe, she has your eyes.

You think so?

Yes, she looks at you just like you looked at me... full of love.

Joe blinks his eyes once for the first time in minutes.

Are you doing okay, Joe?

Silence fills his thoughts.

Can you believe she is real? We always wanted a baby. I wish I were there to hold her.

The doctor says Emma is really healthy, but I'm so worried about her.

Don't be. You will be such a great Dad.

Not that, I'm worried about what her life will be like, here.

Mary laughs. *As opposed to on Earth? You know what will happen there in a few years.*

I know, but I worry about her. What happens if something happens to me?

Silence again fills his thoughts. Joe closes his eyes. He imagines Mary's hands wrapping around his shoulders from behind him. Her fingers press against his chest.

Joe, I will always be with you. I will give you strength. Do not worry. Emma will be okay. Emma will be okay... Emma will be—

A piercing chime echoes through Joe's living area. His eyes dart open. Soft cries come from Emma.

Joe bolts from his bed into the living room. Above the access panel, Joe sees Jacob standing outside in the corridor. The cold condition of the glass awakens Joe.

"Afternoon, Joe. Mind if I come inside?"

No words occur as Joe steps to the side as his father enters.

"I would have stopped by sooner, but I wanted to give you some time to get used to things, here."

Joe grunts.

"Are you sleeping, any? With a newborn, I bet Emma keeps you up at night?"

Joe comes closer to Jacob.

"What the hell would you know about that? You were not there for me?"

"Joseph, let's sit."

Jacob motions him to the sofa.

"I was not there for you and Rachel. And with all of this, with everything that will happen to Earth; I didn't have a choice."

"Didn't have a choice? Bullshit!"

"Like I explained when you arrived, Eden recruited me. I wanted to join to save our family. I was too late for Rachel, but not too late for you."

Joe huffs his breath. His chest heaves.

"There you go. Did Eden recruit me because of my research or because of you?"

"Like I said, your research got you here... okay, so, I was able to highlight your work to get you noticed for recruitment."

Silence joins them in the room. An unknown common bond forces the silence. Jacob holds his apprehension about what to say to Joe, while he holds back thirty-seven-years of sorrow being without a father.

Cries shriek through the quietness of the living room.

"I'll get her, Joseph. Looks like you can use a break."

Jacob stands. His face beaming as he disappears into the bedroom. Joe hears his father.

"Hey, Baby Girl. How's my little Emma? There... there... "

For a moment, Joe's past with his absent father vanishes. His daughter's grandfather is taking care of her. But, as soon as Jacob enters the living room cradling Emma, sadness displaces the normalcy.

Jacob stands swaying, rocking Emma in his arms.

"Where do you keep her food? Can I feed her?"

Exhaustion forces compliance, as Joe points to the kitchen.

"I suppose you know how to feed her?"

"Joseph, I may not have been there for you, but I can feed a baby."

Jacob returns to the living room and sits across from Joe.

"I can't believe how fast she is growing."

"You've not seen her in only three days."

"True, but I can see it. Look how she can hold the bottle with little help from me."

"Huh, yeah, I think she's going to have Mary's independence for sure."

The comment forces Jacob to turn his attention away from Emma.

"Joe... how are you doing?"

"I told you, I'm fine."

"Are you?"

A piercing stare shoots across the room to Jacob.

"If you don't mind me saying, you look terrible. Not only have you just lost your wife and gained a new daughter but the experience of journeying here and living on Mars… this all has to be taking its toll on you?"

Joe rakes his hands through his hair which has not been cut in eight months since Mauritius. His hands follow the back of his scalp to his neck scratching his skin through a thick, uneven beard.

"Can I at least send someone here to clean you up?"

Joe's eyes traced his father's arms to his hands. Emma turns her head to Joe while holding the bottle, almost as if she understood Jacob's request.

"Uh… huh… okay, I guess someone can help me with *this*," Joe said pulling his hair several inches from his head.

"Great. Next, we need to talk about your lab. I hate to press you, but we are literally sitting on a ticking clock with Earth. I need you to start your work there."

Joe looks away. Work is the last thing he is thinking about, now.

"We still have a couple of years to ask Eden to send us equipment from Earth, but you just need to tell us what."

Joe grunts. The thought of cataloging equipment does not entice him.

"Can I ask you a question?" Jacob asks as Emma finishes her bottle, "You've dealt with tragedy in the past; what did you do to push through?"

"Uh… I lost myself in things. I remember Mama's funeral. I was lost in watching a replay of the Moon landing… with Charlie, I buried myself in my work… "

"Then, there you have it. Get lost in your work in the lab. Don't worry about Emma. We have people here with their sole task being to take care of babies and children. In fact, two of them you already know from your trip here?"

Joe's eyes lift upward. "Who?"

"The sisters, Heather and Joanie. I'll ask one of them to stop by with the person I'll send over to cut your hair."

Jacob lifts Emma to his left shoulder and taps lightly on her back. A small burp releases from her carrying a whiff of powdered milk to Joe.

"And, Joseph, we really need you, here. And, I hope you will visit your lab, soon."

Joe releases a deep sigh.

"You're right… it worked before. I need to do something to take my mind off things."

Jacob smiles and holds out Emma to Joe.

"Here, you better come get her. Each time I hold her, I feel myself getting more attached to her than before."

"Yeah, send one of them over here tomorrow so I can see how they are with Emma. Once I'm comfortable leaving her with someone, I'll start my work."

"I know there's still a lot to discuss and work through, but I promise to give you as much space and time, as needed. Even though we cannot tell anyone of our relationship, I don't want this to come between me being a grandfather to Emma."

Joe looks down at his daughter asleep in his cradled arms.

"Let's take it one step at a time. How's that?"

"I'll take it. I'll send someone by tomorrow to help with your haircut. And, I'll check if Joanie or Heather are free to stop by. Thank you for letting me spend some time with you and Emma."

Jacob presses his hand flat against the door panel as it opens, as he has global access to every door in Salvation.

Silence returns to Joe's living quarters. Soft breathing is rhythmic from Emma in his arms.

It's okay, Joe. Emma will be fine. You need to get on with your life.

Joe imagined Mary's arms around his holding Emma together.

You have an important job to do, and Salvation needs you.

A smile creeps across Joe's face as he walks into his bedroom.

"Dim lights."

EARTH DATE: SEPTEMBER 3, 2016 (1 WEEK LATER)

DEPRESSION REACHES A POINT where its toll is too much. One month after Mary's death, mourning still haunts Joe. His saving grace... Emma.

Joe and Mary had been almost inseparable after first meeting when they were ten-years-old. Joe closes his eyes and can recall that day twenty-seven years in the past. A sad day; his mother's funeral.

Rachel had battled brain cancer for months. Her struggle was Joe's inspiration for his genome, cancer research which had brought them to Salvation.

When Joe recalls first meeting Mary, he remembers her first words: *What are you watching?* The memory of seeing a replay of the Moon landing that afternoon brings a smile to him given the current irony of living on Mars.

As Joe remembers Mary's first words to him, her last words chase away his childhood memories.

"Promise me. You will protect our daughter," Mary said as Doctor Johanisson had pushed her out of her medical room for her cesarean operation.

This promise to Mary replays over-and-over inside Joe's mind. Her words comfort him giving him strength.

During the past two weeks, Joe has worked to feel settled into their new living quarters. Via daily walks with Emma through the Salvation complex, the facility becomes more familiar.

To Joe's surprise, a Children's Wing is available for daycare and educational activities. With Jacob's insistence, the staff of this wing assists Joe with Emma.

Normalcy returns to Joe. Today is the day he meets his lab staff — the reason for his selection to join Salvation.

Today also holds another form of significance for Joe. It is the one-year-anniversary of Gabriel sharing to Joe the information about CIE.57.20, the Eden Foundation, and Project Salvation. The meeting which changed his life, forever.

He hid the secret of Salvation for months. They experienced a vacation in paradise with its staged plane crash. They blasted off from Earth and traveled to Mars. He learned Mary was pregnant. Jacob revealed himself to him and is the Salvation Leader. They confined Mary to her bed until her death upon delivering Emma.

Joe welcomes normalcy. He craves this feeling for his own sanity.

Nervousness rumbles through his stomach. Standing outside his laboratory door brings apprehension to Joe as if it was his first day of class.

Joe places his hand flat against the access panel. A green light does not appear. He lifts his hand and replaces it on the panel. Still, the red light teases him.

A few seconds had passed. The glass door slides open to his left. Inside the lab stands an older man. A familiar glint of light bounces off the man's bald head.

"It's great to see you again, Joe," the man said.

Joe's mouth gapes open. Air rushes from his lungs chasing a question which escapes through his lips.

"Professor... Baptiste?"

The man sees Joe sway forward-and-back. He grabs Joe's arms.

"I've got you. Come inside," the man said.

Joe follows the man as he guides Joe to a chair.

"I know. I know, you have a million questions about me."

"But... but... "

"Joe, like you, I was selected to join Salvation," Professor Baptiste said as he pulled a chair next to Joe.

"But, when... when did you know?" Joe asked his former college mentor.

Professor Baptiste looks over his shoulder and lowers his voice.

"We're not really supposed to tell anyone our stories here, but this is a special case since we know each other."

"Know each other."

Baptiste senses Joe's frustration.

"Joe, I'm sure you're aware of how hard it was to keep this secret from everyone. The same is true for me."

Joe leans back in his chair.

"You remember when I approached you about my retirement and moving to Florida?"

"Yeah, it was right after I completed my Ph.D., and you helped Charlie and me get your old laboratory at Stonehaven."

"Yep, that's the time when Gabriel recruited me to join."

Joe widens his eyes.

"Oh, so Gabriel recruited you, too, huh?"

"Yes. The work we started on cancer research and the human genome is what had placed me on their radar as someone who could help Salvation."

A sense of relief intensifies for Joe. Soon after Gabriel had recruited him, the secret ate at Joe. The only person Joe had confided everything he had known from Gabriel was Charlie. After Charlie's death, Joe kept the secret until Gabriel informed him to tell Mary. However, Joe still could not bring himself to tell Mary the full truth.

One year later, Joe sits with his old mentor discussing CIE.57.20, how Earth is doomed, and the excitement of Project Salvation. The conversation is therapeutic for Joe.

"I did leave for Florida... that is true. But, it was not for retirement," Baptiste said.

"What was your role, then?"

A smile beams from Baptiste.

"My role was to help scan potential recruits to join Salvation."

"Scan? Scan for what?"

Baptiste releases a short laugh.

"Well, there will only be ten-thousand people brought here from Earth."

"Yeah, the minimal viable population for gene diversity."

"Exactly. But, after people are recruited based on needs and skill, we have to ensure they have no underlying issues or potential for issues."

"Issues? I'm not sure I follow?"

"Come on, Joe. Think about it. Remember our first class together?"

"Uh… yeah."

"Each person is complex. But, we are unique. We have our own, unique DNA. And, as your research shows, sometimes that DNA is flawed."

"Oh, I get it. You were scanning for defects in their DNA."

"More like looking for genetic markers for predispositions to certain diseases or cancers. If Salvation will truly sustain a population, then we have to weed out those on Earth, who are a potential threat to us, here."

Joe sits in silence both stunned and in contemplation.

"But, isn't it those defects, which helps us, humans, better evolve?"

"Oh, Joe, I've missed our debates. I'm so happy you're joining us. Oh, and my sincere thoughts are with you. I'm so excited you are here, but my first words should have been how sorry I am about Mary."

Joe lowers his head removing his eye contact with Baptiste.

"Thanks," Joe said in a softer tone.

"And, how's Emmanuelle?"

Joe lifts his head. His entire demeanor brightens.

"Oh my God, Emma is fantastic. If it wasn't for her, I'd most likely be looking to walk outside Salvation and suffocating to death."

Baptiste places his hands on Joe's hands.

"Well, then, let your daughter get you through this time. I'm aware it is so hard especially being here, but focus all your strength on Emmanuelle. Oh, I'm sorry, Emma."

"She's definitely saving me, for sure."

Joe pauses for a moment.

"So, how did you scan people's DNA on Earth?" Joe asked changing the subject.

Baptiste laughs. The laugh differs from what Joe remembers.

"Actually, Gabriel told me something that at first I didn't believe, but now, I put nothing past The Eden Foundation to do."

"Oh, you've got my interest peaked, now."

"Well, The Eden Foundation developed a way to extract DNA samples from people through the delivery of vaccines."

"Vaccines? Like the flu shot?"

"Exactly. The flu shot. So, somehow Eden worked with the manufacturers of the vaccines. I don't think they were even aware, but for each vaccine, Eden was able to get the DNA sample. From those samples, I ran our tests."

"Holy shit, really?"

"Yes. I'm not sure if this is true or not, but I have my suspicions— "

"About what?"

"Remember the swine flu?"

"Oh hell, yeah, Mary and I caught that and felt terrible for days."

"Well, I ran tests on the virus strains of that swine flu outbreak. I found DNA marker elements in those samples, which looked like our testing parameters. It was just too convenient for me."

"Hell, not to mention how many people started getting the vaccines."

"Exactly. But, we started to have a problem. Those damn celebrities in Hollywood tried linking vaccines causing diseases which was total bullshit. Hell, I should know."

"How did that cause you trouble?"

"Shit, people are so gullible. They listened to comedians instead of doctors and the numbers of people getting vaccines declined. And, our timeline for scanning people kept marching on as that son-of-a-bitch will still strike Earth."

"So, how did you fix that? I mean, when we left, that was still an issue, if not even worse now?"

Baptiste releases another laugh.

"That's when Gabriel came to me again with another plan. I'm not sure if it was his plan or someone within Eden, but it was brilliant."

Joe leans forward to Baptiste.

"Remember a few years ago when those commercials aired about DNA testing to discover your ancestry?"

"Sure. Mary and I did that test. I'm like seventy percent Scottish. Mary was mostly German."

"It was fun wasn't it, learning your family history?"

"Hmm, yeah, I guess. We got a kick out of... Holy shit. I get it. You used those tests to scan people."

"Joe, you always were my best student. Yes, exactly. And, that was a genius way of getting the information. Hell, Eden didn't even hide the fact we were collecting people's DNA."

"Wow. People are gullible. You're right. Shit, Mary and I were."

"So, is that where Eden got our information to clear us to come?"

Baptiste sits unresponsive. A grin creeps across his lips.

"How long have you been here?"

Baptiste stands and paces the laboratory.

"Today is my one year anniversary of my arrival here."

"Well, then, here is another coincidence. Today is my one year anniversary of Gabriel recruiting me," Joe said.

Baptiste stops his pacing and turns to Joe.

"I can tell you this. With Eden, there is no such thing as a coincidence. I've seen too many things, now."

Joe shrugs his shoulders.

"I mean, look at us. First, I was your professor, then your mentor. How was I to know that years later, I would be the one to come to Salvation to set up your laboratory based on your research?"

Joe stands pacing the opposite side of the lab from Baptiste.

"I've monitored your work and have been so impressed with the advancements you made discovering the genetic marker for glioblastoma."

"Well, thanks to my mom's brain cancer, I was able to identify her RNA codex miR-182 as the gene marker for GBM."

"I'm sure it had to come as a relief when you learned you did not have her same RNA marker?"

"Huh— "

"I have to confess; I had to scan your DNA to clear you. And, your miR-182 was negative," Baptiste said interrupting Joe.

Years ago, what assisted Joe to identify the marker as a predisposition to develop this brain tumor which had killed his mother was his realization he shares the same codex as his mother, Rachel.

Joe turns away from Baptiste. A revelation comes to Joe. Somehow, his father, Jacob, had manipulated Joe's DNA scan allowing him to come to Salvation. Only Joe knew he had this marker as he had purposely omitted this finding in his research.

"Uh… yes, I was relieved for sure," Joe said. His first lie to Baptiste.

Baptiste approaches Joe.

"Well, this will make my transition working at Salvation that much easier with you being here, Professor," Joe said.

Baptiste opens his mouth in silence. He keeps a secret from Joe.

When Gabriel had recruited Baptiste to leave Earth, they both knew Baptiste had nothing to lose. The week prior, Baptiste had been diagnosed with Stage III liver cancer giving him at least a year to live.

Baptiste has beaten this estimate so far by five months but knows he is on borrowed time. With the tragedy Joe has just endured, Baptiste withholds this news, for now.

"So, I have a question. What I'm I supposed to call you? I thought there were no last names here?" Joe asked regaining his mentor's attention.

"I'm called Baptiste, here. As you can imagine there are a lot of Johns in the population. Someone assigns new arrivals their name. It's typically their first name followed by their arrival and living information. Supposedly, common first names are not used, so you can imagine my surprise you are called Joe?"

"Huh, yeah Joe is common, but I'm sure it's because it's short for Joseph, which isn't as popular."

Joe's reply comes fast. He recalls the conversation with his father upon his arrival to Salvation. Jacob's instructions were to never reveal Joe's relationship with him and their shared last name. The instruction is necessary to prevent any thoughts of nepotism influencing Joe's recruitment to Salvation.

"How 'bout a tour of the lab, Baptiste?" Joe asked changing the subject.

20-Baptiste

A ONCE METICULOUS SCIENTIST, chaos has consumed Joe the previous year since his recruitment in Colorado. Order inside Joe's mind has faded.

During the past week-and-a-half, a comfortable feeling of structure returns. Joe immerses his energy into taking over his laboratory from Baptiste and meeting everyone assigned to work with him. Before Joe's arrival, Baptiste had created detailed notes of the expected practices for the lab. These notes have been helpful as Baptiste's time with Joe has declined the past days. His fifty-five-year-old mentor is taking a much-needed vacation.

In the early planning stages, Eden recognized the need for recreation activities to rejuvenate the Salvationists. Rover vehicles capable of transporting six passengers ferry between the main Salvation area and the nearby holiday complex. For those leaving for vacation, the initial thrill is the ability to walk on the actual Martian surface; an experience reserved for maintenance staff and planetary researchers.

While the main Salvation area is functional, the holiday complex is the ultimate in luxury. Attendants pamper guests with various spa treatments and relaxation exercises. Clear ceilings allow for prime viewings of the Martian surroundings; an otherworldly experience in an alien environment.

Each Salvationist wears a bio-suit serving multiple purposes. The suit provides constant measures of heart rate, blood glucose levels, blood pressure, and body temperature. Mainframes in the medical area house the records. Abnormal readings will flash in Doctor Johanisson's tablet alerting the need for potential medical attention.

During Baptiste's travel to the holiday complex, alerts routinely come to the doctor's tablet. Johanisson flips through the readings ignoring them as they are the same abnormalities seen the past several months.

Just as Joe had lost himself in his work at Stony Brook after his best-friend Charlie's death; his Salvation laboratory protects his heart, yet again. His days are full, but he promises himself to come home early — a similar promise he had made to Mary many years ago. But, unlike then, Emma forces him home early in the evenings.

Joe reviews the files containing the DNA scans of every resident at Salvation. Baptiste meticulously had chronicled the specific details in the exact fashion Joe would have executed. This self-realization reinforces Joe's long-held belief he had modeled his work practices from his mentor.

As Gabriel had described during Joe's recruitment in Colorado, Joe is responsible for determining which men and women will pair together to conceive children. He scans DNA records for potential birth defects or reduced proclivities of producing diseases or cancers for the joined couple.

Gabriel had been less than forthcoming with Joe's purpose since the original invitation to Joe was due to his cancer research and the Foundation's willingness to back his academic work financially. However, in some way, Gabriel had told the truth from their initial meeting: Joe's mission is to ensure the survival of humanity.

Eden recruited those chosen to join Salvation based on their capabilities to support the future population on Mars. The evaluation of the potential recruits includes a first-pass assessment of their DNA. At Salvation, Joe performs the second, detailed scan. However, as Baptiste had explained on Joe's second day in the lab, the final approval is made by Jacob.

"So, let me get this straight, Jacob makes the final determination even though he's not a scientist?" Joe said recalling his last conversation before Baptiste left for his vacation.

"If you've not already determined this for yourself, Jacob is in control of everything, here."

"Has he ever rejected a pairing recommendation?"

Joe recalls the laugh released by his mentor; a laugh heard many times during their time at Stony Brook.

"You'll learn soon enough."

EARTH DATE: SEPTEMBER 11, 2016 - AFTERNOON

MARS IS LESS THAN HALF the diameter of Earth and spins at half the speed. This means the Salvationists experience the familiar feeling of the duration of night and day on Mars. At 2:41 a.m., to adjust for the slight difference in rotation, the Salvation clocks change back to 2:00 a.m. across the complex.

One year, or the time it takes Mars to complete one orbit around the Sun, differs from Earth. With Mars being the fourth planet from the Sun, the elliptical orbit takes 687-days versus 365 for Earth. Rather than establish a new system for calendars, Eden indicates the month-day-year the same as on Earth with one extension: the Martian year every 687-days after Earth-date November 15, 1983; the first landing on Mars.

Today is Earth-date, September 11, 2016, Martian Year 17.

This new, but familiar concept of time, conflicts with Joe's intended method of managing his files. To account for the Martian years, he establishes a cross-reference document to avoid unintentional readings within his reports.

Baptiste has left for his holiday, and Joe asked his lab staffers to go home early. The silence allows Joe to concentrate.

Every Salvationist has a record of their sequenced DNA before their recruitment. This mapping provides for easy reference of their genetic markers for predispositions to cancers and certain diseases. The specific pairing of DNA sequences of potential male and female partners will reduce the probability these conditions not developing within the population.

In 2003, the Human Genome Project took thirteen years to sequence the first human DNA. Today, this sequencing occurs in one day. And, given Joe's wishlist of equipment to Gabriel before leaving Earth, Eden has provided the lab with the latest sequencing apparatus.

Joe gets his record among those Baptiste had cataloged earlier. To test the machines, Joe places a cotton swab in his mouth and transfers the material onto glass slides.

A surge of excitement courses through his body. The instruments are next generation ones not even available within the research community on Earth. Joe not only has one but three.

Joe sets the glass slide with his sample inside the sequencer. Reading from the manual, Joe enters various commands on the keyboard attached to his new toy.

As the computer cycles through its diagnostic controls, the DNA sequence develops within the apparatus. The expected completion time is less than four hours.

While the machine performs its processing, Joe returns to his cross-referencing of the Salvationists' records between Earth and Martian dates. One hour passes.

"Huh, that's strange... I can't find his records?"

Joe flips through the files trying to locate the record for Baptiste.

I can't find it, here?

As Joe contemplates reviewing the files again in search of Baptiste's, a chorus of chimes plays from the DNA Sequencer.

"Wow, that was fast."

Joe retrieves his sample and the report taking them to his workstation. A few minutes pass.

Yep, the same sequence as before. At least I know the machine works.

Joe leans in his chair and closes his eyes. Deep relaxing breaths follow. With a jolt, Joe stands. *Where is it? I saw him drinking from it before he left.*

Inside Baptiste's white, desk drawer, Joe finds a familiar object from his days at Stony Brook: a rim-stained coffee mug, a present from Joe on his defense day of his dissertation.

I can pull a sample from this and run it through the machine.

Joe glides from the desk as he swabs the mug's rim. He transfers the trace sample to the glass slide and positions it inside the sequencer.

This will let me know the age capabilities of the machine since this sample is three-days-old.

Joe enters the test protocol commands into the machine and resumes his cross-referencing. Four hours pass.

The latest report lies on Joe's desk. Baptiste's identified genome glares at him. One specific point stands out.

"No... that... can't be right?"

Joe scrolls through his research reports digitized by Eden from his Stonehaven lab.

Baptiste has cancer?

The genetic marker is unmistakable. Memories of his mother's passing from her brain cancer rushes to him followed by peace knowing her affliction had pushed him in his research. Countless conversations with Baptiste during his graduate work about cancer and someday finding a cure; Baptiste's test results taunt his heart.

A vibration rattles his thoughts. The black, rubberized band around his left wrist alerts Joe of the time. The quaking jolts his thoughts away from Baptiste to his daughter, Emma. In years' past, Joe would have disregarded this alarm and continued his work. But, his responsibilities with Emma call.

Joe will have to wait two days until Baptiste's return from holiday to confront his old mentor.

EARTH DATE: DECEMBER 24, 2016
(2 MONTHS LATER)

DEATH COMES FAST to one cursed with Stage IV cancer. The disease has worked its way through the stomach and into the vertebra. Baptiste lays pale and weak in Doctor Johanisson's Medical Wing of Salvation.

A familiar foe to tragedy, Joe has visited his old mentor each day upon admittance to Johanisson's care. Several days had passed after Baptiste's return from holiday until Joe developed his courage to confront his friend.

The unpleasant conversation lingers in Joe's memory as Baptiste had broken down in tears sharing his prognosis. Joe recalls asking if Baptiste had a family history with cancer throughout their studies together in Stony Brook. Baptiste's only reply being he was not sure.

In Joe's graduate studies, Baptiste shared his personal stories. Joe felt a kindred relationship with his mentor with them both losing a parent at an early age.

Baptiste had told Joe of how at only four-months-old, his mom had discovered his dad, Simon, dead on their kitchen floor. Simon had died during the night by slipping accidentally on wet tiles with his bare feet.

Joe also appreciated Baptiste's shared sense of humor as Baptiste always ended this story by saying, *those who say to never cry over spilled-milk are full of shit.*

"I still don't understand how I was approved to come to Salvation?" Baptiste's comment replayed nightly in Joe's thoughts as he scoured through his research hoping to discover a last-minute cure to no avail.

Joe had shared how he discovered Baptiste's cancer. The news struck Baptiste as odd even though he never considered to examine his medical records before Joe's arrival.

The cancer had appeared months before Baptiste left Earth for Salvation. But, The Eden Foundation still approved his departure from Earth.

"The work must have been that important," Baptiste said upon his initial conversation with Joe.

Baptiste fought the disease as best as possible with chemo and cancer-therapy drugs. However, tonight, the battle is ending; and both he and Joe are aware this may be their last talk together.

"Is there anything I can get for you?" Joe asked.

Baptiste's voice has grown frail, which shocks Joe. He often thinks of his first day in class with Baptiste his sophomore year at Stony Brook. Baptiste commanded a lecture hall full of one-hundred-and-fifty students. Now, this authoritative voice is merely a whisper as Joe sits with his head lowered over his friend.

"No, I'm fine," Baptiste said in a soft whimper.

Joe holds Baptiste's bony, cold left hand comforting his dear mentor.

"You know... have I ever told you... "

Baptiste squeezes Joe's hand.

"I always looked up to you as a father figure."

Joe feels Baptiste pet the back of Joe's hand with his thumb.

"I mean my father was... well, you know, wasn't around. And, when we met, I really enjoyed our time together. Not just the lab work, but your personal advice and things."

Joe makes a point not to look at him. While Joe is used to death around him in his life, this moment never becomes easier.

"You comforted me by listening about my troubles with Mary and my work without ever complaining... I really appreciate everything. Hell, if it weren't for you, I would never have been recruited here— "

Baptiste squirms his hand inside Joe's grip. The shocking movements stop Joe. He hesitates his glance to Baptiste fearing death has taken his friend. The squirming continues.

No longer fearing what he will see, Joe turns his head to the bed. Baptiste's eyes are open wide; his mouth moves without a sound.

Joe leans over Baptiste's face. Words escape through whispers from Baptiste.

"I... know... about Jacob... "

The breathy words startle Joe as he turns facing Baptiste.

"What do you know?" Joe whispers remembering the promise he had made earlier to Jacob not to tell anyone.

Joe turns his ear back to Baptiste's mouth.

"He's... your father. I've known... since... "

Baptiste gasps for air into Joe's ear.

"... we first... "

Silence.

Joe turns back to Baptiste, his eyes lifeless.

"Since *we first*, what?"

Joe lifts his head from the bed and pushes with force on his friend's shoulders in successive motions.

"Baptiste... Baptiste... John... John... "

Tears drop from Joe's cheeks soaking into the bed sheets around Baptiste's dead body. As quick as the tears came, is as fast as they stop. Vibrations rattle his wrist.

Joe stands and leans one last time over his fatherly mentor. He presses his lips on Baptiste's forehead while simultaneously using his left palm to close Baptiste's eyelids. With a heavy, deep moan, Joe leaves the room.

On the other side of the one-way mirror in Baptiste's medical room, Jacob stands having watched Joe since his arrival to visit with Baptiste. He heard what Joe had said, however, Baptiste's words were too quiet.

Jacob had remained motionless during Joe's entire exchange with Baptiste. The only time he slumped his posture was when Joe had told Baptiste, *I always looked up to you as a father figure.*

As Joe left, a smile creeps on Jacob's face as his fatherly competitor is no longer.

21-Baby Genius

TIME IS NO MATCH for an aching heart. Sorrow has compressed Joe into his living quarters the past few days. The misery of Baptiste's passing intertwines with his suppressed emotions for Mary.

Unshaven and disheveled, he lays in his dark bedroom. His eyes transfix into the dancing shadows on the ceiling from the glowing LEDs of the room's wall control panel.

Cries from Emma break his trance every few hours. Hunger and her demand for clean diapers create the shrieks from her small lungs.

Insomnia returns. Memories juxtapose against the reality of living on Mars. His mental-state spirals with his absence of sleep.

A faint whimper comes from Emma. Joe props his body up and twists his legs to the floor stubbing his right big toe against her bedside crib.

"Shit!"

Joe's exclamation startles Emma causing her to squeal.

"Ssh… ssh… " Joe slips his hands under her warm body lifting her. "There, there… it's okay; Daddy just stubbed his toe."

A slight swinging motion calms her cries.

"I bet you're hungry."

Joe leaves their bedroom and goes in the open living room and kitchen area.

"Lights, on."

Warm LED lights illuminate the rooms as Joe fixes Emma's formula. As he rests on the sofa with Emma in his lap, he marvels at her facial features as she takes her bottle. As she drinks, he rubs the side of her right cheek with the back of his fingers.

"Emma, you favor Mary every day."

Joe closes his eyes.

"Oh, how's my little girl?"

"She's doing just fine," Joe said as he smiles opening his eyes. His sleep-deprived imagination creates a vision of Mary kneeling on the floor before them. Mary's hand rests on the top of Emma's head.

"I can't believe how big she is getting."

"She really is growing fast for a four-month-old. I was so concerned about how she would develop here. But, she seems to be ahead of where she should be… "

"Joe, how are you doing? I'm so sorry about Baptiste."

A heavy sigh comes as he closes his eyes.

"I should be used to death, but it never gets easier."

Mary grabs his hand. Her hand feels cold to him.

"He was in so much pain for so long. Now, he's in a better place."

Joe opens his eyes staring at Emma in his lap. She has stopped sucking from her bottle. He notices her head turned away from him, her eyes looking upward. Emma smiles.

"Look, Joe. Do you think she can see me?"

Joe opens his mouth. Words fail to come. Confusion fills him.

Is Mary really here?

Before Joe speaks, a chime rings from the door. The figure of Jacob appears on the small screen beside the door.

Joe glances to Emma. The bottle is back in her mouth, and Mary's image disappears.

"Open door," Joe says. The white door slides to the left as Jacob enters, then closes.

"How's my little Emma doing?"

Joe does not reply.

"Can I?" Jacob asks stretching out his hands.

"Uh huh." Joe grunts as Jacob lifts Emma cradling her at his chest.

"I know I've not been around since Baptiste's passing, but I've stopped by to check on you and to talk business."

Joe slides his right leg onto the sofa twisting his body. Throbbing radiates from his big toe through his calf.

"We need you to pull yourself together so you can start the lab work. We have only less than four-Earth years left. And, we need to know what other equipment you might need."

Joe inhales; his chest swells. Hot air presses through his nose as his body deflates.

"I just needed some time to collect my thoughts."

"It's difficult, I know. First, Mary, and now your friend, Baptiste."

Throbbing be damned, Joe slams his foot off the sofa to the floor and stands.

"First, Mary? She's not first. Hell, that would be you, then Mama... " Joe paces the room as Jacob slowly rocks Emma. "Grandma... my friend Charlie... "

Joe releases a long grunt in annoyance as he sways in his stance near the kitchen.

"Joseph, I'm sorry there seems to be so much death around you... but, now, with your work you are responsible for here at Salvation... will help us with new life and possibly help us with keeping people healthy."

Joe stands still. His eyes roll to the ceiling listening to Jacob.

"The first thirty-seven years of your life seems to be full of death, but thirty-seven years from now... hell, for that matter two-hundred years from now, you will be linked with life... you have to look at the bigger picture, here."

Joe places his attention to Jacob and his daughter. Jacob's remarks resonate, not about him, but with his daughter.

"Here, take her." Jacob hands Emma to Joe.

"She's the reason for you, now. I'm sorry about your sadness, but keep your focus on Emma. Pull yourself out of this… this depression you're in and go back to the lab. We'll have people take care of her during the day, so don't worry."

Emma's eyes close. Joe feels her little body breathing. He places her frontside against his left shoulder as he gently pats her backside. Tears form and roll down his face. Jacob puts his large, firm grip on Joe's right shoulder.

"I know I've never been a father to you. And, even though we can tell no one about our relationship, I'm here anytime you need to talk."

"Of course, it's not like you're going anywhere," Joe said with a laugh.

Jacob returns the laugh. "I guess you're right. See, you're stuck with me now," Jacob said squeezing and releasing Joe's shoulder.

"Fine. I'll take Emma to the daycare area in the morning and go back to work."

Jacob returns to the entryway.

"Great… open door," Jacob said stepping into the hall, "oh, and by the way, in case you don't know, happy new year."

The door closes.

Happy new year… oh, that's right on Earth… huh, only three more to go…

Joe returns to the bedroom placing Emma into her crib and goes quietly back to the kitchen ensuring not to wake his daughter. Water refreshes him as he sips his drink.

"Good night, my little Emma," Mary's voice comes in a hushed tone to Joe from the bedroom.

"Ma—ma."

Clanging echoes from the sink. The plastic cup Joe held slips from his hand. He rushes to the bedroom.

"Lights, on!"

The room is empty. Emma lays in her crib; her eyes open.

"Man… I'm hearing things."

"Mama." A small voice came from the crib.

Joe approaches Emma. She turns her head to him.

"Mama."

"Emma?"

"Mama."

Is she saying, Mama?

"Mama," Emma said as she grinned.

Joe takes her against his chest. He does not believe what he hears.

She was born one month early four months ago. She should not be able to speak, yet.

"Emma, did you just say your first word?"

Joe pauses expecting to receive a full response from her.

"Did you see Mary, your mama?"

Joe gently touches the back of shoulders comforting her.

"Mama."

Earth Date: August 1, 2017 (7 months later)

TIME IS BUT A FLEETING MOMENT. Worry and sorrow freeze time making heartache longing. Happiness and preoccupation drive time forward. Joe is stuck somewhere in the middle.

A good day is one he characterizes by working his way through his tasks, lost in his work. No matter how hard he tries, thoughts and memories of Mary or his friend, Charlie, frequent him in unsuspecting moments.

Emma has become Joe's compass providing him direction and purpose. Time for her is unassuming. Her routine is simple and basic: wake with her dad for breakfast, daycare in the mornings, and a mid-afternoon nap. Like clockwork, Joe picks her up each afternoon at six.

The routine is in place. Joe is managing his time. His life moves forward.

Safe at Salvation, a looming countdown hangs over everyone. In three-Earth-years, the end will come for the planet. What preoccupies everyone are their specific tasks in preparing Salvation for weekly arrivals of people and supplies. Salvation sends requests for specific equipment and supplies back to Earth with each return flight. Time moves forward for everyone.

To protect himself, Joe has not attempted to connect with anyone. He takes Emma to daycare and works in his lab. Two staffers assist him, but only through his academic commands. His unwillingness to associate with anyone is his self-defense mechanism.

The current Salvation population is eight-thousand-four-hundred-thirty-four. Ten thousand will inhabit Salvation by Earth-date August 1, 2020, the final arrival to Mars.

If projections hold true for the total population, the expected number of births will equate to one-and-a-half times the expected number of deaths each Martian year. Given the average age and pre-screened health readings for each Salvationist, this expectation is to have approximately fifteen births versus ten deaths annually.

Resources and self-sufficiency dictate what is possible to sustain a population of ten thousand. After Earth-date, September 11, 2020, the Salvationists will be alone in the solar system.

The first week at Salvation, each new arrival undergoes an orientation. The newest Salvationists learn how to maneuver through the complex, safety protocols, and the off-limit areas.

After explanations and tours of the physical complex, the arrivals review their work assignments gaining clarity on their responsibilities. Some are maintenance staff; others are engineers and technical people. Salvation has teachers, doctors, cooks, a police force, and information technology personnel; many recruited from Silicon Valley.

Joe falls within the class of Salvationists designated as scientists. While his specialty is genetics, others specialize in archeology, chemistry, astrophysics, astronomy, agronomy, food specialists, and many others.

To further the Salvation diversity, The Eden Foundation reached beyond the borders of the United States selecting two-thousand people to join. However, the main criteria for selecting a Salvationist was not necessarily one's race or nationality, but what they could bring to the new colony.

After the orientation work review, the new arrivals attend a presentation outlining the laws and punishments established within Salvation. The rules are rather simple based on three levels.

Level-One Crimes include vandalism, theft, assault, and unprotected sexual intercourse. Punishment is prison time plus a reduction of their employment pay based on the degree of the crime. Salvation must support a level birthrate given its resource constraints, hence the strict unprotected sex laws.

Level-Two Crimes include sexual assault, physical harm creating incapacitation of work, and murder. Punishment is a prison sentence determined by the Command Leader, Jacob. Salvation's greatest resource is its people. Any crime which impacts the utilization of this indispensable resource, Salvation will not tolerate.

Level-Three Crimes include any action resulting in physical damage of the Salvation complex which threatens the lives of its inhabitants. Punishment is banishment from Salvation, which means certain death within seconds. The facility protects everyone. Redundancies are present, but any willing damage to the complex is strictly forbidden.

During the presentation of laws, the new arrivals are taught the importance of maintaining order within Salvation. Jacob, as the Leader, is to be respected. His word is the law. Jacob protects the Salvationists.

To help reassure everyone, the instructor explains the thorough examination which The Eden Foundation administered in its selection and recruitment of colonists. The examination not only includes a mental health evaluation of the recruits, but Eden also investigates their family history for any issues related to the propensity of violence.

A portion of the orientation session relates to personal hygiene, eating, and drinking. The new arrivals learn where to get food and drinks in the common areas including a familiar grocery store. The job one holds determines the amount of finances one gains.

Those holding specialized levels of service, designated as *Privileged*, earn more per day than the general population, identified as *Restricted*. Privilege pay is three credits per day while Restricted is two credits. Everyone, upon arrival, receives one-thousand credits in their account using their right-hand palm to authorize payments.

Eden had established during the Salvation design phase that people should be paid for their work. Consumable items would have an associated cost, and therefore this would prevent any one person from hoarding goods used by the many.

Salvation provides everyone with clothes, housing, healthcare, and education. While everyone has the same services, the only exception is with housing.

Privileged live in the enclosed structures on the Martian surface while *Restricted* live in underground structures inside extinct lava tubes running under the surface. The construction of both dwelling areas use the same materials and methods; the only difference is the view. This pancaked layout allowed Salvation to construct a compact area supporting the expected population.

While nothing is a guarantee, the hope for the early Salvationists is one where future generations will be able to terraform Mars. Having the ability to plant and grow crops may create an Earth-like atmosphere. As the green plants flourish, the plants use solar energy to synthesize food from the plentiful carbon-dioxide creating oxygen. As the oxygen levels develop, the Martian atmosphere thickens assisting the decrease of solar radiation striking the surface. Mars may become habitable outside the Salvation complex and their bio-suits.

Of course, this is only a theory. However, the seven billion people of Earth believe the ability to colonize Mars is, also, just a theory.

What neither Eli Bishop nor the early planners could envision is how the theory of terraforming Mars would eventually lead to the facility's collapse in less than twenty years.

Time marches forward.

EARTH DATE: AUGUST 10, 2017 — EARLY EVENING (10 DAYS LATER)

JOE PLACES HIS HAND FLAT against the cold, glass window beside the door. A chime rings on the other side of the door. The light above his hand changes from red to green. A gentle, swoosh sound pushes the white door open to the left. Joe's shipmate to Mars, Heather, greets him.

"Hi, Joe. Emma has been an absolute baby doll, today. She's had a great birthday. Hard to believe she's already one."

Joe enters the daycare area. Four cribs each with a small baby are against the opposite wall.

"Emma doesn't turn one for another six months."

"I know, but on Earth, she would be one," Heather said as she collects Emma's toys from a locker on the side wall next to the cribs.

"So, Emma slept well this afternoon?"

Heather smiles as she approaches him holding his awakening daughter.

"She just fell asleep only a few minutes ago, so she'll probably sleep like real good for ya tonight."

Joe takes Emma's bag from Heather.

"Did you happen to notice anything unusual with her the past couple days?"

Heather squeezes her eyes together. Three small wrinkles etch into her forehead above her nose.

"Nothing out of the normal... she does seem to talk a lot though for being so young."

"So, you've noticed that, too? I thought it was just me. I've not really been around babies before, but I've thought she was ahead of schedule as far as talking goes."

Heather laughs. "Yeah, like at lunch today, I was eating my sandwich, and you know what she said?"

"Uh-huh?"

"I hear her little voice ask me, *how is it?*"

"Really?"

"I know, right? I babysat my nephew and niece all the time, and they didn't start putting together words until they were almost two. In Earth terms, she's one, so yeah, maybe that's unusual. Maybe she's like a genius or somethin'?"

Joe holds Emma tight against his chest. Her tiny body is warm and cozy inside her pink, cotton pajamas.

"Well, Heather, thanks as usual for taking care of her. We'll be back tomorrow at eight."

"Okay, you two have a good night."

The white door swooshes open. As Joe steps into the doorway holding Emma, he hears his daughter speak.

"Good night, Heather."

Swooshing from the closing door behind Joe freezes his forward motion. He looks down into his arms. Emma returns a smile.

"Hungry, Daddy. Love you."

"Maybe you are my little genius daughter, aren't you, Emma?"

His daughter smiles closing her eyes. Her father's arms give safety and comfort. A slow, deep breathing returns to her as Joe carries her to their living quarters.

Happy Birthday, Emma.

EARTH DATE: JUNE 28, 2018 (10 MONTHS LATER)

TWENTY-TWO MONTHS, the age Emma would be if she were born on Earth. But, today, Salvation honors her first Martian birthday. With such a dependence of a successful birth-rate, a day, like today, is a cause for celebration across the entire community.

During Earth-year 2010, also known as Salvation Year 14, the first human birth occurred on Mars. The birth was a modern miracle of science gone unnoticed to Earthlings. A miracle repeated twenty-five times over the last, four Martian years.

Early in Year 14, Jacob had given his consent to the selected couple presented by Baptiste. Upon approach by Jacob, each person agreed knowing this was their condition of recruitment to Salvation.

To be chosen by The Eden Foundation means they passed a set of strict criteria to join Salvation. First, they had to have a skill or service which Salvation needed. A limited network of family and friends was an ideal bonus given the clandestine measures required to leave for Mars.

The second-level criterion relates to their personal health and their family history. Each potential recruit had to pass this level of examination, both physical and mental to ensure the prevention of developing certain illnesses. Of course, no one was aware to the extent which the Foundation had collected this information globally.

The last evaluation came through close monitoring of the recruits. A willingness to leave Earth behind and start an uncertain adventure on another planet was the most challenging hurdle for the recruit to pass. This required close monitoring of the recruit's daily life through an extreme invasion of privacy tactics.

Currently, the oldest recruit was a maintenance technician, one of the first builders of Salvation. And, the youngest was thirteen, a computer-science prodigy, responsible for establishing the network for the Foundation on Earth and on Mars.

Since Earth-year 2009, most recruits were in their mid-to-late twenties; a prime age for conception and childbirth. Joe, now thirty-nine in Earth-years, is an anomaly, as most scientists are at Salvation.

If the recruit did not have a specialized skillset but passed the other criteria, the Foundation recruited them to join for service roles within the Salvation complex. General maintenance, security, teaching, cleaning, daycare, and more were the positions these recruits held. All agreed to join knowing their primary responsibility is to be someday selected in a pairing for conception.

Given the strict Level-One Crime mandate outlawing unprotected sexual intercourse, the control of unplanned pregnancies is possible. This is what the Salvationists are led to believe, however.

Most non-surgical contraceptive medications are available for women. The Eden Foundation sponsored researchers in the U.S., who had believed to be researching with the National Institute of Health, to develop birth control drugs for men.

Through nefarious, clinical trials on unsuspecting prison inmates, the Foundation had their method for controlling births at Salvation. The solution is a gel containing two synthetic hormones: progestin and testosterone.

Progestin blocks the development of natural testosterone produced within the male testicles preventing the creation of sperm. To counteract the hormonal imbalance progestin creates, such as reduced libido and strength, the gel also delivers doses of synthetic testosterone without generating the development of sperm.

Given the hygiene protocols established, the requirement is for all Salvationists to shower daily. The male birth control gel is diluted into the regular shower gel for washing one's hair and body. Sperm suppression lasts about seventy-two hours allowing for any lapse in this required hygiene schedule.

Only three people at Salvation know of this solution: Jacob, Dr. Johanisson, and Joe after his orientation with Baptiste before his death. Just as partial truths allowed for manipulation by the Foundation on Earth, the same ploys occur at Salvation where no one knows about the chemical in the mandated shower.

The pharmaceutical production teams at Salvation develop many drugs for various uses. Different supplies of materials go into a myriad of products manufactured. No one follows the full supply chain of materials as it is not their responsibility. Therefore, the components going into the shower gel go unnoticed.

Once Jacob approves the pairing through Joe's genetic selection process, the paired couple meets for the first time in Jacob's office, a high honor. The couple can build a relationship together or treat the pairing as a business-like transaction. Of the twenty-four couples selected since Earth-year 2009, all chose to cohabitate in the same living quarters to raise their child.

To remain on the strict timetable guidelines, Salvation does not allow for natural conception with its low odds. Both the man and woman undergo preparatory stages for in-vitro fertilization.

Dr. Johanisson administers fertility medication to the woman stimulating egg production. The desire is to obtain multiple eggs because some will not develop or fertilize after retrieval through a minor medical procedure.

For the man, he must abstain from sex of the personal nature to allow for maximum sperm production. Every three days for two weeks, the man provides a sperm sample each capable of inseminating up to four pregnancies. Within four to eight attempts, a successful conception will occur.

Dr. Johanisson places the samples in centrifuges to separate the X and Y chromosome-laden sperm. The denser X-sperm settles at the bottom of the test tube with the lighter Y-sperm suspends near the top.

Jacob approves the selection process of the sperm to assist better the birth of a baby boy using the Y-sperm or a baby girl with the X-sperm. While not an absolute guarantee, this selection process improves the odds supporting the decision for the sex of the baby.

Each month, Dr. Johanisson prepares the samples performing the insemination. He injects the sperm sample into the egg attempting the fertilization process. Johanisson monitors the egg to confirm fertilization and cell division achieving a successful embryo.

Three days after egg retrieval and fertilization, Johanisson inserts a catheter into the woman's uterus transferring the embryo. After six days, the hope is for successful implantation and a continued process of fetal development.

The process of in-vitro fertilization has become a standard practice on Earth. Given the Martian environment and gravity differences, the scientific community had believed this process to be only theoretically possible on Mars.

A few years ago, Dr. Johanisson with help from Baptiste proved it possible. A process which will continue the development of human life outside Earth, and one that eventually will lead to its demise.

EARTH DATE: JUNE 29, 2018 (THE NEXT DAY)

A LONG DAY CELEBRATING Emma's first birthday at Salvation is almost complete. Hundreds of people have visited Emma and Joe in the agricultural community center, an area akin to Central Park in Manhattan.

At the equivalent to twenty-two-months-old on Earth, Emma speaks in complete sentences. Her rapid increase of speech baffles Joe. At this stage in her development, she should speak approximately two-hundred words and say two-to-three-word sentences. However, Joe places her vocabulary as that of a five-year-old on Earth.

Physically, Emma appears as a healthy child her age. With her advanced ability for speech, this shocks new people she meets.

"Hi, Joe," Heather said visiting with him and Emma in the park. "Happy Birthday, Emma."

Emma reaches her tiny hands taking a small, wrapped gift from Heather.

"Thank you, Heather. How's your sister?" Emma asked.

Even though she spends most days with Emma, her question surprises Heather.

"Oh, Joanie's great."

"Emma, can I ask you something?"

A pair of light-green eyes, her mama's eyes, pierce through Heather. Emma's brain focuses on her pending question thirsty for knowledge.

"How do you learn so many new words, so fast? I swear you know all the big words."

Emma smiles. "I don't understand all the big words?"

The logic of Heather's statement made little sense in her developing brain. Emma has not yet learned the meaning of sarcasm.

"Daddy likes to read to me at night. I guess I pick it up that way," Emma said.

More people stop and interrupt their conversation wishing her a happy birthday. Heather kisses and wishes Emma a happy birthday, again, before she leaves.

As the day progresses, Joe and Emma meet the families who had delivered a baby while at Salvation. Twenty-five kids ranging in Earth-age from eight-years to six-months-old visit. They are Emma's classmates in the Children's Wing of Salvation during the day.

Emma is famous within the complex as the first person conceived on Earth and born on Mars. The early fears of possible developmental defects had long vanished. Astonishment replaces the earlier fear given her advancement.

"Happy birthday, Emma," another lady said in the park. "so, who's one-year-old, today?" The lady flicks Emma's nose playfully. "Who's a special little baby-way-by, today?"

"Thanks, but actually I am twenty-two-months-old on Earth. Since Mars has an orbit of six-hundred-eighty-seven days, I am arbitrarily one-Martian-year-old, today," Emma said.

A look of terror encroaches on her face as the lady rushes away in silence

"Emma, that's not nice. Remember what we talked about?"

Tiny light-green eyes pierce Joe. Questions to Emma trigger her complete concentration.

"I know. I don't need to say so many words. People just don't understand how smart I am. But, you know what, Daddy?"

"What, Baby Girl?"

"That's their problem."

Joe erupts in laughter. Emma's chubby cheeks shake while resting in his lap.

"You sound just like your Mother right then."

"I miss Mommy, Daddy."

Joe squeezes Emma's shoulders.

"I miss her, too… I miss her, too."

22 - JACOB

EARTH DATE: SEPTEMBER 11, 2018 — 9:00 A.M. (2 MONTHS LATER)

VIDEO MONITORS THROUGHOUT the common areas of Salvation display various landscape pictures from Earth. Current information and event news scrolls across the bottom.

Jacob uses the monitors to give information direct to everyone providing updates on new arrivals to Salvation. These informational broadcasts are increasing in frequency as the number of arriving ships from Earth continues to proliferate the landing area. With wo-Earth-years until the end, the arrivals of people and equipment surge.

This morning at 9 a.m. every monitor displays a bright, white screen. An image emerges of a red circle outlined in white inside a red triangle, the logo for Project Salvation developed by Eli Bishop decades prior. Jacob's image pushes through the fading logo.

"Good morning, Everyone. I trust everyone is doing well," Jacob said from the monitor.

A horde of people in the common area watches. Emma is asleep in daycare while Joe listens to the broadcast in his lab.

"Today, we will receive two arrivals. The first is needed machinery for drilling into the Martian surface. These are our new diamond cutter tools just developed by a company in Australia for mining. Our scientists are still hard at work developing new methods for creating drinking water. But, I will deliver more information about that soon."

Joe continues to listen to Jacob. Notes and calculations steal his attention from the screen. His first presentation to Jacob is due later in the afternoon for his first couple selected for procreation.

"In the second landing, our newest neighbors will arrive. As a reminder, please review their backgrounds sent to your tablets with their pictures. Please welcome them when you have a chance."

A muffled ping rumbles under a stack of papers covering Joe's tablet. He clears his view of the screen and notices the file from Jacob. He shrugs his shoulders and releases a faint grunt.

"Also, at exactly four o'clock this afternoon, you will hear music played through the speakers across Salvation. This will signal everyone to pay attention to the monitors as we celebrate and prepare for remembrance of those we have left behind. As you know, at eleven-past-four on Earth-date September 11, 2020, our former home will come to an end. This will always be a somber time for us. But, it will also be a cause for celebrating our continued way of life on Mars."

A heavy sigh echoes through Joe's empty lab. He blocks from his mind the inevitable which will occur in two-Earth-years.

"So, please join later today for our reflection of our past lives on Earth and what awaits us here on Mars. Peace be unto you, my friends."

With his final remarks, the red triangle with its circle reappears. After thirty seconds, the logo fades away; the regular programming returns.

Huh, only two years left…

Joe stops his work. He stares at Mary's picture on his desk rubbing her image with the palm of his thumb. Light glistens from his wedding ring on his left hand.

"Mary, if we didn't come here, we would still be together on Earth."

The rubbing stops. Jacob's voice repeating the words *in only two years* replays in Joe's mind. The caressing of Mary's picture continues.

"Hell, I don't know what would be better… two more years with you or us dying together when that planet hits Earth?"

EARTH DATE: SEPTEMBER 11, 2018 – 3:24 P.M.

THE LONG, WHITE CORRIDOR in the leader's wing of Salvation intimidates everyone who walks its path. Over the past several months, special crates from Earth have accompanied each new arriving rocket. Most of the contents have been emptied and lean against the walls along the hallway.

Still, after two-and-a-half-Earth-years at Salvation, the footsteps are heavy for Joe. His magnetized shoes meant to replicate the sensation of gravitational forces of Earth fall clumsy beneath him.

Joe enters the corridor noticing the tall plastic containers. Each is of varying heights and widths with the same thickness of a half meter.

Halfway through the hallway, Joe stops as the door at the end opens. Jacob steps out into the corridor.

"Joseph, I'm happy I caught you out here. You want to see something very cool?"

Joe shrugs his shoulders. "Guess so."

Jacob meets Joe where he had stopped when the door opened. He presses the blade of a knife into the edge of one of the white, plastic containers.

"You know what's been missing here?"

Jacob's question goes unanswered.

"It's quite simple, really. Think about it. Earth will be destroyed soon, and we have escaped here to save human life."

"Not another poetic moment?"

"No, listen. We are bringing people here and the best technology available from Earth… hell, we're even bringing seeds, and we don't even know if they will even grow."

"What's your point?"

Joe's question comes gruff as his presentation, his first about the next proposed pairing for childbirth, is fresh in his memorized speech.

Jacob wiggles the blade across the top of the container. He reaches inside pulling out a thin, white-foam packing material. Joe's interest intensifies.

"Shit, we're bringing all these things to Salvation to carry on our life, here… why not also appreciate some artwork, too, while we are at it?"

Joe takes one step back; his eyes widen.

"Is that a copy of— "

Jacob interrupts Joe in his own excitement.

"*The Mona Lisa?*" Jacob said followed by a bellowing laugh echoing throughout the long corridor. "Copy, hell, this is the real thing… *The Mona Lisa* has always been my favorite."

Joe reaches his hand out stopping short of touching the DaVinci masterpiece.

"Uh… how did you… why is… "

"Do you really need to ask me that? We're responsible for a lot of shit in the past. Taking artwork is the easiest thing we've ever done. Plus, you know, an inferno at the Louvre set by the Foundation doesn't hurt."

Joe scans the corridor. He walks away from Jacob stopping in front of the largest container against the wall. This one is different. While most are rectangular boxes, this is long and cylindrical.

"You mean to tell me that inside each of these are works of art *like that?* What the hell is inside *this one?*"

Jacob joins Joe and inserts his blade into the container's edge.

"I will not open *this one* all the way because it's so large, but it's *The Raft of Medusa* by Théodore Géricault."

Joe peeks inside the container.

"That thing is massive… I remember seeing this when Mary and I went to the Louvre."

"Yes, and this one is a large son-of-a-bitch. It's like sixteen-feet by twenty-three-feet and will just fit the wall in my office," Jacob said referring to his double-level office area.

Géricault created his masterpiece in the Earth-year 1818. The oil painting is an epic depiction of the savagery of men in the direst of circumstances.

His work reflects the true events after the French naval frigate *Méduse* ran aground off the coast of northwest Africa. The blazing heat of the summer, equatorial sun had roasted everyone in the open seas.

Three days had passed with failed tries to free the ship. Of the four-hundred passengers, only one-hundred-forty-seven passengers and ship's crew boarded a flimsily made raft from the wooden ship's debris. With the number of people onboard, food and water had no room.

The passengers onboard a slowly sinking raft attempted the sixty-mile journey to the African coast. After thirteen days, a passing French ship, *The Argus,* happened by accident upon the dreadful raft.

All but fifteen people were left alive. The others had been killed or thrown overboard if they had not succumbed to hunger or suicide first.

The survivors, if you can call them this, endured starvation and dehydration. Their hunger so intense drove them to cannibalism.

A strange choice of painting for Jacob to want in his office.

"Oh, I see... it's rolled up inside this thing."

"Most of the paintings are like that, but the small ones ship flat like *The Mona Lisa*. It's funny. I always thought that painting was much larger as famous as it is."

Joe laughs. "Funny, I said the same thing to Mary."

Jacob leads Joe down the corridor to his office.

"Plus, I've always thought the plain, white walls in this place seem so dull. Why not have all this original art hanging for us?"

"So, a fire, huh?"

"Oh yeah, at least sixty percent of the Louvre is damaged."

"Are they all just paintings? Any statues?"

Jacob ushers Joe into his office with the door sliding closed behind them.

"No, I wish. But, we just don't have the room, and our payload is mostly already spoken for."

"Mostly?"

"Yeah, sure. For each arrival, we leave some space for things we may discover we need here at Salvation."

"Basically, you're placing an order with Earth so to speak on the things we need."

Between short chuckles, Jacob responds, "Yeah, sure. And, our single supplier closes in a couple years."

Jacob sits behind his desk. Joe joins him on the sofa in his office.

"You have the information about your recommendation?"

Joe fumbles the tablet from under his arm handing it to Jacob, who studies the contents.

"Those two that I selected are the two that right now are the best match."

"Best match?"

"Well, yeah, obviously everyone here has basically been pre-screened for diseases. So, that leaves me with studying the DNA to make sure the proper pairings of people given their specific age."

Jacob sits silent. An occasional pop comes from the glass surface as Jacob's fat fingers poke and drag across the tablet's surface.

"I know this is your first choice, but I can't accept this. Did Baptiste not tell you my first criteria the couple must meet?"

Joe looks perplexed. "Huh, no. He said that you would challenge me to make sure we get this right. Eden had already established the criteria when they recruited people to come."

The tablet bounces across the desk back to Joe.

"Look. I know we have decided on a population here at Salvation to yield a genetic diversity. But, can we not at least attempt to pair people of the same race together?"

The question charges to Joe like a long-lost hint of forgotten racism he had seen in his time growing up in Texas. In the academic setting outside New York City, racism had not been as obvious to Joe.

"Huh... uh... well, now... I mean yes... no... "

Joe struggles with his internal battle about how to respond.

"Well, what the hell is it? It's either yes or no!"

The hostility of Jacob's response lunges to Joe across the woodgrain desktop.

"I'm sorry. Either you want me to focus on the science, or you need me to make a false decision based on something as stupid as race."

Jacob leaps from his chair standing behind his desk.

"Stupid? Look, I don't care what the science says. As long as we can, we should keep the races pure. Ours and theirs."

The phrases coming from Jacob pierce Joe's brain. Jacob remains a stranger to Joe having faked his death before Joe was born. But, the overt racist words are coming from his father's mouth.

Joe sits quiet, motionless; he is unsure how to respond.

Jacob releases a lengthy, loud laugh. "I'm just fuckin' with ya, Boy. No, actually, your recommendation is just fine with me. I'll send them the invitation to my office later this week."

Air rushes from Joe's lungs; his shoulders relax. Relief overcomes him.

"Good, because I did not want to debate this topic with you."

Music plays from the speakers in the ceiling inside Jacob's expansive office.

"Awe, shit. It's time for my speech."

Jacob walks to the opposite wall from his desk. A digital camera mounted on tripod points to the blank, white wall.

"You're welcomed to stay and watch, but be quiet."

"No, that's okay. I've got some work to finish in my lab. I'll listen to you from there."

"Okay, I'll stop by to see Emma later this week… " Jacob said nodding his head quickly up-and-back signaling goodbye to Joe.

"Good afternoon, Everyone. Three minutes from now, this will be the exact moment in two-Earth-years that our former world will end. So, please join me across our whole complex for three minutes of silence…"

Joe hears the last words as the office door closes behind him. Two men carry a white rectangular container to Joe placing it beside Jacob's office door. He stops watching the men come-and-go with their work.

"Oh my… so, this is real artwork, huh?"

Joe slips out a pen from his tablet and presses the pen-top pushing out the small, metal ink-tip. He inserts the tip into the edge of the container sliding across opening the flap.

"Holy shit… " Joe shines the tablet's light into the opened container. "… is this Monet's *Waterlilies?*"

The sight of the masterpiece pulls the air from Joe forcing his back against the opposite wall. A quick memory races to him of Mary's childhood bedroom. They had spent many hours under a hanging poster of this painting as they kissed and rubbed against each other throughout their high school years.

"Mary, I wish you could see this."

23 - Exploring Salvation

NORMALCY IS A STRANGE word in an alien place. Life progresses well for everybody at Salvation. Deliveries of equipment and people contribute to a steady influx of newness for the Salvationists. Even to the old-timers like Jacob, one of the first permanent residents since Earth-year 2011, life on Mars is normal.

Eden realized the challenge is to offer familiar food to Salvation and sufficient volume to support the planned population of ten thousand. Stolen technology from NASA and the International Space Station allows food systems to flourish. Hundreds of Growing Modules next to the complex supply freshly grown lettuce, tomatoes, beans, and a plethora of other vegetables with the same nutrients and taste as on Earth.

Bright LED lights replicate sunlight onto fertile Nebraskan topsoil. Underneath the Growing Modules within the million-year-old lava tubes, a vast network of silos house a myriad of seeds and seedlings for planting.

The first missions to Mars after constructing the Salvation complex delivered tons of seeds from the various countries of Earth. From the exotic passion fruit to staples like green beans, with the uncertainty of what would grow on Mars, the seed stores are diverse. As fruits and vegetables grow, Salvation farmers and scientists collect new seeds to replenish their supplies for conservation measures.

Jacob had reached out to an engineer, named Mac, who Jacob knew would entertain Joe in providing an in-depth tour of Salvation. Sensing depression eating at his son, Jacob explains to Mac to take Joe anywhere he would like to visit in, and even outside, Salvation.

Joe meets Mac in the center hub of the complex. A smile, long-departed, curls upward for Joe as Mac introduces himself.

"You must be, Joe?"

"And, you're Mac?"

"Yep, that's me. My friends back home used to tease me by calling me MacGyver because I could damn-near fix anything. Once I got here, I just kept the nickname, Mac. So, here I am."

Mac is a thin, balding man. His stark receding hairline chases the gray-streaks of hair backward running through his thick mullet, a striking hairstyle given his '80s television namesake. An unassuming person, Mac's silver, wire-rimmed glasses shine bright under Salvation's LED lights.

"So, Jacob asked me to show you around."

"Yeah, I've been here almost three-Earth-years, and I've not ventured out much except to my lab, daycare, and the cafeteria," Joe said scanning the floor avoiding Mac's eye contact.

"That's cool, Man. No sweat. It takes some of us a while to get used to our new environment."

"How long have you been on Mars?"

"Oh, wow… so, Jacob didn't tell you, then?"

"No, tell me what?" Mac's eyes meet Joe's as he pulls his gaze from the floor.

"I hold two distinctions at Salvation… I have been living here the longest of anyone else, and I am also the oldest person here."

"Really?"

"Yep, back on Earth, I worked first for Northrop Grumman doing some gnarly government construction projects for dozens of nuclear missile silos. Funny thing is I got tired of all the travel. But, I was lucky enough to get a job with NASA doing various projects to build Skylab."

"Shit, Man, you must be what... "

"I know, I'm an old fart. Don't look it, do I? How old do you think I am?"

Joe studies Mac. His hairline with a gray-streaked mullet is a clue. The fine wrinkles etching across his forehead and around his eyes are another giveaway.

"Hmm, I'm going to guess seventy-two, I mean, if you worked building Skylab, that was like in the early '70s."

"Pretty close. I'm eighty-three."

Joe jumps back. "Get the hell outta here, no way."

"Yep, I sure am. I'd show you a driver's license, but shit, we ain't go those anymore, now do we?"

Mac laughs. Another giveaway to his actual age is his missing front teeth, which until a barking howl escapes Mac's lungs, Joe has not seen earlier.

"So, how long have you been here?"

Mac walks away from Joe down the Maintenance Corridor from the Central Hub. Joe follows with his growing excitement of the tour.

"Well, the Foundation recruited me back in 1979 to supervise module wall construction on the Moon. I know, crazy, right?"

"Yep. Isn't that when Eden first started going there?"

"Sure was at least for construction purposes. Talk about a scary time. I was on the fifth mission and oversaw about twenty guys. That was some weird shit back then."

Mac had Joe's complete attention like a child's first visit to Disney World.

"How were the living conditions?"

Both men stopped their forward motion as Mac stares to the ceiling. He runs his hand across his bald forehead.

"Whew, terrible. I was puking all the time. We lived on what looked like those old Apollo-type lunar modules and wore compression suits all the time. But, we managed."

"How long did you stay there?"

"Oh, you could only live there about six weeks at a time before it got to be too much for ya."

"So, you went back to Earth."

"Yeah, and because all the damn secrecy about what we were doing, I had to live in Eden's facility in Colorado and couldn't go anywhere."

"Outside Denver?"

"Yep."

"I've been there. It looks like a prison."

Mac laughs. "So, you must have only visited the front of the building. The back is where they kept us all between our missions. Shit, I guess you can say it really was a prison."

"If it was so bad, why did you sign up for it?"

The joyful expression disappears from Mac. A vacant stare directs back to Joe.

"C'mon, Man. They told you, right? *No* is not an answer. Once they approached me, I knew I only had one choice… but, shit, who else gets a chance to go to the Moon unless you were one of those hotshot, pretty boys back then."

They continue walking down the long corridor.

"And, you did that how long?"

"Four years on-and-off. Then, they told me about Mars."

"You mean you signed up because of the Moon missions and not Mars?"

"Exactly. They told me we were building a Moon base for the military. Those Eden fuckers never tell you the whole truth, only what they need to tell you."

"And, that's when they told you about the end of Earth and Salvation?"

"Not at first. They explained the U.S. Government had contracted Eden to go to Mars and replicate what we had been doing on the Moon."

"And, just the adventure of Mars convinced you to go?"

Mac laughs. "That and a promise of a million-dollar payday, which never came. I never had a family. Out-lived 'em all. I figured this was a chance to win the lottery so to speak, get a huge paycheck and eventually retire on a beach somewhere. Shit, was I fooled."

"Do you regret it?"

They reach the end of the corridor and enter the room. Lights flicker. Rows of gym-type lockers line a back wall. Joe follows Mac's lead as they rest on a bench in the center of the room.

"Regret, now that's an interesting word, isn't it? How can I regret everything that I have seen and experienced? I have gone to the Moon more often than anyone else on Earth or hell, even here for that matter. I was on the third ever mission to Mars and have lived here since 1990 continuously."

"1990? Wow, that is a long time."

"If we're counting Mar's years, it's only fifteen. But, yeah, twenty-nine Earth-years."

Silence sits between them for a few seconds.

"Huh, so you first arrived in… "

"1984, I know, it gets confusing thinking of the years, here."

"So, you traveled back-and-forth for six years, then?"

"Yep, same setup as on the Moon. Living in rocket ships, assembling the modules that I realized we had built on the Moon because those were my walls. I got used to living in Space, so I could stay up to three months at a time before coming back to Earth."

"Back to Colorado."

"Yeah, that shit-hole. But, on my second return to Earth, that's when the Foundation told me about everything. About that planet coming to Earth and their need to build Salvation. That's when they promised me a spot here because, shit, Man, I built this fuckin' place."

Joe turns his head to Mac.

"I just realized something else."

"What's that?"

"I think you probably have a third distinction, then?"

"Hmm… "

"You have to have lived in Space the longest than any other human?" The genetic scientist inside Joe spins his imagination in excitement. "Do you know my job, here? I would love for you to visit me in my lab some time so I can take some samples?"

Mac stands and turns his back to Joe.

"Sorry, but, one condition I told them up front decades ago was that I ain't no freakin' lab experiment. I've not been sick a day in my life other than just some nausea at first on the Moon."

Joe senses Mac's displeasure of his request and changes the subject.

"So, you said you were with NASA back in the early '70s... "

"Yep, 1970 until '73."

"Maybe you knew my grandfather, Eli? He died in 1979, but he worked at NASA for a long time. He oversaw Mission Control during the Apollo Program."

Joe was careful not to speak Eli's last name under the instructions Jacob has demanded. His question slipped out trying to create nervous small talk.

Mac continues with his back to Joe. His eyes open wide exposing small, red veins in the corners like a red spiderweb creeping from the underside of his eyelids.

"Hmm... Eli, you say... never heard of him." Mac's head remains frozen. His body twitches as his eyes dart side-to-side in a rapid motion. "Nope, that name doesn't ring a bell."

"Here, open this locker and get changed," Mac said seeming to change the conversation back to Joe.

"How does this work?" Joe asked opening the locker and holding a black, rubber-looking outfit. "Looks like a onesie?"

"A who see, what?"

"You know, a onesie that baby's wear."

"Sorry, never really been around any of them."

Mac demonstrates.

"Okay, it's easy. It just slips over our bio-suit. The medical team needs to read our vital signs when we exit the complex— "

"Exit the complex... are we going outside?"

"Jacob didn't tell you?"

"No, he just said you were taking me on a detailed tour of Salvation."

"Well, hell, why do you think we're going outside, then?"

Joe follows Mac's lead by removing his magnetized shoes and sliding his legs into the pants of the black suit.

"Snug fit, huh?" Mac asked.

"What is this material?"

"Well, our normal suits will protect us outside the walls, but it's the radiation that would kill us if we didn't wear these. They used to be made of lead and were as heavy as my ex-wife, may she rest in peace. But, now, they are made of a polymer which prevents the particles from penetrating the fabric."

Joe follows along slipping his arms through the suit and pulls the form-fitting hood over his head. Only his face, hands, and feet stay uncovered.

"The material is black to absorb heat from the sun when it's super cold out there. The crazy thing is the material will turn white to reflect the heat if it gets too hot. This is only my second time wearing these as they just arrived last month."

Gloves of the same material fit firm over Joe's hands with a surprising sense of touch still possible via his fingertips.

"And, what about our shoes?"

"Hmm, size twelve?"

"Yep, how did ya know?"

"I'm good at sizing things up."

"Here, unfortunately, the technology on our boots are about the same as they've always been, just a little lighter, now."

Joe places his boots over his feet with his usual bio-suit material. His stomach churns in excitement.

"So, you said your friends called you MacGyver, when did you find time to watch TV?"

"Never have? The workers were my friends during the '80s. And, by the time the mid-'80s rolled around, that's when they started calling me that."

"The workers, how did they live, where did they come from?"

"Man, you are full of questions aren't ya? How 'bout we talk about them some other time. But, we need to go out, now. There's only a few hours in the day that's perfect out there as far as the amount of light and temperatures go."

Mac stands leading Joe to the wall next to the lockers. He demonstrates for Joe by slipping on a helmet with a clear, glass face-shield.

"Can you hear me, now?"

Joe laughs. Mac's question recalls a memory of a popular commercial from a few years ago on Earth.

"The video and com work just like in the helmets you flew here with. On your face-shield, you should see a small picture of my face in the upper-left corner. And, along the right side, you should see some numbers in white."

"Yep, I see you and the numbers, but they are hard to see."

"Don't worry. Out there, the white letters and numbers stick out very good against the red landscape."

Joe's knees buckle. His stomach churns. On Earth, he daydreamed what the Martian environment must look like. But, given what has happened upon his arrival to Salvation, those dreams had vanished.

"When we get out there, the face-shield will darken a bit to help with the bright light from the Sun. But, if a dust cloud develops, it will lighten automatically. Oh, and the numbers, next to those is a small square in the center of your vision. The numbers on the top-right tell you how far away the object is in that square in meters."

"Cool."

"And, the numbers below that tell you the temperature, wind speed, and the distance away from your nearest entry-point back into the complex."

Joe hears his breathing inside his helmet. His heart pounds through the layers of his bio-suit and black, radiation suit.

"This way."

Mac leads Joe through the locker room. A door slides open as they approach closing behind them as they walk through the opening.

An orange-lit keypad teases Joe with its configuration of numbers like those of his first cell phone. Mac presses a code into the keypad which turns green as he moves his hand from the door.

A massive sound like rushing steam pushes through the door as it lifts upward into a recess in the doorframe. This door is unlike one Joe has seen in his short time at Salvation. At least a foot thick, its gray-metallic exterior encloses a small, thick-paned window at eye-level.

Mac is first through the doorway. The door slips down into a closed position. Another orange-lit keypad illuminates on a duplicate exit on the opposite side of the small room.

Joe peers through the small window of the other door. An eerie reddish tint reflects off his face-shield.

"Oh… my…. God… "

Mac enters another code on the keypad and removes his hand. Billows of white steam and air force their way into the small chamber-like room.

"This operation is the same regardless of our coming or going. It cleans off any dust and radiation particles that tag along when we go out there," Mac said yelling over the rushing air.

Silence fills the chamber as the white haze disappears.

"Are you ready, Joe?"

Another rush of air follows Mac's question. This rush is not from the outside-in, but the inside-out. The vacuum, air pressure of Salvation trapped inside the chamber floods out into the Martian environment.

Mac exits through the opened doorway. Joe inches forward.

What are you watching?

The first words his Mary had ever said to him etch their way into his head. Joe was ten-years-old in front of his living room television after his mother's funeral watching the twenty-year-anniversary of the Moon Landing.

His excitement that afternoon scanning the grainy, black-and-white images of Neil Armstrong stepping out onto the lunar surface had caught the attention of Mary. She introduced herself and sat watching with him on that sad day; a day which changed Joe's life forever.

A single tear from each eye drips from his bottom eyelids with the unexpected childhood memory. The water droplets fall at a slow pace in the Martian gravity seeming to float their way in front of him.

Joe transfixes his vision from the falling tears ahead to Mac. The top-right number in white shines brightly against the red landscape. Mac is ten-meters ahead, outside.

"C'mon, it's just like walking on something that's half sand and half gravel. You'll get used to it, easy."

Joe's left foot steps forward followed by his right. Another inch and Joe will touch the alien soil.

"One small step for a Man, one giant leap for… holy shit!"

Mac laughs bending at his waist and slapping his right-gloved hand onto his thigh.

"You're not the only one who's said that same line as Armstrong did when they step out for the first time."

Joe takes a few steps from the complex. The door remains open as a safety measure for quick entry.

Their black-material suits fade to a gray color to compensate for the outside temperature.

Mac was correct. To Joe, the ground feels like walking on sandy gravel. His steps are lighter given the absence of his magnetized shoes inside Salvation.

The white, exterior walls of Salvation stretch through the valley floor between ranges of mountains on all sides. A location selected for protection against the Martian winds.

A rust-colored haze fills the air as the sun's rays penetrate through the thin carbon-dioxide-laden atmosphere. The distance is challenging to see too far ahead through what looks like city smog to Joe.

Silence fills Joe's helmet except for his heart pounding he senses inside his ear canals. He takes deep, quick breaths. Mac talks to Joe, but his words fall deaf.

It's so beautiful isn't it, Joe.

Mary's voice comforts his nerves as Joe joins Mac standing beside a large out-cropping of reddish rocks.

Yes, yes, it is Sweetie.

EARTH DATE: MARCH 28, 2019 - AFTERNOON

"IT'S AN AMAZING SYSTEM."

"Well, they just send me the designs and parts, and me and my teams assemble everything once the shipments arrive."

Mac scans the length of pipes stretching across the Martian landscape from the Water Harvester Array to Salvation. Rectangular solar-powered devices stand twenty-meters tall across an area the size of two basketball courts. A metal pipe thirty-meters-long extends beneath each harvester into the Martian sub-surface ice.

Inside the box-like structures, the solar panels activate heat-tracing elements within the pipe melting the ice allowing hydraulic pumps to extract a slurry mixture of salt, water, and soil into the harvester. Heaters process the slurry raising the temperature above the boiling point of water creating steam.

Condenser plates pressed into the harvester's side walls collect the steam allowing pure water to flow from pipes running from the plates to the reverse-osmosis membrane filtration system. As water droplets press through the membrane structure, safe drinking water is pumped via heated pipes preventing freezing into the infrastructure system of the Salvation complex.

"How long has *this* system been installed?"

"We completed this not that long ago, a couple weeks before you arrived."

"These systems provide enough water for everyone?"

Mac's hearty laugh fills Joe's helmet.

"Only a part, maybe a third of the future needs for the population. We still rely mainly on our water pipelines coming down from the polar cap. It's a similar concept to how we capture the water with the harvesters, but the volume is higher from there."

Joe scans the horizon. Large black pipes extend beyond the horizon.

"How far away is that facility?"

Mac cleans the instrumentation panels affixed on the harvester array.

"Over that hill you see the pipeline disappearing, it's a day's drive in our rover vehicles."

"That close, huh?"

"Yep, well, hell, it's all relative here, since Mars is about half the size of Earth, ya know."

"Enough water is produced for the expected population, then?"

"At max production from all our capabilities, it's not a problem. We allow for twenty liters of water per person per day. But, that includes water not just used by the person, but to sustain that person in all things like food production, cleaning. Well, ya know, everything water is needed for."

Mac leads Joe beyond the Water Harvester Array. Two hours outside the confines of Salvation, the exhilaration Joe experiences skipping across the red landscape amuses him.

"So, can you guess what this system is?"

Joe studies the various pipes and cylindrical pedestals extending up from the Martian surface.

"No clue."

Mac slaps his gloved hand on top one pedestal. A dull thud echoes around them.

"This is part of the Oxygenator System. One thing Mars has a lot of is carbon-dioxide. These round things sticking up across the field are air inlets sucking the atmosphere just beneath the surface."

Joe turns his body searching across the valley. Fifty inlets stand around him.

"We pump the air through ceramic catalysts materials and heat these up. That reaction converts the air into oxygen, and we pump that into the complex."

"You mean like a catalytic converter on a car."

Another laugh fills Joe's helmet.

"Huh, I never thought of it that way, but yep, exactly."

Mac leads Joe through the pipe inlet field.

"From the air, the entire Salvation complex looks like a wagon wheel. As you can imagine, the Oxygenator and Water Harvesters are vital systems. And, we have six systems of these around the full perimeter of the complex. We need two to fulfill our requirements and the rest are backup systems."

"Have you ever needed to use the backups?"

Silence chases away Mac's earlier laughter.

"Early on, yes, but now our systems are fairly reliable. But, don't worry, we do maintenance every day and test everything constantly."

"But, what happens when we have to rely totally on our own, here?"

Mac places a gloved hand on Joe's shoulder.

"That's why we have strict rations on our water and activities just in case. But, don't worry, we've got a shit ton of experience operating our systems. In fact, we have not received any replacement materials for these systems in years."

Mac turns Joe back to the complex. The sun will set within the hour.

"So, I understand our water and oxygen generation. And, obviously, we get our electricity from solar panels, but what about… "

Joe pauses as he stumbles catching his balance.

"Shit?"

"Oh, no, I'm okay," Joe said.

"You gonna ask me about how we handle our shit aren't ya?"

A rage of laughter consumes Joe's helmet.

"Well, yes, I was. I mean, how is that processed?"

Mac leads Joe to a new area beside the Oxygenator taking a detour before returning inside the complex.

"It's almost the same filtration type systems as back on Earth. Have you not thought to yourself why everyone is instructed to use two different toilets? One for takin' a piss or a shit?"

"Not really."

"Yeah, no one ever seems to care about that because this shit work everyone always takes for granted. Urine is collected and then treated. The captured water is used as potable water for cleaning and washing things in Salvation."

Joe stops his forward progress.

"For cleaning— "

"Yeah, you're brushing your teeth and taking showers in reclaimed water. But, obviously, we don't tell anyone that even though that water is cleaner than probably the drinking water."

Joe continues forward.

"And, what about the other?"

"The potable water cleans the waste down the toilet. Wire screens capture the solids, which we use in our furnace production to help generate heat, and the remaining water is treated like back home and funneled into the potable water system."

Mac leads Joe to the entrance door to the complex they had exited a few hours earlier.

"So, everything is pretty much an enclosed system for the infrastructure," Joe said.

"Look around. This is fuckin' Mars. It pretty much has to be, doesn't it? Like you said earlier, soon, we will only have ourselves here. And, all our systems have to rely on each other."

Their feet fall heavy on the metal floor inside the small entranceway. Mac enters a code on the keypad. The outer door closes down to the floor followed by white steam and air rushing into the room. Twenty-seconds pass as the steam clears.

Mac enters a code on the opposite door's keypad with the door sliding open to the right. They come inside with the door closing behind them.

"Thanks for taking me out there."

"No problem. You got time for dinner?" Mac asked.

Joe follows Mac's actions as they remove their helmets, gloves, and boots. Both rest on the metal bench removing the outer layer suit.

"Sure. My daughter is being looked after this evening, so I have time."

Joe's response surprises himself. For the past six hours, amazement chased away the melancholy of his normal routine.

"Great. I can show you how we manufacture our food before we go to the cafeteria."

Joe replaces his regular magnetic shoes over his bare feet.

"Huh, I never really thought about that."

Mac's laugh flows from behind the closed toilet stall.

"You never thought about it? That's a good one."

Joe enters the empty toilet stall.

"Not really, too many things going on for me, I guess."

Water gushes down the drain as Mac exits.

"Oh yeah, Jacob mentioned a few things to me. Sorry to hear about your wife, Man."

Joe exits as water gushes behind him.

"Thanks. Most of my thoughts have been on my work and daughter. I sometimes forget where we are, and I just don't seem to ever really think about it."

"Well, you are ahead of most people. I hear from a lot who are still freaked out as fuck about being here. It sounds like to you it's just a normal place."

"I guess... that, and a lot of practice of zoning out my thoughts over the years."

"Take it from me as I have lived most of my life either on the Moon or Mars, that's a good thing. It creates normalcy."

Joe laughs.

"What's funny?"

"Most of your life on the Moon or Mars... "

Mac joins Joe in laughter and mimics a robotic motion with his arms.

"Beep beep, I am an alien. Beep. Take me to your leader... "

The two men laugh as they leave the locker room area.

EARTH DATE: MARCH 28, 2019 – EARLY EVENING

"THIS IS MY WORK AREA," Joe said as he follows Mac through a familiar passage.

"Yep, this is the scientific side of the complex."

Various technicians pass them.

"I never really grasped how long this hallway is. My area is up front," Joe said.

"I'm not here much myself. The research labs and medical equipment are near you. But, down here, we have the cool stuff, the manufacturing area."

"Manufacturing? I thought you were taking me to the food production area."

"Sorry. There's no kitchen on this tour."

The solid white walls disappear followed by clear glass. Mac stops with Joe.

Dozens of glass incubator stations connect in numerous rows. A myriad of wires and cables reach between the stations as small robotic arms move throughout the room.

"Now, you're the scientist and probably know more about these processes than I do. But, each of these lines creates different things. Some produce food. Others medications and vitamins and shit like that."

Joe places his nose an inch from the glass.

"You can arrange some time with the people who oversee this area to learn how it works. All I really know is they somehow use sunlight and bacteria."

Mac continues walking to the end of the corridor as Joe follows. At the end, a door opens as they enter the food preparation area adjoining the cafeteria.

"*Those packages there*, they flow down the conveyor from the production room and are stored *here*."

Joe follows Mac into an enclosed area. A robotic arm transfers the packages from the conveyor to various holding bins affixed along the walls.

"On the other side of those bins are more conveyor belts. When someone in the cafeteria places their order, the corresponding package slides down from the holding area to the belt where the food is cooked."

"Cooked?"

"Zapped, microwaved, whatever. Most of it is rehydrated with steam and then served out there."

"Huh, I just thought there were people back here making the food we ordered."

"Really? You think that out of ten-thousand people, some of them will be cooks?"

Joe stands silent.

"I'm jus' fuckin' with ya. Here, let's go eat. I'm hungry as shit, Man."

Mac leads Joe through the prep area placing his hand on the glass panel next to a door. The red light changes to green as the door opens. The familiar sight of the cafeteria greets Joe.

A group of ten people moves quick before Mac and Joe. At the end, each places their hand on a scanning bed as they key in their order on a terminal.

No more than five minutes pass until their food order arrives on a conveyor belt as they wait.

"There's a table in the corner."

Joe grabs his food tray following Mac.

"Do you eat here often?" Mac asked.

"Not really, I usually just eat in my lab."

"Chicken noodle soup. How's that?"

Joe slips the empty spoon from his lips.

"Not bad."

Mac holds a bite of beef steak on the end of his fork. His eyes transfix on his food.

"Crazy to think that this steak is made in a lab."

The bite of meat disappears into Mac's mouth.

"And, tastes just like beef, too."

Joe slurps his soup. Steam rises from the cup encircling his nose.

"Well, I learned how that is made here. One of my first meals was a cheeseburger, and I was amazed at how close that tasted like something from back home," Joe said.

Mac turns his concentration to Joe.

"Do I want to know?" Mac asked.

Joe does not wait to hear Mac's response and proceeds to inform him how stem cells from various animals develop muscle cells. The addition of amino acid proteins to the cell promotes tissue growth inside a cultured bioreactor.

Mac holds his fork before his lips. Juices from the meat glisten in overhead LED lights.

"Very fine strains of the muscle tissue are layered continuously on top of each other forming the meat. Once it grows to the specified size, it is clipped, and the remaining tissue continues to grow."

"You make it sound so delicious," Mac said slipping his bite into his mouth followed by a small chuckle

"That's why it tastes just like beef or chicken, hell even fish and pork for that matter, because it is. Just so happens it's made in a lab."

"I'm not sure about that, but hell, it's a helluva lot better than what it used to be. Those tasteless meals were terrible."

The cafeteria room fills with people as the typical work evening shift starts.

"Well, I should get back to my daughter," Joe said.

Both return their empty food trays to the black, rubber conveyor belt that moves through an opening in a wall.

"Thanks for showing me around, today."

"No problem. I enjoyed giving you the tour. I don't get to do that much with anyone but the workers who will work on those systems."

"Maybe we can meet up again for dinner from time-to-time," Joe said.

Mac stops turning his stare to a small mirrored wall at the entranceway of the cafeteria. He winks at himself.

"Sure. That sounds great. Just let me know."

Joe walks in front of Mac breaking his stare from the mirror as Mac follows Joe from the cafeteria.

On the other side of the one-way mirror, Jacob watches them leave. A crooked grin creeps on his face as he exits and walks the dark corridor from the cafeteria; a walkway only he knows. He passes living quarter after living quarter each with similar one-way mirrors.

24 - Brace for Impact

THE WALLS WITHIN Joe's office vibrate signaling time to log-off his computer. Lab technicians scurry from the area. Joe inhales holding his breath for several moments before following the staffers.

Excitement is electric through the corridor leading to the Arrival Bay. Joe jostles for a position on the viewing platform outside the glass walls as white smoke ruffles from under the rocket engines.

Audience murmurs fall deaf to Joe as he surveys the latest passengers disembarking the ship. The last Salvationists have arrived.

A group of seven walks from the platform as flight techs greet them. Each has the same shock expression.

He really isn't coming.

Satisfied no one else was arriving, Joe forces his way from the platform. Within minutes, he is back to his lab. Alone.

In the years since his arrival, Joe has pushed himself to forget Earth and the event which will befall upon his home in less than two-Earth-months.

His ongoing research and responsibility consume his thoughts. Only his four-Earth-year-old daughter brings him any sanity.

Joe fantasizes of the possibility of his Eden recruiter, his friend, Gabriel D'Angelo, appearing through his office door at any moment. However, today, with the last arrivals, Joe realizes his friend, his recruiter, was true to his word and will not join the ten-thousand population of Mars.

Gabriel's non-arrival does not come as a surprise to Joe. As part of his conception work, Joe has records for everyone at Salvation including those which had not arrived, yet.

With today's arrival, the full population stands at ten-thousand-thirty-two accounting for the last few births. The four rockets used to ferry passengers and equipment are present. One sits within the complex undergoing arrival inspection and the other three rest outside Salvation.

Several chimes ring throughout the lab. A flat-screen panel on the wall illuminates as Jacob's image focuses.

"Good afternoon, Everyone. Today is a special day. Our last fellow members have joined us. We are now complete. As we welcome our new neighbors, we face the harsh reality we have all known for some time. No more return flights to Earth and no more arrivals will happen. My friends, we are now totally on our own."

Joe refuses to watch Jacob. His head hangs in his right hand while his left rubs a picture frame. A photo of Mary jumping on and wrapping her legs around him as they wore their high school graduation gowns brings fond memories of a happier time of pure joy.

"But, there are no worries. We all have our roles to play at Salvation. And, for those that have been here a long time, you know how self-sufficient we have become. It is now that we, soon to be the last humans, continue our new lives here on Mars."

A new picture reflects back to Joe in his hands. In Mary's belongings after her death, Joe had found a picture of them sitting on the front porch of his Texas homestead with his grandmother, Liz. The smiles glow from the faded photo.

"But, with our excitement comes an unfortunate reality, my friends. Those left behind on Earth will soon meet their fate which has brought us to Mars. I assure everyone here, the steps The Eden Foundation has always taken to hide the reality of the planet approaching Earth are still being performed."

Joe returns both pictures to his desk. Jacob's voice captures his attention.

"The people of Earth will only have hours' warning of what is about to happen. We have gone through extreme lengths and maintained protocols to keep the planet hidden from observation. No one will suffer as the event will take place almost instantaneously. So, my friends, while we continue humanity here at Salvation, our hearts go out to those left behind."

A massive sigh releases from Joe.

EARTH DATE: JULY 17, 2020
SARASOTA, FLORIDA – EARTH
(56 DAYS PRIOR TO IMPACT)

"WE INTERRUPT THIS BROADCAST to bring you breaking news," said the voice through the television in the center of the recreation room of the Sarasota Springs Retirement Community.

"What did the President say, now?"

"Oh hush up, you ol' liberal windbag."

"Ssh, you both shut up. Hey, turn it up."

"Reports are coming in from across the country of widespread internet outages. The New York Stock Exchange and the NASDAQ implemented emergency stop procedures— "

The anchorwoman freezes her report placing her right hand to her ear. "Okay, uh… okay," she said to the voice in her earpiece. She returns her hand to the desk.

"This just in… we are now learning that across Europe and Asia, they are experiencing internet outages as well. U.S. Government authorities have made no announcements… we go, now to our reporter, Janice, from the Pentagon."

"They're right… I can't get to *Words with Friends* on my phone."

"Ethel, you're a cheater. I've stopped playin' with you, anyway."

"You Two, quiet!"

"Pentagon officials I've just spoken with indicate a world-wide internet blackout is occurring. Nuclear power plants and most utility companies across the world are shutting down as a safety measure as most are operated by control systems connected online."

"Janice… Excuse me, Janice… we are now receiving reports that telecommunication and cell services around the country are experiencing outages— " The news anchor said interrupting the reporter.

"That's right. An official, who didn't want to be identified, told me that all communication systems appear to be affected. There's even a concern that communication satellites will— "

The voice from the reporter falls silent through the darkening flat-panel television screen. White hair and bald heads reflect in the black mirror of the screen everyone had gathered around listening to the news reports.

"Hey, turn it back on!"

"I can't… " one of the retirement home attendants said pointing the remote control to the television.

Silence and darkness fill the recreation room. Cool air stops blowing from the air conditioning vents. The silence lasts a few seconds.

"This is it! This is how it happens. Are the missiles going?"

An elderly lady takes the man's hand as he shouts. "Now, now, dear… it's okay."

The attendant comes to the pair holding hands. "Sue, is Freddie okay?"

"Oh, yes dear, Freddie's ex-military and always thinks Russia or North Korea will attack us."

Freddie rocks back-and-forth in his chair. "It's time… it's gotta be time… the missiles… "

Sue stands holding his hand. "Here, let me take you back to your room."

The two leave the recreation area as arguments from the others fall deaf behind them. Red light permeates the darkened corridor as Sue escorts

Freddie to his bed. The battery-powered Emergency Exit sign illuminates their path.

Sue pushes open the door to Freddie's room. "Okay, you're back home, now. Do you need me to bring you something?"

Freddie sits mute.

"I'll be next door if you need anything."

He remains motionless. Heat in the room builds this early afternoon in Florida; his sweaty palms grip tight on each side of his wheelchair.

Scars from skin burns run the length of his arms to his chest. Old scars like full-body tattoos etch their way up his neck and across his face.

Freddie opens the top drawer of his dresser reaching inside. His stoic face never veers from its blank expression.

He closes the drawer after pulling back his hand and forces his chair to the window. His frail hand unlatches the lock. Stale, humid air rushes inside his small, single room.

Freddie lifts his head to the sky. The glaring sun blinds him. A small shadow drifts across his eyes as his hand blocks the warm light.

The object from the dresser drawer comes into focus in his hand. A small, yellowing picture of a woman holding a baby shines in the halo of sunlight.

"Tina... Ruth... the end is near... "

EARTH DATE: AUGUST 1, 2020
SARASOTA, FLORIDA — EARTH
(42 DAYS PRIOR TO IMPACT)

A RAPID THUMPING against the door startles Freddie awake. Sweat stains consume his bed sheets. The stench of arthritis rub and stale clothes compress the sultry room.

"Freddie, Freddie, open up... I know you're still here," Sue said from the other side of the door.

"Go away!"

"Freddie! Open this goddam door, now!"

A low groan pushes through the room as he forces his torso up from the bed. His wheelchair waits as he pulls himself into its confines.

He pushes his chair to open the door. A loud creak pops from the warped, wooden frame from the heat.

"You need to come with me."

Sue pulls his chair through the doorway and pushes him to the Recreation Room. Paper and trash cover the floor.

Sweat pours from her face. The layered blush on her cheeks captures the sweat pooling on her jawline. Her shirt tucked into her skirt. A proper lady, Sue never leaves her room without her makeup and wig while wearing her Sunday-best.

"You've not been out of your room in days, and you need to eat something… "

Sue positions Freddie's chair next to the open window. A gentle cross-breeze offers slight comfort.

"You sit here, and I'll be back in a moment."

The sound of her shoe-clapping quietens as Sue leaves Freddie alone. Rustling tree branches serenade him through the window.

The Sarasota Springs Retirement Community encompasses a complex of four, three-story buildings. A greenish pond filled with tropical flowers and plants provides a central focus point to the small campus.

Sue returns to Freddie carrying two bowls of chicken noodle soup. "*Here*, eat this."

Freddie reaches out his hands. The spoon shakes as he lifts the soup to his dry lips.

"It's cold."

"Sorry, but we still don't have any power, and the gas stove doesn't work."

The two sit quiet slurping from their bowls. Each steals a glance to the other.

"Where are the birds?"

Sue rests her empty bowl on her lap. "The what? What birds?"

Freddie places his empty dish on the floor. His sweaty hands slip across the steel of his chair pushing closer to the window.

"The birds... there's always birds out there. Do you hear any?"

Sue stands and walks to the window next to him. She places her hands on each hip.

"Huh, I guess you're right... weird, no?"

Freddie pushes back into the room.

"Now that you mention it, I don't think I've heard or seen any animals out there in a couple days. All I do is sit here and stare out of this godforsaken place."

"What about the nurses... surely, you talk with them?"

"Fred, you haven't been outta your room? We're the only ones left."

The wheelchair slowly spins in the center of the room.

"Since, when?"

"You know, you remember... couple weeks ago, the announcement on TV when we lost all power. Some of them left when their families came and picked 'em up. Others just left. None of the people who work here have returned... guess they went home to their families."

Sue leaves the window. A white rocking chair beckons her.

Sunlight relents its mercy as it sets behind the community buildings. Sue lights two Yankee candles. Passing small talk keeps them company.

"You're former military... do you have any idea what possibly could be happening?"

Freddie sits non-responsive to her question.

"The day we lost power, you kept saying something about missiles... what did you mean by that?"

Yellow, flickering light shines across Freddie's face. He goes to the open window. Silence continues to scream from outside absent even the chorus of crickets.

"Missiles... I don't remember saying that."

"You were screaming something about them, and that's when I took you back to your room."

Heavy breathing belabors Freddie. His lips purse tight together.

"Sue... I've got a story to tell you... my name's not, Freddie."

EARTH DATE: AUGUST 2, 2020
SARASOTA, FLORIDA — EARTH
(41 DAYS PRIOR TO IMPACT)

HOURS PASS. Amusement and disbelief overcome Sue.

"Freddie, uh, I mean, uh… Jackson, is it?" Sue said with her left hand on her hip as she rolls both eyes. "That sure was some story you just told me. Best entertainment I've heard since the blackout."

Jackson turns his back to Sue staring into the blackness of a quiet night.

"Believe me or not, but it's all true."

A hand rests on his shoulder as she slides the rocking chair beside him.

"So, you were once an astronomer, and you saw something back in… what did you say… in 1960? And, someone ran you off the road because of what you had found back then?"

"Been in a chair like this ever since."

"Then, you took your family to Iowa to hide? God, I've been there once. I can understand why you felt safer there."

Jackson laughs. "Felt safer, so you believe me?"

"I believe it's been hot, we've been in the dark too long, and you've got a fantastic imagination."

Sue rubs Jackson's shoulders. Her hand rests against the back of his wet neck.

"Been in the dark… that's funny. The entire world has been in the dark too long that's for damn sure."

"Oh, you mean, this… what did you call it… this Eden Foundation you once worked for?"

Jackson lowers his head. Sue comforts him with her touch.

"Yes, The Eden Foundation. Like I said, they recruited me to join— "

"Because they promised to help with your daughter… Ruth?"

"Yeah… Ruth."

"See, I was listening. In your story, you never explained what happened to her?"

Jackson reaches behind his neck catching Sue's hand in his. He guides her to his face and down the front of his neck.

"*These scars*... they came from the night she died. There was an explosion... and... and... she didn't make it... "

"Oh, you poor thing."

"I was in the back of the apartment when it happened. The explosion pushed me outside."

Repressed memories flood Jackson's mind.

"We were near a university, so the fire department came quickly saving me. The next thing I know I wake up a few days later wrapped head-to-toe in bandages."

"What caused the explosion?"

Jackson pushes his chair away from Sue moving closer to the window.

"The fire department said there was a gas leak from the kitchen. But, I think... "

"What, that the same people you were running from, found you?"

"That's what I think. So, that's why I came here and called myself Freddie."

"No one here checked on that?"

"Not when you pay them thousands of dollars each month in cash. They didn't care to ask— "

Breaking glass and a slamming door startle them. Sue jumps from her chair. Her knees pop loud from her sudden movement. Jackson pushes away from the window out of instinct.

"What was that?"

"Stay here, I'll check it out," Jackson said pushing his chair to the door.

"Hey, anyone here?" a familiar voice said growing louder before Jackson leaves the room.

A man enters the doorway. Several plastic bags with groceries and boxes hang from both hands.

"Oh, sorry."

"Harry, you scared us. Where have you been?"

"I left to go to my daughter's apartment in downtown, but she wasn't there. I waited, and she never came. Have you been out there? You won't believe what's happening? The whole world has gone batty, I tell ya."

Harry sets the bags on the floor. Three stale doughnuts roll out from one box which falls open.

"I brought as much as I could find in the house."

"Why did you come back?" Sue asked.

Harry rests in a rocking chair, his clothes drenched with sweat. Body odor and whiffs of menthol from a mixture of cigarettes and ointment creep upon Sue and Jackson. Harry takes a deep breath.

"I... I... couldn't take it any longer. The screams... the yelling."

"Thought you said your daughter didn't return?" Jackson said interrogating his neighbor, who had occupied the room across the hallway from his.

"No, not from her... from the people outside. Rioting and looting."

"What about the police?" Sue asks.

"First couple of days, I saw some of them trying to break things up. I walked up to one officer and asked if he knew what was happening?"

"What did he say? We haven't heard from anyone since everyone left. It's just been Jack... uh, I mean, Freddie and me, here."

"He didn't know much. But, he did say his son with the Miami/Dade Police Department drove up basically to escape from Miami. The whole waterfront and the South Beach area have burned to the ground. People are just going nuts."

"Wonder what's causing all of this? It's crazy how much the world seems to rely on the internet and information," Sue said.

"I know. When I was speaking to that cop, his partner overheard our conversation and said everything seems shut down, everywhere."

Jackson pushes his chair back-and-forth away from Harry's conversation with Sue.

"But, when I saw the police later shooting into the crowd and people shooting back, I knew it was getting too bad to stay there."

"So, you came here?" Jackson said.

"I had to walk here, but yeah, this has been home for a couple years. Figured no one would come here ransacking an old fart's home."

The three spoke well into the night. Harry carries the conversation as Jackson only listens. Jackson surfs the decades of his memories in his mind.

Puzzle pieces he has searched for since that evening sixty-years ago fall to him. Their intricate edges slip in his mind forming a clear picture.

I knew it. That thing I saw… it's going to strike us. Those things Eden made me do… it had to be all connected…

"I'm not tech savvy, but everything in the world is connected these days," Harry said as Jackson sits silent.

Hmm, no one can communicate… why shut down the internet, now… unless it's going to happen soon…

EARTH DATE: AUGUST 19, 2020
SARASOTA, FLORIDA — EARTH
(23 DAYS PRIOR TO IMPACT)

A LITTLE OVER A MONTH has occurred since communications and electricity ceased to exist at the Sarasota Springs Retirement Community. What drew families to the complex was the security they saw upon entering the campus grounds.

Unlike most retirement communities, Sarasota Springs lies at the end of a quarter-mile stretch of road hidden off Interstate-75 south of Tampa. A tall metal fence surrounds the campus. A fence originally meant to keep its residents inside the campus without worry of one wandering away, now keeps anyone out.

Three days had taken place since Sue went with Harry in a car they had discovered inside the maintenance building. They had traveled north to determine if they could locate knowledge about what was happening. Jackson remained behind refusing to go with them.

Years of hiding and running, the absence of food and water carries limited impact for Jackson. Summer in Florida brings afternoon storms allowing fresh rainwater to satisfy any thirst he feels.

Piles of crackers and cans of Vienna sausage lay on a table in the Recreation Room. He passes his time ransacking the empty rooms of his elderly neighbors knowing their penchant for hoarding and hiding snacks.

Equations and orbital drawings of the Milky Way in white chalk fill a blackboard of a nurse's station in the room. Jackson sits beside the snack-filled table glaring at his work on the board.

The familiar screech of a failing timing belt grows louder from the window. Three days earlier, the same squealing drifted into silence as Sue and Harry drove away from campus.

A few minutes pass. One set of footsteps creeps from the outside hallway coming to the Recreation Room.

"So, you came back?"

Jackson's question comes to Sue as he sits in his wheelchair. His back is to her as she comes in the room.

Sue steps in front of him. Her hair disheveled, her dress ripped. Streaks of blood lay dry across her face and the backside of her hands. She crumples to the floor.

Several minutes pass until she opens her eyes. A cold, wet compress comforts her as Jackson pours water into a paper cup from one of the gallon milk jugs he uses to collect the rain.

"Jack… "

Sue's voice comes soft, weak, and broken.

"Jackson… "

"H*ere*, drink *this*."

She holds the cold cup racing it to her lips.

"Where's Harry? Is that his blood on your clothes?"

Swallows of water come fast from the emptying cup.

"No."

"Is it yours?"

She shakes her head back-and-forth and lowers the water to her lap.

"I don't know whose it is? Jackson… it's… it's so bad out there."

"What happened?"

Three quick breaths push from her lungs. Tears seem like they should fall, but dehydration and exhaustion prevent her sobbing.

"We... uh... we left here. Harry used to live in Tampa, so we headed there."

"What did you see?"

"The closer we got, there were so many cars just abandoned on the streets. We started seeing burned bodies near the cars. We... uh... when we got close enough to see the skyline, all we saw was black smoke billowing above the Bay."

"Did you not see anyone alive?"

"We stopped at a gas station to see if we can find anyone. There were two kids inside, a brother and sister... and... they told us about the riots and fighting that happened. Their parents were leaving the city when the Army passed them going the other way. That's when they heard the gunshots and bombs going off."

Jackson does not interrupt her. He rubs the back of her hands.

"We took them with us. Harry found some gas and put it into our car. We decided to drive to Orlando because that's where I used to live. We only got about halfway there when we came up to an Army barricade."

"Did they stop you?"

"Yes, and we were just happy to see anyone."

"What did they say?"

Sue hesitates. Her bottom lip quivers. Still, no tears.

"It was two young soldiers. I think they were just as surprised to see us as we were them. We asked what was happening. And, they told us to not go any further. The rioting and people trying to stop them, well, they described what we had seen in Tampa."

"Did they say anything... anything about what caused the blackout..."

"They said they didn't know. But only that what is happening in Orlando is happening across the whole country, and they think other countries for that matter... huh."

"Huh, what?"

"They never said why people were rioting though?"

He squeezes her hands into his.

"They didn't have to. It doesn't take long for people to go to their primal behavior when they feel threatened. I mean, if there is no communication or power, and this continues; then the worst in people will start to show."

"But, to riot?"

"I don't think it takes that long. If people don't know what's happening, then it will drive them crazy. We've been connected for too long. Look, it was only, what, a few days here before everyone left?"

A violent cry erupts from Sue. Her chest heaves uncontrollably.

"Why are you crying? It's okay, you're back here, now."

Jackson attempts to calm her.

"Out... out... of nowhere, one of the soldiers was shot right in front of me. That's where the blood came from."

"Who shot him?"

"While Harry and I were talking with them, the brother and sister had stayed behind in the back seat of our car. We didn't see the boy get out of the car holding a gun. And, I don't know... why... but, he shot the soldier."

"Oh my— "

"I fell to the ground. That's whose blood *this* is. I guess. Harry jumped over me going to the boy, I guess to get his gun... and... and... that's when... the other soldier fired his rifle... the bullets just zipped over my head as I watched them... "

Sue's chest heaves as her mouth opens. With nothing in her body to evacuate from her, she collects her breath.

"The other soldier killed them. He then stands over me and places... places the end of his rifle against my forehead... he pulled the trigger... and... and the gun only clicked."

"What?"

"Next thing I felt was his boot slamming against my stomach and chest as he cursed at me. I just closed my eyes and pretended to pass out... shit, it's not like I don't have experience doing that with my ex."

"So, he left, then."

"Yeah, after a couple minutes, he got into his Jeep and drove away. I waited until I thought no one was around and got back into the car and came here."

Jackson hands her another cup of water.

"It's okay, now. You're safe, back here."

Sue closes her eyes. Her breathing slows.

Jackson rubs her face with a moist towel cleaning the blood away. She falls asleep leaning against him on the floor.

"This is not happening by accident. The end must be getting close now for them to create this kind of chaos."

25-A New Secret

SALVATION SPLITS THE daily time into two halves. Ninety percent of the community works during daytime hours, while the remaining work nights. The primary duties of evening workers are cleaning, maintenance, and security.

This separation of work-time helps conserve resources. An unpredictable number of people working varying hours across the twenty-four-hour and thirty-seven-minute day creates challenges in managing the infrastructure.

Most who work beyond the daylight hours are those like Joe conducting research. His responsibility does not require him to be in his lab during the evening, but his bouts of insomnia require this diversion.

Two others within Salvation share Joe's misery: Jacob and Emma. Both never sleep more than two hours per day.

At four-Earth-years-old, Emma is beyond her age. Mentally equivalent to someone in their early twenties, she is competent of complete independent thoughts and retains an entire vocabulary. Her developing brain craves information like a drug addict seeking a fix.

With Joe's constant absences from their living quarters, Emma acquaints herself with her father's patterns. She predicts with absolute certainty when he will return for the evening, often pretending to sleep when he arrives home.

Maintained within the Salvation computer network are six-hundred-years' worth of books and journals created since the Gutenberg printing press. Eden had captured digitally every one keeping a historical record of Earth.

Emma spends hours each day speed-reading volumes of text. Her photographic memory catalogs the information for easy recall at any moment.

Tonight, reading does not satisfy Emma. She leaves her quarters since she does not expect her father's return for another six hours.

A familiar sight, no one stops Emma as she strolls through the corridor to where Jacob lives. An open invitation, Emma hopes Jacob is awake.

The corridor of the Leader's Wing always amazes her as she walks to his door. Hundreds of original, art masterpieces adorn the walls. Mona Lisa's eyes still startle Emma as she pauses to appreciate the portrait.

A few minutes afterward, she comes to the end of the walkway. The coldness of the identification pad's glass jolts through her arm. The light switches from red to green as Jacob has granted her entry any moment she wishes.

The door closes behind Emma as she enters Jacob's suite. She hesitates. An unfamiliar woman's voice comes faintly from Jacob's bedroom.

Emma approaches the open doorway. In one simultaneous moment, the woman's voice disappears as Jacob turns to his granddaughter.

"How's my little Emma, tonight?"

She stands on the other side of the room.

"What are you watching? I thought I heard a woman's voice?"

Jacob motions Emma to him. As she gets closer, Jacob closes the window on his computer.

"Can I share a secret with you?"

Emma stands beside her grandfather's chair looking up to him. His eyes are always trustworthy to her.

"Sure. I promise not to tell anyone."

Jacob lifts Emma on his knee.

"I have access to communication satellites above Earth."

"Can they identify where the access is originating from here on Mars?"

Jacob smiles. "No. It's a blind access point. I can watch any current television station on Earth that I want. But, nothing has been coming from them for weeks."

"Why?"

"I'm not sure. But, what I wanted to show you is that from this tablet only, I can access television programming I have been recording since I've been here."

"TV? I've read about that and have been curious to what that looked like?"

Jacob reaches across Emma clicking on his screen.

"I've been mainly collecting programming about nature. I thought someday I'd make this available to everyone."

"Why wait?"

Jacob hangs his head to Emma as he smiles.

"Well, the people here need more time adjusting to Salvation and making Mars their home. It's too close to the end of Earth, and it may be too difficult for people to see. Maybe someday, I'll share it."

Images of zebras running across the African plains appear before Emma. Golden sun rays illuminate the black-and-white striped animals. Emma's face reflects the sun from the screen.

"Those are zebras. Have you ever seen one of those?" Emma asked.

Jacob laughs. "Not in Africa like this, but I saw them in a zoo one time."

Emma touches the screen. "They're so beautiful."

Her eyes scrunch together. She lifts her stare to Jacob. "I will never see any animals, will I?"

Jacob clicks the window closed. The black mirrored screen reflects their image of her sitting on his lap.

"Huh, I guess you won't, at least in person."

Emma full of confidence replies, "Well, then it's great you have this programming. I think everyone will love to see these images from their home."

"*Their home*... it's your home, too."

"Not really. I was born here. This is all I know. Mars is home for me."

Jacob hugs Emma. "I'm so happy you feel this way."

"Why would I not? I don't know any other way to think. How can I feel bad or miss something I can't even relate with?"

Jacob widens his eyes looking at Emma. "Your Dad told me you were getting really philosophical lately."

"Yeah, I've finished reading *Man's Search for Meaning* a few days ago."

"Huh, I've never heard of that one."

"I finished reading the works by Freud, and I was searching for more contemporary philosophy books."

"Are you sure you're only four?"

"Yes, four-Earth-years, let's be clear."

They share a laugh.

"Anyway, in Frankl's work, he argues that the answer to the meaning of life is that you don't get to ask the question. But, life is the one who asks, and we must reply without actions."

Silence falls between them.

"I can tell by you not saying anything that this is why Daddy tells me not to talk about things like this with people because they'll think I'm strange."

Jacob hugs her. "You're not strange. But, I can appreciate what your father is saying."

"I know. I do get so bored though because I spend my day in class with other children my age or a little older."

"Emma, in a few years, we can move you to another setup with older students, but for now, it's best we keep this charade up."

"Is it because I'm the first born on Mars but conceived on Earth?"

Jacob does not respond with an immediate response. He lifts Emma off his lap as she stands next to his chair.

"Pretty much that's the reason. I don't want to ever lie to you, Emma. We are a small, new community. Even though we've done what we can to make Salvation seem normal to everyone... "

"I'm not normal, am I?"

Jacob releases a deep sigh. "No, you're not. You are very special. And, we just need to keep this secret from everyone for some time to protect you... protect us that's all."

Emma walks in front of Jacob's bed. "I understand. I need to appear normal to people, so no one freaks out more than they already are by living here. I get it."

Jacob stands and approaches lifting her in his arms. "You're young, but I think it's time I can tell you another secret, which will help you better understand."

Emma's eyes widen in his arms as he carries her to a sofa against the side wall. He places her down and sits beside her. The black leather softens against her.

"Emma, there's another secret your dad, and I are keeping from not only you but everyone here."

"A secret?"

"I will tell you this, but you have to promise me you will tell no one, including Joseph that I've told you."

Before she could respond, Jacob continues. "I know you will."

"You can trust me. I promise not to say anything to anyone, not even Daddy. He already has so much on his mind."

Jacob inhales one deep breath. Air slowly bellows from his lungs.

"Emma... my little, Emma... I'm your grandfather. Joseph is my son."

26-Earth Falls Silent

THE DAYS DRAG along hot and muggy. Relentless humidity fails to leave as the daylight grows shorter with each passing night. Thick clouds have settled across the sky the past week acting as a gray blanket over the lush landscape after daily afternoon rainstorms.

Since her return, Sue remains in her room. She sleeps on her right side with her knees to her chest. Deep wrinkles from a life left long behind her furrow across her face and hands. Between bouts of restless, nightmare-filled dreams, she stares through her window from her bed.

Time passes with no update of what is happening outside the confines of the retirement community. The world around them remains in chaos. Serenity finds Sue and Jackson in their hidden sanctuary of campus.

A foul stench emanates from each room of the building. Without an operating air conditioning unit, humidity and temperatures build inside the thirty-seven rooms on each floor. To create cross-breezes, Jackson has opened most windows. However, this allows rainwater to collect on the floor under the windowsills.

Without the presence of birds, which Jackson noticed earlier, the Floridian insects seem to multiply every hour. Hungry mosquitoes dance across the tops of the windows.

To escape the depressing confines, Jackson wheels his chair down the long hallway. At the end, a balcony opens allowing him to sit outside facing east. Without electricity, the elevator does not work. With Sue's incapacity to move, she cannot help him down the stairs. And, he does not dare to drag himself alone downstairs.

As evening approaches, hints of blue sky push away the clouds. For the first time in a week, the clouds vanish. Streaks of red and orange etch across the sky behind the building as the sun sets.

A strange sense of peace settles around him. Without the birds, the creaking of insects and crickets chime louder as darkness encloses the kaleidoscope of the evening sky.

Along the flat terrain of west-central Florida, Jackson views an unobstructed horizon. Before the chaos which has befallen them since losing communications and electricity, he recalls the inability to see starlight even on the clearest of nights. City lights from Tampa to the north and Orlando to the east wash out the stars.

With the darkness, thousands of flickering white dots consume the evening sky. The faint image of the Milky Way caresses the collage of stars and planets rising above the horizon.

Hmm... I wonder where is Columba Noachi in the sky?

The constellation Jackson had studied that night sixty-years-ago still haunts him all these years later.

I know what I saw. I had proof, and they stole it from me.

Images of an object Jackson saw through the Palomar Telescope caused him great concern, then. Hairs on his arms standing and the cold-chill streaming through his body still comes to him as he recalls that night.

And, to think The Eden Foundation knew about this and tried to keep it a secret from everyone on Earth.

Given his plight with his daughter, Ruth, he was desperate for help as she was often in trouble. The situation made it easy for Eli Bishop to approach him when he needed help with her the most. His love for Ruth had created blinders for the activities The Eden Foundation requested him to perform over the years.

Huh, I knew when they tried to kill us in the World Trade Center that I had made a terrible mistake in trusting them.

Jackson had held a growing distrust with Eden. Never able to pull all the pieces together, his instinct pointed to his discovery of the mystery object in Space. He led a shattered life after that evening on the mountain; his legs pinned under the crushed dash of his pickup truck. But, time has been his cerebral equalizer allowing him to connect the loose ends in his mind. He only needed Eli Bishop to corroborate his theories.

Feeling like a fugitive running most of his adult-life; tonight in the open, humid air on the balcony, a moment of total clarity crushes his memories.

This is all connected… everything that has happened… what is happening, now…

Jackson forces his body to the front edge of his chair. He peers down to the ground forty-feet below him. His hands grasp the painted white, rusting metal safety rail. He pulls his body from the chair leaning against the railing.

The small picture of his wife and daughter dig into his left palm as he squeezes his grip. Silent tears race down his scarred face. He places his right hand under his thigh lifting his right leg over to straddle the railing. As he leans back, his left hand pulls his left leg over the railing joining both feet on the outside edge of the balcony above a concrete pathway.

His breathing is slow and deep. The picture crumbles inside his left fist. Jackson closes his eyes. A deep, final breath consumes his lungs.

His fingertips lose their grip on the railing behind him. At the same moment, Jackson opens his eyes staring straight.

"What the hell!"

Jackson screams and reaches quickly behind his back catching his balance. He props his ass on top the railing wiping away his tears clearing his vision along the horizon.

A manic laugh of a crazed man erupts from him. He lifts his legs each across the railing returning to his chair.

"I knew it… I just knew it… dammit, I was right… "

Laughter ricochets across the open lawn.

"I knew it!"

In the distant horizon, a quarter-Moon rises; a regular occurrence for this time of the month. Although he no longer had possession of pictures from that night in February 1960, the mysterious object in the photo had seared itself in his memory. The same object now rises with the Moon visible from the balcony.

What was only a smudged dot on a screen sixty-years-ago, the planetoid appears nearly the same size as the Moon on the horizon. A reddish-orange glow encases the elongated space rock.

Jackson pushes his chair from the railing. His mouth holds open. Speechless.

Along the flat horizon as far as Jackson can see from his vantage point, thousands of fire streams push their way up from the ground to the sky. Atop each stream, a nuclear warhead rushes to the heavens.

"The missiles… the missiles will protect us… "

Jackson whispers into the night air.

"I knew it… I am not crazy… "

A breeze off the Gulf of Mexico rushes across the humid landscape. Clouds push across the sky from the West until reaching the horizon like the closing of a movie theater leaving a cliffhanger.

The object approaching Earth is as far away as the Moon. All available nuclear missiles launch for a rendezvous midway before the planetoid reaches Earth. The cliffhanger awaits until tomorrow to see if this last-minute approach is effective in stopping the inevitable.

EARTH DATE: SEPTEMBER 10, 2020
SARASOTA, FLORIDA – EARTH
(1 DAY PRIOR TO IMPACT)

"SUE! SUE!"

Jackson's calls go unanswered.

"Sue! Dammit, Sue!"

Jackson wheels down the hallway separating the fire extinguisher from the wall. He comes back to her locked door.

"Sue, open the door!"

He waits a few seconds and turns his chair sideways. The extinguisher is heavy in his arms as he contorts his torso to his right. With a swift motion, he swings the end of the tank to his left as hard as his strength allows against the doorknob.

Success. The door opens to Sue's room. Jackson wheels inside as she props herself to the side of her bed. He grabs her hands in his.

"Have you seen the sky... It's so... so, beautiful... "

Dense clouds overhead illuminate with a haunting, orange glow in the middle of the day. Jackson remains by her describing the beautiful colors to coax her to leave her room.

"This is it, isn't it... the End?" Sue speaks in a soft, defeated tone as she raises her head to meet his gaze.

"I don't know. Last night, I saw all those missiles take off headed for that thing."

"You think that's why the sky's so orange, right now?"

Jackson releases his grip and rolls to the window pushing open the musty curtains. His face lights up orange reflecting the sky.

"It's too hard to say. Those damn clouds... I can't see shit."

"What's that?"

Sue jumps from the bed and grabs Jackson's shoulders behind him. A low rumble shakes their building.

"Is that an earthquake?" Sue asked.

Jackson grabs the blanket off the floor and pulls Sue's hand.

"Quick, we need to get under the doorway. Feels like it."

Anyone who has lived in California will not mistake the sensation of an earthquake even after sixty years since leaving the state.

"We don't have these in Florida?"

"Here, put the blanket over us and cover your head with your arms!" Jackson yells.

The low rumble lasts for one minute but never gets worse. Pictures and books fall from the shelves as white dust from the overhead tiles drift to the floor.

"That was a weird feeling."

Sue kneels by Jackson's chair as they stay in the doorway.

"You think we'll have more of those?"

As a trained astronomer, Jackson knows the answer but lies instead.

"Don't think so. Could be coming as a result of all the nuclear explosions."

"You think?"

Instead of responding, Jackson stays silent.

"Maybe we should get out of the building in case there are more of those?"

Jackson refuses to resist Sue's recommendation. She stands pushing him from her room down the hall to the stairs. She slips her arms under Jackson's sweaty body lifting him from his chair to the floor.

"Let me take your chair down, and I'll be right back."

A combination of wheels bouncing against the steps and creaking knees follow Sue into the darkness of the stairwell.

"Okay, I'm coming back— "

Her voice trails off seeing Jackson halfway down the first section of steps pulling against the railing for support.

"Here, I've got you."

She slips her hands under his shoulders pulling him down. A faint orange hue illuminates their way through the darkness as the daylight slides under the ground floor door frame.

"Okay, we've made it."

Sue's chest heaves. Sweat streams from her forehead pooling under her eyes.

A low rumble approaches. Another earthquake.

"Shit! Let's get out of here!" Jackson yells.

Sue slams open the door pushing Jackson outside the building. Their bodies glow orange from the sky.

Jackson's chair bounces on the ground as Sue holds on to him. The rumble does not last as long but feels stronger.

"Where should we go?"

"Push me to the courtyard. It's an open-air space, so nothing should fall on us out there."

Sue cries. The chair squeals across the concrete walkway. Another rumbling chases them to the center of the yard.

"Okay, we should be all right, here," Jackson said trying to comfort her.

The rumbling grows constant but never feels worse. A sensation of riding in the open bed of a pickup truck pulsates underneath them.

Hours pass. The rumbling continues stopping every few moments. Thick clouds obscure their view of the other side of the blood, red sky.

At 11 p.m., the sky should be dark. However, it is as bright as before — an eerie mix of red and orange. The rumbling does not stop as their bodies stretch-out on the grass beside the concrete path.

Jackson's eyes fall heavy. He finds the rumbling sensation relaxing. Sue's faint sobs lull him to sleep.

"Oh my God, Jackson! Wake up!"

EARTH DATE: SEPTEMBER 11, 2020
SARASOTA, FLORIDA – EARTH
(DAY OF IMPACT)

AN EARLY 3 A.M. MORNING should come peacefully. The shrill emanating from Sue startles Jackson awake. A wet sensation consumes his backside drenching his clothes and hair.

"Jackson, there's water rising in the courtyard. We gotta get up!"

He props his torso on his elbows. In a swift motion of surprising strength, Sue lifts Jackson from the ground to his chair. Water sloshes from both wheels as Sue runs pushing the chair to their building.

"Where's the water coming from?" Sue yells.

Jackson realizes what is happening from his knowledge of astronomy and astrophysics but does not divulge the terrifying answer to her.

"We need to get to the top of the building."

A heavy breath escapes from Sue.

"Now?"

"Yes, I'm pretty sure a tsunami is coming in from the ocean."

"But, we've got to be at least ten miles from the shore."

He grabs her right hand. His grip crushes her getting her attention.

"We need to go, now!"

She spins his chair facing backward against the stairs.

"I can help pull the chair up, but I need you to push the chair."

Sue steps in front of Jackson holding the sides of his chair and pushes. He spins his wheels back lifting the chair painfully up each step. Water seeps under the ground floor door rising over the steps behind them.

"Oh my God, the water's coming inside."

"Sue! Focus on me and the chair. We'll take each step one at a time."

Grunts from them both echo in the enclosed stairwell. The humid air thickens as the water level climbs behind them catching them.

"Halfway!"

Sounds of glass shattering push into the stairwell as water rushes into the building. The sudden crash startles Sue as she releases Jackson's chair.

He turns his head to hers. Fear looks back to Jackson.

White from her eyes brightens her face. He releases his left grip on the wheel and grabs her arm before she falls backward into the water.

"I've got you!"

They continue upward. The building rumbles as another earthquake shakes. Large ripples of water slosh around them.

"We're almost there, just a few more steps."

"Will it stop?"

"Just keep pushing."

Their weakened muscles ache through their arms across their shoulders and down their backs. Blood slips from Jackson's hand cut against the dulling rim of his wheels.

A black door stands closed at the top of the stairwell. Jackson pushes. "It's locked."

Sue pushes against the door. A guttural scream releases from her body as the door pops open. The extreme heat and shaking building had caused the doorframe to deform.

Thick, humid air rushes passed them escaping through the opened pathway. They dump out onto the open roof of the building.

"Oh shit, we can't get any higher," Sue said looking over the edge.

The blood, orange light shines across the water. The neighboring buildings submerge entirely. Their building, being the tallest, spares them from the rising water which stops a few feet before cresting the roof.

Sue screams crying as she runs from edge-to-edge of the flat roof. Jackson grabs her arm as she passes him.

"Stop! Stop it! Sue, stop!"

Jackson's pleas catch her attention. She looks down at him.

"There's nothing else we can do. Here, help me out of my chair."

Sue slips her arms under Jackson's armpits. She lifts him from the chair laying him flat on his back on the roof.

"Lie beside me."

She complies. The building rumbles beneath them. Water splashes over the building's edge from the waves created by the earthquake.

Sue catches her breath. "The tsunami… the earthquakes caused them?"

Jackson hesitates but realizes there is no reason to lie any longer.

"What I think is happening is the object is getting closer to Earth. It's large and has a gravitational pull just like the Moon does creating our tides."

"But, this isn't a high tide, and is it also causing the earthquakes?"

Their bodies glow orange reflecting the sky which should experience a sunrise, now.

"As this object gets closer, it's basically pulling at the Earth. That's why the water has risen so fast, and it explains the earthquakes."

"How long will this last?"

Heat increases on their exposed skin. Jackson hesitates his fatal response.

"I don't know. But, I suspect if we could see Earth, it's looking more like an egg instead of a sphere."

"Really?"

Jackson balls his fist showing how the approaching mass with its own gravity will pull against the surprisingly pliable Earth.

"So, it'll pull one side of the Earth, and our planet will be egg-shaped."

Sue stares to the sky in silence. The heat builds roasting their exposed skin. Searing, sizzling sounds pop around them.

"Wha... what will happen next?"

Jackson squeezes her hand tight. He knows but does not want to tell her their pending fate.

"Do you think the missiles worked?"

Silence from Jackson. The heat continues to build. Steam rises from the roof.

Sue spins her body onto Jackson's chest closing her eyes.

"I... I don't want to look anymore... just hold me."

Jackson squeezes her arms pulling her closer to his chest. She quivers on him.

Excitement overcomes him. A smile widens across his face. He stops blinking. The whites of his eyes shine brightly in the thick, red air engulfing them.

In an instant, the total cloud-cover pulls from the sky as if a colossal hand has drawn a cover from a bowling ball. The approaching object sucks away the clouds covering Earth.

While the Earth bulges on the Western Hemisphere facing the approaching object, the eastern half has a sudden collapse. This immediate expansion and compression of Earth create plumes of molten lava exploding into Space across the planet.

With the absence of clouds, the planetoid comes into full view for Jackson. The object fills at least eighty percent of the sky from horizon-to-horizon. The heat becomes too intense pulling the air from their lungs.

Jackson feels Sue's body heave her last breath. The ear-piercing rumble muffles her cries.

Lava streams across the sky into the stratosphere. Jackson quickens his breathing with shallow breaths trying to keep his consciousness. His smile remains etched on his face.

The object fills ninety percent of the sky. Streams of lava spin in torrents in the air above them. Boulders the size of Mount Everest slam through the molten liquid. Jackson's eyes follow a dancing lava stream as it spins above them below the approaching object.

Through Jackson's smile, a guttural scream erupts from his body as the lava stream falls back to Earth across Sarasota Springs eviscerating Florida, the East Coast, North America, and the Western Hemisphere.

CIE.57.20 slams into Earth. In the same instant, the molten interior of the planet mushrooms through the Eastern Hemisphere flipping the inside of Earth outward.

Twelve-and-a-half-minutes later and thirty-eight-millions-miles away, a basketball-size of bright light pulsates where the Earth should be above the Martian horizon. Everyone at Salvation watches on the television monitors the horrific light show along the horizon from the outside cameras.

One minute passes. Jacob's voice comes through the speakers.

"Everyone, our hearts go out to those left behind. Your way to honor their memory is to carry on your work, here. By showing the event live from our external camera focused on the horizon, we hope it brings you some closure."

Joe sits with Emma in their living quarters.

"It's okay, Daddy," Emma said holding Joe's hands as he cries. "We've been saved, here at Salvation."

27-There Will Be Order

THE TIME FOLLOWING the destruction of Earth had brought a lull of mourning and sadness for everybody at Salvation. Gone was knowing another shipment of people or supplies would soon arrive. Gone was Earth; a realization all had known was coming, but until that fateful date was painful to believe.

Like a teenaged child leaving the comfort of their parent's home, Salvation must survive on its own.

Out of respect for those left behind and their lost home planet, life at Salvation flourishes. People perform their work duties. Children go to class. Day-to-day life is normal absent any bright blue skies and the inability to walk outside without the presence of a bio-suit.

For Joe, he has two responsibilities: to be a father to his seven-year-old daughter, Emma, and to continue his research carried over from Earth. Both, Joe performs well.

An unfamiliar feeling has befallen Joe the past three years. Sadness is absent. Serenity has taken ahold of his thoughts. Time passes allowing depression to flow away after Mary's death. Joe still longs for her, but being a father drives him to be present for Emma. She truly saves Joe from despair.

His main work continues to be his scanning of young, fertile male and female Salvationists for potential birth pairings. Joe performs a monthly review of men between the ages of eighteen and forty-five and women eighteen and thirty-two.

The Eden Foundation had selected every Salvationist based on their initial role on Mars. Some have technical and scientific skills vital in an alien world. Others recruited to ensure the continuation of the human race.

Everyone had to pass thorough health evaluations identifying any potential family history of disease or mental disabilities. The Foundation collected each potential Salvationist's health and family records unbeknownst to the candidate.

Eden approached those having cleared the health and mental assessments with the technical or scientific need for Salvation. Sexual orientation was not a factor. Nor did the Foundation try to balance a specific ratio between men and women. This group represents approximately sixty percent of the Salvation population.

Conversely, those not possessing a technical or scientific need, The Eden Foundation had recruited them for one specific purpose: reproduction. Their recruitment involved identifying those likely to accept the adventure of living on Mars while not informing them of the real intent.

Salvation assigned these people non-technical job functions upon arrival to Mars. While not technical, they perform essential jobs such as teachers, maintenance, security, and others.

Before Joe's arrival, Baptiste held the job of scanning potential pairings. His earliest accomplishment was convincing Jacob of a fallacy held within the Foundation's selection process. A need was present to ensure scientific capabilities continue within the lineage of the Salvationists.

Though never proven scientifically, a child may inherit a professional ability. Jacob decided not to risk these crucial skills resulting from genetics extending the selection process into the scientific community.

Baptiste kept meticulous records of everyone. Joe cross-references these in his pairing recommendations he presents to Jacob every month. Once Jacob approves and informs the chosen man and woman, Joe works with Doctor Johanisson and his team in preparing the selected couple for conception.

Normal births and natural deaths occur. People perform their daily responsibilities. Society develops… but, at what cost?

EARTH DATE: SEPTEMBER 2, 2023 (1 YEAR LATER)

WORK AND ALL ACTIVITY have halted for the day. Excitement has been building for days within Salvation. Rumors circulate why Jacob has summoned everyone to their living quarters for a live event on their viewing monitors.

"What's this about, Daddy?"

Emma joins Joe on the sofa in their living room. Through the black mirror of the video screen affixed on the opposite wall, Jacob's image appears.

"Hello, Friends. This is only the second trial in our history of an accused Level-Three Crime."

Emma tugs at Joe's arm. "When was the last one?"

"Ssh, Emma. I don't know."

The video zooms out. Jacob sits on a small stage behind a podium. Before him, Joe sees the backside an athletic-built man with a cropped haircut sitting between an older woman to his right and another woman on his left.

"The accused, Heinrich 17E127, was found two nights ago in Restricted Zone Alpha trying to disable the oxygenation system of the West Wing area of Salvation. Security apprehended him after alarm systems were activated."

"That's why that siren was blaring the other night," Emma said as she watched her dad's attention not break from the screen.

"Emma, I know that man. He came here with us from Earth."

"How does the defendant plead?"

The courtroom sight is familiar to Joe from what he remembers from home. As Eli Bishop and later his son, Jacob, developed the laws and regulations for Salvation, they had modeled the administration and judicial system used within the United States. The only exception… Jacob serves as judge and jury.

The older woman on Heinrich's right stands. "Your Honor, the defendant pleads not guilty, Sir."

A laugh bursts from Jacob behind his podium. "Surely, you're joking. He is on video."

"Your Honor, if I may, the defendant was under duress during his actions."

"Duress? From whom?"

The woman clears her throat. "Sir, the defendant claims you, Sir… you caused his duress. Therefore, the defendant requests to enter a claim of not guilty due to a moment of insanity."

Jacob's face turns stern. His eyes squint above a glowing red face; his brow embeds deep with wrinkles.

"Fine. We will go about the proceedings and hear the defendant out."

Jacob turns his attention to the other seated woman on Heinrich's left.

She rises and clears her throat as Heinrich's attorney returns to her seat beside him. "Your Honor, the prosecution is quite simple."

Video surveillance plays in a split screen in Joe and Emma's living quarters.

"Two nights ago, two hours before sunrise… the accused, Heinrich 17E127, tried to deactivate the oxygen systems in Salvation. The video is quite clear, Sir."

"Yes, yes, it is," Jacob said.

"The alarm system alerted Security and apprehended the accused, identified by fingerprint and retina-scan as being Heinrich 17E127, without a doubt."

Jacob watches the replay of the security feed on his personal monitor. He holds a tablet with the identification information of the accused. He places the tablet on his table and studies the defendant.

"Okay, one last time… how do you plead? This is a Level-Three Crime and based on your plea it will help me determine how lenient the sentence should be."

Silence comes through the video screen to Joe and Emma. Several seconds pass.

"Sir, Your Honor, the defendant still wishes to enter a plea of not guilty for reasons of momentary insanity."

Jacob's left eyebrow raises. "Very well then, plead your case."

Heinrich's attorney approaches Jacob. She stops halfway and turns to the video camera. "Ladies and Gentlemen— "

"I will remind the attorney that you are speaking to me. Everyone watching is doing so because we vowed to maintain transparency in our proceedings."

The attorney stares into the camera. "Ladies and Gentlemen, the defendant… Heinrich is a victim of the harsh laws here at Salvation preventing people who love each other from being together."

"Janet 14E23! You will face me directly! That is an order!"

Joe watches on his screen. Heinrich's lawyer, Janet, swells her eyes. Her bottom lip trembles. She complies with Jacob's command turning away from the camera.

"Heinrich was accused and found guilty of a Level-One crime eighty-seven days ago," Janet said.

"Remind me, again, of that crime."

"Your Honor, Heinrich was found with Joanie 17S47 in his room after Security had observed her entrance to his room on eight, consecutive nights."

"Joanie 17S47, she was my teacher's sister who died seventeen days, ago," Emma said to Joe who holds his stare on the television screen.

Joe shakes his head and stands. "I know, Sweetheart. Joanie and Heather were also with us on our arrival to Salvation."

"Level-One Regulations stipulate that unless paired, no one within Salvation may live with anyone else in their quarters unless granted strict permission by you."

"So, the defendant had already broken a crime and now has committed another," Jacob said interrupting the lawyer.

"Yes. Heinrich is guilty of committing a Level-One Crime. Both Joanie and he were found guilty and served their punishment with seven days in detention and a reduction of their salary."

"Pretty standard sentence for a first offense… apparently it should've been stronger," Jacob retorted.

"Your Honor, their punishment fits the crime— "

"But, tell Him it caused my Joanie's death," Heinrich said in his thick German accent.

"I will remind the defendant to remain quiet unless spoken to," Jacob said.

"The punishment prevented Joanie to be reassigned to the Maintenance Staff, where Heinrich works, from the Food Server Staff. Each was fitted with bracelets alerting Security when they came within ten meters of each other."

"Hardly a reason to cause death?"

"Have you ever been in love, Your Honor?"

Jacob pushes his chair back from his podium. "Janet 14E23, you are treading on a thin line with your question to me."

"Have you ever been in love?"

"Janet 14E23!"

"Have you ever been in love, Your Honor, answer the question!"

Jacob pauses.

"Janet 14E23, I am not on trial, here. Your defendant is. To answer your question… no."

"What?" Both Joe and Emma said at the same time. Their shared response is due to the answer relating to his mother, Rachel, Emma's grandmother.

"Well, Your Honor… " Janet turns her back to Jacob and returns her stare into the camera. "Heinrich and Joanie were in love. So much in love,

Joanie could not stand being kept away from Heinrich. Her angst caused her to kill herself seventeen days ago by exiting the Landing Area's exterior air-lock."

"Janet 14E23! You will turn and face me, now, or I will cite you with a Level-Two Crime assaulting me and the audience with these lies."

Heinrich's lawyer immediately obeys returning her attention to Jacob.

"Good. Now, you may continue, but I'm warning you."

Janet's shoulders lift and relax with a deep breath. "Your Honor, with Joanie's death, Heinrich became so distraught that he temporarily became insane. This insanity enraged within him causing his access to the Restricted Area."

"See. It was easy wasn't it?"

"Excuse me."

"To admit he did it, commit a Level-Three Crime, which I may remind you and everyone watching that if he had been successful, we could've lost our oxygen-creation system to the West Wing of the complex."

"Sir, we are not pleading guilty to this."

"Why, yes... yes, you are. If Security had not caught him within the next several minutes, thousands would have been impacted."

"Sir, no one was or would have been harmed. The backup systems would activate."

"And, what if Security had not caught him when they did... how much farther would the accused have gone?"

The lawyer returns to her seat. Her shoulders round, her head lowers.

"Will the defendant please stand?"

Both Heinrich and Janet rise.

"I, Jacob, Leader of Salvation, find you, Heinrich 17E127, guilty of a Level-Three Crime, on this five-hundred-thirty-second-day in the Year 18. I hereby sentence you to an immediate banishment from Salvation."

Three large members from Security surround Heinrich and take him from the courtroom. As Heinrich leaves, Jacob continues speaking into the video camera.

"Neighbors, I know the result is upsetting. But, again, I want to maintain complete transparency with everyone. We have established our rules to protect us, to protect us all. We have a fragile environment, here, and we will maintain our order within Salvation. Let this be a warning, however. We will do everything to maintain the security of Salvation and to you. With that, have a productive rest of your day."

The video feed ends, Blackness emerges in the screen.

"So, Heinrich is banished from Salvation, Daddy?"

"Yes."

"Where will he go?"

Joe does not respond. He knows how intelligent Emma is.

"Oh… never mind… I understand."

Emma hangs her head down.

"Sweetheart, you understand, don't you? We must follow the rules here for everyone's safety."

"I know… but, it just doesn't seem fair… they were in love."

"You don't even know what love is?"

"I love you, Daddy. I would do anything for you."

Instant dryness forms in Joe's throat as if he had swallowed a glass of sand. Ringing from the intercom system interrupts their awkward silence.

"Answer the call," Joe said triggering the automated action.

"Joe, this is Doctor Johanisson."

"Hi, Doc, what can I do for you?"

"Can you come by my office? I've had two patients stop by with strange fevers… I've not seen anything like that before, here."

"What does this have to do with me? How am I supposed to help?"

A momentary pause came through the audio connection.

"Joe, they are children."

"Okay, I'll be right there."

"Thanks, and, hurry."

The line dies. Joe stands to leave. "Emma, we'll talk more about the hearing and sentencing when I return, okay?"

"Okay, Daddy. I love you."

"Love you, too."

The door opens and closes as Joe leaves.

Fevers in children… why is Johanisson needing me?

28-THE SICKNESS

"THE NEXT SAMPLES are complete. How should we proceed?" a lab assistant said to Joe.

"Send the results to my computer."

Joe stands at his corner workstation of his laboratory comparing the latest data-set to the earlier fifteen collected.

"Not again." Joe rubs his hand against his forehead. "I can't figure out what is happening."

The lab assistant joins Joe.

"I followed the new testing protocol you established. Do you think we should perform the next test on the latest patient?"

Joe paces the lab. Light steps long have replaced his once heavy gait on Earth. The latest testing protocol requires the magnetic floor, meant to offer a sense of gravity within the Salvation compound, turned off within the laboratory. An unknown source of the anomalies in Joe's samples has frustrated him for weeks.

"Let me think about it. I'll review the past sample runs when I get back from my meeting with the Leader."

Joe grunts as he returns to his workstation collecting his reports on his tablet.

Why is the decay rate speeding up in the cell samples?

"While you're gone, I'll clean up the sample stations."

"Okay, I'll be back in an hour. We can set-up the next test run then."

Halfway across the lab, Joe stops as his Earth-age, ten-year-old daughter stands in the entranceway. Her short, auburn hair contrasts against her light-green eyes, her mother's eyes. Joe smiles.

"Emma, why aren't you in class?" Joe asked taking her hand. "You know you are not allowed out of the Children's Wing."

"I know, but I'm so lonely, there." Emma wraps her arms around Joe's legs. "Plus, I was with Jacob."

Joe kneels beside Emma.

"Do you know what's today?"

Emma smiles. "It's Mommy's birthday, Daddy."

Joe hugs Emma. "Yes, you're right."

"Can we visit her?"

Joe sighs feeling the heaviness in his chest.

"Let me take you back to your area. After my meeting with Jacob, I'll come to get you, and we will go visit Mommy."

She kisses his cheek. "I love you, Daddy."

"I love you, too, my little Emma."

Joe stands and holds her hand exiting his lab. As they approach the translucent door of the Children's Wing, Joe places his hand flat against the scanner.

They enter the room and Emma places her hand on a scanner affixed atop a pedestal. Red letters scroll across the panel: *Emmanuelle 17WD21*. The scan records her attendance in class.

The Children's Wing accommodates up to one-hundred students younger than thirteen-Earth-years-old for classes during the day. Emma hugs Joe and joins the thirty-two others who are left remaining in class.

"I'll be back. I love you."

"Love you, too, Daddy."

The translucent door swishes closed as Joe exits. He fumbles his tablet almost hitting the floor. The screen illuminates with a list of the latest numbers of sick children.

Three more this week… So far, Emma is healthy, but she's not been sick a day in her life… What's causing this?

Joe closes his tablet and places it under his arm as he exits the Children's Wing. His feet fall firm against the floor walking on the magnetic floor following the way to Jacob's wing of Salvation.

He pauses as he does every time in the hallway outside Jacob's living quarters. The artwork masterpieces adorning the walls trap him lingering more than usual. His hand caresses his chest.

Emma wants to visit you, today.

An image of his wife, Mary, comes to him as she does most days. She never ages, however, the gray streaks in Joe's hair reveal his forty-seven-year-old body. This conversation, like most, remains inside his mind. He is fearful of being thought to be crazy if caught speaking to himself.

How is my Emma doing?

She is great as usual… always happy and full of life… she gets that from you.

Emma is so smart. She gets that from you, Joseph.

He shuffles his feet continuing to rub his chest.

What's wrong? I can always tell when something's bothering you?

I can't figure out what's causing the increasing death rates in the children born here on Mars.

Oh no, Emma—

No, don't worry. I've checked her, and she is completely healthy.

Thank God.

I noticed a pattern last year developing in those conceived here at Salvation dying sooner than the healthy population.

But, you perform those tests, the genetic ones to make sure the correct pairings of couples conceive.

Exactly. And, my tests are correct.

Joe slides his back down the wall sitting on the floor. His imagined Mary joins beside him.

I work with Doctor Johanisson and his team of specialists taking samples of those that have died. I examine their DNA looking for any clue to figure out what's happening.

Have you noticed anything so far?

Joe pauses. His thoughts jumble in his mind.

It's strange, because it's not there in the initial genetic scans but shows up during the autopsy.

What shows up?

A mutated gene marker. I haven't been able to link it to a specific illness. But, it seems to start the same way. The person comes to Johanisson's office complaining of a fever which lasts a few days.

How bad is the fever?

That's just it, it's only a mild fever, but everyone here knows the protocol to see the doctor for even the slightest feeling of not being well.

So, this fever seems okay, then.

And, we thought that. It goes away, then a few weeks later it returns much worse, and by this point we notice tumors developing either in the brain or stomach.

Oh, poor thing, I know how much you've struggled with studying brain tumors since that's how your mama died.

Mary's arm drapes around his shoulders. He imagines feeling her warmth across his body.

But, these tumors advance into the body so rapidly. Johanisson and his teams try to remove the tumors and perform rounds of radiation and chemo, but it only drags out the inevitable so long.

What happens?

Within a month of first having symptoms of the fever, they have all died. Every single person.

And, this just started?

A little over a year ago.

Then, there must be something different that has triggered this, don't you think?

Joe stands up quickly.

That's it. I've been trying to examine what's happening, and I've not looked for possible causes.

Mary's image joins him standing.

But, you said, our Emma is okay?

Joe gazes into Mary's light-green eyes.

Yes, she is. There have been deaths of people born before her and after her. And, she is exceptionally healthy which possibly coincides with her genius development.

Mary smiles.

You said she wanted to visit me?

Joe face changes. He had reflected her smile with his, but her question pulls the momentary happiness from him.

I hate going there. Seems like I've been going there too frequently with the recent deaths.

Mary takes Joe's hand to her face. *It's okay. Just like Earth, it's good to have a place where people can go to mourn and remember.*

Her image fades. Joe pushes his hand through Mary's disappearing face. He fights back the longing of wanting to yell out to her, *don't go.*

A deep sigh fills the hallway as Joe stands before the large *Waterlilies* painting from Monet. He places his hand against the glass wall panel and enters Jacob's area.

EARTH DATE: JUNE 23, 2026 (THAT AFTERNOON)

"SO, THESE ARE THE LATEST pairings based on your tests?"

Jacob sat at his desk reviewing Joe's genetic scans. What had been a monthly review occurs weekly given the increasing death rates in children conceived on Mars.

"I've re-run the scans for everyone, here."

The red encased tablet flies across the office landing on the sofa.

"Then, why in the hell are these deaths occurring? I brought you here because you were the expert in this type of analytics on Earth— "

"But, I did not select these people to come here."

Jacob charges as Joe steps backward. He places his hand firm on Joe's shoulder.

"Look, I'll calm down. Everyone chosen to join Salvation passed our initial tests. Baptiste personally oversaw that. It's got to be something here that's causing the deaths."

Joe relaxes his body realizing he will not have to fight off a confrontation with his father.

"Trust me; I'm losing sleep trying to figure out what's happening."

Jacob paces the office mumbling to himself.

"Well, so far, it's only happening to those conceived at Salvation and not to anyone from Earth."

"Right."

Jacob stops his moving and turns to Joe.

"You don't see what's happening infecting those from Earth, do you?"

"Whatever is happening, it is not contagious. Johanisson and his doctors have tested those initially when they come in complaining of a fever. And, it is not a virus or bacteria. Those tests come back negative."

Several seconds pass in silence.

"We need to figure this out soon before the people here begin to suspect a pattern or become concerned."

"Exactly, that's why my team has been working non-stop the past weeks."

"I mean, right now, those that have died have few connections between the other families."

"That's why when I present the suggested pairings to you, we spread them out across the population to help with the diversity."

"But, soon, people will start making certain connections and asking questions… I need to be able to offer comfort to them… to us all."

"Well, I suggest you grant permission with these pairings so we can start their process. It takes time to get them ready for conception."

Jacob retrieves the tablet from the sofa and reviews the statistics.

"Okay, you've got my approval. Make it happen. And, let me know if you need anything to help out your research."

Joe tries to take the tablet from Jacob, who holds it without releasing it.

"And, Joe... above anything else, make sure Emma is okay. She's one of them, you know."

The tablet releases to Joe.

"Absolutely."

EARTH DATE: JUNE 23, 2026 (EVENING)

"DADDY, DO I NEED to be worried about you?"

Joe leads Emma from the Children's Wing to the Central Hub common area of Salvation.

"Why do you say that?"

Emma's left hand feels comforting inside his loose, right fist.

"I know you don't sleep too much, but lately you're not sleeping any?"

"Oh, don't worry, Sweetheart. I'm fine. Just a lot of work stuff going on."

"With your gene study? I wish you would show me that some time. I mean, I've already read every book, here."

"Every one?"

"Yes, well, almost everyone. There are a lot of romance novels and books written about vampires that seem over-played."

Joe laughs.

"Even, *Twilight*?"

"Okay, that series was pretty good, but it seemed like so many authors tried to copy that plot too often... no, I'm talking more about I've read most of the non-fiction and technical type stuff."

"Emma, you sure you're only ten?"

"Yes, Dad, we do this all the time. I tell you about something I've read or done, and you come to me with that."

"I'm sorry. You just still amaze me that's all."

"Well, at least you've stopped testing me to recite memorized text from specific page numbers in a book I've read."

"I know. But, your memory is amazing, and I'm a scientist."

"You're not cutting me open."

Emma laughs pulling her father through the Central Hub. Clear glass walls and ceiling offer an unobstructed view of the Martian terrain. Green plants adorn the interior of the central park-like area, a favorite place in the complex.

"I play along with yours and Jacob's wishes about not letting people know about my abilities, but it's making me feel insane."

"Is that why you skip class a lot? Yeah, that's right, I know about that."

Emma lowers her head.

"I know why I have to play along because people here may not quite understand my brilliance."

"Oh, modest, aren't we?"

"But, I'm so bored in class. At least I've been placed with the older kids, but still, they're only doing Calculus or reading Shakespeare in class."

In the center of the park area, a cylindrical glass elevator rises from the floor to an overhead Rotunda. Joe places his hand flat against the access glass panel. He and Emma enter the elevator with the door closing behind them.

"I'll make a deal with you."

"Sure, what?"

"How about next week, after class, I bring you to my office, and I'll explain my research to you."

"Awesome. I can't wait."

The elevator door opens. A solid, black floor provides a stark contrast to the entire Salvation complex with its combination of white and translucent floors, walls, and ceilings.

Brilliant LEDs shine along the pathway stretching from the elevator to the edge wall. The Rotunda encircles the elevator and accommodates up to twenty people by appointment. Tonight, Joe and Emma are alone.

A clear glass dome stretches across the floor. The evening Martian sky lights up brilliant. Stars twinkle as they walk closer to the dome wall.

As they approach the glass, the stars are not the source of the twinkling lights. Hundreds of small diamonds rest against the glass wall. Each diamond is a memorial to those which have died at Salvation.

When someone dies, the medical team cremates the body. Technicians administer a chemical process extracting carbon elements from the ashes. Through heating the carbon to fourteen-hundred-degrees-Celsius and applying a pressure of eight-hundred-seventy-thousand-pounds-per-square-inch, a diamond forms.

The final resting place for the diamond is against the domed glass. A brilliant source of light, the beauty of the diamonds represent the beauty of those who have gone before the others at Salvation.

Joe brings Emma each year on Mary's birthday to pay respects to her mother.

"Daddy… I can't find it."

"Are you sure?"

Emma flashes a smirk to Joe.

"You know I don't forget anything, and it should be *right here*."

Joe approaches Emma from behind.

"Huh, you're right… I wonder where it could have gone?"

Emma lifts both clenched fists to either side her hips. Huffs of breath rush from her lungs.

In one quick instance, a flash of blue brilliance distracts her field of vision. A shrill releases from her.

"Mama's necklace. I love this."

"Emma, you're getting old enough, now… so, I want you to have *this*."

Joe clasps the gold chain together. The blue-diamond, heart-shaped pendant falls heavy against her chest. She takes the necklace in her hands as she turns crying to her father.

"Oh, don't cry. Your mom looked so beautiful wearing this, and now, it's yours."

"But… but, you wear this to remember her."

Joe places his hands around Emma's shoulders. Her light-green eyes look up to his.

"I've got the best remembrance of her in you, Emma."

Her bottom lip quivers.

"Press the little knob on the side."

Emma follows his instruction.

"Is… this… "

"I spoke with Jacob and asked if I could have your mom's diamond."

With a gentle touch, she presses her index finger on the light-blue diamond affixed in the middle of the left side of the opened pendant. On the right, a picture of Joe holding Emma as a baby rests inside.

"This way, your mom… "

Joe holds back his emotion not wanting to cry.

"My Mary, she will always be with you and watching over us."

Emma closes the pendant. In the same quick motion, the necklace falls against her and presses against her father as she embraces him.

"I love it… oh, do I love it… thank you," Emma said with a muffled voice as her head presses against him.

She releases her grip. Joe lifts the pendant from her chest. Emma's hands join his.

"Wearing *this* when your mom passed away brought me so much comfort… and, now, she's with you and can save you whenever you need her."

Sparkling diamonds surround them inside the Rotunda. Joe holds his daughter in a tight embrace as both cry releasing the anguish of a lost love, a lost mother.

29-Discovery

THE BLACK FLOOR chills Jacob and Joe alone in the Rotunda. Hundreds of sparkles tease their view around the glass dome. Technicians add dozens of new diamonds each month. A tablet in a red casing rests between father and son.

"We've got to figure this shit out," Jacob said leaning his back against the glass wall.

A guttural roar pushes through Joe's unshaven face.

"Goddammit!"

The tablet slides fast across the floor with a violent push from Joe's foot.

"Get a hold of yourself. We need you, now. Don't lose it."

"I've run all the tests I can think of, many times... something is causing a specific gene to trigger the cancer development."

"And, you've checked everything associated with our environment here... can the gravity difference cause it?"

Deep, short breaths force through Joe's flaring nostrils. Thin, gray hairs surrounding his mouth flicker.

"No… it shouldn't. Salvation had many people living either on the Moon or Mars for a long time… I mean look at Mac, that son-of-a-bitch lived to what… eighty-seven."

"Yeah, but he died from cancer."

Jacob stands pacing around Joe still resting against the wall. Like a defense attorney, Jacob grills Joe with questions.

"The cancers are always the same?"

"Yes. They develop fast after the patient acquires a fever."

"And, it's either in the brain or stomach?"

"Yes, and there doesn't appear any connection to why one person develops cancer in either location."

"And, it kills quickly?"

Joe pauses. "Yes. It's extremely aggressive. The longest anyone has lived after a diagnosis has been four months."

A panel of diamonds catches Jacob's attention. The tiny points of light are so close together blocking most of the outside view.

"I know your next question," Joe said.

"Well, let me go ahead and ask it… why have the cancer deaths spread to others, not just the children conceived here at Salvation?"

Joe stands joining his father.

"It seems to be developing much earlier now. Couple years ago, the youngest patient was eleven. Now, they are lucky to make it to two-years-old."

Condensation forms on the window. Joe stands a few inches from the glass.

"To be honest… I can't figure out what's causing it now in those from Earth. The difference with those is an absence of a precondition fever."

Jacob turns and walks across the black floor returning to the elevator. In a sudden motion, he spins back to Joe. "Shit!"

Joe jumps. His magnetic boots momentarily come dislodged against the floor. He floats returning to the floor turning to Jacob.

"What the hell?"

"Wicked Charley horse in my calf… "

Jacob bends massaging the back of his lower, left leg.

"I was just going to say... I have faith in you to figure this out. You were the smartest in this field on Earth, so we have the right person."

"Thanks for the encouragement... are you okay?"

"Getting older."

"You're what... only sixty-seven... you're probably not drinking enough water. That will cause muscle cramps."

Jacob left through the opened elevator only returning a grunt to Joe's advice. The door closes leaving Joe alone.

Silence fills the void in the Rotunda. Diamond lights sparkle on his face forcing his attention back to the glass wall. His slips down to the floor lying on his back.

Old Man gets a Charley horse... hell, I've not heard it called that in forever...

Chills across his backside from the floor comfort Joe. His eyes droop closed.

"You can figure this out, Sweetheart."

Joe opens his eyes. His image of Mary curls her head and shoulders on his chest.

"You need to shave and take a shower."

Her response startles Joe. He is aware she is not real.

"Emma's still okay?"

"Yes. Still as healthy as ever. In fact, she's been helping me with some of my research."

"Really? She'll be only twelve in a few months."

Joe laughs. "Maybe, but she's as smart as anyone I've ever met."

"What father wouldn't say that about his daughter?"

"No, I'm serious. I don't know how she does it, but if she reads anything, she remembers it verbatim. And, not only that, she can apply what she learns."

"Not just a memory recall ability?"

"No, she's way beyond that trick."

Joe imagines her breath on his neck.

"Remember when we used to lie in bed in our little apartment on campus and daydream about our children someday?"

Mary's hand rubs his chest.

"Those were great times. We were so young then."

"We used to hope for two things, that when we did have children that they were smart and healthy."

"Huh, well, she's both of those for sure."

A small laugh grows from Mary.

"What's so funny?"

"Nothing... I was just remembering the evenings we used to have with Charlie and Becky... "

"I just remember all the hangovers I woke up with after going out with those two. Oh my God, I've not thought about them, about Charlie, in years."

"What do you think Charlie would say about this place?"

Joe belts out a deep laugh he had not released in months.

"He would have figured out a way to set up a golf course outside, by now."

Memories with Charlie flood Joe's mind. His eyes fall closed as Mary rubs his chest. His breathing slows.

In an instant, Joe wakes. He bolts to his feet as Mary's image disappears. With a deep breath, Joe lunges across the floor pressing the elevator button.

"Come on! Come on! Goddammit!"

The door opens as Joe presses his body between the opening.

"Charlie! Why didn't I think of this before... his research... biologicals in the city water... maybe that's what's causing— "

The elevator door closes bringing silence in the Rotunda. Joe rushes out on the main floor of the Central Hub running to his laboratory. A faded memory covered by a tremendous heartbreak before leaving Earth had kept its secret from Joe... a secret which may save everyone at Salvation.

EARTH DATE: MARCH 15, 2028 (2 DAYS LATER)

DATA SCROLLS ACROSS a computer monitor in the corner of Joe's lab. Stench propagates the cramped office. Alone, Joe has allowed no staffers to enter the past few days.

He has repeated the DNA sequencing of three-hundred-thirty-two samples, the number of abnormal deaths; ninety-six of these are children conceived and born the past eight-Earth-years at Salvation.

The glass panel by the door chimes. Emma enters carrying a tray of vials full of clear liquid.

"Daddy, you need to take a shower. It smells awful in here."

Emma's attempt to catch Joe's attention falls deaf.

"Did you collect them all?"

The glass vials rattle as Emma lifts them to the table beside the DNA Sequencer.

"Yes, this is the fifth time I've done this."

Emma catches the cold stare Joe gives her.

"Yeah, they're all here. I did have a little trouble with Heather though?"

"Your teacher?" Joe returns his head to his numbers.

"She saw me in the Common Hub collecting samples from the plant irrigation system."

Joe's right eyebrow raises. His head remains in his numbers.

"I told her you gave me a little science project to give me a chore."

"She buy it?"

Emma laughs.

"Yeah, but don't be surprised if she stops by and talks to you."

"Why?"

"Something about me being only twelve and working. I so wanted to retort and tell her no one here would litigate you over the job I'm doing."

Joe laughs. A laugh which had been absent for weeks.

"Yeah, you should have said those words *retort* and *litigate* to her... that would have put her in her place."

Emma joins her father in laughter.

"But, seriously, when can I stop this charade? I know I'm a child in body, but my mind is not."

Joe stands joining Emma by the Sequencer.

"Soon, Emma... "

"Daddy, leave. You stink. I'll run these samples. You showed me how."

Emma leaves the samples on the table. She turns to Joe placing her small arms on his pushing him to the door.

"Okay, okay... run those samples, and I'll be back, after."

"Go! Try to take a nap, too. I know you've not been sleeping."

Emma puts her palm on the panel. The door opens as she pushes Joe into the corridor.

"Go!"

The door closes between them. Emma returns to the samples taking cotton swaps, one into each vial, and smearing the water onto a glass slide.

Three DNA Sequencers operate simultaneously. Emma sits behind her dad's computer monitor. Data scrolls from the simulation Joe has programmed.

Numbers appear in rapid, random order. Emma's eyes scan left-to-right across each line as they arise. The scrolling information captures her attention, her brain a supercomputer.

Chimes from two of the Sequencers break her trance from the monitor.

"That was fast."

Emma goes back to the two machines. The chimes indicate the sample run is complete while the third machine continues operation.

Hmm, these machines stopped. So, they didn't find any biological material to take a DNA sample.

Emma turns to the third Sequencer.

But, this one is still going.

She presses a small button on the top, left corner of the machine's control panel. A small screen illuminates. Numbers scroll across.

"Yes! It found a sample."

Emma runs to leave the lab. She taps her foot waiting the seconds for the glass door to open. Her footsteps fade quick down the corridor as the door closes.

EARTH DATE: MARCH 16, 2028 (THE NEXT DAY)

ONE OF THE EARLIEST characteristics of the human species is its sincere desire to explain the meaning of life. A search for purpose drove the development of religion, which led to a more fundamental question: Are we alone?

Long-held beliefs by billions over millennia provided theories. But, no matter the technological advancement, the real answer has never been solved. That is, until today.

Earthlings became the aliens living on Mars. While little green men are not found, a discovery is made nonetheless proving life exists beyond Earth. Microscopic life.

During the early 1990s, The Eden Foundation extracted the first water samples from the northern polar icecap region of Mars. Results of a myriad of tests proved the water safe for human consumption. This led to the ability for the Salvation Complex, which had started construction, to support the planned human civilization beginning in the next decade.

Joe and Emma sit dumbfounded in the laboratory. The results from the DNA Sequencer has identified something in the sample. A protein is present, which the machine sequenced.

"So, what is it?"

"I... I can't believe this. If we were still on Earth, this discovery would make us famous."

"Daddy, we don't need to worry about that."

"But Emma, you've just discovered the first alien life. Do you understand what this means?"

Even though she is a prodigy, Emma sits silent unable to comprehend her father's question.

"It's only a single-cell amoeba, but the evolutionary theory of life on Earth is that everything evolved from these. And, if this particular amoeba exists on Mars, what others do… what about on other planets in our solar system… or the billions of other planets for that matter."

Emma places her small hands on her father's arm. "So, is this what's making everyone sick?"

Joe stands holding the glass slide with its sample into the light.

"It's difficult to say, for now. We need to find other samples of this or other amoeba structures."

"Well, hypothetically if it is, how does it cause cancer?"

"Hmm, the single-cell of the amoeba creates a copy of itself and forms another, separate structure. The culture of amoebas grows and multiplies. A protein food source provides the energy needed for cell division… it's quite remarkable."

"But, have they been known to cause cancer before?"

Joe lifts his eyes upward trying to recall his biology classes.

Charlie, if you were here, you would know the answer.

"Sweetheart, I need to research this more."

Emma copies her father by staring into the clear, glass slide.

"What would you be looking for?"

Joe returns to his workstation. Tens-of-thousands of lines of DNA-sequenced data stream across the computer monitor.

"What I'm trying to determine is if any specific patterns or something abnormal is in the DNA. Possibly something's common in the DNA between those that died. This commonality or abnormality may be the trigger point for the cancer development."

"Huh… "

"What's that look for, Emma?"

"Well, when you went to take a shower, and I waited on the DNA Sequencers, I was staring at your monitor."

"Okay, so?"

"I saw a pattern in the numbers."

"Oh, I'm sure you did. All our DNA is basically the same with small exceptions which determine if your hair is blonde or black or eye color... things like that."

"Yeah, but wouldn't those commonalities be easy to identify?"

"Of course."

"No, I'm talking about a sequence I saw repeating in at least thirty people's data I watched."

"Huh, come show me."

Joe stands allowing Emma to take his seat behind the computer. She reruns the data scroll. Twenty seconds pass.

"Okay, here, let me pause the run. See *this* short string... AGT?"

"Now, I will resume the scroll."

Ten seconds pass. Emma stops the program after hundreds of lines pass.

"Look, the string appears, again."

"Emma, AGT is an extremely common pairing— "

Emma continues the scroll.

"I know that. But, if we go to the next person... scroll the dataset... wait... then, stop, *there* it is again... let me start it, again... wait... stop, *there* it is again. Do you see it?"

Joe releases a short laugh.

"Well, yeah, the AGT repeats, but like I said, it is prevalent. See, *there* it is again."

"No! That's not it. The pattern occurs every eighteen-thousand-four-hundred-twenty-second pairing combinations that are the same between the two AGT sequences in these two people's DNA... and, if we run a third person's... *there* it is again."

Joe pushes Emma's hands from the keyboard.

"What the hell? Is that true?"

"Continue the run, Daddy. You'll see the next AGT string will follow the same pattern... "

"Oh, shit! That can't be... "

"Can't be what?"

"Let me sit."

Emma stands complying to her father's request. Joe continues the data runs for the next six people… six other children who have died.

"Wow, Emma, you're right. There is a pattern here. I can't believe I couldn't see it."

"Well, you've not been sleeping, plus you know how my brain works. I can memorize and recall anything."

Joe sits stunned. His mouth holds open.

"What does that pattern mean?"

"Uh… well… in my research to what's causing this, I… I never looked for this pattern before, because… "

"Because, why?"

Joe runs his hands through his hair.

"Because, why, Daddy?"

"Because… well… this pattern is not supposed to show up between these children."

"Then, that's what's wrong, isn't it? It's not supposed to be, but it is."

"Not exactly, Emma."

"Why is it not supposed to show up, then?"

"Because this means that these children who have died are… "

Joe can not believe this preliminary finding.

"Are, what?"

"…are related."

Joe stands and lumbers to the door.

"I need to go. I'll be… Emma, I just need to go."

The door slides open, Joe runs out, as it slides closed. Emma continues the data runs.

"There it is, again… there it is, again… and, again… and, again… "

Emma completes the data run for the ninety-six children with the same results.

"Yep, that pattern repeats in all of them… they are all related? How can that be?"

30-DEATH COMES

SHORT SPURTS OF heated breath exit Joe's flaring nostrils. His feet push off the floor with each step. The force so strong Joe breaks the magnetic reaction of his boots. He stops at the end of the corridor placing his right hand on the access panel and slams his left fist against the glass door.

"Open up! It's me! We need to talk!"

"Hold on, hold on," the voice said on the other side.

A second later, the door opens.

"Joe, what's wrong? Why are you here so late at night?"

"Johanisson, we need to talk. I found something in my research that I need your help with before I approach Jacob."

The doctor sticks his head into the corridor scanning behind Joe.

"Quick, come inside. You know Security is limiting open access at this time of night."

Doctor Johanisson's living quarters are spacious. Twice the usual size of those belonging to a family of three which is odd given the doctor has no partner or children.

"What's got you so troubled that couldn't wait until morning?"

Joe stammers through the living room mumbling under his breath.

"Jesus, Man, get it together. Why did you come here, tonight?"

"I was re-scanning the DNA runs for all the deaths… looking for something, anything that I may have missed… "

"And, you found something?"

Joe holds the tablet with its red leather case to Johanisson.

The doctor scans the results. "Okay, help me out, here. DNA sequencing is not my forte."

"The sequencing data you have on that tablet is for the ninety-six children that were conceived and died here at Salvation."

"And… "

"I was looking for a pattern or something common between them… a common mutation or something identifying what triggered the deaths. I was so concerned about looking for this commonality that I totally missed the complete obvious identification marker."

"Joe, you need to help me. All I see are different orders of the DNA elements and their letters."

"Exactly. There is a repeating combination here that's the same for each child."

"What does that mean?"

"It's a paternal marker, meaning that each of the ninety-six children has the same father's DNA."

Johanisson drops the tablet from his hands as it lands on the sofa.

"That can't be, right? You and Baptiste scanned the potential male and female pairings. All of them were different."

A piercing stare comes from Joe across the room to the doctor.

Yes, and after they were approved, you administered the inseminations… "

The doctor exhales rubbing his hands across his balding head.

"Is there something you need to tell me?"

Johanisson turns to Joe.

"I... you need to re-run these samples to be sure there's no contamination in these."

"That will not happen. It's clear what this data is telling me. My problem is I need to figure out who the father is."

"And, how do you do that?"

"This is the paternal marker. I only need to cross-reference this marker to the male inhabitants here at Salvation. I haven't done this, yet, because I need to come to you. If you know something, please, please tell me. We can figure out what's happening and stop these deaths."

Johanisson collapses to the sofa. The tablet bounces up as Joe catches it sitting beside the doctor.

"Please... what is it?"

The red-coloring of the doctor's skin fades. His face becomes pale. Beads of sweat encroach on his brow.

"I... I never thought it would come to this?"

"What?"

"Joe, there's so much you still don't know about."

"I know the work we have done to attempt to procreate a diverse gene pool has gone to shit. Forget about all the children already dying. Hell, if they had lived and eventually had children, so many birth defects and deformities would have occurred. In two generations, there would be no more human life."

The doctor sits emotionless. Sweat drips from his eyebrows.

"I can tell by the way you are reacting that you know something about this... are you, the father?"

"Uh... no... hell, no! Not me!" Johanisson shakes his head.

"If not you, then who?"

Joe's stare pierces through the doctor's trembling body. He stands to escape Joe's entrapment.

"Wait a moment. Let me get something. I think this will give the answers you are looking for."

Joe watches as Johanisson enters his bedroom disappearing into the darkness. He stands unsure what the doctor is retrieving. The doctor emerges from the room with a silver USB drive in his left hand.

"There are some documents on *this* you need to see."

"*Here,* give it to me. I'm reading it now because I don't trust you at the moment."

"Very well," the doctor said handing Joe the drive.

The tablet opens a folder entitled *Eden.* Various JPEG files entice Joe.

"Click on *that one,*" the doctor said pointing to the top file.

A few seconds pass as the JPEG file opens revealing a picture of journal pages.

"What's this?"

"This information came from Baptiste. It's from a journal his father, Simon, had kept."

"Simon? Baptiste told me that he died when he was a baby."

"Yes, that's true. But, did he share with you that Simon was a founding member of The Eden Foundation?"

Joe scans the doctor's face.

"No. John knew my parents had died when I was so young. We understood each other's pain. So, we never really talked about our parents."

Johanisson grabs Joe's hand tight.

"I've read this when Baptiste gave this to me when he found out I knew about his cancer. We kept his illness a secret from everyone for a long time, even Jacob. Baptiste wanted me to have this in case something happened to him."

"What's in the journal? It has to be from the early Sixties."

"As a matter of fact, the last entry is from February 17, 1961, hours before Simon's death."

"Did Baptiste ever mention an Eli Bishop?" Johanisson asked.

Joe's eyes bulged returning his attention to the journal entry on the tablet.

"Um… no?" Thumping from his heart pounds in Joe's throat. "Who?"

"Eli Bishop... Jacob's father... Eli and Simon were the founding members of The Eden Foundation. They were the ones that discovered that goddam planet coming to Earth."

Shocked hearing his grandfather's name, Joe remains calm unsure if Johanisson knows Jacob is his father.

"From the journal, it seems Eli and Simon had different plans for Salvation. Simon wanted to inform the governments about the planet to take action, and it appears Eli didn't believe that was the best plan. See, read *this entry.*"

Joe scrolls the pages as instructed by the doctor and reads out loud.

"*I don't know what it is about Eli. He thinks the government will screw this up. People will not come together to develop plans to divert that planet or to prepare the human race. Eli wants to proceed with his plans. I'm worried he's already moving forward with those...*"

"I can't read this part? Okay, um, here, he continues... *I will approach the President to alert him on what's happening before Eli's plan gets too much traction.*"

"See, they had a different approach. And, since we are here, we can figure who's plan worked out."

"But, wait, I'm not following why this journal entry or anything like this has to do with ninety-six children having the same father, here?"

"That was Simon's last entry. Later that night, he fell— "

"Yeah, I know... he fell on a slippery floor in the kitchen and hit his head killing him."

"Or, as Baptiste believes, Eli killed Simon."

Joe resists the urge to defend a story about Eli Bishop, his grandfather, who supposedly had died when his father, Jacob, was only ten-years-old. But, knowing how the Foundation faked his and Mary's death, and meeting his apparently dead father, Jacob, upon arrival at Salvation, this journal entry feels true.

"So, let me get this straight... this Eli person is Jacob's father, and he killed Baptiste's father, Simon?" Joe asked.

"Yes."

"And, if you believe this, that means Jacob is aware of Eli's actions in developing Salvation."

"Exactly. We've never really talked about our pasts, but hearing this description of events does not surprise me. Hell, it reminds me of my recruitment to Salvation," Johanisson said.

"What do you mean?"

"I was a resident at Johns Hopkins Hospital when Eden recruited me. I went into medicine because that was the profession my father was in. He was killed in early December 1963."

"So?"

"So… my father was recruited by The Eden Foundation to be President Kennedy's doctor, and you remember what happened to the president that December. Many years later, I found a letter to my father welcoming him to the Foundation signed by Eli."

"And, you think Eli had something to do with your father's death, too?"

"Look at the journal entry three days earlier."

Joe scrolls to the entry and reads.

The things Eli is recommending we do to protect Salvation are too much. We can't get involved in assassinations and wars. He thinks this is the best way to get funding for Salvation and to divert everyone's attention to what the Foundation will do. This is wrong. I have to find a way to talk Eli out of this.

Joe rakes his right hand through his hair.

"And, when Baptiste talked about this journal and his thoughts about Eli killing his father, that's when I realized it was Eli who had my father killed."

"Wow, you still need to explain to me then how you got from that to the ninety-six children dying here?" Joe said.

Johanisson stands pacing the floor.

"The more Baptiste and I spoke, the angrier we got. We both had lost our fathers. Whether Eli killed them or had them killed, their involvement with The Eden Foundation… with Salvation was the reason they died… the reason neither of us knew our fathers."

"Okay, I lost my father too, but you don't see me impregnating multiple women?"

The doctor jerks Joe's arm lifting him off the sofa.

"Look, here, Joe. It's not that simple. I'm an old man. Baptiste was dying. And, we… well, we wanted revenge."

"So, you sacrificed Salvation because the Foundation killed your fathers?"

"Yes."

Joe pushes away from Johanisson.

"What the hell?l Do you realize that if I didn't catch this, then the survival of the human race is over?"

"Fuck him. Fuck the Foundation. Fuck this goddam place!" Johanisson screams ranting through the living room.

"Tell me what you did… maybe, it's not too late… we can figure it out."

"No, it is too late."

"Why do you say that?"

"Because no matter what happens, now, I'm assured as dead anyway. Jacob will kill me."

"No. We need you. You're the head doctor here and are important."

"My team can do what I do."

Joe senses the doctor's frightened state. Johanisson's pale face returns.

"Let's you and I go to Jacob. Explain what you have done. We can work out a plan to correct this… it's not too late."

"Joe, you don't fuckin' understand."

"Please, I'm trying to help out, here. Jacob will listen to me. It's not too late."

"No, it is. Jacob will not understand… he will be too angry with Baptiste and me."

"C'mon, Man. Calm down. Let's go see Jacob."

Johanisson fights off Joe's hand.

"No, I'm not going. He will kill me because… those children… he is their father."

Joe's knees fall weak. He collapses to the floor. The room spins as his vision darkens to blackness.

The floor of Johanisson's living room sends shivers through his body awakening him. To the best of Joe's recollection, he had been unconscious for at least thirty minutes.

Joe is alone unsure what to do or how to react. He stands.

"Johanisson… Doctor Johanisson… "

No response comes.

The lights in the bedroom are off. Joe activates the LEDs in the ceiling. A horrific image scorches his brain.

Heavy footsteps lunge from the bedroom to the living room. Joe places his hand on the communication panel beside the front door.

"Hello, Johanisson, why are you calling me so early in the morning?"

"Uh… Jacob… this is Joseph… you need to come here immediately… the doctor… he's hung himself."

The line clicks dead. Joe's knees weaken pushing him to the sofa.

What do I say? Is what Johanisson told me even true?

A lump presses against the bottom of his right thigh. Joe slides his hand under his leg pulling the tablet out from under him. The USB drive is missing. Small electronic parts are scattered on the floor.

Joe reviews the tablet. The JPEG files have been deleted. No evidence of the journal is present. One file is open with two words typed: *I'm sorry.*

"Dammit!"

The door swooshes open as Jacob rushes through the entry.

"What the fuck happened? Why are you here?"

Joe sits, his head lowers to the ground.

"I… uh… I came here wanting to run some data by Johanisson… we were talking and, I fainted… when I came around, I found his body hanging in the bathroom doorway from his bedroom."

Joe knows not to divulge the conversation he had with the doctor. The sensational claims are too much to believe to approach Jacob. Their immediate concern is the doctor's body. Joe needs more information before confronting his father… information that only the DNA can answer.

EARTH DATE: MARCH 17, 2028 — 2:00 P.M.

POUNDING FISTS AGAINST the desk echo in the laboratory. Emma jumps frightened by her father.

"Can I help?" Emma asked recoiling in her chair.

"I need to work alone tonight. Just need some time with my work. I feel like I'm getting close to an answer."

"Okay. If you need me, I will be at Jacob's. He's invited me to watch a movie... ever seen *Forrest Gump*?"

Joe lifts his head from the monitor.

"Uh... yeah, it was one of your mom's favorites... mine, too."

A quick smile overcomes Joe.

"You should come with me. I'm sure he won't mind."

The perpetual frown returns to her father.

"No, I've gotta finish this up."

A warm, light kiss touches Joe's forehead.

"Love you, Daddy. Stop working so hard and get some sleep."

Joe catches Emma's gaze.

"You sound just like Mary."

"That's because Mama was a smart lady... okay, I'm going... love you."

Silence returns to the lab. Joe continues his frantic hunt for one missing DNA record... his father's.

Two hours pass.

Hmm, I've looked and can't find his records anywhere... can't think of why I never looked before... guess I had never considered needing his DNA in my work... that's it...

Joe stands leaving his lab. His feet move fast across the floor. A few minutes later, the long corridor belonging to Jacob's living quarters appear. The masterpieces of art fly pass him.

His chest heaves until he calms down. Joe places his palm against the access panel.

"So, you decided to join us for the movie?" Emma said as she smiles.

"I needed a break, and I've not seen any kind of movies since coming here... not to mention my favorite one."

The living room is dark. Light flickers from the television monitor.

"Happy you can join us, Joseph," Jacob said as he extends his right arm to Joe to sit.

Emma joins sitting between them.

"Forrest said his friend is missing his legs, Daddy."

Joe laughs remembering a simpler time when he first saw this movie with Mary. A sudden crash of Forrest Gump's shrimp boat into the pier behind Gump and Lieutenant Dan startles Emma.

"Jacob, do you like shrimp? I'll never be able to taste it?"

"Oh, no, Emma. I can't eat shrimp. I'm so allergic to shellfish. My face swells up like a balloon."

Joe grunts.

"Huh, me too... Mary had an EpiPen in her purse when we used to go to the Shore."

Emma smiles. Her eyes dart between both her father and grandfather, who she had promised Jacob to keep their secret.

The movie continues.

"Jacob, mind if I get some water... can I get you or Emma any?"

"Sure."

"Yes, thanks, Daddy."

Joe stands and enters the kitchen returning a few minutes later.

"Took me a few minutes to figure out your water faucet."

"Yeah, it's different from yours, everyone else's, too, for that matter... one of the first ones built."

Each sips their cold water. The movie continues. Minutes pass.

Joe hears the character of Forrest Gump talking about how he misses his wife Jenny, who had died earlier in the movie. His heart pounds, and his throat swells moving upward to his mouth. Sad, soaring music plays as Gump rides his lawnmower the next morning.

"Okay, I need to go back. Jacob, thanks for the invite."

Emma lifts her head to Joe. A small tear trickles down the bridge of her nose from watching the movie.

"Thanks for coming. I must have you both over some time, and we can watch something else," Jacob said.

"Here, let me get those."

Joe reaches for the empty glasses from Jacob and Emma returning them to the kitchen.

"See you at home, Emma."

The door opens. Joe leaves walking down the corridor. He pauses in front of Monet's *Waterlilies* painting.

I had forgotten how good that movie was. Joe thought speaking to Mary.

Me too.

I almost lost it when Jenny came back.

Joe imagines Mary's hand holding his as they stand beside each other.

I know why you had to leave. That ending is too much. You cried when we first saw it. I can only imagine, now.

No, well, yeah… uh, that would have been too hard to watch… but, I needed to leave because of this…

Mary's eyes widen.

Oh, Jacob's glass… you can get a DNA sample from that…

Exactly. Love you, Mary, but I need to go.

Her image disappears. The door closes behind him as the lights dim along the corridor. The *Waterlilies* fade into darkness.

The DNA Sequencer hums with the sample Joe has taken from Jacob. Joe's foot pats the floor fast as he shifts his weight side-to-side.

"Come on… come on… "

Three quick chimes release from the machine before powering down. He returns to his monitor.

He studies the results. A loud rap from his hands slaps against his forehead.

"It's a match… Johanisson was telling the truth."

Joe paces his lab.

What do I do next? How do I approach him?

Ringing from the communications panel interrupts his thoughts. "Hello?"

"Joe, we need you in the medical facility."

"Why? I'm sure the doctors there have everything under control."

Silence comes through the panel for several seconds.

"Joe, we have a problem… twenty people are here… they have a fever and are showing symptoms of the same sickness… we need all the help we can get, and Doctor Johanisson is not responding to our calls."

What? I thought Jacob was going to handle the situation with him?

"I'll be right there."

The communication panel turns off. Joe hides Jacob's DNA results in his desk.

Jesus, what's causing this with the people from Earth?

He logs off his computer.

Even if Jacob was the father to all those children, this isn't explaining why this sickness is moving to the others, now.

The overhead LED lights dim as he leaves.

EARTH DATE: MARCH 20, 2028 (3 DAYS LATER)

A FRIGHTENING ALARM shrills throughout the Salvation complex. An alarm tested once each year, now signifies a dire emergency.

Patient beds strew the full length of the corridor of the Medical Wing. Each holds someone afflicted by fever. The earliest ones having arrived with this symptom two weeks ago, now suffer from rapidly progressing brain or stomach cancer.

The medical staff including all research scientists attend to everyone as best as possible. But, it is overwhelming. Some attending physicians work with their own internally growing fever.

Joe remains healthy as he draws blood samples from everyone searching for the answer to what is causing the deathly scene. Sleep comes to him only through his body's forced passing out spells at his desk every few hours.

The alarm ends. Jacob's voice comes through the speakers throughout Salvation.

"Until further notice, everyone is required to stay in your living quarters. Maintenance and Security will continue to work under *A-Protocol* conditions meaning our facilities will continue to operate and be secure as usual. Everyone at Salvation… you are safe."

Joe rolls his eyes listening.

"We are restricting everyone to their rooms to prevent further spreading of an apparent infection that is occurring within the facility. If you begin to feel ill with fever, please do not come to the Medical Wing. Instead, use your communications panel and call the medical staff. A doctor will visit you."

Joe grunts. *How many doctors do we even have left?*

"Anyone caught outside their living quarters will receive a citation from Security. A second citation will force us to quarantine you inside your quarters. We are taking these steps as a measure to limit exposure and is part of the normal emergency drills we have practiced before."

Yeah, but this is real. Joe thinks to himself.

"Once we have further information, I will come back to you, immediately."

Jacob's voice disappears into the speakers. The shrill of the alarm and Jacob's same message repeats two additional times before ending.

31-Is It Too Late?

JOE TAKES A FRESH blood sample from the most recent patient, and the one nearest death admitted three weeks earlier. He observes the difference in deterioration of the body's cells between the two people.

An hour later, the most-ill patient succumbs to her cancer. Joe continues taking samples each hour from the other patient, who grows worse in condition.

Emma works alongside Joe. Her knowledge of genetics and microbiology is on par with her dad and the hundreds of digital, medical textbooks she has read the past month. Even only at twelve-years-old, her genius and photographic memory serve Joe well. His capacity dwindles given his unpredictable hour-long naps exhaustion forces.

"Here's the latest sample," Joe said returning to his lab.

"Okay, I've run the diagnostics. Just like the last samples, each is getting exponentially worse in degradation," Emma said not looking up from her microscope.

A metal tray clangs across the floor startling Emma. She leaps in her seat and rushes to Joe, who collapses to the floor. Worried, she lifts her hand to his forehead... no fever.

Joe remains unresponsive as Emma places a pillow under his head. She drapes a lab jacket over him hoping he will get at least a couple hours of rest even if it is on the middle of the floor. Her small body does not have the strength to lift him to the sofa even in the Martian gravity.

She collects the undamaged sample from the floor placing it by her workstation. Before resuming her work, she sits closer to her father at his workstation watching Joe to make sure he is doing okay.

"Your desk is messy. No wonder you can't ever find anything quickly."

Emma often continues conversations with her dad when he passes out to comfort her.

Though being a prodigy and never being sick a single day, Emma has self-diagnosed one mental illness she possesses: a mild form of obsessive-compulsive disorder. But, she attributes her need for things to be in a complete order as being a perfectionist instead of being OCD. To allow her to consume as much information as quickly as possible, Emma requires structure.

Emma arranges the samples in date-order on Joe's workstation. The tabletop becomes visible after weeks of hiding. Three tablets remain untouched on the corner of the desk.

"Here, I'll charge these up for you. That way, when you wake up, they'll be ready... "

Emma searches the desk.

"Hmm, there are four of these... maybe it's in here?"

She opens the top drawer of the desk. The tablet with Jacob's DNA results joins the other three in their docking stations.

Electricity from the station awakens the tablet taken from the drawer from its sleep mode. Strings of DNA code illuminate against the white screen. Any pattern of numbers or letters will capture Emma's attention like a deer on Earth crossing a road at night with approaching lights.

Emma stares at the letters. She instantly knows they are DNA-encoded structures.

"Hey, that's the same pattern I showed you a couple weeks ago taken from the children… "

She removes the tablet from the docking station.

"Hmm, but this pattern does not repeat in this sequence. It just is the first part."

Emma closes her eyes while holding the tablet. In an instant, her eyes open. She turns to her dad who still lies on the floor.

"This is the original DNA structure common to all the children. That means this belongs to either the same mother or father for all of them… that can't be, right?"

Emma takes the tablet to her workstation. The DNA sequence teases her. She scans her computer. Three minutes later, the tablet drops from her hands onto the desk. The sudden sound wakes Joe.

"Uh… how long was I out?"

Joe sits up from the floor. He moves his mouth open-and-closed, then side-to-side.

"About twenty minutes. Daddy, you need to see this. I found something and have a theory I want to test."

Curious for any answer, Joe stands. Blood rushes to his head. He bends over his knees as he takes two deep breaths before joining his daughter.

"What is it?"

"Well, while you were asleep, I was cleaning up your desk. Started to charge your tablets for you and found *this one*."

The tablets look the same. However, as Joe saw the DNA sequence, he knew this was the one from his desk drawer.

"You remember me showing you the same, repeating pattern in the DNA samples taken from each of the children who have died here?"

"Uh— "

Emma does not allow Joe to answer.

"Well, this sequence from this tablet shows this belongs to the same donor-parent for all the children. I can't tell if this is from the father or mother, but it's the same person."

Emma looks at her father as he returns a stare to her.

"Do you know who's sample this is on the tablet?"

"I'm still working on that."

Joe's response comes quick. He knows Emma can read him, anyone for that matter. He needs to be firm in his response to help hide the truth he knows.

"Well, regardless… that's not what I wanted to show you. Instead, I wanted to show you *this*."

Grogginess churns in Joe's head.

"What's that… oh… that's the amoeba sample you found a few weeks, ago."

"Yes, yes, it is."

"What does this have to do with the DNA sequences?"

"I have a theory that I would like to test. Seeing this common parent to the children, what if there is some common defect in the DNA sequence that somehow this amoeba exploits?"

"Well, even if that is somehow true, how can you make the leap from finding this amoeba to it being a potential cause of death for the children?" Joe asked.

"I'm not sure, yet. It's a hunch. Seeing the parent DNA and knowing that is the missing link between all the children's samples… I don't know… it's like a puzzle in my head. I instantly saw DNA molecules forming in my mind and connected it to what I've also been studying about amoebas… and… there's some reason the children were the first ones to get sick."

"So, what's your theory?"

Emma pauses.

"On Earth, there was an amoeba identified as *Naegleria fowleri.*"

"You mean, the brain-eating amoeba."

"Yes, that's the common name of it… but, what if this one is like that, and somehow infected the children, who all had the same gene defect? That could make them susceptible to the same illness."

This theory from his prodigy daughter catches his interest.

"Huh, so the parent could have passed on the same gene defect to all the children. In turn, this amoeba influenced this defect… this could be the same causation event, which led to the children dying in the same way... but... "

"I know what you're going to say... but, that should mean the parent should have died also given they have the same defect?"

Joe steps away from Emma. A realization hits him. His knees buckle returning him to the floor.

He knows what the gene defect is... it is the one he has studied his entire adult life... the RNA codex miR-182... the same gene defect location, which triggers glioblastoma multiform (GBM), an aggressive brain tumor. The same cancer which took his mother's life and sent him on his path of study in college... the work that brought him to Salvation.

For years, Joe thought he carried the same defect as his mother. But, what if, his father had this same defect as well? Since Joe had thought Jacob had died before he was born, he never had a sample from his father... until, now.

"Emma, see if you can find in the sequence a marker for RNA codex miR-182. It's identified with— "

"I got it. I know your research... hold on, let me look... "

Joe remains on the floor; his head hangs low. Three minutes pass.

"Yep, there it is... that same codex is in the parent sample... and, let me check... also in child one... child two... child three... "

"You can stop. It will be in all of them."

"So, that means we have found the commonality of a defect from parent to all the children. Now, we just need to prove that this amoeba sample can influence this defect causing the illness."

Joe stands.

"That means, we need to find more samples of that amoeba."

Emma joins Joe as they collect vials and wire baskets.

"Take me to where you found the amoeba sample."

EARTH DATE: AUGUST 13, 2028
(5 DAYS LATER IN THE LATE EVENING)

THOUSANDS OF TINY lights flicker around the Observation Rotunda. Small boxes lie on the floor under the windows. The incoming volume of new diamonds outpaces the rate technicians can install them on the glass walls.

Jacob and Joe sit on the floor between the boxes; their backs rest against the wall. Silence is their companion.

A growl releases from Jacob as he pulls the closest box to him. Dozens of diamonds spill over rolling to the elevator.

Jacob stands pacing the floor. Light twinkles across his face.

"This is unacceptable... this is unacceptable... "

Joe listens as his father mumbles as he walks.

"This is unacceptable!"

With the yell, Jacob kicks the now, half-empty box. The lower Martian gravity allows the diamonds to float longer in the air before settling to the floor.

The pattern of light in the air mesmerizes Joe if only for a few seconds before Jacob continues his rant.

"We worked too long... we sacrificed too much... for what... a fuckin' amoeba... a goddam amoeba!"

Joe stands and approaches Jacob.

"It's in our water system. And, that's what's caused the deaths," Joe said in a calm voice in trying to tame Jacob.

Jacob kicks the dented, empty box, again.

"So, we close off the infected water source, clean the systems, and use only water from the Harvesters... what I don't understand is... we've used the water from the polar caps for decades without issue. What's changed?"

Joe turns his back to Jacob. He stares out the window as his father continues his pacing.

"I can only guess that the amoeba has always been there... with the full population here on Mars, now, we used enough of the water and lowered that water table to the area where the amoeba thrive."

A strong grip springs upon Joe's left shoulder. Jacob stands behind him.

"If that's true, then why have we all not died?"

Joe steps to his right to dislodge the uncomfortable hold.

"Of the four-thousand or so who have died, from what I can determine, their bodies were an excellent host for the amoeba. It's the type similar on Earth in Australia with brain-eating ability... I can only speculate that somehow the amoeba here on Mars is related to what was in Australia... and do you know what that could mean?"

Jacob does not respond.

"That either life from Earth once populated Mars or the other way around—"

"Joseph! I don't care. What I care about is the other six-thousand of us still alive... why are we not sick?"

Joe lowers his head approaching Jacob.

"That's just it... it's hard to say if we all aren't sick already and just not showing signs, yet... some people have systems that can fight invading cells better than others... it may be just a matter of time."

"Are there tests you can run to determine if this amoeba has infected others?"

"There's no need. We're all infected."

Jacob slaps the wall. The lights twinkle violently as the glass shutters.

"So, you're saying we're all a damn time bomb waiting to go off?"

Joe does not respond.

"Well, I can tell you one fuckin' thing... I'm not getting sick."

"Why is that?"

"Let's just say I have my own stash of water I drink from."

Joe cocks his head to the left staring at Jacob. "What do you mean?"

"Shit, I never trusted the Foundation and this water design. My water is bottled water from Earth."

"Get the hell outta here."

"No, it's true. All the water I drink and use comes from Earth."

"Then… then, you've got to let us use this water to bridge the time it will take to sterilize our systems."

"No! I have enough to last another few years… even my supplies will empty… but, I will share what I have with you and Emma… no one else… from what you're saying, it's too late for them, anyway."

Joe huffs several breaths quick through his nose and opened mouth.

"It's too late for Emma and me, too."

Jacob turns to Joe.

"Emma! She's not sick, is she?"

"No. In fact, from the tests I have performed on her… she is actually the only one I can find where the amoeba does not survive within her cells… I'm trying to see what's different about her to possibly come up with some sort of cure or preventative— "

"What's different about her than everyone else?"

Joe slides his back down against the wall. The floor cools his legs as he sits.

"Of everyone who either came to Mars or was born here, she is the only person who developed inside the womb in zero gravity of space. My speculation is that during the fetus development inside Mary that the zero gravity caused mutations within her cells."

"Is this why she's a genius?" Jacob asked joining his son on the floor.

"Well, Mary was about four weeks pregnant when we left Earth. That's about the time the embryo develops the brain and spinal column. We usually think of something happening during this time of embryonic development as the time most susceptible to birth defects."

"That's some helluva a defect."

"Exactly. We always think of bad results, but this turned out completely the other way. If all of this weren't happening, I would love to do more research on her."

"So, you're saying her development while traveling through Space is somehow protecting her against this infection?"

Joe lifts his head to the ceiling. The multitude of stars catches his attention.

"Is that it? Is that why?... Joe... Joe."

"Sorry... uh... yes, that's my guess."

"You hesitated."

"Well, she has something else unique about her?"

Joe returns his attention to Jacob turning his body to his father.

"You probably don't recall my cancer research at Stony Brook?"

"Of course, I do... that's why you were selected."

"But, the details of it... the gene marker identified causing the same type of brain cancer Mama died from."

Jacob darts his eyes from Joe lifting them to the glass ceiling.

"There is a marker in her gene that indicates a strong likelihood of developing cancer... and, it's passed through heredity— "

"So, do you have it?"

"Yes, and so does Emma."

Jacob returns his vision to Joe.

"That means you and her will develop cancer? That's ironic isn't it considering what's happening here... why haven't you, yet? You're older now than when Rachel... uh... um... died?"

The memories from his childhood lift Joe from the floor.

"I don't know, why? When I turned twenty-eight... the age Mama was when she died... I seemed to count the days until I was diagnosed. But, as time passed, I guess I just felt like it would not happen to me... but, then again, it's only a marker... it's not a for-certain predictor."

"Well, you're what, now... "

"Forty-nine."

"Yeah, forty-nine, I knew that... I think you're okay."

"It's not about me, though... I'm talking about Emma."

"What about?"

"It goes back to her development in zero gravity. She has that gene marker, but hers seems mutated. And, that mutation is what my theory is as to what is fighting off this infection for her."

Jacob rejoins Joe pacing the floor.

"Can't we replicate this marker from her and inject others… kinda like a vaccine?"

Silence comes from Joe.

"Isn't that what's done with like the flu vaccine?"

"Not exactly, but I understand what you're asking… we have a problem though here."

"What's that?"

"Even though we have all the equipment needed for the research, it takes years of study and research to develop gene-therapy type of vaccines. They did this on Earth in developing immunotherapy treatments for colon cancer… but, that took a decade with dozens of research teams across the United States and Europe to develop— "

Jacob runs to the dented, empty box. He lifts his leg backward and forces it forward. The box flies bouncing off the opposite glass window.

"Then, that's your mission… you've found the amoeba… we'll act to stop the water flow from the caps and sterilize our infrastructure… your complete focus now is using her cells to come up with a treatment for."

"It's not that simple."

"Why?"

"I need to continue my original work in pairing couples for childbirth… we need to start this again before it's too late?"

"Too late! Too late! Joseph, look around… all these diamonds… if we don't start soon, there will not be any humans left to fuckin' worry about any cure."

Joe's shoulders slump. His eyes drift to staring away from Jacob.

"I tell you what I will do… I'm lifting this regulation about controlling who's selected… let them all fuck for all I care at this point. We can later stop it once our population gets back up to where it needs to be."

Air fills Joe's lungs. His body lifts upward.

"Go on… I can see you want to say something."

Joe approaches Jacob.

"Well, I can say that, at first, I didn't agree or like the fact I felt like I was playing God… but, I came to realize we do need to pay attention to the selection of people for childbirth to prevent— "

"Let me stop you right there. What the hell are we preventing, now? If we don't start having births in the next few years, all this shit doesn't matter anyway, and we'll just die off. All the other children have died and didn't make it to adulthood, but at least you've found what's causing these deaths."

Joe turns away from Jacob. Silence follows him. The quietness lasts too long for Jacob.

"Well?"

Joe continues with his silence.

"Well, Joseph… "

"There's something else I need to tell you," Joe said turning back to Jacob.

EARTH DATE: AUGUST 14, 2028
(THE NEXT DAY IN THE EARLY MORNING)

ORANGE LIGHT SHIMMERS through the diamonds embedded into the Observation Rotunda walls. The rising morning sunlight lifts the veil of darkness in the room. A crumpled box rests in the middle of the floor. The black floor intensifies the tiny orange reflections from the dozens of loose diamonds from the box.

The cold floor soothes Jacob as he lies motionless on his back staring to the stars through the ceiling. Joe sits with his back against the glass wall beside his father; the same position both men have remained for the last hour.

"I can't believe it… I mean, I've done some pretty fucked up things in my past… but, to trick me… for me to have fathered ninety-two children and not even know about it… that's some fucked up shit."

"And, neither Baptiste nor Johanisson gave you any indication they were doing this?" Joe asked.

"No, to my knowledge, everything was going to plan. Baptiste brought me the recommendations, and I approved them, then Johanisson did his thing… and, you didn't know what was happening when you took over from Baptiste?"

"I was just following his protocol he had set up. Since he was my mentor at Stony Brook, I basically followed along. I never looked at the gene structures between the different children to identify a link to a common parent… or hell, even to confirm the genes from the parents… I mean, why the hell would I need to at that point?"

"Wouldn't you need to confirm— "

"What? That the parents were who they were supposed to be? I had no reason for that… my only follow-up with the newborns was to collect their sample for a record when they would be of age for future pairings."

Heavy sighs come from both in unison.

"Didn't you think it was odd to give a sperm sample a few times a year?"

"Joseph, I can say that everything that had to happen to construct Salvation I knew about. But, when a doctor… Johanisson tells me to provide a sample as part of my normal check-up visits, how I was supposed to know… hell, I do remember the first time he mentioned it, he said it was part of a full battery of tests to ensure I am healthy… "

"You knew nothing about this? I mean, everyone faked their deaths to get here… there is a shit-ton of secrets you and others had to keep, but you knew nothing about what they were doing with your sperm samples."

Jacob is quick to sit up from the floor.

"Look. I've done some shitty, crazy things for Salvation… and, I'll admit, I thought about having a child or two born by me, but I have always kept to the greater mission about this place… the survival of our species… "

"And, inbreeding would have stopped that over time."

"Exactly, I, at least, know that. That's why we set up this damn protocol and had those laws established in the first place… to protect just that."

Jacob lifts his body from the floor. He bends stretching his back.

"Plus, I know I have a huge ego, but what happened is even beyond my comprehension… shit, I give Baptiste credit… a fuckin' great idea to get his revenge."

"So, you're not denying Grandpa Eli killed his father, then?"

Laughter swells through the Rotunda.

"Killed his father… shit, Boy, that man is the true creator behind all of this. Of course, he did, I'm sure."

Joe stands joining Jacob.

"Can I ask you?"

"What?"

"I know there are a lot of things you've not told me about Grandpa, what happened to him… all the shit leading up to 2020… can you at least tell me, now?"

Jacob drapes his arm across Joe's back. His father's touch is a feeling Joe had daydreamed as a child to experience.

"What the hell… I might as well tell you everything… guess there's no more reason to hide anything."

The sun rises above the horizon. Warmth envelops father and son from the growing light.

As Jacob confesses the complete information he knows about Grandpa Eli and The Eden Foundation, Joe witnesses his father's shoulders lift. He senses the relief his father must be experiencing as Jacob reveals one dark secret after another.

Nothing is held back. Hours pass. The small, orange dot of the sun lifts high into the sky.

"… the President… you killed him?"

"I didn't do it, but we convinced others for sure."

The stories continue as if Jacob was reading from a fiction novel. Joe sits on the floor; his mouth remains open.

"Did you know Mary, and I were on our way to New York on 9/11?"

"No, but we made sure the people we had involved only took domestic flights… it was easier to make sure it could happen so soon after take-off… those bastards would have had too long to think about it on an international flight."

"But, how… why? What motivated them to do something like that? Or anyone else in those things you've told me."

Jacob laughs.

"We got extremely good at getting people to do what needed them to do. You tell a group of people one thing. It leads to an eventual invasion over time. Then, the people who were invaded are motivated by revenge, and they become even easier to manipulate."

"Oh my God... something like that had to take years."

"Try decades. We knew 2020 was coming... we needed funds to build this place... we needed distractions to hide our activities... with that kind of time, it becomes a very long con, and we got our work done."

"But, why not just come clean with the government? Surely, if the planet came together, there was enough time to develop a way to at least deflect the planetoid from hitting Earth."

"And, that's just what your grandpa started to say... he began to change his mind... he just wouldn't listen to our scientists who had confirmed everything he knew to be true when they first discovered that motherfucker."

"I know... that planet was too big and moving too fast to deflect... but, even still, with all that time... what... sixty years— "

"What? Build more places like Salvation on Mars? Look around... we designed this place for ten-thousand people... but, seven billion people were on Earth... that's over seven-hundred-thousand of a similar sized Salvations. Shit, Mars isn't even big enough for that."

"But, that's just it... what about other planets... or hell, even moons of other planets."

"Well— "

Chimes echo violently inside the Rotunda stopping Jacob. The Communication Panel beside the elevator illuminates. Emma's voice comes through the speakers in the ceiling.

"Daddy... uh... Jacob... are you up there?"

Joe walks from Jacob to the elevator's panel.

"Hi, Emma. Yes, we're up here."

"Can you reactivate the elevator and let me come up? I need a break from the Medical Wing."

Joe places his finger over the control-lock feature on the panel.

"I'm coming up."

A few seconds later, the door opens. Emma staggers into the Rotunda. "I'm so tired."

"How long have you been working?" Jacob asked.

"I've been helping out for three days straight. I'm so sick of seeing death. That's why I wanted to come up here and get away from everything for a while."

Joe catches a glance from Jacob. Emma stands between them.

"So, what have you been talking about?" she asked.

32-Revelation

THE SPACIOUS CAFETERIA is vacant. Plastic scraping echoes from a lone fork across a food tray. Artificial, juice-flavored water refreshes Emma as she finishes her birthday dinner, her sixteenth in Earth years.

With a deep sigh, she stands; her shoulders hunch forward. A conveyor belt moves from the motion detector as Emma returns her empty tray.

Sound-effects of birds chirping ring loud throughout the Central Park Hub. In years' past, the number of people admiring the gardens suppressed the sounds. Now, the noise is deafening. The cackle of flying geese startles Emma as she roams through the hub.

The central elevator dings as she enters. Within a few seconds, Emma steps out into the Rotunda. Silence. Shimmering light blinds her forcing her gaze to the floor. She lies with her back against the cold floor as she stares through the glass-domed roof.

Flickering light fades as the sun sets low on the horizon. The nine-thousand-seven-hundred-thirty-four diamonds fade to black against the night sky.

Tears spill down the sides of her face filling her ears. Her chest heaves deep and fast. She rubs her necklace pendant seeking comfort.

Emma wipes her face dry with the dings emanating from the elevator.

"There you are. I've been looking everywhere for you."

Footsteps grow loud above her head.

"Mind if I join you?"

Emma does not answer.

Joe grunts as he bends his knees to the floor. He positions himself on her left side as he mimics her position staring up through the ceiling.

"Daddy… "

"Yes, Sweetheart."

"Are we going to die?"

Joe grabs Emma's hand bringing it to his chest.

"Don't think about things like that, especially on your birthday."

Emma jerks her hand free.

"Some birthday. What does it even mean, anyway?"

Joe props his torso up onto his right elbow as he twists his body to his daughter.

"What does it mean? Baby Girl, you are one of the smartest and strongest people I've ever met, or for that matter ever heard of."

Emma maintains her gaze through the ceiling. Twinkles of light dance across her face.

"When your mama and I used to daydream about having children, we never imagined how beautiful and amazing you would be… if she were here, she would be so proud of you."

Her chest expands taking in a deep breath.

"This is not what I imagined my sweet sixteen birthday to be like?"

Joe smiles.

"How did you think it would go?"

"I've watched those movies from the '80s a lot recently— "

"*Pretty in Pink?*"

"Yeah, that one and others, but… "

"Emma, those are just movies… they're good ones, but still, just movies. Plus, those movies weren't set on Mars."

She does not laugh along with him. "I guess what I've been so sad about is that I'm so lonely here. I've been lonely my whole life."

Joe lifts his body and sits with his legs crossed facing Emma.

"It's my fault. We kept you isolated so long as a child away from the children."

"You didn't understand why they were dying... you only tried to protect me."

"Yes, but, you've not had a normal childhood... but, then again, what's normal about any of this?"

"Daddy, this place is normal to me. I've never been anywhere else."

"I wish you could've seen Earth. There were so many beautiful places to see."

"What was your and Mama's favorite place?"

Joe lifts his eyes to the ceiling. Emma joins him sitting up facing him.

"There were so many places we wanted to visit, but money was tight for us. But, Paris will always be a special place for me... that's— "

"Where you proposed to Mama?"

"Yes."

"What was the *Eiffel Tower* like?"

A tremendous smile etches across Joe.

"You've seen pictures and learned the history of Paris."

"Uh, huh."

"It's hard to explain... but, we came from Texas. And, we just never had seen buildings like that... and, then to go to the top of the tower at night and see all of Paris... it was so... magical."

"I wish I could have seen it."

Joe takes Emma's hands.

"Well, you've seen something here that almost everyone on Earth never did."

"Oh... you mean, Mars?"

"Yeah."

"The place where we are all going to die, so it means nothing, anyway."

Joe lifts his shoulders. As they lower, a heavy breath escapes his lungs.

"Look... " Emma points around the room, "all these diamonds.... almost everyone has died, here."

Joe's head follows her hand around the Rotunda.

"I know... and... I thought we could stop it... but, no one here seems to be immune from this."

"You, me, and Jacob seem to be okay... but, not anyone else."

Joe rubs the back of her hands with his thumbs.

"Sweetheart, there's something I need to tell you about Jacob. I made a promise not to tell anyone because that could have caused us problems here... and, I didn't want to tell you earlier to protect you."

Emma looks at her dad's eyes. A piercing gaze comes from her.

"But, Emma, it's time you know... Jacob... well, he's your— "

"Grandfather... I know."

Joe jerks his head from Emma. The whites of his eyes brighten.

"What? How... long have you known?"

Emma tightens her grip in his hands. She slips a smile on her face.

"Well, he told me a long time ago. I was four."

"Four!"

"Yeah, but don't be mad. He promised me not to tell you."

"What did he say?"

"That he was your father. I mean at first, he just told me he had to leave you as a baby because of the responsibility to build this place. But, he later told me about faking his death like everyone, who came here, had to do."

Joe sits silent.

"Grandpa told me you knew, and that he was so sorry for what he had to do to you and Grandma."

"Yeah, it was so hard growing up for sure."

"So, I promised him not to talk to you about it because you had to work out your issues with him and with everything else happening, here."

"But, you were so young. How can you keep that a secret?"

"You said it yourself, I'm amazing," Emma said with a laugh. "But, I knew you had so much on your mind with your research about the deaths... I just felt like I didn't want you to worry about anything else."

"That's why you've spent a lot of time with him over the years, then?"

"Yep, when he told me, he promised to make up for lost time with you."

"And, don't get me wrong, I appreciate everything he has given you."

"I liked being able to visit his place any time I wanted to watch movies... we never really talked too much about things though. I sensed something troubled him with everything going on, here."

"Troubled?"

"Well, yeah... he's responsible for everything. I mean there were times I wanted to tell you, and we would act like a larger family... but, there's just been too much going on for him to worry about. I didn't want him to worry about us."

"Worry? Why do you think he would worry?"

Emma glances to the glass ceiling before returning her gaze to Joe.

"Well, here lately... I'll go over at night... and, before he knows I'm there... I hear him talking to himself."

"So, why does that make you worry?"

"Because there's also a woman's voice. It's always the same conversation. But, when I enter the room, there is no one there except Jacob. It almost sounds like he's playing two parts when he's talking."

"What's he saying?"

"It's hard to hear exactly because it's pretty low. But, it sounds like he's talking about that planet that hit Earth. Then, it sounds like every other word is being said and they are saying something about not being able to talk anymore because power systems are failing."

"Huh? Are you sure he's not talking to someone else?"

"No. Plus, there's no communication system in his room except the normal Comm System."

"Does he do that often?"

"Not every time I'm there. But, it's the same conversation I've heard a few times over the years."

"So, that makes you worried about Jacob?"

"Of course, he's talking to himself. I've read about schizophrenia, and maybe he's dealing with that?"

Laugher billows through the Rotunda.

"Schizo… no! I can say this about the man… I may have only known him in person as my father for the last sixteen years here, but I can honestly say of all the conditions he could be inflicted by that's not one of them… maybe, he's like you a little?"

"What do you mean by that?" Emma takes her hands from Joe.

"You said you were lonely? I can only imagine how lonely his life had to have been leaving us? I mean… I've spent so much time alone with my research that I've talked to myself at times… I think that's pretty normal."

"Maybe so… yeah, I guess I do that, too."

"Yep, see… we're all related and share that same trait."

Emma retakes Joe's hands.

"What else do you think we share? I mean, is there something about us that seems to protect us here compared to everyone else?"

"I should show you my research sometime… the three of us share a part of our DNA."

"Of course, we're related, so obviously we do."

"No, not exactly. I'm sure you've read about RNA codex and sequencing components that make up the DNA structure."

"Uh, huh."

"Well, we share the RNA codex miR-182, which is a genetic marker for the potential development of a certain form of brain cancer."

"Like what's killing everyone here?"

"No. That's the amoeba structure, which has caused that. But, for some reason, it appears the thing in our DNA which should elevate our chance of contracting this brain cancer is protecting us against the amoeba attack."

"So, Jacob gave it to you, and then you gave the codex to me?"

Joe squeezes Emma's hands.

"Yes, but, here's where it's interesting… from my research on Earth, this codex is extremely rare… something like literally one-in-a-million people has this. I mean, there are other reasons brain cancers can develop, but this codex seems like almost a certainty it will happen."

"But, you and Jacob haven't?"

"I know... my theory is that it's something about the gravitational difference between Earth and Mars impacting this development."

"So, what's strange about that... Jacob has it... he passed it to you, then to me."

"Well, your grandma, Grandma Rachel."

"Your mama?"

"Yes. She died when I was ten from brain cancer."

"How old was Grandma?"

"Twenty-eight. I was able to identify through her DNA she had that codex, which I also found in mine."

"How did you get her sample?"

Joe laughs.

"Funny thing... when my grandma died, she sent me a box of old pictures and a scrapbook that my mama had started when I was a baby. In that, she had a lock of my hair taped to one page and a lock her hair beside mine. She had written a note saying something about how my hair looked like hers."

"So, you used her hair from that book?"

"Exactly. And, I remember at the time being pretty clever with finding and testing it."

Silence sits between them a few moments.

"Wow, I get it now... Jacob meeting Rachel was like a one-in-a-million chance, then."

"Huh, guess so... but, at the time of my research, I didn't even know about his DNA and wasn't even aware he shared it, too."

"So, when you were twenty-eight, were you concerned about cancer?"

"Emma, I've always been afraid of that... I think I used to fool myself thinking that my research was because I was attempting to understand what happened to Mama, but in reality, I was afraid of dying myself from it."

Emma reaches across the space and grabs Joe. She rubs his back as she embraces him.

"But, you didn't."

"And, that's just it... I have had a new theory the past few years that since both my parents... your grandparents had the same codex that instead of being a precursor of contracting brain cancer, the combining of this same codex in our DNA is doing the opposite."

"Well, if that's your theory, is there a way to transfer our DNA into those left alive here before it's too late for them?"

Joe's shoulders heave up-and-down in Emma's arms.

"Daddy, it's okay. What's wrong?"

Joe pushes away from Emma.

"We don't have the one machine here for that... I never requested it... I've looked through all my notes... and, before the end of Earth when it was possible to still get equipment here... I... uh... "

"What is it, Daddy? Why are you so upset all of a sudden?"

Joe wipes his face dry.

"I wrote down in my notes the exact machine I needed... but, I didn't ask for it... I had written it down on your first birthday... "

"Oh... I see... the anniversary of Mama's death."

Tears and heavy crying comes from Joe. Emma slides next to him burying her head into his chest.

"It's okay, Daddy... it's okay... "

"No, it's not... if I had that machine here... I could have tried...."

The words come slow between gasps of breath from her father.

"I could have... extracted our DNA and... created an immunotherapy treatment... "

"I've read about that in the medical journals... that treatment was developed in the early 2000s."

"Exactly, if I had those machines... I could have tried... to save everyone."

Emma rubs her father's back and shoulders.

"Oh, Daddy, but you don't know if that would even work?"

"But... but, I could have tried... maybe, I could have saved some of them."

"Or not, you don't know. Don't beat yourself up over that."

"Too... too late... that's why I've been working so hard... since I've been here... I feel so guilty... all I needed to do was show Jacob my notes... we would have this machine and have tried."

Emma continues to comfort her father holding him, reassuring him. But, hours pass into the night until Joe falls asleep in her arms. She cannot recall the last time seeing her father sleep as she runs her fingers through his hair.

33-A Grandfather's Love

THIRTEEN YEARS... the time since the destruction of Earth. Thirteen years... the time needed for almost everyone at Salvation to die.

Today, only three survive after the death of a technician from the South Wing of the complex.

Emma leaves Joe alone in their living quarters as he has knocked himself out purging the last of the alcohol delivered to Salvation over a decade ago. The past several weeks have taken their toll for Joe as he has kept away from her and Jacob.

Late into the evening, Emma walks through the corridor of art masterpieces. Lights illuminate her path activated by her motion outside Jacob's living area.

She places her hand flat against the access panel as the door opens. The room is dark as the door closes behind her.

A light shines through a short hallway connecting Jacob's office to his main living room. Faint voices come through the light attracting Emma closer.

The voices are not new. They are the same she first heard many years ago when Jacob confessed his secret of being her grandfather. Years had passed since she had heard them again. But, during the past few months, the voices come nightly.

Tonight, the voices are different… they are much louder than she recalls. Emma knows Jacob's voice, but, the woman's tone is unfamiliar.

Emma enters the hallway staying firm against the wall. With each step further into the light, the voices increase in clarity. Emma stops and listens.

"The countdown has started," Jacob said.

"How are things there?" a woman asked; her voice crackles.

"They could be better that's for sure," Jacob said. "How about there?" Emma heard Jacob ask.

"Our… communications… seem to be working… but, we still have problems with… "

Frustration builds for Emma. The woman's voice cracks and is difficult to understand.

"We corrected our problems with our power and water systems," Jacob said.

Emma comes to the edge of the hallway. She stands the closest she has done so in hearing the conversation.

Her face shivers against the wall. She peeks her head around the corner peering into Jacob's bedroom.

Jacobs sits on the foot-edge of his bed. He holds a tablet on his lap. A small image of Jacob's face is inside a small square on the lower-right section of the screen.

On the screen, Emma sees a woman speaking to Jacob. Her gray hair is short on the sides and feathered back on top. Wrinkles appear through the screen from the woman's face. Emma tries to focus better on the screen.

"Jacob, is someone there with you?"

"Emma, is that you?"

Jacob presses the tablet closed. The woman's image fades as the black mirrored screen emerges. Emma sees her reflection in his tablet. He stands and turns to his granddaughter.

"My little, Emma… how long have you been standing there?"

She marches to Jacob. "Who was that? Who were you speaking with?"

Jacob places the tablet on a table by the wall. Emma stands close giving him no room to move. She reaches for the tablet as he grabs her hand.

"Don't touch *that*… I've let you have your run of this place… but, you are to never touch *that*, do you understand me?"

Emma shakes. "Yeah… yes, I understand. It's yours. But, who were you speaking to?"

"Emma, sit."

Jacob points to a chair in the corner of his bedroom as he retakes his seat on his bed. Emma complies.

"What I'm about to tell you, your father doesn't even know."

"Should I go get him?"

"Where is he?"

"He's passed out, but I can wake him."

"No, let him sleep it off."

Jacob slumps over on the edge of the bed. A violent cough overtakes him.

"Are you okay?"

Jacob regains his composure wiping his mouth.

"I'm fine. I've not slept in days… and, what I'm about to share with you… well, it's something I should have told you when this all first started."

"When all what started?"

"The deaths… when they started… we should have planned for this, but there were still too many people, here."

Emma slides to the edge of her chair. She restrains her body from lunging in frustration to her grandfather.

"A plan for what?"

"To leave Salvation."

"Leave… what? From here?"

"Yes."

"But, I don't understand."

Jacob turns his head to his tablet still on the table.

"The person I was speaking with… she is the Leader of another place like our Salvation."

"Another place… there's another Salvation complex, here?"

Jacob clears his throat. Large gulps of air caress down his body.

"Yes, there is another Salvation-like place… it's called Atlantis."

Emma stands marching to the hallway. She stops and turns to Jacob.

"That's it. I'm going to get Daddy. Salvation… Atlantis… you are going crazy, I knew it. Really? Atlantis?"

Jacob stands. His lungs intake a deep breath as his chest swells.

"Sit down!"

The terse tone of his voice pulls Emma back to her seat.

"The Eden Foundation, the group responsible for this place and everything we've done, developed a backup location. Our mission has always been to ensure the survival of the human race."

"Okay, if this is even true, why haven't we gone there, or someone come here to help us in all this time?"

A grin emerges on Jacob's face. The smirk is unfamiliar to Emma.

"It's not that easy."

"Why? Can't we use the terrain vehicles to go there?"

"No."

"Why not? Are they that far away from us?"

"Yes."

Emma stands.

"If you're going to tell me, then tell me, already."

"The Foundation designed another facility like ours. It's called Atlantis, and we constructed it during the same time as Salvation but smaller."

"How much smaller?"

"They don't have as much room as we have here, but it's designed for a population of seven-thousand."

Emma returns to the chair.

"Seven… well, can we go, there? Do they have the same problems we have had?"

Jacob pauses. He looks to his tablet, then to Emma in the corner.

"Now that there's only three of us, we can go."

Emma stands, again. "Let me go get, Daddy."

Jacob coughs clearing his throat more.

"No, there's more I need to tell you."

Emma sits beside Jacob on the bed. She grabs his hands. They are freezing inside her fists. She squeezes hard against his hands.

"Tell me."

Jacob lifts his eyes to meet hers.

"What do you know about Europa?"

Emma relaxes her hands as she lifts her eyes inside her eyelids. She tightens her grip.

"You mean Europa, as in one of the moons of Jupiter?"

"Yes… that's where Eden built Atlantis."

Emma releases Jacob's grip. A dull thud raps against the mattress comes from his falling hands. She rushes to the hallway; her back remains to Jacob.

"I'm getting, Daddy. You're crazy."

"Look, Emma, here are the pictures."

Emma stops. The overhead LED lights illuminate her. She turns back to Jacob approaching him as he holds the tablet.

"Here is Atlantis. These are their facilities."

Emma takes the tablet from Jacob and swipes her finger across the screen. Familiar white-walled structures appear on the scrolling pictures.

"Are these real? It looks like places, here."

"Keep going. You'll see the differences at the end. Yes, the walls should look familiar, as they used the same construction design."

Emma stands, her mouth opens.

"What's *this*?"

Emma holds the tablet out to Jacob.

"It looks like the outside of Salvation, but the picture is wavy."

"That's because ice covers Europa. We have a small station on the surface. Below that is a two-kilometer tunnel straight down. That's how thick the ice is. At the end of the tunnel is a sea of fresh water."

"So, you're saying we have a Salvation complex like this one here on Mars, but it's on a moon of Jupiter?"

"Yes, but, it's under the ice and water."

"But— "

"What? There's no difference building Salvation in a Martian atmosphere or building Atlantis under water on Europa."

"Why Europa? Why under the ice?"

"I'm sure you've read the theories about colonizing different places in our solar system."

"Yes, Mars was always considered the obvious choice."

"Exactly, and that's why we are here."

"Venus, it's too intense there, and the only way was building some sort of cloud cities," Emma said.

"Yep, too futuristic for us on Earth to design beyond theory."

"The Earth's moon is obviously not a good choice because it would be destroyed with Earth… that leaves the moons of Jupiter."

"Yes, Titan and Europa. But, Europa was chosen because building under the ice protects the complex from radiation."

Emma continues scrolling the pictures on the tablet.

"It's the same concept as getting here. The same rockets visiting Mars also traveled to Europa. The people chosen filled the same roles as here."

"So, Atlantis… they are okay, there?"

"Yes, they had some technical issues given their depth below the surface, but worked them out."

"That's why the woman's voice was crackling?"

A surprised look creeps across Jacob.

"Uh, yeah. How much did you hear?"

"She asked how things were here and they were working through their communications issue."

Jacob stands.

"Now, that there are only three of us left... it's time for us to go to Atlantis."

Jacob bends at his waist. A sustained grunt bellows from his gut.

"You okay?"

A laugh pushes his hands off his knees as Jacob stands up.

"You'll be seventy-two, someday. I'm just old... I can't believe I've lasted this long."

"Grandpa, you've got more life to live for sure... you've gotta get us to Atlantis."

Emma stands joining Jacob.

"How are we getting there?"

Jacob laughs.

"In all this time, no one has ever asked me why do we keep one of the rockets standing in the Launch Bay."

"Probably everyone is like me and think it's more of a monument for us coming here."

Another laugh erupts from Jacob.

"Yes, that's true. But, it's also programmed to travel to Atlantis from here."

"Really?"

"In the Control Room down there, the instructions for leaving are on a tablet."

"Hasn't anyone found that before and asked questions about leaving?"

"No, that's because to access that tablet requires my palm print. And, it has the commands to create the rocket's trajectory protocols. It also can communicate with the satellite still in orbit above Mars, which pulses the lasers to push the rocket to Jupiter."

"Do you know how to fly the rocket?"

"Don't need to... once we enter the commands in the computer, it flies itself," Jacob said.

"Jupiter is what... ten times farther away than Mars is... sorry, uh was to Earth."

"I know what you are trying to calculate… it took three weeks to travel to Mars with the photonic propulsion system… to Jupiter will take us twenty-eight weeks."

"Seven months?"

Another laugh comes from Jacob.

"Yes, but it took the Galileo spacecraft to get there in six years in the nineties… so, we've made a little progress."

Jacob laughs through small coughs.

"You know what… maybe you should go get Joseph. I can tell you both more about it. We should make our plans to leave soon."

Emma starts again to the hallway. Jacob returns to the edge of his bed.

"I still don't know if I believe you or not, but I'll go get him. It may take me some time because I need to sober him up."

"Emma… "

She stops and turns back to Jacob.

"Yeah?"

Jacob stares at her and smiles.

"Uh… never mind… I tell you when you return."

Jacob watches Emma as she continues into the darkness through the light on the other side of the hall.

EARTH DATE: SEPTEMBER 12, 2033 (NEXT MORNING)

HE'S STILL ASLEEP.

"Daddy! Wake up!"

Emma pushes Joe's bare feet dangling off the bed's edge. Heavy snoring grunts from Joe.

"Please, please wake up… I need you to come with me."

Joe stretches. His mouth opens wide.

"Wha… what time is it?"

"Come on, Daddy, please get up… come with me to Jacob's… he has officially lost it, now."

A pillow muffles Joe's amusement.

"Lost it, now… that man lost it years ago."

Emma slaps Joe's naked foot.

"Dammit, Daddy, get up, now!"

Joe pushes his body up from the mattress. His hair spreads in different directions. Creased wrinkles mark the left side of his face.

"What's he doing?"

Emma paces the floor.

Should I tell him? Do I even believe him?

"Well, are you going to tell me, or what?"

Emma stops and turns to Joe still sitting on the bed.

"Do you know about Atlantis?"

Joe jerks his head backward.

"The lost city?"

"No, Atlantis… another place like Salvation."

"Should I?"

Stop playing games with me. Please tell me what you know.

"I don't know… Jacob told me that The Eden Foundation developed another Salvation where others from Earth also live," Emma said.

Joe stands. He rakes his hands through his dirty hair.

"No, I've never heard anything like that… you said, Atlantis?"

"Yes, Atlantis."

Joe now paces as Emma watches.

"Frankly, it would not shock me. With all the secrets that man has kept and all the shit Eden did to set up Salvation… I could believe another place like us here exists on Mars."

Emma catches his hand as he passes her in the middle of the bedroom floor.

"Dad… it's not a place on Mars."

Joe stops and stares at his daughter.

"Then, where is it?"

"Europa."

"Europa… Europa… oh, Jupiter… a moon… Are you positive that's what he said?"

Emma releases his hand. Joe continues moving to wake his body.

"Yes."

"But, it's gotta be much harsher to live there than here as far as is from the Sun?"

"Yes, at its closest orbit, Jupiter is five-hundred-eighty-eight-million-kilometers from Mars."

"How do you know... uh, never mind."

Joe plops onto a chair in the corner of the room.

"Did Jacob say how many people are there and how they are doing?"

Emma mirrors Joe's reaction and sits on the unmade bed.

"Seven-thousand people... Jacob said they seem okay but have had communication issues."

"Probably, because of the distance."

"That and the ice."

"Ice?"

"Yeah, like you said, it's a cold environment there. Thick ice covers the moon and oceans of water lie underneath."

"Huh."

"There's a benefit with the ice because it protects Atlantis from radiation."

Joe erupts with laughter.

"I get it, now."

"Get, what?"

"Atlantis, the name. Supposedly, the lost paradise which sank under water never to be found... pretty clever."

Stay with me, Daddy. I need your help with Grandpa because I don't know if he is crazy or not.

"So, he is in contact with them?"

"Yes, Atlantis is led by a woman, but he didn't say her name. He said the three of us should leave Salvation and go to them."

Joe leaps from his chair.

"Go to them?"

"Yes, the rocket in the Launch Bay... we can program it to travel there automatically."

"Travel there. Do you know how long that will... oh, of course, you do?"

"Twenty-eight weeks using the photonic propulsion system."

Joe lifts his head to the ceiling.

"So, that satellite is still up there... guess it would be."

"And, next month is the perfect time since we will be as close as we will get to Jupiter."

"You believe him?"

"That's why I need your help. I don't know. He sounds crazy... but, what if?"

"What if? You mean, what if we go there and they are all dead or dying?"

"Oh, like *here* you mean?"

Joe joins Emma on the bed.

"Yeah, good point... it's not like they can come here?"

"That's why Jacob said he waited to tell us until now because we are the only three left."

Joe releases a loud groan and falls flat against the mattress.

"With our issues here... everyone dying... he could have told me about this Atlantis place... maybe we could have contacted them and shared information or something."

Emma stands pulling her dad's hand.

"Come on... let's go. We can ask Jacob all our questions and figure out what to do next."

Ten minutes pass during their walk from their living quarters to Jacob.

"Is he expecting us back? It's so early in the morning?"

"Daddy, look around... who cares... there's no one else here... come on."

Emma places her hand against the access panel. Joe and Emma enter Jacob's dark office. Light from the hallway guides them to his bedroom.

"Come on... Jacob, I brought Daddy with me."

They enter the bedroom.

"You woke me up and brought me here, and he is asleep himself."

"Jacob, we're back."

No response.

"Grandpa?"

Emma shakes Jacob's exposed foot.

"Grandpa... Jacob... we're back."

Joe comes to Emma's side.

"Jacob... the old man is asleep... see, we could have waited... I don't believe him anyway... "

Emma touches Jacob's face placing her hand under his jawbone near his ear.

"Oh my God!"

Emma places her hands to her mouth and backs away from the bed.

"He's... he's dead."

Joe bends to Jacob placing his ear over his father's nose. He repeats Emma by putting his finger under Jacob's jawbone. No pulse.

Joe stands and turns to Emma. He grabs both her arms pulling her closer to him.

"Ssh, it's okay... Sweetheart, it's okay... "

Emma buries her head into her father's neck and left shoulder. Between bursts of air through chattering teeth, Emma said, "Is it the cancer?"

Joe rubs the back of Emma's shoulders.

"I will check... but, it may have just been his time."

Emma cries in the arms of her father. Tears fill both Joe's eyes but never fall.

"It'll be okay... we will figure out what we will do, next."

34-Escape

I SHOULD HAVE NEVER LEFT GRANDPA ALONE.

Emma follows her father as he pushes Jacob's covered body on a gurney. The once-busy Medical Wing is dead-silent. Two of the four wheels spin and squeal echoing through the corridor.

"I'll run tests on him tomorrow to find his cause of death… Emma, you don't have to come with me."

Where else am I going to go?

Joe places his hand on the access panel of the Morgue pushing his father through the opening doorframe. Emma hesitates.

It's too creepy.

"There, I'll leave him, here… I'll come back, tomorrow. I just can't handle this now."

Emma steps to the side as he passes by her in the doorway.

Why is Daddy acting so normal about Jacob?

"Let's go get breakfast. I'm hungry."

They continue back through the Medical Wing. As they approach the cafeteria, Emma speeds up passing him. She stops impeding his forward motion. She turns to him.

"Daddy, what's the matter? Why are you not reacting to his death? You want to have something to eat, now... it's only us left, and we need to take action to leave for Atlantis."

Joe steps to his left passing Emma. He does not respond.

What's up with him?

"Come on... I need to eat. I've got an awful headache."

You shouldn't be drinking at night.

Emma follows.

"Let's talk about what we're going to do as we eat," he said.

Emma stands silent watching her dad.

Eat? I'm not hungry.

Joe grabs for a food tray dropping it on the floor.

"Here, let me help."

"Thanks. It just slipped."

"No problem. I'll eat, but I want to talk about what Jacob told me. We need to figure out how to leave."

Joe takes his food and juice-flavored drink. Emma follows him to a table.

"I hope we can find a seat."

A small laugh follows him.

"That joke never gets old... here, let's sit there," he said.

Silence joins them at the table as they eat their breakfast.

"You're not going to eat *that*? I thought you were so hungry?" Emma asked.

Joe pushes his fork through the powdered eggs.

"We should have eaten a burger for breakfast... you wouldn't believe how the real thing tastes... there was this place, where I grew up... Hillbilly's Burgers... now, those were the best burgers."

"Dad!"

Emma slams her fists onto the table. Joe shuts up and lifts his head to his daughter.

"You are not yourself. I know it's shocking your father is dead… they're all dead, and it's just you and me, but you have to get it together."

Joe sits without expression. A few seconds pass.

"My favorite was the chili burger with fries… now, that was a goddam burger."

That's it… I can't take this.

Emma pushes her tray toward Joe. With a huff, she stands and walks away from him.

"Emma! Come back, here."

I'm out of here.

As Emma left the cafeteria, footsteps follow behind her.

"Where are you going?"

"Jacob said there were instructions on a tablet in the Control Room of the Launch Bay."

"Hold on. I'm coming."

Emma stops allowing Joe to catch up. They continue walking.

"Sorry, 'bout that back there."

"That's okay. I know it's hard on you."

Joe grasps her left hand stopping her progress.

"Emma, that man has never been my father. He was never there for Mama and me. And, Grandma… she had to raise me. That son-of-a-bitch can never replace all the hurt and pain he brought to me."

Emma's shoulders shake. Her chest heaves in-and-out. A terrible frown forms under her squinting eyes as she breaks down crying in the middle of the corridor.

Joe pulls her to him embracing her.

"Oh, Sweetheart, I'm sorry… I know… uh… he meant something to you… he tried making up for my shitty life with you… I'm sorry, I didn't even think about how you must be taking this."

Joe's chest muffles her response.

"That's… okay… I've never cried over anyone… before… "

"There, there."

They stand silent in an embrace. Joe rubs Emma's back as she cries. Two minutes pass.

"Fine. Let's go see if we can find this tablet... what do you say?"

Emma looks up to her father. Her eyes swimming in tears.

"Okay."

Joe takes her hand leading Emma to the Launch Bay.

EARTH DATE: SEPTEMBER 12, 2033 (1 HOUR LATER)

"DID HE DESCRIBE what the tablet looks like?"

Joe and Emma open-and-close every drawer and locker inside the Control Room. Expansive windows surround the room for complete visibility of the Launch Bay.

"No, only that it was here and had the instructions for the rocket."

"It looks like no one has been in here in a long time."

"There has been no reason for years to be in here."

Where can it be? It would be hidden, wouldn't it?

Emma searches the opposite area in the room from Joe.

He said no one knew about Atlantis... only him... so, it can't be just out in the open...

"Did I tell you about this desk Grandma gave me when she died?"

"No... you never talk about that time in your life."

Joe laughs.

"Yeah, in her Will, she had written that the *truth is in the desk*, and for years, I never knew what that meant."

A minute passes with no additional explanation.

"And?"

"And, what?"

"You were just telling about a desk and Grandma."

"Oh yeah, that's right. God, I swear, I'm losing my mind. Yeah, so Mary and I always thought she was giving us a clue about hidden money or something in the desk. One day, I came home from work in a bad mood and pounded on it. Next thing I know, a hidden drawer popped open on the bottom."

"Was there money inside?"

"No, only a picture... of my high school graduation."

"Why did she hide that picture there?"

"I don't know and never figured it out. I looked so happy in it though."

"You've never shown it to me before."

"Remind me tonight. I'll find it and some others I have. There's one from that night with your mama that's always been my favorite."

Several minutes pass. The tablet remains hidden. Joe and Emma sit frustrated behind the computer control systems.

"Why did you bring up the desk earlier?"

"Huh... oh, searching for this tablet reminded me of the last time I was looking for something hidden."

"And, you said Grandma didn't explain her reason for hiding it?"

"No, and it was just so weird."

"Weird?"

"Her message was about truth being in the desk then finding my picture, but the weird part was an old man had taken it. And, I never figured out who he was or how Grandma got it?"

"So, you think there's a hidden compartment in this control panel?" Emma asked.

"Let's find out."

Joe slams the top of the table holding the computer terminals.

"Anything?"

"No... try it again," Emma said.

Joe repeats harder.

"Nothing... but, there's a slot, *here*." Emma points to a horizontal opening on the front, edge of the table.

"Hmm, it looks like a CD slot."

"Uh, what?"

"CD music... uh, never mind... Let's power on the table and computers."

Emma presses the *power* button. A slow hum radiates under her palms flat on the table.

"What are you looking for?"

He presses various buttons around the computer monitor on the table-top.

"Maybe, there's a way to open— "

A mechanical zipping noise rattles within the slot as a glass tablet emerges.

"Maybe that's it?"

Joe removes the tablet from the slot pressing the power button. Two words appear at the top of the screen: *Flight Protocol.*

"This has to be it? Jacob said it was a flight protocol tablet with the programming information needed for the rocket."

"Oh, no… look at this."

"Looks like the outline on the door access panels here in the complex."

"It's not working with my hand… how about yours?"

Emma places her hand on the tablet switching to the other. Nothing happens.

"We need to take this to Jacob's body. I'm sure it will work for him," Emma said as she stands. "Come on."

Joe stands and then sits back down.

"Are you okay?"

"Yeah, just tripped. I got too excited."

They leave the Control Room making their way through the Salvation Complex returning to the Morgue in the Medical Wing. Joe enters the room as Emma stands in the doorway.

"*Here*, you take *it*… I don't want to go inside."

Emma gives her father the tablet as he uncovers and places Jacob's right hand flat against the glass. The tablet flashes *Access Denied.* Joe tries again without success.

"It's not working."

"How cold is his hand?" Emma asked.

"His? Oh, that's right. The scan won't work if his body temperature is too cold."

Joe slaps his hands together and rubs them hard for several seconds placing them together over Jacob's hand. He puts the tablet under Jacob's palm. *Access Denied.*

He repeats his action. *Access Denied.*

"Wait, I'll be back in a few minutes," Emma said as she disappeared from the doorway.

Joe stops trying to heat his father's hand and looks at his closed eyes.

"You miserable, son-of-a-bitch. I hate you. I hate you!"

He slams his closed fists onto Jacob's chest. Words no longer come from Joe, instead only screams with each punch.

Emma returns running into the Morgue pulling her father off of Jacob. Joe backs away as she wraps Jacob's right hand in a white cloth. Steam rises from her hands as she presses the fabric.

"Here, give me the tablet."

Joe complies as she removes the cloth from Jacob. She presses his palm onto the tablet. *Access Granted.*

"Look, see, it worked," she said. "Can we review the tablet out of here? I don't like this place."

"Sure."

Emma leaves as Joe follows her. They continue through the maze within the complex returning to the Control Room.

"You read the files. You'll memorize it better than me, and that will help in case something happens to the tablet," Joe said.

The tablet has multiple files with instructions for the rocket for flights between Earth and Mars, between Mars and the Moon, but nothing concerning Atlantis. Ten minutes pass as Emma commits hundreds of pages to her memory.

"Huh, the rocket controls seem easy enough. I will need to sit in the Command Module and see the controls, but I can program it."

"And, Atlantis?"

Emma quickly scrolls through the pages, again.

"Nothing's here about that."

"Do you see anywhere to access the files on the tablet?"

The tablet turns in Emma's hands as she scans the glass.

"Ah, maybe, this?"

Emma presses her finger within the outline of a small, white box on the lower-left part of the screen. The white screen with the Flight Protocols shrinks to the bottom as a program opens listing the files.

"Okay, I'm at the file explorer... hold on... okay, I read *that*... and *this*... huh, what's *this one?*"

She presses her left index finger on an untitled file. A second later, a flight protocol opens, which was not included in the earlier list.

"Daddy, this is it? The destination is unnamed, but given the protocol description of distance and time... this has to be between Mars and Jupiter."

"Are you sure?"

"Yeah, in the ones I read, it provided the coordinates for the flight path. And, if I do the geometry, I can figure out distance... so, *see here...* "

Two pages of calculations and coordinates scroll pass as Joe reviews the screen over Emma's shoulder.

"It would take me a couple hours to do the calculations."

"Trust me, I can see the calculations in my head, and one of them indicates a destination almost six-hundred-thousand-kilometers from here."

"Atlantis?"

"That's what we have to assume... let's go into the Command Module... if I input this information in the system, the onboard computer will highlight the flight path, and we will know for sure."

EARTH DATE: SEPTEMBER 23, 2033 (1 WEEK LATER)

JOE AND EMMA HAD CONFIRMED the flight protocols would get them to Jupiter's moon, Europa. This verification made for an easy agreement to leave Salvation. Emma studied the orbits of Mars and Jupiter. Jacob was correct. Within the coming weeks, the two planets will be at their closest point meaning a twenty-eight-week sojourn.

They worked to collect supplies and identify items to bring with them. Joe based his decision of things based on his three-week flight experience over seventeen years ago.

"Okay, this will be enough food and water for us when we leave next week," Joe said.

"You look a little pale."

"Looking at this food packed into this machine brings back memories when Mary and I came here. I recall it doesn't taste as good as what's in the cafeteria, but at least it will give us calories."

They leave the rocket climbing down the steps. Mary reviews the flight apparatus of the connected hoses while Joe heads to the Control Room.

"Let me try to reach Atlantis, again," Joe said as he enters the glass-walled room and rests behind a computer terminal.

They have failed in getting through with anyone with Atlantis. Only static comes through each frequency.

"Are we doing the right thing in leaving?" Emma asked entering the Control Room.

Joe spins in his chair to Emma.

"As you said, they have communications issues... we just have to have faith that they are there and that everything's going to be all right."

"Daddy, that doesn't sound like you. I don't think you've ever talked about faith before."

Joe's shoulders slump.

"With everything that's happened in my life, it's just something I've lost."

"So, why, now? Why do you have faith we will make it there and that they're not having any issues like we have here?"

Joe rubs his forehead and clears his throat before answering.

"Emma... we have two options... either we live and die alone here, or we seek-out others. The Eden Foundation and Salvation have a lot of bad things about them, but... our mission is something I started to trust in a long time ago."

"What's that?"

"Earth is gone. We have to have faith in this Atlantis and that our fellow people are there, because if not, then our mission to save the human race is lost… and, everything that we've done… was completed in vain."

The words coming from her father inspires her. An overpowering sense of loneliness and sorrow have been her companions her entire life. Atlantis brings her hope… it brings her possibilities… it propels her forward to follow her father… to fulfill their ultimate mission to save humanity.

EARTH DATE: OCTOBER 3, 2033 (2 WEEKS LATER)

I CAN'T BELIEVE IT. Today's the day. I'm so nervous… Dad seems okay… at least he's traveled in this before.

"Are you ready?"

Emma does not respond.

I'm so scared, but I can't tell him. This is my home… this is the only place I know.

"I've checked all the supplies… the fuel… and reviewed the checklist from the Control Room at least a dozen times," Joe said.

Maybe we should just stay here. At least we are familiar with this place… what happens if there is a problem during our flight…

"Have you checked the flight program, again?"

Emma shakes her head acknowledging the rocket is ready for launch.

"What should we do with the memorials?" Emma asked.

"The what… oh… you mean in the Rotunda."

"Yeah, each of those diamonds is someone who lived and died here… should we just leave them?"

Joe pauses from his pre-flight list of items he is checking.

"What do you want to do? We can leave them behind. This was their home, and it's their final resting place."

"But, if we take them, we can create a memorial at Atlantis for everyone… do you think anyone will ever come back here?"

Joe sits rubbing his forehead.

"I'm too tired to think about that… but… we must assume that if we are going there, someone someday may come here."

"But, if they do and aren't prepared for the amoeba here, then, they may eventually die, too," Emma said.

"Oh, you haven't noticed the signs?"

"What signs?"

"The past couple of nights, I've left signs with notes about what has happened here. They're in multiple places in case something happens to one wing of Salvation. This way, if someone arrives, there will be a record."

"Good idea… but, as you were talking… I realized what I want to do about the memorials," Emma said.

"Yeah, what?"

"We have these canisters we are loading with supplies… can you help me load them on this cart… I'm going up to the Rotunda, and I will bring them all with us."

A smile overcomes Joe.

"Sounds like a great idea. I'll help you with the canisters… if I wasn't so tired from not sleeping the past weeks, I'd go up there to help you."

"No worries. I've got it," Emma responded.

A few minutes later, she pushes the loaded cart to the door of the Control Room.

"We're leaving in three hours. If you aren't back in two, I'll come up there to help," he said.

Emma leaves. Joe continues walking through the checklist accessing the computer to double-check Emma's programming.

Two hours pass. At the same time Joe opens the door to leave, Emma stands in the hallway to the Launch Bay.

"Here, let me help."

The weight from the diamond-loaded canisters makes pushing the cart a challenge.

"How was it?" Joe asked.

"They just popped right off the wall. It was easier than I thought."

"Okay, I'll take these out to the rocket and load them in the supply hull. You, go ahead and get ready," he said.

Twenty-minutes later, her father returns

"Are you okay?" Emma asked.

"I'll be honest… I've been trying to keep a brave face, but I'm pretty nervous," he said. "Well, you look really pale, too."

"Am I pale? I'm beyond nervous… I'm so scared," she said.

Joe hugs her

"It'll be okay. I've flown in that before. It's amazing in Space. And, these rockets have flown many missions, so we'll be fine."

"I'm still scared… I'm leaving my home… and— "

"Emma, I know how you feel. You are feeling exactly how your mama and I did when we left Earth. But, with your quest for knowledge, just think of all the new things you will learn once we get to Atlantis."

You always know what to say to make me feel better.

"Thanks, that helps me. I just wanted to tell you how scared I am," she said.

"You will be just fine. You are the smartest, bravest person I've ever known… I love you, Emma."

Joe kisses the top of his daughter's head. "Now, we need to get ready to leave… "

Several minutes pass as they make their final arrangements in the Launch Bay. They climb up the stairway to the opened Command Module. Emma sits in the pilot seat inside the module. Joe takes his position in the navigation seat. Each progress through their checklist for take-off.

"Fuel level, full… " Joe said.

"Check," Emma responded.

"Photonic Propulsion Shield, operational…. "

"Check."

"Power systems…. "

"Check."

"Oxygenation synthesizer… "

"Check."

"Control signal… control signal… "

"Hmm… control signal… Daddy, we have a problem."

"What's wrong?"

"I'm sure I checked the control signal with the Control Room earlier this morning, but I'm not getting a signal now?" she said.

"Hmm."

Joe reviews the checklist on her tablet and turns the knob responsible for tuning to the control signal.

"You're right… no signal."

"Without that, we've lost the ability from the program loaded in the Control Room to relay the launch signal to the rocket… I'll go back— "

Joe grabs Emma's arm.

"No, I'll go. I'm done with my checklist. You go ahead with yours, and this will keep us on schedule."

"Good point. Okay, if you need anything from there, just ping me on the radio."

Joe kisses the side of her right cheek.

"I love you, Emma. I'll be back in a few minutes."

"Okay, love you, too."

The vertical descent through the Command Module into the Living Module is a challenge. Even with the lighter Martian gravity, over the years, Joe's muscles have adapted by weakening. His hands shake from holding his weight as he traverses his way down the rocket. Joe opens and closes the access door as he leaves the rocket.

Minutes pass. No response comes from Joe. Emma completes her checklist.

He should be back already.

Emma unsnaps her harness.

I'm going down to the Control Room… maybe he needs my help.

As she presses her body from the flight seat, a rumbling shakes the rocket. The vibrations force her back to her seat.

What is that?

Emma reaches for the communication headset to call the Control Room.

"Daddy! Daddy! Are you there?"

Through the front window, the red haze of the Martian sky grows. The roof of the Launch Bay slides open retracting to the side wall, which descends into the floor.

"Daddy!"

Emma screams for her father though her headset as the Launch Bay becomes fully open to the outside atmosphere.

Through her headset, she hears him cough.

"Daddy, is that you? Are you okay? What's happening?"

"Emma… " Joe's voice is soft and low.

"Yes," she responds.

"Emma, I have activated the launch sequence."

"But, you aren't back, yet."

"Yes… I know… I need you to go without me— "

"What! No! I'm coming out and down there to you."

"You can't. In thirty seconds, the rocket will take-off. You won't have time, and you need to be in your seat."

"No! You can't!"

The rocket vibrates violently. Emma's teeth chatter.

Oh God, oh God…

A survival instinct forces her return to her seat as she fastens the buckles.

"Daddy, no! Stop the sequence."

"I can't. I've deactivated the abort function from your control. I'm controlling the launch from here."

White smoke surrounds her from the rocket engines firing below her. Her visibility reduces. The red sky shines brightly through the smoke.

"I love you, Emma… I can't go with you… I'm… I'm dying."

"What!"

"I didn't want to tell you… you wouldn't have left."

"But, you can leave with me. Once we got there, they can help us." Emma's words come fast.

"No... I won't make it... I will die onboard... and... and... I can't do that to you."

"No... stop this... let me out... close the Launch Bay."

"I'm sorry Sweetheart I love you. I will call you back in five minutes once you are in Martian orbit."

"Daddy? Daddy!"

Emma's screams for Joe become silent through the roar of blasting off from the Martian surface. Her body shakes side-to-side. Her amazement of the growing black sky filled with stars silences her screams. She feels her body become weightless as she loses consciousness.

Minutes pass.

"Emma... Emmanuelle... are you there? Emma?"

Joe's voice becomes louder in her headset. Emma opens-and-closes her eyes fast regaining herself.

"Emma?"

"I'm... I'm here."

Her voice comes back to Joe like a little girl. Joe hears her crying.

"Don't cry, Emma. My Emma... I had to do this... you have to go on... there's nothing left here."

"But, you're there. I don't want to leave you?"

"I know... and, I hate leaving you... but, you must go. I'm going to die, and then you would be here all alone, and I just can't have that."

Her father's words pierce through her crying. She lifts her head and clears her throat.

"But, why didn't you tell me?"

"You wouldn't have left, or if you decided, later on, to leave I wouldn't be able to help. Plus, if you wait, you will miss the window in traveling within the capacity of the rocket system."

Sobbing fills the communication line both ways.

"I should have seen the signs," Emma said.

"Signs?"

"Yeah, the headaches, coughing... you had been dropping things... I just thought you were your normal self and that came from not sleeping."

"I know, Sweetheart, I diagnosed myself with a brain tumor two weeks ago... it was so hard keeping that from you."

"But... I could have helped."

"No, there's nothing you could have done... it's just my time... my whole life I knew this was how I would die with my mother's genes... I'm just lucky that it didn't develop until now because of my dad... "

"Huh, that's the first time I've heard you call him that?"

"I guess you're right... but, the greatest thing I have ever done is raising you."

"Daddy... bring me back... "

"You are the miracle that your mama and me had always dreamt about. She would be just as proud of you as I am."

As Joe speaks to Emma, she caresses her mother's diamond pendant floating above her chest in zero gravity.

"Emma, you are so smart... so beautiful... you are my everything, and I'm not worried about you... you are so brave and strong... and you will be with others in Atlantis."

"Oh, Daddy, I love you."

"I love you, too... now, we only have a few minutes left."

"Why?"

"The satellite we are using to have our conversation only works without the laser propulsion system operating."

"So, when that starts to push me forward, we won't be able to talk?"

"Yes, I'm afraid so."

"But, can't you delay it?"

"You know the answer... you know all the answers of everything you've ever read," her father said.

"It's automated... once the rocket completes its orbit, the satellite will identify the alignment between it and Jupiter and fire its laser," Emma responded.

"Yes, the photonic shield behind the rocket will receive the laser's energy pushing you exponentially forward."

"Will you be okay there?"

406 ◆ CHAD JOSEY

"Don't worry about me, Emma. I will complete all the records here... eventually, someone will return, and I don't want our experiences to be forgotten without no one knowing what happened."

"Daddy...... I'm scared... I will be alone."

"It's almost time, Emma. There's one other thing... in my flight bag on the side of my seat, I've left a box for you. In it, you will find– "

Before Joe finishes his sentence, the force of the rocket propelling forward startles Emma. The laser from the satellite collects within the photonic shield. In zero gravity, friction is absent. With each subsequent laser pulse, the rocket exponentially speeds toward Jupiter.

"Daddy! Daddy! Daddy!"

Emma screams into her headset. Nothing. Silence. Only her massive breathing returns in her earpiece.

She unbuckles her restraint and lifts herself into Joe's absent seat. Disconnecting the straps, Emma reaches inside her dad's travel bag pulling out a silver-colored, metal box, which fits in her right hand.

Emma snaps open the lid. Tears roll from her eyes suspended in front of her face.

Three pictures? Daddy told me about these.

She holds the top one.

Oh wow, he looks so young. This is his graduation picture coming down from the stage.

She flips it over and reads her father's handwriting.

The truth was in the desk.

The second picture which came later after the graduation ceremony shows her mother, Mary, jumping up onto Joe, her legs straddling his.

That's Mama... Daddy was right. They look so happy.

Tears flow streaming out suspended from her face.

This... this must be from the Eiffel Tower... look at those smiles... that's when he proposed.

Emma clutches her mama's pendant.

Oh, Mama... I love you.

She rubs her fingers across Joe's pictured face.

Daddy... I promise you... I will not let you down... I love you.

Emma lifts the third picture to her face. A light kiss leaves a lip print on the color paper. She returns the picture to the box.

Huh...

A small, metal USB stick floats from the box. Emma grabs it.

What's on this? Why did Daddy leave me this?

35-Coming Home

FIVE WEEKS HAVE PASSED.

Salvation remains quiet. Joe wanders the corridors entering each room. With each visit, he leaves a note about each of the past occupants. The letter states their name where they were from on Earth with their birth and death dates.

Someday, someone will come back, here... they need to remember who we were.

The activity gives Joe something to consume his thoughts.

How is Emma doing onboard the rocket? How much longer do I have?

Of all the places in the Salvation Complex, there is one that remains personal to Joe. For hours, he lies on the floor of the corridor leading to Jacob's living quarters. Monet's *Waterlilies* reminds him of his teenage youth.

With each visit, Joe envisions Mary lying beside him admiring the masterpiece.

"Don't you find it crazy?"

"What's that Joseph?" Mary said in his imagination.

"How we used to make-out on your bed, and you had a poster of that painting on your wall."

"I must have been a terrible kisser."

Joe kisses the back of Mary's hand as he laughs.

"Why do you say that?"

"If I were a great kisser, then you would not remember that poster."

"Oh, I remember every night… every time we spent together. I know there were times my research took me away too many hours, but I loved you so, so much."

"Joseph, I know. And, I loved you."

Reflections of a happier, simpler time preoccupy him.

Time… Joe has lost this concept. If he thinks about time too much, terrible sadness overcomes him. The time since Emma had left… the time until the end comes for him.

"Joseph, so how do you think Emmanuelle is doing?" Mary asked.

"I'm sure just fine. She's incredible… but, I miss her."

"So, this Atlantis… you don't remember Gabriel or anyone ever telling you about it?"

"No… Gabriel and later Jacob shared everything with me."

"Everything? All the secrets… all the conspiracy… maybe it's a good thing you didn't know. Could you have chosen between Salvation or Atlantis to go?"

"Huh, I don't know… I only saw pictures of this place, here. If you think about it, Salvation is truly a miracle. I mean, other than everyone dying, it's amazing here… we live on Mars."

"Pictures… didn't Emma tell you that Jacob showed her pictures of Atlantis?"

Mary's words jolt a memory through his body. His cancer-riddled body jerks to his feet.

"Oh my God… we were so shocked by his death and then finding the launch information for the rocket, we never looked at those."

Joe places his hand flat against the door access panel of Jacob's home. The door opens.

"Wait for me, Joseph," Mary said following behind him.

The lights flash on as Joe runs into Jacob's bedroom. Mary is already there, waiting for him.

"Emma told you Jacob showed her the pictures on his tablet," Mary said as Joe searched the room.

"There it is on the table."

He opens the tablet. A picture of a white building suspended in water pushes through the awakening screen.

"This must have been the last one she saw... "

Pictures scroll pass as Joe flicks his finger across the screen.

"Crazy... these look very similar to the pictures I saw so long ago in Colorado. Gabriel shared with me the construction photos from the site on the Moon and then the pictures from here... these look very similar."

Thirty pictures later, he stops scrolling.

"Huh, that looks like all of them."

Joe presses the small, white-outline square on the lower-left of the screen. The file explorer opens.

"Okay, this lists all the pictures I just opened... huh, what's this... look at the size of that file... "

The file does not open.

"Dammit, password... password... what the hell could this be?"

"Are you sure it's asking for a password and not a palm print?" Mary asked.

"Well, a palm print won't do any good... Jacob's body is no longer available... password?"

"Hmm... E-M-M-A... shit... what about... E-M-M-A-N-U-E-L-L-E... Shit! Shit! Shit!"

"Oh, Joseph, it could be anything. Maybe look around... maybe Jacob left a hint somewhere."

EARTH DATE: NOVEMBER 17, 2033

ONE WEEK PASSED.

Joe's strength fades. Yesterday, something new happened… he started coughing up blood.

"H-O-U-S-T-O-N-1-9-6-9… ugh… I can figure this out."

In a quiet, lonely place, Salvation yields a new torture as he works to solve the puzzle of guessing the password.

EARTH DATE: NOVEMBER 24, 2033 (1 WEEK LATER)

JOE FLIPS A CALENDAR on his lab desk, which he updates each year to coincide with the dates on Earth. Today is Thanksgiving.

The memory of this holiday, even now, devastates Joe. At fifty-five-years-of-age, the memories of the pain his Grandma Liz experienced when Grandpa Eli died still come vividly to him.

For most of the year, Joe keeps his memories, especially those of his youth, away from his thoughts. But, Thanksgiving is different. They rush to him.

An unusual feeling of sadness invades his thoughts. Memories suppressed for decades, Joe's time is fading, and his feelings flow like a raging river after a thunderstorm.

Grandma was a special lady… she looked after me… if it wasn't for her, I don't know what would have happened.

A memory returns to him of his grandma rushing passed him at church when he was ten-years-old. Chocolate and peanut-butter from the candy his mom, Rachel, had told him not to eat salivates his dry mouth remembering its taste.

That's my worst memory as a child… I remember the horror on Grandma's face when she ran to Mama. Minister Greene held her, but it was too late.

Joe closes his eyes. Feelings of air rushing across his face as a child from the open windows of the new Oldsmobile refresh him. The remembered smell of farm pastures between their home and the church returns.

Mama sure looked so pretty that day. That's the happiest I ever remember her being. But, then a couple hours later that was it…

"Shit! That's it!"

Joe jumps from his desk chair retrieving Jacob's tablet from the table beside the DNA Sequencer.

"R-A-C-H-E-L... you son-of-a-bitch, that's it... that was the password."

The desk chair provides comfort to his frail bones as he rests. He holds the play-button on the video file.

"Huh... it's a recording from the week before Earth ended according to the date, *here*."

The video plays. White numbers scroll indicating the passing time of the video beside the date.

"Who is that?"

An older woman appears on the screen. Deep wrinkles etch across her forehead. Her hair is completely gray, kept short and feathered back on top.

Jacob's face appears in the lower-right of the screen, inside a small box.

"This must be the woman Emma told me about who she heard Jacob speaking with... she is the one in command at Atlantis."

The video continues... the sound is intermittent and choppy.

"The countdown has started," Jacob said.

"How are things there?" the woman asked as her voice crackles.

"They could be better that's for sure," Jacob said. "How about there?"

Do I know this woman? She seems very familiar?

"Our... communications... are working... but, we still have problems with... "

"We corrected our problems here with our power and water systems," Jacob said.

Joe closes his eyes. Mental flashcards scroll as he tries to identify the woman.

I know I have seen her somewhere, before?

Dull thumping in his temple, which has grown worse each day, throbs behind the tumor. The video continues.

"Jacob, is someone there with you?"

The woman's voice slices through Joe's pain. His eyes force open returning his attention to the screen.

"Emma, is that you?" Jacob said in the video.

Joe hears Jacob's question forcing the tablet closer to his eyes. To his amazement inside the small box, Joe sees Jacob turn. Behind him, hiding on the floor is Emma.

Oh my God, she's so adorable… what, she was four, then?

"How's my little Emma, tonight?" Jacob asked.

Joe sees Emma remain on the other side of the room.

"What are you watching? I thought I heard a woman's voice?" Emma asked.

Joe sees in the video Jacob motion Emma to him. As she gets closer, the video shrinks.

"Can I share a secret with you?"

Those are the last words Joe hears from the video file.

"Huh, Jacob must have closed the tablet stopping the recording… oh my, I need to watch that again… Emma was so cute."

Joe presses the play-button, again. The video starts from the beginning. A smile comes to Joe as Emma appears on the screen. He replays the video five-times, one-after-the-other.

"I understand, now… Emma said she thought Jacob was going crazy and talking to himself. She even said he sounded like a woman."

Joe erupts with laughter.

"Hell, I just watched this five-times-in-a-row… maybe, I'm crazy? I must be, I'm talking to myself."

The desk chair creaks as Joe leans back replaying the video file.

"This was probably the last communication Jacob had with Atlantis… if they were having communication issues then, they must not have fixed them, either that, or it was a problem on our side."

A violent cough erupts from Joe as the video plays. His hand presses the glass screen accidentally freezing the playback.

After a few seconds, he regains himself as he wipes his lips with the back of his closed hand. His head cocks to the side. His eyes narrow.

On the tablet, the video stopped. The gray-haired woman's image has frozen. A feature Joe missed during the earlier, multiple playbacks was of a brief one-second smile, gone unnoticed. Unnoticed that is until the video paused from his cough attack

A strange, warm sensation consumes Joe's chest rushing to his face. The woman looks beautiful to him. Her smile is familiar.

"Mama! Oh my God... Mama! Is this you?"

Like a small child, Joe rushes to hug his mama, even if it is only a flat, glass tablet of a video recorded thirteen-years-earlier. Joe lowers the tablet into his lap.

"Mama? It is you, isn't it? You... you are at Atlantis? Mama, your granddaughter is coming... I wish I could have made it... Mama, I love you."

Tears fall like they never have before from him. At fifty-five-years-old, seeing a video of his mama, Rachel, made him feel like he was ten, again.

"Mama, I love you... I miss you... "

Joe repeats these words several times. With each attempt to speak between gulps of air, his words come out softer and slower.

"Mama... I love you... "

Air pushes from his lungs. The image of Rachel freezes in his mind as the light in the room dims. Her picture remains bright until darkness fills his complete vision.

"Joe... Joe... "

His name becomes louder in his ears as light enters his eyes.

"Joe... Joseph... are you okay... are you still with me?"

Joe opens his eyes. Cold wind hits his face. The image of his wife, Mary, focuses in his mind.

"Here, let me help you up... you fainted," Mary said.

"I... uh... fainted?"

The bite from the cold wind intensifies as he stands. Clouds cover the orange sky of a sunset. Buildings and streets are three-hundred-meters below them.

"Uh, where are we... what happened?"

"Joseph, are you sure you're okay? I mean one minute you propose to me, and the next you pass out."

"Propose to you?"

"What? You can't take it back, now. My answer is already yes... I love you, Joseph."

Joe shakes his head.

"Uh... I don't understand... what... uh... Salvation... uh... "

Warmth surrounds him. He feels the embrace of Mary standing behind him. Her arms stretch under his coming together on his chest.

On the horizon, the orange sun sets. The sky fills with shades of red and purple. Paris never looked so beautiful.

"Joseph, I love you."

"I love you, too, Mary."

Through the horizon, a bright, white light grows. Like a growing tidal wave, the white light engulfs the Paris cityscape in front of them.

"What is happening, Mary?"

In his left ear, he hears Mary's whisper. "This is the place where we were our happiest... we had our whole lives ahead of us... we are back here, before we go."

"Go... go, where?"

Mary does not reply.

"Joseph?"

"Yes, Mary."

"I will love you, forever."

"I love you, Sweetie."

Joe turns to Mary. Both mirror a smile as their lips join together in a passionate kiss.

"Time to come home," Mary said parting a moment from Joe before returning to his lips.

The brilliant, white light surrounds Mary and Joseph disappearing with them as the Eiffel Tower's lights twinkle in the night sky over Paris.

END OF BOOK TWO

Epilogue

"WELCOME HOME to the States, Gabriel."

"Jacob, thanks. It's so great to meet you in person finally."

The morning had turned bright in the foothills of the Rocky Mountains outside Denver. Golden and rust hues encircle the compound The Eden Foundation had completed in the remote countryside.

Jacob leads Gabriel inside an unassuming building absent any windows or decoration. Down a dim-lit hallway, they enter a small room.

"You have done an exceptional job with your position with *Sauvage*. I'm sure Paris has treated you well, but I need you to take on more responsibilities for Eden."

A cold, metal chair presses against Gabriel's gray Armani suit. Jacob stands between him and a hanging television screen.

"I have been nothing but honest with you, Gabriel. For you to assume command of Eden, I need to bring you up to speed on our activities we have underway and planned."

Jacob paces the floor.

"I cannot believe you're leaving Earth. I've known about Salvation for years, but it always seemed like science-fiction," Gabriel said.

"It's time for me to assume command at Salvation. We have built several sectors of the complex, and I need to oversee the next stages of construction."

The television screen comes to life tuned to a financial news, cable network. Two rows of stock symbols and prices scroll right-to-left across the bottom of the screen.

"The information I need to share with you is in the red folders on the table."

Gabriel grabs the top folder from the stack.

"The first thing to discuss is our funding. Eden has many entities around the world, like *Sauvage*. As you know, we set up these companies with fake operations. Their real value is their ability to trade in the financial markets."

Jacob steps closer to the screen.

"You see the Dow, *here*?"

"Yeah."

"This afternoon, it will close at an all-time high, over fourteen-thousand."

"But, how do you… oh?"

"We're able to manipulate the markets, in fact, all the global markets. People are so greedy that it's been the easiest thing we've done for financing."

Gabriel laughs. "I'm sure funneling the government defense spending budgets were challenging."

"Actually that was easy too because of the bureaucracy, our redirection of funds was easy to hide."

Jacob joins Gabriel at the table.

"We're still involved there, but this global bull market has been fantastic," Jacob said pointing to a tabbed-chapter in the folder.

"How are you manipulating the markets?"

"I mentioned greed, didn't I? Well, the housing markets have gotten out of control. Banks will give money to anyone these days. We developed a new trading vehicle where we combine hundreds of junk mortgages and sell them as secured derivatives to companies for their pension funds... hell, we've even sold these to countries."

Gabriel flips through the pages.

"The beauty of this is other financial institutions copied us, and this has fueled the housing and stock markets even more."

A slow laugh comes from Jacob.

"But, tomorrow morning, we're dumping all those products, and we'll watch the dominos fall."

"I don't quite understand."

Jacob stands and approaches the screen.

"All these talking heads are hyping up the markets. Even every-day people are buying stocks. Once we dump all of our financial instruments, the value will collapse. Banks will recall the funds from the securities, and there will be a run to pay for everything."

Gabriel studies the pages in the red folder. He lifts his head and watches Jacob pace in front of the television.

"But, the mortgages that back those funds are way upside-down. In a few months, the banks will start repossessing homes from people, and the banks will fail no longer providing funds to companies. The companies then will start massive layoffs of people. And, the damn snowball really grows. More mortgages will go into default, and more companies will go under."

Gabriel lowers his gaze from Jacob back to the folder. "Holy shit. What you are describing is a complete melt-down of the global economy."

A loud bang slaps against the television screen from Jacob's hand.

"You're absolutely fuckin' right... a complete melt-down. And, we are hedging this by taking the money we dump from the mortgage-back derivatives and will wait. We will buy properties and stocks for next to nothing this time next year."

Jacob flicks the screen with the back of his fingers.

"And, those sons-of-bitches won't even see it coming."

Gabriel motions Jacob to rejoin him at the table. Questions come fast to comprehend the records within the folders.

Hours pass. Jacob shares the details of how Eden has structured every funding vehicle globally and the next steps to continue sending money to Eden and Salvation. The financing of complete operations encroaches the trillion dollar mark for the first time in 2007.

"Gabriel, this is enough for today." Jacob again approaches the screen. "See… what did I tell you? The Dow closed at an all-time high, today at 14,164. Are you ready to watch to bottom drop?"

Gabriel stands and joins Jacob.

"Tomorrow, I will review with you how we monitor people to join us. We still have a tremendous amount of work to do for Salvation."

About the Author

CHAD JOSEY is an engineering project manager by day and a writer by night. Originally from North Carolina, Chad resides in New Jersey after living and working four years in Germany.

Chad attended North Carolina State University obtaining his Industrial Engineering degree. Upon graduation, Chad pursued his MBA from Queen's University of Charlotte.

Chad has traveled to sixty-two countries documenting his travels and his American Expat life with his wife and their dog at his travel website WorldThruOurEyes.com. Chad weaves his travel experiences and professional life into his writing.

The Salvation Trilogy:
Book One: *SECRET SALVATION*
Book Two: *SALVATION CONSPIRACY*
Book Three: *PROMISE OF SALVATION*

Please consider leaving a review on Amazon to share your impression of **SECRET TRILOGY** with other potential readers.

Follow Chad on social media for updates for Book Three:

Website: https://chadjosey.com

Facebook: https://www.facebook.com/AuthorChadJosey/

Twitter: https://twitter.com/chadjosey

Pinterest: https://www.pinterest.com/chadjosey

www.ingramcontent.com/pod-product-compliance
Lightning Source LLC
Chambersburg PA
CBHW030547020726
47494CB00005B/1520